A Dead Man's Chest

A Dead Man's Chest

Bruce Banta

Copyright © 2011 by Bruce Banta.

Cover and author photos by Deb Banta.

Library of Congress Control Number: 2011907795
ISBN: Hardcover   978-1-4628-7253-4
           Softcover   978-1-4628-7252-7
           Ebook   978-1-4628-7254-1

All rights reserved. No part of this book may be reproduced or transmitted in any form or by any means, electronic or mechanical, including photocopying, recording, or by any information storage and retrieval system, without permission in writing from the copyright owner.

This is a work of fiction. Names, characters, places and incidents either are the product of the author's imagination or are used fictitiously, and any resemblance to any actual persons, living or dead, events, or locales is entirely coincidental.

This book was printed in the United States of America.

To order additional copies of this book, contact:
Xlibris Corporation
1-888-795-4274
www.Xlibris.com
Orders@Xlibris.com
97364

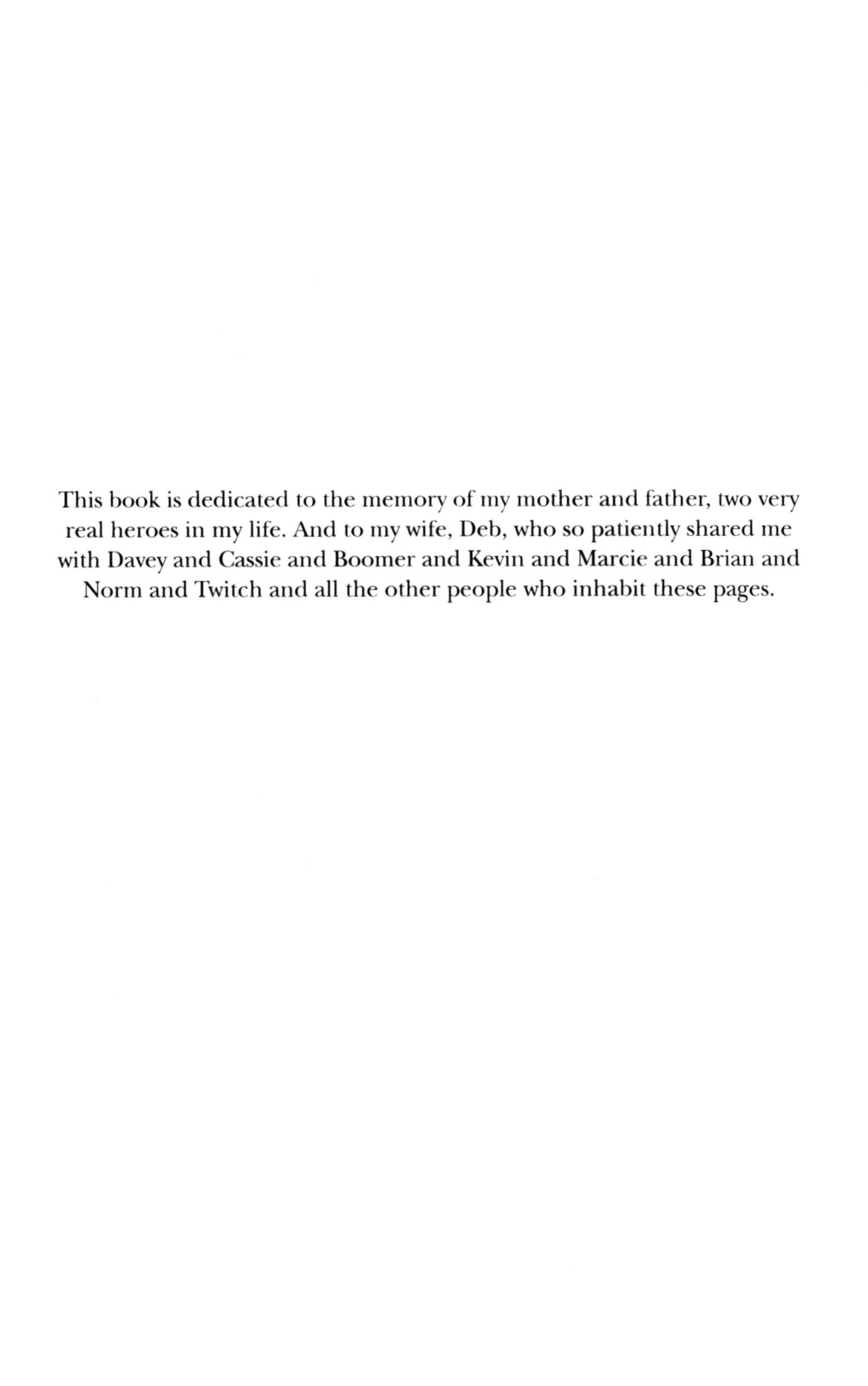

This book is dedicated to the memory of my mother and father, two very real heroes in my life. And to my wife, Deb, who so patiently shared me with Davey and Cassie and Boomer and Kevin and Marcie and Brian and Norm and Twitch and all the other people who inhabit these pages.

Chapter 1

*T*hey killed Keith in the early afternoon. Shot him from helicopters in a blue summer sky.

Lord Greystoke was the first one aware of the helicopters. Davey and Lorraine were preoccupied. Lorraine sat in a wicker chair in the shade of the house, getting stoned and droning on about how the moss retained moisture in her hanging planters. Seated beside her, Davey was gazing at Lord Greystoke with a glassy sort of envy. The benefit of moss to hanging planters was not currently of deep and engaging concern to Davey.

His Lordship, unencumbered by either drugs or self-pity, was sprawled in the dusty August sunshine, no doubt dreaming innocent dreams of small furry things struggling in his mouth. He lifted his head and looked around with that expression cats use to convey equal parts of annoyance and alarm. He rolled onto his feet, crouched low, flattened his ears, and twitched his tail.

"Come on, Greystoke," Davey said to the cat, only partly in jest. "Don't you be leaving me too."

"Christsake," said Lorraine, chuckling. She was chasing pot with white wine on the rocks, and her voice was slurred with it. "You got a burr up your ass, take it up with Frank. What's Greystoke got to do with it?"

The cat, Davey sulked to himself, doesn't have to hear about the construction and management of hanging planters. The cat, you see, wasn't stuck out here listening to stoned gibberish while Frank and Keith were cloistered in the house, engaged in discussion to which Davey was pointedly uninvited. The cat didn't have to sit and chat with Frank's wife like one of the girls, pretending he was fine with it, while his partners in pot held secret counsel. And that, my dear, is reason aplenty to snipe at the fucking cat.

"What's that?" said Lorraine.

Davey blushed. Had he been sulking out loud? The old tongue spilling a bit of leakage from the locker where nice guys keep their complaints? Thirty-two years of being a nice guy, that locker was stuffed full. Be a lot of spillage, it ever started leaking.

But Lorraine cocked her head and lifted a wisp of graying auburn hair off her left ear. "There it is again," she said.

The faint chop of a helicopter rotor came and went so quickly Davey could've imagined it. He looked at Lorraine, opened his mouth to ask if that's what she'd heard, and then it came again: a deep growl beneath an undulating chop. The sound filtered through the forest to the west, growing louder by the second.

"Mounties?" Davey said, rising from the lawn chair, searching the western sky.

The house crouched in the southeast corner of a roughly cleared acreage. Second-growth conifers, a hundred feet high, surrounded the clearing. To the north, west, and south, the forest stretched into the distance; to the east, it formed a thin strip between the clearing and the sea. The brackish scent of low tide was sweetened by the smell of spruce and balsam and marijuana.

In front of the house, Frank and Lorraine's rust-decaled van was parked on the gravel beside their daughter's white Samurai. Beyond that was the six-acre clearing where Frank's ganja sprouted betwixt and between sawed-off tree stumps and west coast scrub brush.

Lorraine stood up and peered westward, shading her eyes with her hand as if that would help her see through the trees.

"Frankie!" she called out, setting her drink on her chair where it tipped and tumbled to the ground. Apparently, she'd decided that an approaching helicopter overrode her husband's do-not-disturb request. "Frankie!"

Lord Greystoke leaped to his feet and hightailed it into the bush, and Davey figured the cat had the right idea—fade into the forest and let the Mounties have the crop. Unlikely the cops would chase them through the trees over Frank's little outdoor grow-op.

Keith came out of the house first, his face searching the sky. He was Davey's age plus a few months. At five foot ten, hundred sixty pounds, with his dark hair and eyes, he looked enough like Davey that it wasn't uncommon for people to think them brothers. And the way their parents had chummed around, who knew?

Frank came out a moment later. Half a generation older, Frank was an aging hippie with a thinning gray ponytail and a short-barrelled pump-action shotgun.

"Are you *nuts?*" Davey cried, staring at the shotgun. The chopper noise was loud enough that he had to raise his voice. "Cops see that we're fucked. Let them *have* the damn crop."

Then Keith was in his face. "Sorry, Davey, might not be the cops. We thought we had more time."

"What do you *mean?*" Davey yelled above the chopper noise. "Who *else?* More time for *what?*" His words were swallowed by the noise.

The treetops to the west were flattened by rotor wash, and two helicopters roared in over the clearing. They were large and black, with extended nose cones and boxy cargo bays. The windows were tinted dark. They showed no markings.

They hovered in the blue summer sky three hundred feet above the clearing where Frank's marijuana was coming into bud. The cargo doors slid open. Canisters the size of beer kegs tumbled out, four of them. They glinted in the sunlight as they fell, then hit the earth and detonated with the deep basso cough of exploding gasoline. The noise seemed to start inside Davey's head and blow outward, like the pattern of the explosions—great fiery circles blasting outward from the point of impact.

Davey stood there as if pinned by the mass of the noise, the solid waves of heat, the whirlwinds of smoke and dust, the impossibility of what was happening. He heard tiny popping sounds to his left. Frank was pumping and shooting the shotgun. That's it, piss them *right* off.

The choppers turned toward the house. Men stood in the cargo doors, looking down over automatic rifles. Davey suppressed a ludicrous urge to wave at them. Then the house started coming apart. Windows shattered and splinters flew from the walls.

Frank grabbed his wife's arm, and they ran around the house toward the woods. Davey started to follow, but Keith took his shoulder and turned him the other way.

"To the boat!" he yelled.

"What the hell—"

"Not *now*, for Christsake!" Keith screamed, and they ran.

They headed for the trail that led through the forest to the ocean; the trees would hide them from the choppers. Just before they got there, Keith stumbled. Davey helped him up. There was blood everywhere.

"Fucking shot, man," Keith said.

No way, Davey thought, his brain standing there shaking its head. *This ain't really happening.* But his body wasn't listening. His body surged with adrenaline and listened to nothing.

He got Keith's arm over his shoulder and half-carried him down the trail, where the crowd of trees dulled the roar of the choppers. They met

Cassie running up the trail toward them. She'd been sunning down on the dock and, either in haste or in shock, had forgotten her bikini top. She stopped when she saw them and stared at Keith. Her eyes grew huge and her jaw dropped.

"Back!" Davey yelled. "Go back!"

Cassie stood gaping at Keith.

Keith told them he was fucking shot, man.

The helicopters growled at them.

Davey grabbed Cassie's arm and spun her around, shoved her back down the trail. At the trailhead, a series of wooden steps sloped down over the rocky shore leading to a floating wharf, the planks and beams all rough cedar, silvered by weather. *Small Wonder* was moored out at the end of the wharf. Davey never stopped to consider that a thirty-six-foot sailboat on the open water was not a really good refuge from armed helicopters. He scampered toward her much as a field mouse scampers to his little hole in the ground when a big iron plough bears down on him.

He lifted Keith into the cockpit and laid him on the starboard bench, then looked around for Cassie. She was on the wharf, still naked but for the yellow bikini briefs, meticulously packing a tote bag with towel, sunglasses, sunblock, and other such shit that was scattered around her tanning station.

"Cassie!"

She responded to her name, but there was an unsettling vacancy in her eyes.

"Come on!"

She looked back toward the shore. Toward the racket of aircraft engines and the thick black smoke rising above the trees.

"Never mind! You can't go there!" He leaped onto the wharf and tugged her to the boat. "We have to leave. Now!"

She stepped aboard and said, "Mom?" But she wasn't asking Davey. Maybe she was asking the sea or the sky or the second growth forest. "Daddy?"

Her eyes fell on Keith, and she groaned. Her face went pale, and she shook her head in rapid little arcs.

"Go below!" Davey fumbled the mooring lines free. He jumped into the cockpit and gave her a nudge toward the companionway. "Go below." Clutching her bag as if it were a life ring, she stumbled below.

Davey fired the engine and got *Small Wonder* headed into Queen Charlotte Strait, guiding her between circular net pens teaming with salmon. As soon as she was past the pens, Davey tied off the wheel and kneeled beside Keith.

Jesus, he really was shot. A couple of bullets had passed through him back to front. There was an exit wound on the right side of his chest, another on the left side of his belly. A lot of stuff that was supposed to be inside him was on his outside. His breath was shallow. It gurgled through pink foam on his lips. He blinked and swallowed, and his body made sounds a body's not supposed to make. Clearly, this was not a first aid kit sort of thing.

"Fuckin' shot," he said, and the concept seemed to amaze him, as if he'd just won a lottery or something. "Believe that shit?"

Davey took his hand. He had no idea what to believe.

"Sorry," Keith said. "Had to try."

What? Davey wondered. *What did you have to try? And with whom?* But he didn't ask. Maybe he didn't really want to know.

He looked shoreward and saw that against the tide they'd made little more than a cable's length. A fat column of dark smoke was billowing up over the trees. Two men appeared at the trailhead. One cradled a rifle; the other lifted something to his face. *Binoculars,* Davey thought and flipped him a bird.

The men turned and hurried back up the trail. Back, no doubt, to the helicopters. Davey nudged the throttle to make sure it was fully open. Like an extra half a knot was going to make the difference. He heard the rising note of the chopper engines. The flesh at the back of his neck tingled and tried to crawl up under his hair. But when he peeked over his shoulder, the choppers were speeding inland. He found he'd been holding his breath. When he let it go, it came out shaky.

Davey took his friend's hand again. "They're gone."

Keith shook his head and muttered, "Uh-uh." He closed his eyes and blew pink bubbles. His body shuddered, like a weight lifter trying to press too much, and he called out for Boomer.

"Boomer's not here," Davey said.

"Boomer's got it," Keith said, using all his strength to suck in enough air to make the words. "No cops, Davey. Boomer's got it."

Keith's sweat soaked his hand. Or maybe it was Davey's sweat. He stroked Keith's forehead. It was cold.

"Promise," said Keith. "No cops."

"Sure," said Davey, scared sick and sure about nothing.

Keith swallowed noisily and blinked his eyes. Mumbled something about his chest. Davey glanced at the ragged seeping hole there and looked away. Keith babbled on. Mentioned his chest again and something about a gun. Simply his mind, Davey supposed, tripping through the place where minds go when their bodies get great bloody holes shot in them.

Keith's grip tightened. "Davey?" he asked, and the fear in his voice made Davey sob. Davey wrapped his arms around his friend and held him close. Keith's eyes were wide and full of fear. His pupils dilated, as if trying to see through sudden solid blackness, and he let go a sigh that stretched out forever and ever, amen.

Davey sat there holding Keith. His mind was spongy, saturated with the whisper of the water on *Small Wonder*'s hull and the muffled chug of her engine. The imminent danger seemed more of a nuisance than a concern, a chore to be put off while he curled up in a corner and listened to the swish of the water and the chug of the engine and waited for Keith to come back.

Some lost amount of time later, he heard a low moan. Looked over his shoulder. Cassie was standing in the companionway hatch. A beige watch sweater from Davey's closet hung around her like a sack. God, she was pretty. Even with her hazel eyes all puffy from crying and her hair tangled into chestnut-colored rat's nests she was pretty.

Course she was. Didn't have holes shot in her, did she? Anyone without holes shot in them was pretty.

"Is he dead?" she asked, her voice thick with mucus.

Davey opened his mouth but couldn't find his voice. He nodded. Prised his hand loose from Keith's grip and closed Keith's eyes for him.

"Mom and Dad?" she asked.

"I don't know," Davey said.

"Oh god." She shook her head. Her face tightened, and Davey was afraid she'd start crying again.

She didn't, though. She closed her eyes and clenched her jaw. She opened her eyes and glared at him. "What happened?"

"I don't know," he repeated, sounding even to himself like a half-wit.

Cassie leaned her weight on the bulkhead, and her right hand came into view. Davey looked at the pistol in it, his old Llama 9 mm automatic. She must have found it while digging through his clothes for the sweater.

"We don't need that," he said. There'd been enough shooting for one day.

She looked down at the gun, then at Keith, then Davey. "We should go back."

Davey looked shoreward. The column of smoke billowed over the trees a couple of miles back. Fire crews could be there already, police to follow shortly.

No cops, Davey, promise.

"I'm going to Boomer's," he said. "I'll drop you at Alert Bay." She could take the ferry from Alert Bay and get back home in a couple of hours. If she still had a home.

Cassie looked at the body, shook her head, and looked away. Her shoulders trembled with silent sobs.

Davey wanted to go to her, hold her, and tell her it would be okay. Wanted her to hold him and tell him it would be okay. Human contact and murmured lies, that's what he wanted. But the truth lay in a bloody mess on the sole of his boat.

When he stood up, his legs trembled. He hoped Cassie didn't notice. Pretending to be in charge of himself, he opened the locker under the starboard bench. He pulled out a large flag, black with a white Jolly Roger on it.

"What are you doing?" she asked.

"I'm going to bury him."

"What? You can't."

Davey laid the flag out on the deck. "I'm not going to pull up to the dock with Keith lying here like this."

Cassie turned and went below.

The pirate flag was about eight feet by ten. Keith liked to run it out when they were carrying pot. Said that the Mounties would never suspect a boat flying the Skull and Bones, man. Davey had never really followed the reasoning behind that, but producing a trail of reason to follow was not a concern for Keith. He'd gone after life with a childlike immediacy; reasons came and went along the way. He was a thirty-two-year-old little boy playing pirates: flying the Jolly Roger was a given, like the sea chest in his cabin and the macaw he'd named Captain Kidd.

Davey remembered how disappointed Keith had been when the bird turned out to be a landlubber with no tolerance for the discomforts of life on board: *"Captain Kidd, my ass. Parrot fucking stew is what you are."* But of course, there'd been no parrot stew. Captain Kidd now squawked and shat in the office of Boomer's Boatworks.

Davey burrowed deep into the memories, where Keith still lived and laughed. It was the only way he could work with the slab of cooling meat that had been his friend.

Cassie came back, minus the gun, and started helping him. She was weeping softly, but she was getting it done. They got the thing wrapped and strapped and dragged it aft to the swim grid. Davey looked at it, thinking there should be some last words, but there was a feverish heat in his head, burning up thoughts like rubbish in a furnace.

"What if it floats?" Cassie said.

Davey, trying to think of a eulogy, almost laughed. It was a crazy, cackling laugh that fortunately burned up in the fever before it got started.

But she was right. Bodies afloat tended to stay afloat. He went back to the locker, got a six-foot length of boom chain and shackled it to Keith's legs. Still lost for words, he bent down and kissed the head of the thing in the flag. Then he pushed the chain off the swim grid and gave Keith to the cold deep waters of the Queen Charlotte Strait.

Chapter 2

*D*avey hung up the phone, pulled out his pack of Player's, and lit one. Medicinal smoke. Adrenaline control. He stepped from the phone booth and glanced around.

He was in Alert Bay, a cluster of wooden buildings clinging to the rocky shore of Cormorant Island as if spawned from the debris of some ancient shipwreck. A glance and a half covered the whole village.

Tourists in bright clothes prowled the main street, a narrow strip of blacktop separated from the shoreline by a concrete seawall. Davey walked with his head down, his eyes on the sidewalk. Before coming ashore, he'd washed himself and changed his bloody clothes, but still, he felt Keith's blood on him like a neon stain. He crushed his cigarette and hurried out along the public dock to his boat.

Aboard *Small Wonder*, he found Cassie sitting huddled on the V-berth in the forward cabin. She looked small and formless draped in Davey's track pants and watch sweater. Afternoon sunlight spilled through the portholes and pooled in her eyes. She still had the Llama automatic, clutching it the way a child might clutch a doll as her home burned down. Maybe if he gave her some comforting words, she wouldn't need the talismanic comfort of the gun. But he had none to give. Davey Jones didn't do comfort; he'd never learned how.

He said, "I need to get going."

Cassie sniffled loudly, cleared mucus from her throat.

Davey leaned into the head, tore a length of toilet paper from the roll, and offered it to her.

Cassie took the tissue, mumbled, "Thanks," blew her nose, wiped her eyes, cleared her throat.

"What did Boomer say?" she asked. "Does he know what happened? What's happening?"

Davey shook his head. "Just that Keith left a message for me."

"What message?"

Again, Davey shook his head. "Boomer wouldn't say. Just said that Keith left it on Linda's answering machine two days ago. Boomer and Linda are taking the tape to their cabin. I'm meeting them there. I need to get going."

Cassie looked at the gun in her hand. She dropped the clip from the handle and disarmed the chamber. Set the empty gun on the bunk. "Did Boomer say anything about Mom and Dad?"

"No. Sorry. No word."

She nodded once. "I'm coming with you. They'll call Boomer as soon as they can."

"Okay then," said Davey, thinking, *If they can.* Cassie maybe thinking it too. Neither of them saying it. "We'll cast off, then."

Three hundred and fifty kilometers long, Vancouver Island lies soft against Canada's west coast. Four times a day, a tide that ranges as much as eighteen feet pushes countless tonnes of water through the narrow passage between the island and the mainland. *Small Wonder* left Alert Bay on the flood. The following current rushed her east through Blackfish Sound, named for the killer whales that meet at Robson Bight to plan mayhem and slaughter, and into Johnstone Strait. To the right, the sun was setting behind the forested slopes of Vancouver Island's Franklin Range. High to the left the day's last light glowed pink on the snowy peaks of the mainland's Coastal Range. Cold air rose off the water; the temperature plunged. Davey wrapped himself in a cruiser jacket.

The night was soon black under a canopy of stars. The settlements of Port Neville and Kelsey Bay passed by on the shoreline, tiny lights in the massive night. Davey steered by radar and GPS until the moon came up. It was a three-quarter moon, and it spread a copper-colored carpet across the water. Just past Sayward, the tide turned against him. To his left, it rushed out between the Discovery Islands, creating chutes with names like Surge Narrows, Hole in the Wall, Whitewater Passage, and the Sink. *Small Wonder* struggled against the current in the dark for six hours and reached Seymour Narrows, the granddaddy of all rapids, on the turn of the tide. Slack water lasted for just twenty minutes, then the flood surged from the north, bearing *Small Wonder* through the Narrows and around Race Point and scooting her past the lights of Elk Falls and Campbell River. To the east, the sun cracked open the horizon.

Two hours later, Davey was squinting, his eyes burning with fatigue. Sunlight poured over the port bow, glittering like bits of glass on the choppy waters of Georgia Strait. Fifteen hours after leaving Alert Bay,

Davey steered into an unnamed bay on the Vancouver Island shoreline midway between Comox and Campbell River. Among his friends, the bay was known as Boomer's Bight. Second-growth rainforest crowded the shoreline. Deep in the curve of the bight, about half a mile from the headland, Boomer's cabin squatted among the trees above the beach.

Davey guided *Small Wonder* along the deep channel that lay between the bay's north shore and the jagged sprawl of Gunner's Rock. As they neared the T-wharf, Cassie deployed the fenders astarboard and readied the mooring lines. Boomer, all six and a half feet, two and a half hundred pounds of him, came out onto the floating wharf to meet them. He wore a checkered shirt and blue jeans big enough to make a decent sail cover. His red hair and beard looked like fire with the sun in his face. Or maybe that was just his expression.

He took the lines and tied them, then helped Cassie from the boat. Held her. Murmured sympathies to her. Milk of human kindness. See how it's done, Jones? Ain't that tough. Maybe take notes or something.

Not fair. Boomer had known her since she was a child, had an avuncular relationship with her. Davey had an avuncular relationship with no one. Anyway, Davey wasn't sure that he could hug her strictly for her comfort. The image of her breasts was still there, popping up, as it were, in the back of his mind.

Linda came out to the boat too, her fine blonde hair wisping in the breeze. She was in her midthirties, but her soft blue eyes and peaches-and-cream complexion gave her five or six years for free. She was about five foot four, plump in a sensual sort of way. She gave Cassie a hug, then took her hand and led her toward the cabin.

"Look, Boomer," Davey began, but Boomer held up his hand, stopping him like a traffic cop.

"You got nothing I want to hear," Boomer said, "until you listen to the tape."

Davey gave him a look. "Why not just tell me?"

"Because I'm hoping, I'm really, really hoping that *you* can tell *me*."

The living room in his cabin was furnished in what Boomer called contemporary garage sale. A couch and two armchairs upholstered in heavy earth-toned fabrics of textured pile, none of them matching. Two end tables were wooden packing crates with decals on the sides depicting broken wine glasses. A large burl coffee table centered it all like a compass rose. Boomer, Linda, Cassie, and Davey stood around it like the cardinal directions. On the coffee table were a crossword puzzle book and Linda's little white answering machine. Boomer leaned down and activated it.

The machine made a low whispery sound, as if clearing its throat, and said, "Linda, it's Keith." And it was. The same voice that had said, *Fuckin shot, man.* Davey shivered. "I hate to do this to you," it said as traffic noises ebbed and flowed around it. "But I'm running out of options. I may have to leave in a hurry, and if I do, there's something Davey has to know. If I disappear, let Davey listen to this tape. Thanks, you're a sweetheart. Hopefully, next time I see you I can ask you to erase this nonsense."

The machine beeped to signal the end of the message.

Davey looked at Linda. "He left this on Monday?"

"That's right," said Linda. She carried a slight British accent, like a memento she hadn't the heart to get rid of. "Three days ago."

"Shshsh," said Boomer and raised his hand. The machine was rolling again.

"Hi, Davey," said Davey's dead friend. "If you're listening to this, things have gone from bad to worse. I can't give you any details in case the wrong people hear this, and quite frankly, I don't know who the wrong people are anymore. I have to warn you that things might get a bit hairy. You might be tempted to go to the police. Believe me, you really don't want to do that. You want to get in touch with Marcie Dennison, only her."

There was a phone number, repeated twice.

"I acquired something for her," Keith continued. "And the people I acquired it from are a wee bit pissed off. Marcie was going to protect me, but I'm not sure she can anymore, so I'm keeping the item in question in case I need something to bargain with. If things don't work out for me, you'll have to find it and get it to her. Think of my sea chest and Treasure Island. You'll say, nah, can't be. But it is, it's there. Gotta clock, man. Places to go, things to do."

But the tape kept rolling, recording the traffic in the background. There was a polite double toot, almost apologetic, road rage by Milquetoast. Then Keith took a deep shaky breath.

"Oh boy," he said. "I wanted to say something, you know, special, just in case. Cause you and me, Davey, we had some times, didn't we? Can't think of anything poignant to the occasion. Kind of a word is that? Poignant? Where the hell do we get words like that? Christ, I'm babbling. Never known me to babble, have you? Ha ha. Don't want to say good-bye. Gotta. Remember, Davey, *illegitimus non carborundum.* I'm sorry, man. So fucking sorry."

The machine whirred and clicked and shut down.

From behind the cabin, the genset thrummed. To Davey, it was the sound of a heavy gauge drill bit penetrating his skull, turning his brain into a block of wormwood. He looked inward, as if peering down the holes, imagining a sea of grief, like molten lava, seething down there. But that was just imagining. Blink your eyes and look again and there's nothing. The unbearable weight of emptiness.

"Well?" said Boomer. "Treasure Island? Marcie Dennison? Protection? Talk to us, Davey. What the hell's going on here?"

Davey stared at the answering machine. Felt their eyes on him like heat lamps, burning his ears and his cheeks and the back of his neck.

He shook his head. "I don't know. Means nothing to me, none of it."

"C'mon, Davey, you're saying Keith had something going that you didn't know about? That's a tough sell."

Davey recalled the private meetings between Keith and Frank. *Trust us on this, Davey. We'll fill you in as soon as we possibly can.* Their last meeting interrupted by helicopters and exploding gasoline and gunshots. *Fuckin shot, man.* Meeting adjourned.

He said, "I didn't see much of Keith for the last five, six weeks. He'd got himself a girlfriend. He'd show up when we had a delivery to make, and then back to Lily."

"But you saw him yesterday. He left this message on Monday. How come he never told you about it yesterday?"

"How the fuck can I know that?" Davey snapped. But his eyes skittered away, went to the window. Out on Georgia Strait, the morning sunlight spread like fire on the water. He stared at the yellow glare till it hurt his eyes. He thought of Cassie. Wondered if Frank had shared with his daughter whatever confidence Keith had deemed Davey unworthy of. He looked at her. She'd gone and sat at the base of the stairway—limp, wrung out, her face glazed with exhaustion. So goddamn pretty it ached. Davey shook his head.

Boomer was watching him, one eyebrow cocked, still waiting for an answer.

"Keith was in a mood yesterday," said Davey. "Didn't say much of anything." At least, not to Davey. "I figured his mind was down in Campbell River with his girlfriend."

"This girlfriend, you said Lily. Obviously not the Marcie Keith mentioned in the message."

Davey shrugged. "Could be. He called her Lily White, but I suspect that's a stage name."

"Even so, the number he left for this Marcie is a Victoria number. You said his girlfriend lives in Campbell River."

"No, she doesn't live there. She has a gig there. At JJ's. She's a dancer. You know—a stripper."

Boomer grunted. "What did he acquire for her?"

Davey shrugged.

"Why couldn't he go to the cops even when he found himself drowning in shit?"

"Case you missed it, Keith and I've been moving Frank's pot for the last few years."

"That don't cut it, Davey. No one goes to jail for pot these days. Cocaine, on the other hand, or heroin—"

"We shouldn't jump to conclusions, Lawrence." That was Linda. She was the only one Davey knew who got away with calling Boomer by his given name. She was sitting on the stairs beside Cassie with an arm around her. "We've got a name and a phone number. We should gather as much information as we can."

She looked at Davey. "What about Treasure Island? Any idea what Keith means by that?"

Davey nodded. "Seems unlikely, but he said it would. Place we used to stash product when we did a Vancouver run. It's on Granville Island. We called it the Treasury."

"There we go," said Linda. "If we can find out who Marcie Dennison is and what Keith got for her, we can make decisions based on information rather than oh my god."

"Or," said Boomer, "we get Davey a lawyer, take all this crap to the cops, and let them sort it out."

Davey picked up the crossword puzzle book and tore the corner off a page. He wrote on it Marcie Dennison's name and phone number. "Use your truck?" he asked.

The phone company had never felt disposed to service Boomer's remote property, and Boomer considered the cell phone a high-tech ball and chain. The nearest phone was the pay phone at Casper's out on the highway.

Boomer dug a set of keys from the pocket of his jeans. "Believe I'll tag along," he said.

Boomer's waterfront retreat was linked to the real world by a four-kilometer stretch of dilapidated blacktop that went by the name of Crabbe-Levy Road. Ages ago, someone had paved it, but the works department had ignored it over the ages, leaving the pavement to deteriorate into a moonscape of heaves and potholes.

"Cassie looks about done in," said Boomer as he guided his old Chevy pickup around the worst of the broken surface. Morning sunlight glinted through emerald branches of hemlock and Douglas fir.

"I don't think she's slept or eaten since it happened," said Davey. "Be amazing if she wasn't done in."

"How about you? You holding up okay?"

"I'm fine."

"Right. Found out Keith was dealing dangerous goods behind your back, buried his shot-up body off the swim grid. Sounds fine to me."

As Crabbe-Levy Road neared the highway, the forest gave way to neglected farmland. Mounds of brambles swallowed rotting fences. Groves of saplings, like nature's claim stakes, sprouted in pastures gone wild. Davey stared out the side window at a decaying barn, its gambrel roof crippled with age. He supposed some poor sap named Crabbe-Levy had worked his fingers to the bone clearing the land, stringing the fences, raising the barn. Now he had a busted-up road named after him.

"Are Frank and Cassie tight?" he asked.

Boomer glanced at him. "Tight as any father and daughter, I guess. Why?"

"Does he confide in her?"

"You think she might know something? Think her dad might've told her something? Should be asking her, not me."

"First thing she did when she got on the boat was dig out my old pistol."

"After her home got bombed and shot at? Seems guilty as hell to me."

"She knows her way around a gun," Davey said, ignoring Boomer's sarcasm. "How many university coeds can load and strip an automatic pistol?"

"Given Cassie's lifestyle, it'd be strange if she didn't know her way around a gun."

"You mean, being raised on a pot plantation."

"I mean, being raised on an isolated fish farm. I mean, learning how to hunt instead of how to ride a bike. I mean, having to use deadly force to protect the fish pens from sea lions and bears."

Casper's Mohawk station took up the southeast corner where Crabbe-Levy met Highway 19. As Boomer drove into the sprawling gravel parking lot, he was explaining that Frank's open-air potarium did not constitute a drug cartel and that Cassie's familiarity with firearms did not make her a gangster moll.

"They came in helicopters," Davey said. "With bombs and automatic weapons. It wasn't about a few pounds of homegrown pot."

The parking lot was empty. By noon, it would be full of motor homes and fifth wheels, but nine in the morning was too early for tourists. Boomer parked close to a pair of pay phones attached to the cinder block wall.

Davey fed the coin slot, punched in the number, listened to the ring tones. His hand was clammy on the receiver. Suppose Marcie Dennison didn't *care* if Keith was dead and Frank chased to ground by armed helicopters, they owed her a chestful of cocaine and she aimed to collect?

"Good morning," said a pleasant female voice with an Asian accent. "Crown counselor's office, Victoria."

Davey took the instrument away from his face and frowned at it. Had he misdialed?

Boomer raised an eyebrow, mouthed, "What?"

"Hello?" the phone insisted. "May I help you?"

Davey brought it back to his cheek. "I'm, ah, looking for Marcie Dennison?"

"Counselor Dennison is busy at the moment, sir. May I have her return your call?"

Davey's mind reeled in an effort to change direction. A crown counselor? "Can you tell her it's from Keith Stoddard?"

"One moment, Mr. Stoddard. I believe Counselor Dennison will take your call now."

The moment was a quick one. Evidently, Counselor Dennison wasn't too busy to take a call from Keith Stoddard.

"Keith," she said, her tone not nearly as congenial as the receptionist's. "What in God's name happened up there?"

Whatever happened, Davey doubted it was in God's name. He cleared his throat. "I was hoping you could tell me," he said.

There were a few seconds of cautious silence, then, "Who is this? Please identify yourself."

So Counselor Dennison knew Keith well enough to recognize his voice. Curiosity wormed its way into Davey's confusion.

"A friend of Keith's," he said. "Keith suggested I get in touch with you."

She seemed to think about that for a moment and then said, "I need you to identify yourself and come to my office." It was a directive, not a request.

Davey shook his head. "Not until I know what business you had with Keith."

"What has he told you?"

"He died before he got to that part."

That took the wind out of her sails. It left with a muttered, "Good Lord."

The operator broke in to inform Davey that his prepaid time was up. Dennison talked to the operator and accepted the charges at her end. When she'd got rid of the operator, she said, "Hello? Are you still there?"

"Still here," said Davey. "Still waiting for an answer."

"I'm sorry," she said, not sounding it. "But I'm unwilling to discuss this over the phone with a stranger. If you don't want to come to my office, we can meet at a location of your choice. Either way, if you are a friend of Keith's, I can guarantee your safety."

Marcie was going to protect me, but I'm not sure she can anymore.
Fucking shot, man.

Davey broke into a cold sweat and almost hung up again. But Dennison could tell him why Keith was dead, and she wasn't going to tell him over the phone. He said, "Can you be in Nanaimo tomorrow afternoon?"

"Yes. I can do that."

"There's a pub called Muddy Waters, just off Stewart Avenue near Departure Bay. Be there at one tomorrow afternoon. Tell the bartender you're looking for Davey."

"Davey?"

"Right. Just wait there. I'll be along as soon as I'm sure there are no cops. If I suspect a cop anywhere near there, even if he's just getting donuts, I won't show."

"If you *are* a friend of Keith's," she said, "you have nothing to fear from the police."

No cops, Davey. Promise. No cops.

He quietly hung up.

Back on Crabbe-Levy Road, Davey rolled down his window and lit a smoke. "I'll go to Vancouver tonight," he said. "See what Keith left in the Treasury before I talk to this Dennison."

On the drive back, Boomer scowled at the road, dodging potholes with the thoughtless ease of someone who was used to the job. He failed to offer Davey a ride to Nanaimo, making Davey asked for it.

"So can I bum a ride to Nanaimo with you or Linda?"

"Take the truck," said Boomer through his scowl. "Linda and I are staying."

"What about your jobs?"

"Don't worry about that. Eddie can run the Boatworks as well as I can, and Linda's got sick days owed at the law firm. Wouldn't leave Cassie alone in any case. You just worry about getting this mess fixed."

Davey realized he didn't want the smoke, crushed it in the ashtray. "I take it you still think the best way to do that is through the Mounties."

"Silly me, huh?"

"You heard what Keith said—"

"Keith's *dead!*" Boomer slammed the steering wheel as if it were the wheel that was too stubborn to understand.

The two men kept any further thoughts to themselves until Boomer pulled into his driveway. He parked behind the cabin, close by Linda's white Prelude. Davey opened his door to get out, but Boomer's hand dropped on his shoulder.

"I won't let you put Linda in the path of this thing," he said. "The minute I see it heading her way, the cops are here like that." Instead of snapping his fingers to emphasize *that*, he squeezed Davey's shoulder. Hard.

"Of course," said Davey, and at the time, he meant it.

Chapter 3

$\mathcal{D}$avey considered Nanaimo, with its eighty thousand souls, a city; Vancouver, with its millions, was a bludgeon to the senses. Dusk was falling by the time he debarked the ferry and flagged a cab at Horseshoe Bay, yet Vancouver seemed to be just waking up, some great nocturnal beast emerging from its lair rested and hungry. As his taxi made its way through West Van toward Lions Gate Bridge, the immensity of concrete seemed to tower over him with an eerie awareness, the constant motion and racket to jabber at him.

Apparently unaffected by Davey's phobia, the driver, a dark young man in a purple turban, whistled softly as he steered the car through streets like canyon floors. None too soon for Davey, the cab found its way out of the looming labyrinth of downtown skyscrapers and took the Granville Street Bridge over False Creek. It followed the cloverleaf back down to False Creek and took a smaller bridge over to the sandbar they call Granville Island.

Created largely from a century's buildup of industrial slag, Granville Island was discovered by the arts community a few decades ago. The industries were pinched out. Warehouses and ironworks became theaters and art galleries and public markets. The cab rumbled over a cobbled street half hidden by wisps of ground mist and, at Davey's bidding, stopped at the public wharf. Davey pulled out a hundred-dollar bill, leaned over the back of the seat, and looked at the driver's name tag.

"Tell you what, Dahli, keep the meter running and take a little tour. Meet me back here in about ten minutes and I'll catch a ride back to Horseshoe Bay."

Dahli took the hundred and gave Davey a salute.

Davey lit a smoke as he watched the black-and-gold North Shore cab drive away. He'd left Boomer's pickup in Nanaimo, at Miller's Landing, a pub next door to the ferry terminal. Crossing as a foot passenger eliminated the risk of being left behind by a ferry overburdened with long weekenders. Of course, it also eliminated the option of taking Keith's chest with him, but that was okay. If the chest contained what he feared it might, he wouldn't want the damn thing with him. He'd simply open it and take a peek. When he met with Dennison, he wanted to know what Keith had acquired for her.

He looked up and down the cobbled street and glanced out along the wharf. The racket from downtown, like the glitzy city skyline, skipped across the shiny black water of False Creek, but on Granville Island, the markets were closed and the theater crowds were wrapped up in act 2. It was about as quiet as Vancouver ever got. Satisfied that he was alone, Davey crushed out his smoke and stepped off the street.

Clambering over the shoring of granite and limestone boulders, he made his way under the wharf ramp. He laid his hands on what looked like about a thousand-pound chunk of pink limestone. It even had the grainy, dusty feel of rock, he thought, as he pushed it aside. Amazing what they could do with plastic these days.

He and Keith had bought the "rock" from a landscape supplier. It weighed about eighty pounds. Behind it was the small cave in which they stashed product when they had business in the big city—a little hollow in the rocks they'd come to refer to as the Treasury. Davey pulled a palm-size flashlight from his jacket pocket and shone it into the cubbyhole. He sat there until he heard Dahli's cab returning, shining his flashlight into the empty Treasury, as if expecting Keith's sea chest to materialize.

Dahli got him back to the ferry terminal ten minutes before departure. With the August long weekend looming, Thursday's final sailing was predictably crowded. Hundreds of cars and trucks were crammed onto the three-vehicle decks. The lounges and promenade decks were swamped with vacationing humanity. Davey waded through the human tide until he found a breezy corner on the upper deck where he could smoke in peace while he nursed a disappointment as bitter as the tobacco.

Keith had left the message on Linda's answering machine on Monday, presumably after stashing the chest. So the chest had been there at least three days. Some wino could've crawled under the ramp to shelter from the night. Or a couple of kids could've gone down there to neck. Or to pass around a bootlegged bottle. Maybe one of them leans against the plastic rock. It shifts. What have we here? Buried treasure in a dead man's chest. Yo-ho-ho and a bottle o' rum.

Davey shivered. Even in midsummer, the night wind sweeping across the deck was cool enough to numb his cheeks and his fingers. He zipped up his jacket, pulled up the collar, and buried his hands in the pockets.

On the upside, he could truthfully tell Dennison that whatever Keith had acquired for her was gone, swallowed, as it were, into the belly of the nocturnal beast. And good riddance to it. Right?

Wrong.

He opened his jacket, used it as a windbreak to light another smoke. The truth was, he'd been counting on the sea chest. Never even considered that it wouldn't be there. Still counting on Keith to show him the way. At thirty-two, he'd accepted that he was a follower, a career second-stringer. Always willing to put his shoulder to the job provided someone else told him what the job was.

"I'm no good on my own," he said to the cigarette. "Hell of a thing for a man to face."

Maybe that's why his grief felt so barren and cold. Maybe it wasn't grief at all, but rather self-pity.

He flicked the cigarette over the rail, and he hoped, the philosophical bullshit with it, certain that both were equally unhealthy. He looked at his watch, saw that he'd been wandering the deck for an hour. No wonder he was cold. He headed inside.

He was lined up at the coffee counter when the guy behind him moved in too close, breaking into his space, reminding Davey why he hated crowds. He turned his head to make eye contact, let the guy know his rudeness was unappreciated. He was a big man, several inches taller than Davey, with the shoulders to go with it. His tanned face was all lines and angles, like an artist's rough sketch. His eyes, so dark they seemed all pupil, wouldn't meet Davey's. Telepathically, Davey told him to back off.

Turned out the guy wasn't telepathic. He followed Davey to a vacant table, placed his cup beside Davey's, and sat down. He stared at his coffee, as if studying the ripples set up by vibrations from the ship's engines.

"Good night for a boat ride, yes?" he said, finally looking up.

He had a deep mellow voice despite coming from a face that could've been carved by a chainsaw from a block of mahogany. Part of the mellowness was due to a thick accent that Davey couldn't place. But mellow voice or not, Davey was in no mood for conversation. There were several other vacant tables. Davey started to rise, but the guy put a hand on his arm.

"My employer," the man said, "invites you, yes? Likes you company, yes? Tonight."

What the hell? "You talking to me, buddy?"

The guy frowned. "Sorry. My English." He flip-flopped his hand to demonstrate his English and then smiled. "But who else I'm talking to, Mr. Stoddard?"

Davey felt the blood drain from his face. *Mr. Stoddard? The guy thinks I'm Keith!*

He forced himself to smile. "There you go," he said. "You want a Mr. Stoddard. My name's Jones. No harm done."

They guy's hand closed on Davey's forearm. "Name is no matter, yes? Name is easy." He shrugged. "The boat docks, you and me, we are walking together off, yes?"

Davey felt his guts go hollow. "Tell your boss thanks," he said. The forced smile was causing cramps in the hinges of his jaws. "But my calendar's full. Maybe if your boss calls my secretary, something can be set up in a month or two."

The guy smiled back. His smile didn't curve up at the corners but slashed straight across his face, like a scar. He shook his head and opened his leather jacket. Davey saw a pistol holstered under his arm. The guy reached in with his right hand.

Jesus!

But the guy didn't bring the gun out; he brought out a cell phone.

"I make arrange of transport, yes?" he said. He opened the phone, looked at it, and frowned. "Ah. Is interfere."

He showed Davey the faceplate, as if worried about whether or not Davey believed him.

"I try outside," he said. He got up, stepped toward the outside door, and then turned back.

"Is ocean," he said, sweeping his arm to show Davey where the ocean was. "Is no place to run, yes?"

Outside, the guy went straight to a window. He smiled at Davey through the glass, held up the phone, and made an okay circle with his thumb and forefinger.

Davey waited until the guy was dialing, then got up and trotted to the staircase. As he turned down the stairs, he glanced back. The guy was talking into his phone, but his eyes were on Davey.

Davey sprinted down the stairs, crashing through the flood doors that separated the decks. He went all the way down to the lower vehicle deck, where they keep the overheights—the touring motor homes and the semis plying trade between the mainland and the island. He darted into the maze of rigs. If he could find a sleeper unit with an unlocked door, he could get off the ferry as a stowaway. He'd worry later about explaining things to the driver.

He heard the staircase door clang as it opened and closed, echoing through the cavernous hold. He heard footsteps echo across the steel deck, and he realized that the sound of a truck door would produce similar effects.

He stood still and listened to the footsteps. Maybe they didn't belong to the gunman, could just as easily be another passenger or one of the crew. Right, and maybe if Davey closed his eyes, he'd be invisible.

He was standing between two trailer trucks parked side by side about five feet apart. One of the trailers was a container with the Radio Shack logo on the side. The other was a flat deck with a solid roof over it and canvas curtains drawn between the roof and the deck. Davey found a seam between the tarps and peeked through. The deck was loaded with coils of sheet metal laid sideways on pallets. He could hide inside one of those coils, ride off the ferry on a load of steel. He was fumbling with the tie-downs between the tarps when he heard the footsteps change course and draw closer.

"Ah, Mr. Stoddard." The guy's voice was unraised. Either he knew Davey was close or he was afraid of attracting the attention of any crew who might be down there. "Sooner than later," he said, "we all leave the boat, yes? Can be easy, can be hard."

Davey considered calling out to attract help from the crew but quickly dismissed the notion. He was certain that this guy was linked to the helicopters, and the people in the helicopters hadn't carried guns merely to threaten. They'd used them. Davey himself might be under some sort of temporary protection from this guy's employer, but not so any crewmember that came upon them.

He crouched and peered under the truck, saw a pair of tan loafers close enough to spit on, had he any spit to spare. He stood and backed up against Radio Shack. His muscles tensed, and his mind stopped making silly plans and focused on what had to be done.

As soon as the guy stepped between the trucks, Davey grabbed his jacket, spun him, slammed him into the flat deck, and threw his forehead at the guy's nose. With a sinking feeling, Davey realized the gunman was not only stronger than himself, but faster. He dodged the head-butt with ease. His arms shot up between them and pushed like pistons. Davey flew backward. The gunman's hand went under his jacket.

The space was too confined for Davey to go far. With a bruising jolt to his back, he bounced off Radio Shack. He rebounded with his knee rising, slamming up between the gunman's legs. The guy grunted in pain. His hand dropped from his jacket in a reflexive attempt to cover his parts. Davey's knee struck again, harder, as if gaining momentum from the first strike. Coffee-scented breath exploded in his face. Davey's knee came up for a third strike, aiming again for the groin. The guy bent low, either protecting himself or doubling over in pain. There was a moist hollow thunk as Davey's knee hammered the guy's head into the chrome bell of the wheel hub. The gunman went limp and folded onto the deck.

"Fuck you, man," Davey hissed, pacing on his toes around the crumpled form, panting, adrenaline buzzing through him. "Said fuck you, man."

He fought to get his breath under control. His heart pounded in the back of his head. His palms were clammy. The big muscles in his legs and arms twitched spastically. His throat burned with acidic bile, his mouth was dry as sand. He clenched his teeth and dry-swallowed.

He undid the tie-downs, holding the tarps together on the flat deck. He had to stop and shake his hands to keep his fingers from trembling. Hoisting buddy was a chore. The guy weighed over two hundred pounds and was in no condition to be helpful. Unable to push him up, Davey took one of his hands, climbed onto the truck, and pulled, twisting and bending the arm as much as he had to. Or more.

In the dim privacy of the trailer truck, the air thick with the smell of canvas and oily steel and engine fumes, he went through the guy's pockets. There was a billfold with a fistful of cash. Davey gave that back to him. There was a passport for one Dominic Slavos, citizen of the Republic of Turkey. Good shit. Davey gave that back as well.

But he kept the gun, a Beretta automatic. Finding a round in the chamber, he ejected it, replaced it in the clip, tucked the gun into the back of his jeans, and pulled his Windbreaker over it.

And he kept the photograph. It was a telephoto close-up of *Small Wonder*'s cockpit. Glaring at the camera was a grim-faced Davey Jones. His white T-shirt had blood splotches on it, like a poorly done tie-dye. His right hand was raised, middle finger extended. It was a pose Davey would remember for the rest of his life. What the camera angle missed was Keith's body lying beside him on the deck.

Davey folded the picture and slipped it into his pocket and then checked on Dominic. His breath was even, his pulse steady. A nasty purple welt was rising on his brow. Davey hoped the guy would wake up with a headache big as the great outdoors.

"Have a good trip, Nicky," he said, hoping the truck was headed for some remote outpost like Port Alice or Winter Harbour.

Chapter 4

*B*ack up on the passenger deck, Davey went to the midship's head. It was crowded. It seemed like every guy in the room was staring at him. He backed out and made his way aft, eyes down to avoid the stares he was certain he was getting from the crowded seats. He checked the front of himself for blood. Saw none, but still. The gun at the small of his back felt huge. Should've tossed the damn thing overboard. Surely they could see it through the jacket. Or suppose his jacket had got tucked inside it? He didn't dare check.

Flushed and sweating, he hurried into the aft men's room. It was mercifully empty. After relieving himself, he went to one of the sinks and splashed his face with cold water. He looked in the mirror and thought about Dominic Slavos from Turkey. Who had carried a photograph of Davey Jones. Whom he'd thought was Keith Stoddard. Whose company Dominic's employer would like. Yes?

The public address system cut through Davey's confusion. Between bursts of static, a metallic voice informed the passengers that they would soon be docking in Nanaimo, asked them to please return to their vehicles, reminded them that smoking was not permitted on the vehicle decks, hoped that they'd enjoyed their passage aboard the *Queen of Coquitlam*, and thanked them for choosing BC Ferries, as if there was another way to get to Nanaimo.

Nanaimo. Where Dominic Slavos had phoned to "make arrange of transport, yes?"

At the Nanaimo terminal, foot passengers had to file down a closed corridor and through a small foyer out to the parking lot. That's where they'd wait, the people Slavos had phoned. Would they too have a photograph of Davey Jones?

Davey felt the prickly heat of panic and cooled himself with another splash of water. It was too late now to go back down and join Dominic in the steel coils. He could stay aboard and return to Vancouver, but he was on the last sailing; this ship wouldn't be going back to Vancouver until the next morning. Cleaning crews and safety inspectors would be swarming through it all night.

He jerked when the washroom door opened. A tall young man came in. He wore a floppy brimmed hat over curly black hair and brown eyes, an army surplus jacket over faded brown T-shirt, cut-off jeans and hiking boots over woollen socks. His backpack identified him as a foot passenger.

Davey towelled off his face. "How you doing?" he asked.

"Good enough," the young man said in an accent that Davey thought came from New Zealand. "How's yourself?"

"Not too good, actually." Davey made a sheepish grin. "Seem to have got myself up the creek."

The Kiwi laughed as he stepped to the urinal. "Been there myself a time or two."

"Two women meeting me at the terminal. Neither knows about the other. Not yet anyway. Could get tense."

The Kiwi finished his business and went to the sink. In the mirror, he gave Davey a grin, but it didn't drip with sympathy.

"I wonder," said Davey, "if, ah, if you'd be willing to let me use your hat and jacket and backpack?"

The young man's eyes narrowed with suspicion.

"Just till we get out of the terminal," Davey said. "I can make it worth your while. How's a hundred sound?"

"What, dollars?" The Kiwi's expression changed from suspicion to interest.

"Yeah." Davey pulled out his wallet. "Here, you can hang on to this. When I give your stuff back, you return the wallet less a hundred bucks."

The Kiwi riffled through the bills, gave Davey a frown, shrugged, finally laughed. "What the hell. Why not?"

Davey kept his back to the wall as he switched jackets. He pulled the floppy hat low over his brow, shouldered the pack, and checked the effect in the mirror.

"Should get me through," he said. "Can't thank you enough."

"Sure, and a hundred bucks is enough."

Davey stayed centered in the stream of passengers that flowed down the gangplank, through the corridor and into the foyer, where it merged with a crowd waiting to receive friends and relatives.

Outside the foyer, a dozen or so cars idled in the loading zone. Davey scanned them from under the hat brim. A gray sedan caught his attention.

Two large dark-featured men stood with folded arms beside it, frowning as they perused the crowd. Davey tugged the hat brim lower and angled away from the overhead lights. The Kiwi followed him across Zorkin Road, down the knoll, and into the parking lot at Miller's Landing.

In recognition of its heritage as a mining town, Nanaimo maintained a high *per capita* ratio of drinking establishments. Miller's Landing was one of several located near the ferry terminal. Davey and the Kiwi blended with the migratory groups of pub crawlers ebbing and flowing through the parking lot. When he got to Boomer's truck, Davey opened the passenger door and set the backpack and the hat on the seat. With his back to the open door, he exchanged the Kiwi's army jacket for his Windbreaker. The Kiwi extracted five twenties from Davey's wallet and handed it back. He carefully rearranged the brim of his hat before setting it on his head. He looked at Davey, grinned, and said, "What now, buds?"

Davey frowned. "What now, what? Go blow the hundred bucks on a good time."

The Kiwi's tanned face crinkled with some inner amusement. "Yeah, I probably should. But those people you were shy of, well, to a poor old boy from Down Under, they looked more like hoods than lovers. And if I had that sort looking for me, even if they were lovers, I'd want to carry a gun myself."

Davey felt his cheeks heat. Groups of people were strolling by, some close enough to touch. Not a good place to discuss carrying guns.

His first instinct was to get in the truck, slam the door, and drive away. But the Kiwi might pick that particular moment to be an upstanding citizen and phone the cops. Tell them to watch for a dun colored Chevy pickup. Driver's a white male, five-ten, dark hair, brown eyes. Got a Beretta automatic tucked in his pants.

"C'mon," said Davey, "let's get off the street."

The Kiwi shouldered the pack and followed Davey into the pub. They found an isolated table out on the smoking deck. A blonde waitress took their order. Young and shapely, she wore a white apron over a black form-fitting minidress. A tag on her bosom said, "Hi, I'm Janie."

The young Kiwi never took his eyes off her as she went into the bar and returned with two mugs of beer. He whistled softly between his teeth as she went off about her business. His eyes slid reluctantly away from her hips, sparkling with a youthful overload of hormonal synapses. His eyes, not her hips. Well, maybe her hips too.

"Imagine Janie," he confided to Davey, "wearing nothing but the apron."

While that was certainly worth imagining, Davey's mind was otherwise occupied. "How did you know about the gun?" he asked.

"In the gent's room." The Kiwi smirked, proud as Punch. "You were standing next to a mirror."

Davey lit a smoke. Hiding his back in front of a mirror seemed to nicely sum up his ability to cope with armed helicopters and gunmen from Turkey.

"D'you mind, buds?" The Kiwi pointed to the pack of Player's.

Davey slid the cigarettes toward him. "You saw I had a gun and you decided to play along anyway?"

The Kiwi gave a lopsided shrug. "My first thought was to clear out. But a little voice spoke up and said, 'Kevin, old buds, you're ten thousand klicks from home and close to broke, and a hundred bucks is a hundred bucks.'"

He paused to light the cigarette he'd taken.

"Then I saw those goons waiting at the terminal and I thought, hi-ho hi-ho, there's a couple reasons to carry a gun and buy a disguise."

Davey glared at him while the Kiwi gulped beer from the mug with as much zeal as he'd fantasized about the waitress.

"God, that's good," Kevin said to the mug.

Davey leaned toward him. "Are you retarded?" he said. "Because I got to tell you, Kevin, old *buds*, I can't think of another reason why you would want to stir through shit like this when it's got nothing to do with you."

The Kiwi drew on his cigarette and closed his eyes with the pleasure of it. "Been awhile since I had a proper smoke," he said, as if lung cancer and heart disease were urban myths. "Ain't the same, piecing together other folks' leavings."

He leaned close to Davey and said, "What it is to me, buds, is an employment opportunity. Stop me if I'm wrong, but those guys waiting for you, they weren't cops. And for whatever reason, you can't go to the cops, or they won't help you. So you and those guys have got something going, a little hide-and-seek. Looks to me like the game's for keepsies and there ain't no home free."

Kevin paused to quaff more beer. Davey wrapped his hands around the cold mug. "And you're what? Dudley Do-good?"

The Kiwi put the cocky smirk on his face again. "No, buds, I'm busted is what I am. And you got money. Enough that you're not worried about handing your wallet to a stranger. Don't mind saying that I've been around the block a few times."

Kevin tucked his chin and raised his fists in a pugilist's pose. "You could have a worse mate when you're up against it. And I don't give a shit why the cops won't help you. All I care about is getting a ticket home."

He emptied his mug and held it up for Janie to see. She smiled at him and waved.

He looked back at Davey. "So what say, buds? I got to find work anyway, and it seems you could use a mate to watch your back."

"Cutting through the bullshit, you're applying for a job as a bodyguard?"

"Beats picking fruit or pitching hay. And I bet you pay better than Farmer Jack."

Janie arrived with round 2. Davey's first mug was still nearly full, yet his belly felt bloated, a condition due to nervous acid rather than draft beer. For a moment, he felt Kevin's spiel pluck at the corners of temptation. There was a bag of cash in *Small Wonder*'s chain locker—not a fortune; homegrown pot didn't generate the abundant revenue often associated with the drug trade. But enough to buy the Kiwi a ticket home. And his encounter with Mr. Slavos argued strongly in Kevin's favor, which was quite the coincidence, wasn't it? Being offered a bodyguard within minutes of being threatened with deadly violence. It wasn't in Davey's nature to trust anyone he'd just met, and coincidence was always just met.

Still, his decision wasn't based on distrust. In all likelihood, Kevin was just what he claimed to be—a cocky young opportunist. But Davey decided that he didn't need his back watched, and he didn't want the encumbrance. All he needed or wanted was to meet with Counselor Dennison.

When the waitress left, he put enough money on the table to cover the tab and leave a tip. "You're better off pitching hay," he said, and he walked away.

Had he seen Kevin abandon the beer and head for the pay phone, Davey might've thought the Kiwi was going to sic the cops on him after all. But Davey didn't see it. Davey was already out on Zorkin Road, waiting for the light to let him turn onto Stewart Avenue. He'd forgotten his concern about being reported for carrying a restricted weapon. His mind was too crowded with concerns to hang on to new ones that he picked up along the way.

Stewart Avenue cut across the hillside above Newcastle Channel. Above the street, big wooden houses, built back when lumber was cheap and miners wealthy, were being phased out to make way for ocean-view condos; downhill, the slope between the street and the docks was packed shoulder to shoulder with boat yards and chandlers. Davey drove half a kilometer up Stewart Avenue, U-turned across the wide pavement and parked at the curb under the Boomer's Boatworks sign. He sat in the truck thinking about tomorrow's meeting with Dennison. All things considered, maybe tomorrow was too far away. Maybe he should try to reach her tonight. Her office would be closed, but maybe she had an answering service that could get a message to her.

He stepped from the truck and lurched as a spasm ripped across his back, right where Radio Shack had stopped him and pushed him back at Dominic Slavos.

God*damn* it.

He was going to be stiff as a plank in the morning. Unless he was sadly mistaken, there'd be a bottle of single malt muscle relaxant in the lower right-hand drawer of Boomer's desk. He took the bundle of keys out of the truck, found the door key, and let himself into the boatworks.

The windows let in streams of moon-colored light from the street lamps, light that was quickly absorbed by the prevailing gloom. Davey was reluctant to turn on a lamp and risk arousing the spirit of duty in some passing patrol car, so he navigated through the dark around the reception desk to the door of Boomer's inner office. A soft chuckle caused his heart to leap up into his throat. He spun to his left. Captain Kidd chuckled again from his perch in the corner.

"*Jesus*," Davey hissed. Things weren't bad enough; he needed a parrot giving him a seizure.

The macaw's brilliant plumage was muted and blotchy in the dim light. Davey stepped toward the perch and held out his hand. The parrot rubbed his head against Davey's fingers. Davey decided not to tell Captain Kidd about Keith's death.

"Good one, Jones," he muttered to himself. "Right on top of it, aren't you? Sharp as a fucking pancake."

The bird chuckled.

"Yeah, well, it's been a shitty day, Captain. Could really use a drink." He left the parrot and continued into the inner office.

Boomer's private office stretched the entire width of the building. Indicative of Boomer's priorities, there were no windows looking into the reception office, so Davey could have turned on a light without it being seen from the street. He didn't, though.

Boomer's Boatworks was built on the steep slope between Stewart Avenue and Newcastle Channel. While the office was at street level, the floor of the shop was thirty feet below. In keeping with Boomer's priorities, the back wall of his office was solid glass. His could observe the cavernous shop like a ship's master observing his vessel from the bridge. From that vantage point, Davey saw a light glowing down in the shop. The light came from a gooseneck lamp illuminating the surface of a workbench. Someone's shadow loomed over the workbench. The hands of the shadow person were fishing through papers scattered across the bench top. Davey thought it must be Eddie, burning the midnight oil to catch up on the paperwork.

Eddie Roe was fortyish. A thoroughbred Haida, born and raised in a village in the Queen Charlotte Islands, he'd been with Boomer since the birth of the Boatworks. If Davey made his presence known, he'd have to explain it, and he really didn't want to get Eddie involved. He was about to turn and leave when he saw the hands sweep the bench top clear. They reached down and pulled out a drawer, dumped the contents onto the bench, and started fishing through it. Not Eddie after all.

Davey tried to tell himself that he'd stumbled into a burglary in progress, but he wasn't buying it. No way. The guy turning the workbench inside out was somehow linked to Dominic Slavos and the deadly helicopters, to Keith's sea chest and Crown Counselor Dennison. Davey stared through the window while fear buzzed through his thoughts like static, filling his mind with white noise. Through the static, he screamed at himself to get the hell out of there. Go to the truck and drive away. Right now.

But up above the white noise, up on the bridge of the brain where reason looks down on emotion like the master of a vessel portraying calm command in the midst of chaos, Davey realized he was looking at someone who could provide some answers. He reached back and pulled Dominic's gun from his waistband, worked the slide to arm the chamber. He opened the door and crept down the heavy wooden stairs, keeping his eyes on the shadow person beside the pool of lamplight. When he felt concrete under his sneakers, he stopped. The guy was about four big steps away, surely close enough to hear Davey's hammering heartbeat.

He tried to moisten his mouth, but there was no moisture to be had. He dry-swallowed to loosen his throat. His mind screamed, *Are you nuts? You can't do this!* But his arm pointed the gun and his mouth cried, "Right there, fuckhead! Don't move!"

The guy jerked away from the bench.

"I said don't *move!*" Davey cried. He closed the distance between them and pressed the gun to the back of the guy's head. "Lean on the desk. Do it!"

The guy leaned forward, placing his hands on the bench top. Davey kicked the guy's legs apart until they were spread far enough to be uncomfortable.

"Don't fuck with me," Davey said as he searched under the guy's jacket. He hoped his voice didn't sound as squeaky as it felt. "I'm scared shitless and I'm not used to guns. My finger's on the trigger and it's shaking like crazy. You understand?"

He found a short stubby revolver and put it in the pocket of his Windbreaker. For a split second, he was aware of a soft hissing sound behind him. Before he could turn, his head exploded with a pain as stark as a sheet of polished steel, then imploded toward darkness. Out on the perimeter of the collapsing darkness, his grip tightened. The gun in his hand jerked. There was a distant popping sound.

Chapter 5

*I*t was a liquid sort of darkness—tidal, with a suctioning swell to it. Voices gurgled up through it like bubbles from a diver's regulator. One was a surly voice, speaking the vernacular of the gutter. The second was calm, controlled, oiled with a milder version of Slavos' accent.

Behind Davey's eyelids, small bursts of light began to punch holes in the darkness. With the bits of light came pain. Nauseous waves of it rolled up from his testicles. Sharp blades of it stabbed into his ribs with each breath. It gripped the back of his head like a vice and rasped like a hot file in his throat. Confused stupid, Davey moaned.

"Mr. Stoddard awakes," said the calmer voice.

The tilting bursts of light coalesced into one great light shining directly onto Davey's face. The backs of his eyeballs burned, as if hot grit had gotten into the sockets. He blinked and tried to turn away, but he found himself tied to a chair. Beyond the light, all was blackness. The familiar mixture of scents—wood, oil, paint, the sugary smell of fiberglass—told him he was still in Boomer's shop. Shapes moved through the blackness, seemingly huge.

"Now if you haven't damaged him too much, perhaps we shall get some answers."

"Cocksucker blew my fucking *ear* off!"

"Do cease your whining, Chambers. You lost an insignificant little piece of flesh."

A flame flared in the darkness. There was a cadence of sipping sounds. Cigar smoke swirled around the lamp.

"A small price to pay for this unexpected visit by Mr. Stoddard."

In the darkness, a chair was shifted, its legs scraping on the concrete floor. The glowing cigar tip descended to Davey's level.

"That is how one pronounces your name, is it not, Mr. Stoddard?"

As Davey's consciousness solidified, so did his memory. Confusion gave way to awareness, and with the awareness came fear. Fighting his fear with anger, Davey told the cigar smoker to fuck off. Except he didn't tell him anything because all that passed his damaged throat was a muted rasp.

"Yes, well, that's neither here nor there. What matters is that you took something that belongs to our employer, and he wishes very much to have it back." The voice sipped its cigar for a moment. "A colleague of ours who was to open negotiations with you seems to have disappeared. The gentleman who spoke with you on the ferry, he seems not to have gotten *off* the ferry."

A dense cloud of smoke swirled around the lamp. The cigar tip flared into an angry red glow.

"Suppose we start with that, Mr. Stoddard. Suppose you tell us all about your excursion on the ferry this evening."

A large-knuckled hand appeared from the darkness, holding the cigar like a street fighter's knife. The hand was attached to a thick hairy forearm, ropy with muscle, protruding from the rolled-up sleeve of a black shirt. The cigar moved forward, sending up a puff of smoke as it burned through Davey's T-shirt and into the flesh of his belly.

The pain filled his eyes with tears, turned his muscles to wood. He opened his mouth to scream, but neither the blistering pain nor the stench of his own burning flesh could force the scream through his damaged throat.

The cigar lifted away, hovered for a moment, moved to the left, and burrowed again into Davey's belly.

Davey had imagined pain to be finite; like the terminal velocity of a falling object, it would reach a certain level and remain stable. It wasn't like that at all. It grew, expanding like circles of exploding gasoline across his stomach. And it penetrated, lancing into his guts like something wild and hungry. The need to scream was overwhelming. It erupted like magma from his lungs, but his throat turned it into a gurgling moan.

The cigar was withdrawn, yet the pain remained, a searing thing that rippled over his flesh as if it was alive and glad to be there. Too exhausted to fight it, Davey slumped, whimpering, against the ropes and let the pain have its way.

"Well, Chambers, it appears as if your mindless vengeance has rendered him speechless. Were I you, I should very much hope that this is a temporary condition and that he finds his voice by the time we reach the lodge. Sebastian shall have little use for a mute. Do you suppose you can manage to bring the car round to the back door without making a mess of it?"

Davey heard the sound of retreating footsteps and a softly muttered, "Up yours."

"Amateurs," the cigar smoker lamented to Davey. "I *do* so detest working with amateurs. But Mr. Lazuardi insists on using local talent in whatever form it presents itself. Likes to create a sense of community, does Mr. Lazuardi. And Mr. Lazuardi will have his way. I promise you that, Stoddard, Mr. Lazuardi *will* have his way."

The footsteps returned, too soon to have gotten a car from anywhere.

The cigar smoker said, "Oh, for God's sake, Chambers, what is it now? Don't tell me you've lost the keys? Or is it the car you've lost?"

There was a solid, moist *thud*. The cigar went skidding across the floor, tossing out a light spray of sparks. Bulky weight hit the concrete. A moment later, the light swung out of Davey's face. On the other side of it was Kevin.

"Bastards!" Kevin spat. Gone was the cocky amusement he'd been so full of at Miller's Landing.

He knelt behind the chair and worked on the knots binding Davey's wrists. Davey's arms fell to the sides. Hot needles of blood shot into his fingers. Cramps bit into his shoulders. Kevin untied his legs. They were numb, lifeless. Davey began to slide off the chair. Kevin grabbed him under the arms, and Davey sobbed as pain ripped across his ribs.

"Easy, buds. Easy does it." Kevin helped Davey lie on the floor, balled his jacket up, and placed it under Davey's head. "You got first aid in here?"

Davey opened his mouth and rasped. He considered the possibility that his larynx had been permanently damaged. Nodded his head.

Kevin touched his shoulder. "Just rest. I'll find it."

Kevin picked up the lamp and splashed its light around the shop. Dizziness came over Davey like a breaking wave and started to carry him off.

The sharp foul odor of ammonia brought him back into the world of pain. Kevin was holding a vial under his nose.

"I know it hurts, buds, but you have to stay awake. You have to tell me what to do."

He salved the burns on Davey's stomach and taped gauze pads over them. Pointed to the right side of Davey's chest. "Nasty bruise coming up here. Any ribs broken?"

Davey didn't know, so he shook his head.

Kevin misinterpreted. "That's good. They really worked on you, didn't they?"

He dabbed hydrogen peroxide on the cut on Davey's head. "This doesn't look too bad. Your throat worries me the most. It's swollen something awful. How's your breathing?"

Davey nodded.

"If you keep swelling, you might get into trouble. Keep any ice around?"

Davey oriented himself from the workbench, taking what comfort he could from the image of Chambers's ear splashed on the wall beside it, and pointed to the back of the shop. Kevin aimed the lamp that way and found the fridge. A few minutes later he had ice cubes wrapped in a rag. He placed the makeshift ice pack on Davey's throat. The cooling relief was immediate.

"Can you hold that for yourself? Good, man. I'll haul the trash out to the alley."

Davey held the ice to his throat and listened to Kevin drag something limp and heavy and then grunt as he lifted it. He wondered if the Kiwi wouldn't rather be pitching hay.

Davey moved slowly. Heeding the sensation that any sudden movement might rip the muscle tissue off his bones, he dragged himself into the chair. He closed his eyes until the vertigo spun itself out of his head and then rummaged through the desk for a pen and a piece of paper. Writing the instructions was a chore. His hand kept cramping up with pins and needles, and his mind kept wandering off to a place less painful. He was reading it back to make sure it was legible and logical when he felt Kevin's hand on his shoulder.

"How we doing?"

Davey nodded. The great pain had subsided to the point where he could feel its components—the sting of split flesh, the constricted pulse in his head, the damaged hinges of his joints, the heavy ache in his balls, the shrill scream from the burns on his belly—and he thought he could deal with it like that, one bit at a time.

"I put your buddies in the alley," Kevin said. "They'll be asleep for a while, so I figured they wouldn't need these." He laid two pistols on the bench top—Chambers's snubbed-nosed revolver and Slavos's automatic.

Davey held up the instructions he'd written. Kevin read them and frowned. "You want me to drive you to this Eddie's place? Should be driving you to the hospital."

Davey was unable to summon the energy or the focus to explain that Eddie Roe held an advanced first aid ticket. He insisted by tapping the note.

Still frowning, Kevin shrugged. "Just don't pass out on me."

Davey disarmed the automatic and stuck it back in his waistband. He offered the revolver to Kevin. Kevin looked at the gun, then looked at Davey. Maybe he was thinking about picking fruit and pitching hay. Davey picked up the pen and added to his note: *Still want the job?*

Kevin shook his head a few times, but he was grinning again. He picked up the gun.

In the truck, Davey sat slumped with his shoulder against the door, forcing himself to remain cognizant enough to guide Kevin to Eddie's place. The core of his body was burning bright beneath an epidermal layer of ice. His head was suspended in a nauseous sort of free fall. Bitter dribbles of bile kept osmosing up his gullet, threatening to unload his stomach all over the cab of Boomer's truck. He was tempted to open the window and let fly, but he was afraid it would be like setting a blowtorch to his throat, so he clenched his jaw and swallowed.

Perhaps to encourage Davey to stay awake, Kevin babbled on about how he'd been flirting with Janie until he'd gotten into a fight with her boyfriend, which he didn't know she had until the fists started flying, which seemed like a good time to fade out. He was walking up the street when he recognized Davey's truck parked by the boat shop and figured he might be able to pester Davey into lending him a bunk for the night since he wouldn't be bunking with Janie, who was his first choice—no offense, buds. He'd walked down to the back of the shop where the door was open, and when he saw what was happening, he dropped his backpack and picked up a handy length of two-by-four and put in a little batting practice. The Kiwi's voice blurred into an indecipherable drone as Eddie's little bungalow came into view.

Eddie's was the smallest house in a suburb of large split levels built in the early seventies, when architecture was horizontal and heating fuel was cheap. Thank Christ, Eddie's Toyota pickup was parked in the gravel driveway and his front window was lit with the flickering blue light of a TV set.

Kevin walked to the door and knocked. When Eddie answered the door, Davey felt his will finally relaxing, felt the fine relief of not having to hang on any longer. The world around him began to take on a diffuse underwater aspect.

Eddie pulled on a jean jacket, flipped his thick black ponytail, and strode toward the truck. The gravel crunching beneath his cowboy boots seemed horribly loud, and Eddie's movement caused Davey a curious sense of motion sickness.

Eddie opened the truck door. "Davey, Davey, Davey," he said, as if from some distant place, "look at you."

Without the support of the door, Davey began to teeter outward. Eddie caught him by the shoulders. He saw Eddie's cowboy boots. They were directly below a sudden spew of vomit. He'd been right. It did feel like a blowtorch in his throat. But it didn't matter because before he'd finished, blackness closed in and took him away from it all.

Chapter 6

$\mathcal{D}$avey woke up coughing. Each cough blasted through his throat like a shotgun loaded with bile-flavored shards of glass. He rolled onto his side and tried not to cough, which was like trying not to breathe.

A hand touched his shoulder. "Easy, chief," said Eddie's voice. "Here, drink this."

Through tear-clouded eyes, Davey saw a glass of milky liquid, pale yellow. He propped himself on an elbow, and Eddie brought the glass to his lips. He sipped. It was cool and viscous and tasted of egg and honey and rum. The cough reflex backed off. He drank more.

His senses gathered up bits of the room, Eddie's spare bedroom. Green drapes were drawn across the window, but daylight dribbled through. Carved masks and paintings by Haida artists hung on the walls. Davey saw his clothes stacked on the nightstand under a driftwood lamp. He noticed that they'd been laundered, and he wondered what he'd done in his life to deserve friends the likes of Eddie and Boomer. Kevin was standing in the doorway, watching him with a concerned frown. Eddie was sitting on the bed, grinning.

"Hurts like hell right now," he said, just in case Davey didn't know that. "But you'll be okay. Pulled people out of alleys in worse shape after some good old white boys had some fun with them."

Eddie's high cheekbones gave his face a chubby appearance, but he had a lean wiry build that made him seem taller than his five and a half feet. His grin demonstrated the easygoing nature of his race, but a few missing teeth and a slightly crooked nose hinted at a wilder side.

Davey took the glass and drained it. The viscous drink coated his throat, and the rum loosened his stiff muscles. He eased his legs off the bed and sat up, causing his testicles to ache dully, as if they were tired of aching. He got up and hobbled across the hallway to the bathroom. Under the shower, he let the warm jets of water massage the stiffness

45

from his joints. The running water encouraged his bladder to let go. The pee burned on its way through his penis, and he noticed a tinge of red in it. After the shower, he mentioned this to Eddie. When he spoke, his voice croaked and there was a sensation of gears not quite meshing, but at least he could speak.

"Bound to be some interior damage, beating you took," said Eddie. "I wouldn't sweat it. You're showing no sign of shock. Cellular perfusion seems fine. If you still got blood sign in twenty-four hours, check yourself in. But something a lot of doctors don't advise you of, the body's designed to heal itself with the proper rest and nutrition. Neither of which doctors can bill for."

On the night table beside Davey's clothes were his wallet and his watch. And the photograph. The photograph of himself, bloodstained, flipping a bird from *Small Wonder*'s cockpit. He picked it up and stared at it.

"Nice picture," Eddie observed. He handed Davey another draft of his potion. "You'll want to give it to someone special, I guess."

Davey sipped the drink to lubricate the gears in his throat, and as he dressed, he gave Eddie a brief account of the mess he'd landed in. Eddie had heard news of the attack, but his grin quit trying when Davey told him Keith was dead. When he got to the part about Dennison, he remembered he was supposed to meet her at one o'clock. He looked at his watch. Twenty to five.

"Rest," Eddie said as Davey hurried Kevin out the door. "You need rest."

As pubs go, the Muddy Waters was bright and roomy, with a vaulted ceiling, a sprawling floor plan and lots of glass looking out over Newcastle Channel. Being just a block from Boomer's Boatworks, Boomer and his friends were well-known to the staff. Davey zipped up his jacket to hide the burn holes on his T-shirt, but there wasn't much he could do about his split lip or the bruises on his cheek. The bartender frowned at him and asked what the other guy looked like.

Davey shook his head. "Like a flight of stairs, Sid."

His eyes drifted over the spacious floor, now packed with the supper crowd. "There wouldn't happen to be a woman in here asking for me, would there?"

Sid winked at Kevin. "Ah, now there's a question for the ages."

A stocky Scotsman, Sid's accent rolled from his tongue much as his broad shoulders rolled with his stride. "You missed her by an hour, Davey. Sat here all afternoon. Wee bit pissed off when she left. Said to tell you she'd drop by later."

Davey and Kevin took stools at the bar and nursed glasses of beer. Davey felt a sense of returning wellness, the aches easing from his muscles and the stiffness from his joints. He recognized this as a symptom of rising blood alcohol rather than rapid healing, but was nonetheless grateful. While the alcohol numbed the aches in his body, the familiar, friendly atmosphere of the pub eased the tension from his nerves. The past two days began to seem unreal, as if he'd awoken from a weirdly vivid dream.

"That's why they call it impaired," he muttered to himself.

"How's that?" asked Kevin.

"How much rum did Eddie feed me?"

Kevin chuckled. "Catching up on you, buds?"

"I better go out and get some air."

"Be right with you. Got to find the gent's room first before I spring a leak."

"Just around the corner," Davey said, pointing.

Around the corner, Kevin found himself in a short hallway. On the walls hung pictures of old tugboats. Brass plates on dark wooden doors on either side proclaimed ladies and gentlemen. He bypassed the doors and went to the end of the hallway, where a pay phone clung to the wall. The number he called was answered by a clipped, efficient female voice. He identified himself and waited a few seconds.

A gruff male voice said, "Cronk here. Tell me what you've got."

Kevin spoke quickly. "Two things you should know: first, Keith Stoddard is dead. Second, Jones missed his meeting with Counselor Dennison."

"What do mean, Stoddard's dead? Dead since when? And how?"

How dead can you get? Kevin thought, but he kept the sarcasm to himself. "Shot to death," he said, "in that helicopter business."

"That his blood trail up there, through the bush and down the dock?"

Constable Kevin Purcell shook his head. "I wouldn't know about that, sir. Haven't been to the scene."

"'Cause we've still got people missing, including an officer, and if that's not Stoddard's blood trail, it's someone else's."

There you go, thought Kevin. *Why he's an inspector.*

"Where's Stoddard's body?" asked Cronk.

"Jones got him onto their boat. Buried him at sea, somewhere in the Queen Charlotte Strait."

"Buried him at sea? Jesus Christ, what the hell does he think this is?"

Kevin rather sympathized with Davey. In those circumstances, who'd want to cruise around with a shot-up body leaking all over the boat? But

Inspector Cronk wouldn't want to hear that. Kevin kept his mouth shut and waited.

"And what's this about a meeting with Counselor Dennison?" Cronk asked.

"Jones missed it."

"What meeting?"

Kevin frowned. "I assumed you knew, sir. He said he talked to her yesterday and set up a meeting."

"And you didn't see fit to tell me about it last night?"

"I didn't know about it last night," said Kevin and wondered why Inspector Cronk hadn't known about it and why the counselor and the inspector working on the same case wouldn't know about meetings with witnesses. Being buried undercover, Kevin had to assume that the people in charge of things were all reading off the same page.

"I'll look into it," said Cronk.

Sure, thought Kevin, *you look into it. Load off my mind, that is.* He licked his lips.

"What about our two visitors last night?" he asked.

"Collin Chambers," Cronk said, "local felon, lengthy sheet, mostly break and enter. Picked up three months ago, faced repeat offender status, charges dropped when the evidence disappeared.

"The other one rang bells at Interpol. Jermaine Monkton, a.k.a. the Monk. Believed to have worked for a number of Mideast and European extremist groups. Abduction and interrogation a specialty. Learned his trade in the Turkish secret police. Daddy was some mucky-muck in the Turkish hierarchy. Sent Jerry to school at Oxford, then got himself and Mrs. Monkton killed by communist rebels. Jerry went home with issues. Joined the secret police so he could torture communist rebels. Liked his job too much. Let go for excesses. Now he works for whoever pays the bills."

"Lovely crowd gathering here in lotus land."

Cronk grunted. "We got these two on ice, at least for now. Officially, we're treating it as a tourist mugging. Nanaimo General Hospital is holding them for forty-eight-hour observation. Standard procedure for head injuries and like that. Be nice if we could meet them at the door with a warrant. This meeting Jones had with Dennison, be nice if he was going to pass her the stick."

"I doubt that," said Kevin. "Jones knows Stoddard had something for her, but from the way he talks, I don't think he even knows what it is. Maybe we should tell him."

"Negative on that, Constable. I'm not convinced Jones is an innocent bystander, not when he's dumping murder victims in the ocean. Until I am so convinced, he's a suspect. Your job, Constable, is to stick to him like a wet shirt."

"Right." *A wet shirt*, Kevin thought. *That's me.*

Left alone, it hadn't taken long for Davey's mind to slip into one of those funky sinkholes of depression that an alcohol high often undermines itself with. That nonplace from which you stare without comprehension at the televised ball game and the background noise of conversation and clinking glasses might as well be the sound of so many fairies dancing on the head of a pin. Davey was slipping into such a place when Kevin stepped up beside him.

"Hey, buds? Davey? You still with us?"

Davey pushed his remaining beer away. "Only just."

Kevin laughed. "C'mon, let's get some air."

On his way out, Davey assigned Sid to apply his Scottish charm if Dennison showed up again. "Just keep her here. I'll either come back or call back."

As Kevin drove up Stewart Avenue, Davey noticed Eddie's blue Toyota pickup parked outside the boatworks. The shop was closed for the long weekend; Eddie must've come down to clean up the mess. Davey suggested they stop and give him a hand since they were the ones who'd left the mess.

But Eddie wasn't there. They searched the building. In the yard, Davey called Eddie's name while he pounded on the blocked-up hull of a forty-foot ex-seiner that was being converted into a pleasure craft. He went down the gangplank to the crowded docks, through a forest of masts, out to where Boomer kept his wooden tug, *One Across*, and called out. Half a dozen gulls rose squawking from pilings and hovered in a lazy manner, as if fulfilling an obligation even though they had better things to do.

"He's probably down at the Bluenose," Davey said, "or Tugboat Annie's, getting a bite to eat. Might as well start cleaning up while we wait for him."

Back in the shop, they went to the workbench. There were two wooden chairs beside it, one of them toppled over. A length of half-inch rope lay in an untidy coil on the floor. Three of the bench's four drawers lay empty and discarded. Their contents—work orders and requisition forms and time cards—were scattered across the bench top. Many had spilled to the floor.

Davey pulled out the fourth drawer and fingered through the contents, looking for God knew what, and thought of Chambers's earlobe. Was that laying somewhere among the mess? That insignificant little piece of flesh, the loss of which had frightened or angered Chambers enough to cause him to kick the living shit out of an unconscious Davey Jones.

What's it all about, Counselor Dennison? With these creeps after him, why couldn't Keith go to the police? Tell me, counselor, do you answer to the attorney general, or do you answer to a Mr. Lazuardi, who likes to create a sense of community?

"What was the name of that buddy of yours?" said Kevin.

Davey looked up. Kevin had been sorting the papers on the bench top. He was holding a sealed envelope. Davey reached out and took it. *Keith Stoddard* was written on it in neat, precise handwriting, like that of a primary grade teacher.

The envelope contained a single sheet of paper. Written in the same school-marmish script were five words: *the Indian is with us.* Beneath that was a phone number.

There was a phone on the bench, half-buried under papers. Davey pulled it free and dialled the number.

"Keith Stoddard?" asked a soft throaty voice.

Davey opened his mouth to explain that he was not Keith Stoddard, that there'd been a horrible mistake. Instead, he said, "What do you want?"

"You know what we want. There's a rest stop off the highway at Oyster Bay. If the Indian's life is of any consequence to you, be there at midnight. Be alone."

The connection broke with a click. Davey depressed the disconnect cradle on the phone and looked at Kevin. The Kiwi's tanned face looked pasty and drawn. Maybe he was thinking that hay fields and apple orchards weren't so bad after all.

Davey redialled the number. Bastard was going to talk to him whether he liked it or not. Kevin was saying something about being in over their heads, and maybe it was time to get the cops involved. But Davey wasn't listening. Davey was listening to a recording. A melodic disc jockey-like voice told him that his call could not be completed as dialled and suggested that he check his listing and dial again or call the operator for assistance. Davey opted to check his listing and dial again. And again his call could not be completed as dialled.

"Cops'll be able to trace that number," Kevin said.

Davey looked at him. Shook his head. Held the phone out so that Kevin could hear the recording. "Can't trace a number that doesn't exist," he said.

Kevin licked his lips. "You dialled it right?"

"Twice."

"Muddy Waters," said the phone, "Sid speaking."

"Hi, Sid, Davey here. Did the lady show yet?"

"She did too, Davey. Just gave me a dirty look when she heard me say your name. Here you go."

There was a short pause, then Marcie Dennison said, "Davey, where are you?"

"A pay phone. I haven't much time. What can you tell me about this?"

"Over the phone, nothing. I have to meet you."

"Well, now that's too bad, sweetheart. Since I talked to you, I've been threatened at gunpoint, beaten, and tortured. Right now, I really need to know why."

She hesitated, and Davey thought she was going to relent. Then she said, "Sorry." At least this time she sounded sorry. "I've got nothing to say to a voice on the phone," she continued. "If you really want answers, you'll find a way to meet with me."

"Not today. Something happened that needs my attention. I may be tied up for a while." A little pocket of humor in the back of Davey's mind allowed him to grin at the macabre pun, which helped him rein in his anger or fear or whatever it was. "If I can't get back to you," he said, "a friend of mine will. He calls himself Boomer."

"Look, Davey—"

"One more thing, Counselor. I tried to find whatever Keith was supposed to give you, but it's not where I believe he hid it. I'm afraid you'll have to consider it gone. Have a nice day."

"Davey, if you can just calm down," she was saying as Davey hung up the phone, so he took her advice and tried to calm down. Tried to let go all the extraneous crap and focus on what he had to do. Get Eddie. That's all. Nothing else.

Back in the store, he bought a couple of shrink-wrapped sandwiches, two Styrofoam cups of coffee, and a pocket pack of aspirin. He also picked up a small notepad and a Bic pen. While he waited for the price of the gas fill, he asked the counter girl if Casper was around. The girl fetched him from the back office.

"Hi, Davey." Casper's eyes wandered over Davey's face, pausing on the bruises and the split lip. "How's tricks?"

"Tricky," said Davey. Casper always put Davey in mind of a chipmunk, with his wide jaw and his eyes up high on his narrow forehead. He looked like he was pushing seventy, but Davey had known him for a dozen years, and he'd looked like he was pushing seventy a dozen years ago. "How's Casper?"

"Good. Real good. Love those tourist dollars. Whatcha up to?"

"Got a favor to ask," said Davey, stepping to the front window. "See the guy out in Boomer's truck?"

Casper moved up to take a look.

"He's a friend of mine," Davey said. "A good friend. Name's Kevin. I want you to remember him. If Boomer should ask, I want you to tell him Kevin's a good friend of mine. Okay?"

Casper frowned at him in the way people do when they suspect their leg is being pulled. The pump attendant came in and rang up the price of the gas. Davey paid and headed for the door. He gave Casper a friendly slap on his stooped bony shoulder.

"It's okay. It's not a practical joke. Just remember him. Kevin. See you later."

"Go on," Casper said, not at all convinced that he wasn't being set up for a practical joke. "Get outta here."

Back on the road, Davey gave a sandwich to Kevin and opened the other one. The best-before date on the package was indecipherable, possibly faded with age, and the flavor was uncertain, but he made himself eat it. He washed down four aspirins with black coffee and then took out the notepad and pen. Kevin glanced across at him. Davey told him to keep his eyes on the road.

He'd filled three sheets of paper by the time the truck trundled over the Oyster River Bridge. A gentle left curve brought the highway back alongside the ocean at Oyster Bay. Davey pointed Kevin into the rest stop.

It was just past nine o'clock. Dusk was settling into the sky. A few kilometres to the north Campbell River, a logging town that was rapidly eroding into a city, was flicking its lights on. Quadra Island was a purple blotch across Discovery Passage. The light at Cape Mudge winked at them. Davey lit a cigarette, gave one to Kevin.

"This is it," Davey said. "End of the job. It was good meeting you, Kevin. Too bad it couldn't have been under better circumstances."

"What are you saying, buds?"

"You've more than earned a ticket home. Remember where we stopped for gas? There's a road there called Crabbe-Levy. Raunchy as hell. Drive right to the end of it, far as you can go. Friend of mine lives there. Big redheaded guy. Name's Boomer. This is his truck. He'll be glad to have it back. Anyway, you give him this."

Davey handed over the note he'd written, the pages folded in half. "Give him this and he'll see that you get your ticket home."

"Look, Davey . . ." Kevin held the note as if it was something that might bite him. "I don't know . . ."

"If, for some reason, Boomer gives you a hard time, tell him to ask Casper. Casper will vouch for you."

Davey took a deep drag from his cigarette. The aspirins had calmed his headache, but his guts were wrestling with the sandwich.

"If Boomer's not there," he said, "you'll see my boat out on his wharf, thirty-four-foot sloop. Her name's *Small Wonder*. There's a chain locker in her forepeak. You'll find a green plastic garbage bag in the locker. Be enough money there for your airfare. And take some pocket money. You've earned it."

"This is wrong, Davey. This is all wrong. You're about to do something really stupid. For Christsake, let me help you. That was the deal."

"It's over, Kevin. Doesn't matter anymore if it's right or wrong. It's over. Go home."

Davey crushed out his smoke and stepped from the truck. He thought of the two guns Kevin had stashed under the seat but dismissed the notion out of hand. The most challenging things he'd ever shot at were tin cans. The notion of engaging the likes of Dominic Slavos in a gun battle was ludicrous.

Kevin's expression was that of a child with a mouthful of turnip; whether he swallowed or spit, the consequences were equally dire. Davey tried to find some words that would ease Kevin's dilemma, but his mind had gone blank. He was smiling as he closed the truck door, but it was the sort of smile that fools new parents when their babies get gas pains, a rictus caused by the cramps in his guts.

He watched the truck until the taillights disappeared. The sudden loneliness almost suffocated him. His lungs seized up like unoiled machinery. He forced them to draw air until the feeling passed, as feelings always do.

He walked across a shrub-studded sand dune, stepping over beached logs, until he reached the small crescent beach where, in the daytime, tourists let their kids run off pent-up energy. The beach was lonely now, left for the cleaning crew of phosphorescent breakers to roll in and sweep away the day's footprints. He sat in the sand, cool and dry and granular against his butt, and rested his back against the weathered smoothness of a large log. The aches in his body had become familiar, and like love and hate, familiarity had diluted their power. Or maybe it was the aspirin.

Darkness closed quickly. The starlight became murky and haloed, foretelling a drift of marine cloud, and he hoped it didn't start raining on him. He tried to think, but his mind was obscured by a cloud of its own devising, contemplating the notion of its own death, the actuality of not being alive. How bad could it be? His father had done it. Keith had done it. Everyone who's ever born does it. Life's great irony—no one gets out alive.

Davey recognized the defeatist aspect of his cloudy thoughts, and he tried to fight back. He tried to feel anger again—or fear. But you can't fight clouds. Clouds don't care about anger or fear. They just float around and block out the sky.

Eventually, his eyes folded close, and he drifted off into the purgatory that separates consciousness from sleep, the warm dark womb where reality impregnates fantasy to conceive those creatures, both lovely and horrible, which are born into dreams. But his mind, perhaps glimpsing the creatures being created, steered away from dreams and practiced being dead.

Davey's eyes snapped open, bringing him wide-awake. The sky was black; not a single star showed through the cloud cover. His ears were trying to perk up as if they thought they were dog's ears.

A car.

Not the dopplering whoosh of a vehicle passing by out on the highway, but the soft whisper of an idling engine and tires creeping slowly over gritty blacktop.

Davey brought his left wrist close to his face. The luminous hands on his watch said quarter to twelve. His mind struggled to accept it. It felt like he'd closed his eyes only moments ago. It was too *soon*. He wasn't *ready*.

Move!

He stood. His left leg was full of pins and needles that crumbled under his weight. He hobbled over the sand dune toward the parking lot.

A dark sedan rolled to a stop at the edge of the blacktop. The car and its two occupants were backlit by the overhead lamps at the entrance to the rest stop. Davey worked his way to a Scotch broom bush about twenty feet from the car. The driver's window was open, and Davey listened to a running monologue while he massaged the feeling back into his leg. The driver was immortalizing his sexual prowess in a chattering voice, the vocal equivalent of a toothache.

The passenger was a large man. His head nearly touched the roof of the car. He had long dark hair, unkept so that it had the appearance of oily hemp. His contribution to the conversation consisted of the odd grunt, and Davey could almost feel the guy restraining himself from telling the driver to shut the fuck up.

Just the two of them. No Eddie.

Considering their moronic lack of vigilance, Davey had trouble associating them with the likes of Dominic Slavos and the cigar smoker. Could be they were just a couple of yokels out drinking beer and shooting shit. Nothing to do but ask them.

"Where's Eddie?" he said, but the driver of the car talked right over his words.

"What's the deal with you and Twitch, anyway?" the driver was saying.

"Shut up," said the passenger.

"C'mon, Rockwell. The guy's fucked. Way you stick up for him, think you're queer for him or something."

"Shut up, Cuchera."

"Oh, what's the matter? Hit a sore spot, did I? You and Twitch—"

"Shut up, fuckhead, there's someone out there."

"Huh?"

In the ensuing silence, Davey repeated, "Where's Eddie?"

The driver yelped and jerked. The passenger shoved his door open and stood, extending his arms across the roof of the car, pointing a huge pistol out over the sand dune.

"You want to see Eddie, asshole," he said, "you come get in the car."

The driver searched around in the car for several seconds, eventually found a gun, and pointed it out the window at nothing in particular.

"No," said Davey, "I think not. I didn't come here to deal with a couple of fuckups. Go tell your boss that I want to see Eddie. And I want to see someone who can make a decision."

As he spoke, the guns turned, homing in on his voice. He crouched low behind the bush, scampered to his right and rolled behind a log.

"You're getting in the car, asshole," said ropy hair. "Clean and easy or broken and bloody, it's all the same to me."

The guy's voice was on edge, like a car going too fast around a corner, and it occurred to Davey that these two might be every bit as scared as he was. It was a thought without much comfort. They had guns. A combination of fear and firearms had cost someone named Chambers an earlobe, had come that close to costing him the side of his head.

"C'mon," said the big man, the one named Rockwell. "Prick's going to make us look for him."

"You look for him, you want to," said the guy named Cuchera. "I'll watch the car."

"You really want to split up, him sneaking through the dark, the guy who took out the Monk?"

"All right, all right, I'm coming. Wait up."

The driver's door slammed shut. Rockwell sighed. "Cuchera," he said, "get the fucking keys out the fucking car."

Davey crawled over a concrete curb onto the blacktop parking area. The blacktop made a big oval around a grassy picnic area spotted with shade trees. Crouching low, Davey scampered to one of the big concrete picnic tables and crawled beneath it.

Rockwell and Cuchera spent maybe ten minutes going up and down the beach, crashing through brush and stumbling over logs, before making their way back to the car.

"What's he going to do?" said Rockwell. "We still got the Indian. We better go tell Sebastian."

"Nuh-uh. *You* tell Sebastian."

Davey watched them get into the car. Cuchera slammed his door, and the car peeled out onto the highway.

Chapter 8

"Slow down," said Norm Rockwell. He shrugged to adjust the weight of the .357 magnum in the shoulder harness under his black leather motorcycle jacket. "You don't *want* to explain a speeding ticket to Sebastian."

"Fuck you, Rockwell," said Cuchera as he slowed to the speed limit. "Who made you god? I'm the fucking wheelman here."

Wheelman. Give it a fucking rest.

"Don't tell me how to do my job after fucking up yours," Cuchera rattled on. "You're supposed to be the enforcer, and I can tell you that was some fucked-up enforcement. Sebastian shits down someone's neck, Rockwell, it ain't going to be mine."

Norm looked at the driver, gave a pathetic shake of his head. Donny (call me Wheels) Cuchera, a never-was stock car driver from Ladysmith. Mouthy little fuck is what he was. Wasn't so long ago Norm would've used his size 14 engineer boots to shut Cuchera's mouth for him, mess up his pretty face a bit. Good old days.

They passed over the Oyster River Bridge and turned right. As they went through the sleeping village of Oyster River, Cuchera leaned over, used the light from the street lamps to check himself out in the mirror. Patted his trim blond hair and fingered the starched collar of his pale blue shirt. Pretty himself up after his excursion on the beach. Way he talked, he'd nailed every skirt in the country; way he acted, he was more inclined to chase pants than skirts. Maybe that's how he got the job, a little bum work with Sebastian.

The thought of it made Norm chuckle.

"The *fuck* are you laughing at?" Cuchera said. "We're about to get our assholes chewed to sawdust 'cause you couldn't handle fucking Stoddard."

"Drive, wheelman. Just drive."

Norm knew that no one was going to chew his ass for not nabbing Stoddard, but he was in no hurry to share that bit of knowledge with Cuchera. Let the mouthy fuck sweat.

Intimidation was something Norm knew about. In the School of Hard Knocks, Norm had *majored* in intimidation. Norm had fucking *degrees* in intimidation. But when he'd stood before Sebastian about an hour ago, he'd felt himself withering into the floor. And it wasn't as if Sebastian had Norm's intimidating size. He was a little blow-away-in-a-windstorm guy. There was the hulking bodyguard who always flanked him, but that boy's lightbulb was too dim to be intimidating. Looked like the sort of half-wit had to learn how to tie his shoes every morning. No, it was Sebastian's eyes. Like blue steel ball bearings. Eyes that drew a guy and repulsed him at the same time. He'd aim those eyes at you and you'd feel them inside your head, worming through the soft pulp of your brain.

"The important thing," Sebastian had said as Norm's eyes kept sliding off those blue steel ball bearings, "is to make certain that the person waiting there is indeed Mr. Stoddard and that he is indeed alone. If he agrees to accompany you, by all means, bring him along. But I very much doubt he will. In either case, Norman, he is not to be damaged. You understand, do you?"

Norm was maybe undereducated, but he wasn't stupid. He'd understood exactly why he was being sent.

West of Oyster River the road surface turned to gravel as it headed up into the Strathcona Wilderness. In his distress, Cuchera's foot was getting heavy on the gas again, pushing the car too fast for the loose surface. Pebbles rattled like hail off the fenders, and the rear end fishtailed on the curves.

"Will you relax?" said Norm. "No one's going to chew your ass. Not unless you crash us."

Norm pulled the picture from his pocket and held it under the dashboard lights—the picture of Stoddard in his sailboat, cheeky son of a bitch giving the camera the old one-finger salute. Guy had balls, give him that.

"Sebastian never expected us to take him," Norm said.

It took a few seconds for Cuchera to react. "What?" he said. "You telling me we were pissing around in the dark out there for nothing?"

"Wasn't for nothing," Norm said, his eyes still on the photograph. "Was to flush out any cops might've been there."

Cuchera's foot eased off the gas. The car slowed to a more suitable speed. "The hell are you talking about?" he asked.

Guy was dense as a chopping block. Visions of being a wheelman for the mob. Didn't get it that he was nothing but bait.

"No way," Norm explained, "is Stoddard getting in the car till he knows the Indian's okay. Sebastian knew that. He sent us to spring any trap might've been set if Stoddard had taken his troubles to the Mounties."

"No shit?" Cuchera said. He looked at Norm and apparently saw no shit. "He expects us to bend over and spread our cheeks for the cops? Faggoty little bastard."

Norm smiled. "Want I should pass that message to him?"

"Up yours," said Wheels Cuchera, king of the comebacks.

"One other thing, Cuchera. You ever bad-mouth Twitch again, you'll spend the next six months eating through a straw."

Davey didn't lie in the sand this time as he waited. He didn't close his eyes and drift off into purgatory. He paced the parking lot and chain-smoked. He scampered out onto the sand dunes whenever a car sped down the highway through the night. Convinced that his bladder was full, he tried twice to pee but could release no more than a dribble.

Scared pissless.

He still had no plan, and the void where the plan was supposed to be kept filling up with panic. He tried to displace the panic by concentrating on the job at hand. He had to get Eddie out of it. Whatever else he'd gotten wrong, he had to get that one thing right. They wanted Keith Stoddard; he'd give them Keith Stoddard—straight across for Eddie Roe.

Another car was coming up the highway from the south. Davey crushed his cigarette and stepped out onto the dunes. He crouched behind a large root system attached to a beached log. Peering through the holes in the twisted root wood, he saw the car slow and pull into the parking lot. As it passed beneath the overhead lights, he saw that it was the same dark sedan. It pulled to the edge of the pavement, near the same spot it had parked before.

Davey was farther from the car this time, about sixty or seventy feet, but he saw that the driver was the same young blond man, the one named Cuchera. The person in the passenger seat was considerably smaller than the man named Rockwell. There appeared to be at least two people in the backseat, obscured by shadows. The car sat there for a moment, as if thinking things over, and then the front passenger door opened.

The small man got out. Collar-length wispy hair, white blond. Sharkskin suit over an open-necked white shirt. Despite his small size, he was clearly in charge. Authority fit him like his suit. Deference was something he took for granted. Had to be the guy Rockwell and Cuchera had referred to as Sebastian.

"Mr. Stoddard?" he said. He hadn't seemed to raise his voice, yet it reached out. The same throaty voice Davey had heard on the phone.

Sebastian's head swivelled, scanning the dunes, and for a moment, Davey thought his eyes actually *glowed*, like the eyes of a nocturnal hunter. Trick of the overhead lights. And Davey's spooked imagination.

"Where's Eddie?" Davey called out.

Those weird eyes passed over Davey's hiding spot and then came back to it. They stared at the gnarled root network for a few seconds and then turned toward the backseat of the car.

The back door opened. A broad-shouldered weight lifter type got out. He wore a T-shirt and loose trousers done in matching camouflage. In his right hand was a large automatic pistol. On his left wrist was half of a handcuff. The other half was on Eddie's right wrist.

Davey fought through a debilitating mixture of fear and guilt. "You okay, Eddie?" he said and almost sobbed.

Eddie's ponytail had come loose. He flicked his head to get his hair off his face. "Hell yeah, chief. Having a great old time here."

Davey closed his eyes and swallowed, hoping to get the sob out of his voice. "Eddie walks free," he said, "and I go in his place. That's how it has to happen."

"Very noble, Mr. Stoddard," said the suit. "However, not very practical." He stepped off the blacktop and walked through the bushes and logs that littered the dunes. "Allow me to explain something to you."

He walked a few paces past the root system and stood gazing out at the ocean, his back to the spot where Davey crouched.

"I assume, Mr. Stoddard," he said to the ocean, "that you have not brought the stolen property with you. Only an imbecile would have done that. Although foolishly exuberant, you are not an imbecile. So we have two choices. Either you accompany us with Eddie to a place where we can continue our negotiations or we leave you both dead on this beach. The former is preferable all around. The latter would certainly be a setback, but an insurmountable one only for you and Eddie."

"There's a third option," Davey said as he stood. "I put my gun to your head. You ever heard of a Mexican standoff?"

Still looking at the ocean, the man chuckled. "I am familiar with the term, but it hardly applies to this situation. I am an employee, Mr. Stoddard. Every bit as expendable as the man you bested in Nanaimo. A feat that, by the way, impressed me as much as it amused me. I don't much like that fellow, but he is very good at what he does. Mugged in a dockyard and confined in a hospital will not enhance his résumé. But the point is, if you put a gun to my head, that large fellow by the car will shoot Eddie and turn his gun on you. If I die in the crossfire, believe me, no tears will be shed."

That's it? Davey asked himself. *That's the plan?*

He'd just hid his back in front of a mirror again. Let's face it. He had no idea how this game was played. Maybe he should've taken a gun from the truck. Then at least he'd have the option of calling this creep's bluff. Wasn't as if he'd be jeopardizing a future of bright, bright sunshiny days. On the other hand, this Sebastian didn't come across as the sort who'd waste time bluffing.

"I need a smoke," Davey said. When he reached into his pocket, he heard from the direction of the car the distinctive click of a cocking pistol.

The little man in the suit raised his hand like Moses parting the sea. "Slowly, Mr. Stoddard," he said.

Slowly, Davey pulled out his cigarettes. "I don't even have a gun," he admitted.

They searched him anyway. Then they let him have his smoke, standing there beside the car. Apparently, Sebastian didn't allow smoking in the car. Offended his sensibilities. Davey gave the cigarette to Eddie.

"Convincing them to let us go, are you?" Eddie asked. "Working on their conscience, like?"

Davey was lighting a smoke for himself when he noticed a set of headlights barrelling up the highway from the south, coming on well ahead of the speed limit. The vehicle weaved slightly, indicating it carried members of the local drinking team that Davey had suspected Cuchera and Rockwell of belonging to.

"Otherwise," Eddie continued, "the bad guys would be shot to pieces and I could smoke this thing while walking off into the night. Tom-toms beating in the background, that sort of thing."

The big guard attached to Eddie had a round childlike face to go with his bowl-over haircut and his childish attire. He was grinning away as if they were all good friends having a late-night chuckle.

"I was thinking more along the lines of *running* into the night," said Davey. "Never figured you'd gain two hundred and thirty pounds in a single afternoon," he said, indicating the bulky guard attached to Eddie's wrist.

About ten feet away, Sebastian was leaning on the car, talking to the driver through the open window. Davey looked down the road at the approaching party car. It was no more than twenty seconds away. How lucky would he have to be for the drunks to wreck their car right in the entrance to the rest stop?

Eddie lifted his right wrist and gave the handcuff a shake. "Neither did I," he said. "Although I haven't had a smoke all day. They say quitting can lead to rapid weight gain."

The big guard's foolish grin never flickered.

"This guy know anything?" Davey asked. "Or is he one of the push-button models?"

"Don't let his appearance fool you," said the man called Sebastian.

Davey turned and found Sebastian standing a few feet behind him. Past Sebastian's head, Davey saw the approaching headlights. They seemed to be slowing.

"His facial muscles," Sebastian was saying, "suffered damage in a nasty little situation in Kosovo. A situation from which I extracted him and which earned me his undying loyalty."

"Good boy," Davey said to the guard in his best doggy voice. "What a good boy."

"Smoke break is over," said Sebastian. "We have work to do."

"Shit," said Cuchera out the driver's side window. "We got company."

The approaching vehicle had slowed enough, just enough, to make the turn into the rest stop. It rattled and thumped over the speed bumps. Under the overhead lamps, Davey saw that it was a pickup truck. An old dun-colored Chevy pickup.

"What's this?" said Sebastian.

Davey was standing close enough to Eddie to feel his body tense. Eddie too had recognized Boomer's truck.

"It's your plan," Davey said to Sebastian, trying to distract his attention. "If you don't know what's going on, don't expect me to."

Sebastian ignored him. "Mr. Cuchera," he said to the driver, "give me your gun."

The approaching pickup throbbed with the driving bass beat of old time rock and roll. A whooping yell erupted like a rocket over the music. An arm came out of the driver's side window in a tossing motion. A beer can arched through the light from the street lamps and disappeared down toward the beach.

"Drunks," Sebastian said. He passed the pistol back to Cuchera. "Keep this out of sight. But not too far out of sight. Yours as well, Marco."

To Davey, he said, "No tricks, Mr. Stoddard. The lives of the people in that truck depend on it. In fact, you'd better get in the car. Marco, get them in the car."

The pickup came to a sloppy stop beside the car, about a dozen feet away. Kevin leaned out the passenger's side window, his hands drumming on the door panel in approximate beat with the blaring music.

"Hey, buds," he yelled. "Beach party?"

Eddie was standing far enough off to keep Marco's left hand from reaching the door. Marco had tucked his gun into his waistband to free up his right hand.

"Police business," Sebastian said, his voice rising above the music. "Fuck off!"

In the driver's seat, Boomer was tilting a beer can to his mouth. Kevin turned to him and said something. Boomer tossed the beer out the window and gunned the truck forward. He broke with a screech of rubber, shifted into reverse, and spun the wheel right.

Davey grabbed Eddie's left arm and pulled him away from the side of the car. Marco was stretched out, his right hand on the door handle and his left hand attached to Eddie, when the rear end of the pickup hammered into the far side of the car. The car leaped sideways at Marco, smashing into his right arm and right leg. With a cry of shock and pain, he fell to the ground, dragging Eddie with him. Off balance, Davey stumbled backward. His legs tangled with a bush and he fell ass first to the sand.

Like Davey, Sebastian had seen it coming and leaped out of harm's way. Unlike Davey, he didn't have Eddie and Marco throwing him off balance. Before the echo of the crash had faded, he was going for Marco's gun. Eddie and Marco were tangled together, Marco incapacitated by his injured arm and leg; Eddie incapacitated by two hundred and thirty pounds of Marco. By the time Davey got back to his feet, Sebastian was pulling the gun from Marco's waistband. Sebastian raised the gun, his cruel blue eyes already taking aim. Then he crumpled into a heap on top of Marco. Boomer stood behind him, examining the stock of his shotgun as if to make sure he hadn't damaged it on the back of Sebastian's head.

Boomer reached down, grabbed Sebastian one-handed by his jacket and pulled him off Eddie and Marco. Eddie was cursing; Marco was moaning.

Davey remembered Cuchera. He turned and looked toward the front of the car. The driver was flailing at the inflated air bag. Kevin was leaning on the roof of the car, taunting Cuchera.

"Watch it!" said Davey. "He's got a gun in there."

Kevin grinned. "So do I, buds."

He held up an automatic pistol, the Beretta Davey had taken from Dominic Slavos. Kevin pointed the gun at the open window and fired. The air bag popped and Cuchera screamed. Kevin opened the door, grabbed a handful of blond hair, and threw Cuchera to the ground. He reached in and took the pistol off the seat.

"Don't follow instructions very well, do you?" Davey said.

"Not especially," said Kevin, smiling like it was all a big joke. "About as well as you express gratitude."

"Or did you have it all under control?" Boomer said to Davey. He wasn't smiling; he was scowling. "I got a hacksaw in the truck for Eddie's bracelet. Here." He pushed the shotgun into Davey's hands.

It was a pump action Remington. Davey gripped it hard to keep his hands from shaking. He wondered if the shotgun was made by the same Remington that made the electric shavers. Close as a blade or your money back.

Chapter 9

"Two more for the arsenal, buds," said Kevin, displaying Marco's gun and Cuchera's. He was standing over Cuchera, smiling as if he still thought it was all fun and games.

Boomer plucked the two guns from Kevin's hand and stomped through the sedge and dunegrass down to the beach, scowling at Davey as he went by him. At the water's edge, he flung the guns as far as he could into the ocean.

"Or not," said Kevin.

Cuchera's car was pinging to let them all know there was an improperly closed door. Davey reached in and pulled the key from the ignition. The pinging stopped.

Back from disposing of the guns, Boomer asked after the welfare of the two men lying on the ground. Sebastian was still out; Marco was moaning through a grin.

"Little guy's going to wake up with a headache," said Eddie. "Big guy's got a broken wrist and a gash on his leg. I set the wrist and wrapped the leg. Nothing to trouble the ambulance service with."

"How about you?"

"I'm fine. Treated me good, allowing for the gunpoint abduction. Went through worse at the residential school. At least none of these guys tried to bugger me."

Boomer nodded. He went to his truck and drove it forward. There was a screech of wrenching metal as the truck's heavy rear bumper and trailer hitch disengaged from the side of the car.

Sebastian's driver, Cuchera, was sitting in the sand with his arms around his knees. Davey squatted down in front of him and said, "Tell your boss to back off. This kind of shit is getting no one nowhere."

"You're fucking dead, man," the kid said. He couldn't have been much older than twenty, and despite his tough talk, there were tears not too far from the surface. It occurred to Davey that young Cuchera would likely take the brunt of the blame for what had happened here. In that, they were kindred spirits.

"You coming," Boomer called, "or you going to play some more with your friends here?"

Davey looked at the keys he'd taken from the car. They were attached by a slender chain to a white rabbit's foot. He bounced them in the palm of his hand and then tossed them down onto the beach.

"Tide's coming in," he said. "Better go find them while you can."

"C'mon," Boomer called with a growl, "quit dinking around!"

"Fucking dead," said Cuchera. He scurried sideways a few meters, then turned and scampered down after the keys.

Davey approached the truck from the driver's side, fully exposed to Boomer's ill-tempered scowl. Eddie was in the truck beside Boomer. Kevin was holding open the door on the far side.

Davey took another look at Boomer's expression and said, "I'll ride in the back."

"Good," muttered Boomer.

It was after one in the morning by the time they got to the end of Crabbe-Levy Road. The cabin was dark. Boomer parked in such a way that the headlamps shone on the generator shed. He asked Eddie to take Kevin and go fire up the genset. "Me and Davey," he said, "want to talk."

Davey clambered out of the truck bed, barely aware that he still held the shotgun until Boomer took it away from him. He was exhausted, sore all over, and nauseous with the residue of fear. He really didn't want to talk, but he supposed Boomer had earned it.

"What do you want to talk about?" he said. "How I fucked up and you saved my ass?"

Boomer released the safety on the shotgun. "I thought you were going to hand all this shit off to that crown counselor?" he said as he disarmed the gun and tucked the shells into his shirt pocket.

"That didn't quite work out," Davey said. Thirty meters away, the generator started up with a growl and a puff of black smoke. Davey had to raise his voice. "Where's Linda's car?" he asked. "She go back to town?"

"Took Cassie up to the farm," Boomer said. "But we were talking about the crown counselor, not Linda's car."

A stab of disappointment took Davey by surprise. He wondered if Cassie was going to stay at her parent's place or come back to Boomer's.

"Here I am," Boomer was saying, "thinking you've scraped this whole mess onto the attorney general's plate when some stranger, whose identity I have to confirm through old man Casper, for Christsake, drives up in my truck and says Davey's in trouble, needs our help, you got any guns. That's what we were talking about, not Linda's car."

The diesel growl of the genset steadied into a deep rumbling purr.

"He wasn't supposed to do that," Davey said. "Kevin. He was supposed to clear out. I told him to get some money out of *Small Wonder* and go home. I was going to get these people to trade straight across, me for Eddie."

"And why the hell would they do that?"

The rumble of the generator changed pitch when Eddie threw the switch. Three overhead yard lights flickered on, illuminating the cabin, the yard and the dock. The kitchen window lit up from inside.

"They think I'm Keith," Davey said.

Boomer opened his mouth and started to say something. Davey thought he was going to ask why they thought he was Keith, but Boomer just sighed and shook his head. In the overhead lighting, his hair looked like a copper halo. His frown had changed from one of indignant anger to one of resigned bewilderment. He leaned into the truck, doused the headlights, and shut off the engine. He shut the door and said, "But they don't want *Keith*, Davey, they want something Keith *took* from them."

"Yeah, I'd figured that out just about the time you guys showed up." Davey watched Eddie and Kevin chatting together as they walked to the cabin. He was embarrassed that Boomer had so quickly worked out what he'd needed Sebastian to tell him, that his heroic gesture had been a fool's errand from the start.

"I could use a drink," Boomer said. He put his hand on Davey's shoulder and steered him toward the cabin door. "And an explanation or two. I'm going to smash my truck and knock folks on the head, I'd better know why."

In the cabin, Eddie and Kevin had helped themselves to beer from the fridge. Boomer thought he could do better than that, and he did, digging an unopened bottle of scotch from a kitchen cupboard. He carried it to the front room and put it on the burl table, along with four water glasses.

"Strictly self-serve," he said. He poured about three ounces into a glass and sat back on the couch. "Okay," he said. "Davey, what was in this treasury of yours and what happened to Crown Counselor Marcie Dennison?"

Davey poured a large whiskey and took a grateful drink. He sat in the armchair, holding the glass with both hands on his lap so the guys wouldn't see his fingers trembling, and he told Boomer about the empty treasury and his encounter with Dominic Slavos from Turkey. Davey swallowed his drink and poured another. The whiskey steadied his hands.

Or impaired the part of him that cared whether his hands were steady or not. He took out the photograph he'd taken from Dominic Slavos and laid it on the table. Boomer, the only one present who'd not yet seen it, picked it up.

"That was taken during the chopper raid at Frank's place," Davey said. "We'd just cast off. They think it's a picture of Keith. In a way, it is. He's lying in the cockpit bleeding to death. But they think the guy flipping the finger is Keith."

"The guy flipping the finger," Boomer said, "being you."

Boomer set the photo back on the table. He got up and went to the fridge in the kitchen. Due to the on-again, off-again nature of the cabin's electrical power, the fridge was fuelled by propane. No light came on when the door opened. Boomer asked Davey if he wanted a beer. Eddie said sure, thanks. Kevin said he was fine, buds. Davey decided to stay with the whiskey. Boomer poured his beer into a stein and drank half of it while the head was still foaming. He used the sleeve of his shirt to wipe the foam from his flame-red beard. Didn't take much imagination to see him clad in Viking furs quaffing a tankard of mead.

"You considered telling these folks," Boomer asked, "about the mistaken identity here?"

Kevin had already heard the story. He was wandering around sipping beer and looking at the walls. Boomer kept no art at the cabin. It was unoccupied for weeks at a time, so Boomer never left anything valuable enough to tempt the underprivileged poor. On the walls, in lieu of art, were groups of framed photographs, mostly of Boomer's family. Boomer kept frowning at Kevin as if he had reservations about Kevin knowing his family.

"I almost did," Davey said. "But I'm not sure it would be beneficial to our cause."

"So now we have a cause?" said Boomer.

Eddie chuckled. Davey drank.

Boomer looked at Eddie. "What's your story? What brought you out there tonight?"

"Three big goons with skin darker than mine and a language that sounded like a mob of consonants jostling each other downhill. They walked into the Boatworks like they owned the place. Put a gun in my face and took me for a ride."

"The little guy wasn't there?" Davey asked. "The guy they call Sebastian?"

"Nah, didn't meet him till we got to the lodge."

"What lodge?" said Boomer.

"Mountain resort sort of thing. Way up the Oyster River, through a maze of logging roads, up into the Strathcona Wilderness."

"Could you show the Mounties where it is?"

"No cops," Davey said. "Keith was adamant about that."

Boomer shook his head. "Christsake, Davey, it ain't about Keith anymore."

Davey thought Boomer was wrong about that, but he was too tired to argue the point. He said, "Frank and Lorraine could be up there. If the cops go in, Frank and Lorraine could be in trouble."

"If they're there, they're already in trouble. They might be glad for a change to have the cops show up." But Boomer's tone belied his words, as if he realized that people who dropped bombs from helicopters weren't likely to be squeamish in the disposal of hostages. To Eddie, he said, "Did you see them up there? Frank and Lorraine?"

Eddie shook his head. "It's a big place, eh. Main lodge and half a dozen out buildings. They never gave me the grand tour."

Kevin cleared his throat and turned his head toward the other three. "Don't mean to bud in," he said. He turned back to the wall as if speaking to the picture he was looking at. "But doesn't it seem unlikely they'd take the chance of snatching Eddie if they already had hostages?"

Boomer frowned at Kevin and then frowned at his beer, as if wondering of both why they were there. He put the glass to his lips and drained the beer in a series of swallows.

"Doubt they were there to snatch me," said Eddie. "They didn't know I'd be there. Probably just went to finish whatever they were up to when Davey and you interrupted them. That I happened to be there was a happy coincidence."

Kevin nodded in a way that reserved judgement on Eddie's explanation and then moved on to another set of photographs. He had to shuffle around three cardboard boxes on the floor. The sort of boxes liquor was shipped in. But they didn't contain booze; they contained clothing. Davey noticed a lot of silk and lace, giving him the impression of a goodwill package from Victoria's Secret.

"This you and Keith?" Kevin said. "You guys bag a seal?"

Davey got up and went to look at the picture: he and Keith in wet suits at the water's edge, the seal between them.

"That's Gunner," Davey said. "And he's not bagged. He hangs out in the bay here. Named Gunner's Rock after him."

"Looks pretty tame. A pet seal?"

"He likes to swim with us and bum food off us. Toss up, I guess, whether we've got a pet seal or he's got pet humans."

Boomer had moved in close behind them. "How did you know that was Keith?" he asked.

"Elementary," said Kevin from behind one of his patented cocky grins. He looked back at the photo. "They're hardly twins, but the resemblance is close enough to cause a mistaken identity. Mind if I have another beer?"

"It's in the fridge," said Boomer.

"He's saved my ass twice," said Davey when Kevin was gone. Boomer grunted. "And it's not the first time Keith and I were taken for brothers."

Boomer lifted his glass as if to drink, but it was empty. "Get me one," he called over his shoulder. "You want one, Eddie?"

Eddie was lying on the couch with his eyes closed, holding a tin of beer on his belly. He wiggled it to judge the contents and mumbled, "Not yet."

Davey toed the boxes at their feet. "What's all this?"

"Lily White's stuff."

"Keith's girlfriend?"

"You know a bunch of Lily Whites?" Boomer looked at his empty glass. "Went up to Campbell River yesterday. Had a chat with the manager at JJ's. He was a wee bit pissed off at our Lily. Seems she skipped out on him on Sunday, having never teased a strip nor stripped a tease."

"Last Sunday? Day before Keith left the message on Linda's answering machine?"

"Yeah. Manager's certain that's the day. He had to get the other girls to cover her shows. Cost him double wages."

Kevin returned with a beer in each hand. While Boomer poured his into the glass, Davey asked, "Did the manager report her missing, or was he too upset by the double wages?"

Boomer handed Kevin the empty can. "Put that in the sink for me?" Kevin frowned at him but took the can. "Upside down," Boomer said, "so the dregs drain out."

Kevin walked away and Boomer said, "He didn't *have* to report her missing. Cops came asking about *her*. He figures that's why she powdered on him. She had some kind of trouble with the law."

"Did the law explain to him the nature of her trouble?"

"He didn't say. But he figured they weren't very snoopy, not for cops. Didn't even ask to see her belongings." Boomer looked down at the boxes. "When he hired another dancer he cleared out Lily's room, boxed up her stuff."

"So now you've got a bunch of sexy clothes."

"And this." Boomer reached down and pulled an envelope from one of the boxes. "A letter from Keith. Reads like a love letter, but that ain't all it is."

The flap on the envelope had never been sealed. Davey pulled out and unfolded two sheets of paper covered with Keith's bold, block letter printing just as Kevin returned from his task. Davey noted the way Boomer kept his body between Kevin and the letter. He'd just started reading when Eddie opened his eyes, swung his legs off the couch, sat up, and put his beer can on the coffee table.

"We got company," said Eddie.

A few seconds later, light came through the kitchen window and splashed across the wall as a car turned into the driveway. Boomer frowned, stepped into the kitchen.

Davey looked at Eddie, looked at Kevin, shook his head. *Can't be them*, he told himself. *No way. I'm too tired. We're all too fucking tired.* But he looked at the shotgun, empty, propped against the wall by the door.

"Shit," muttered Boomer from the kitchen window. He hurried back into the front room. "It's the girls," he said. His tone indicated that he might have preferred it to be a carload of Turkish gunmen. "I thought they were spending the night up island." He picked up the shotgun, bent, and slid it under the couch. Shells slid from his shirt pocket and rattled on the floor. "Listen, you guys," he said, pushing the shells under the couch. "What happened out there tonight, Linda never hears about it. Right?"

"Right," said Kevin and Eddie. Davey thought they might have been smirking.

"Davey?"

"Yeah, sure." Davey had absolutely no intention of discussing it with anyone, ever. His body tingled as the adrenaline dissipated. He corrected the imbalance with another glass of whiskey.

Linda and Cassie carried shopping bags into the cabin. Linda, in blue jeans and a loose beige sweatshirt from Bamfield, was obviously caught by surprise. She stood for a few seconds taking it in, this 2:00 a.m. beer and whiskey fest, then strode through to the kitchen, activating every light in the place as she went. Boomer glared in turn at Davey, Eddie, and Kevin, reinforcing his demand for silence, then followed his girlfriend to the kitchen.

Cassie had the faraway look of someone who might never again be surprised by anything. She was wearing a light cotton dress, pale blue with tiny turquoise flowers. The bodice hugged her bosom, and the skirt flowed around her legs. Her long auburn hair was held off her face by a barrette the same color as the flowers on her dress. Her feet were laced into thong sandals. She was gorgeous. When she looked at Davey, he turned away, self-conscious of the bruise on his neck and his split lip, his unkept hair coarse with sweat and road dust. He finished his drink, muttered good night, and went out to his boat.

Chapter 10

*D*avey trudged up out of sleep, shedding it the way a long-distance swimmer sheds water as he trudges from the ocean, feeling as if he'd come through an ordeal rather than a night's rest. Every muscle in his body ached. He lay on the V-berth in the dim light in the forward cabin and stared at nothing. His waterlogged brain retained only a soggy memory of last night's fiasco. There was one thing he did recall vividly: As he'd made his way out the door, he'd seen Cassie and Kevin in conversation, Cassie smiling at the handsome young Kiwi. The image tugged like a barb in the middle of his chest.

"Get a grip, Jones," he told himself, speaking out loud to make sure he heard. "You got bigger problems."

He looked at his watch and saw that it was just past six. No wonder his brain felt soggy. He swung off the bunk, stood, and stretched. Boomer's generator was inactive, but *Small Wonder*'s battery bank was fully charged. Davey turned on a light and examined the yellowing purple bruise on his ribcage. He touched it, surprised to find it more tender than it had been the day before. He looked lower and was glad to see that his scrotum no longer looked the size of a grapefruit.

He walked aft to the shower cubicle abaft the galley. In the shower, the rope burns on his wrists stung a bit when he soaped them as did the cut on the back of his head when he shampooed. The hot water excited a burning sensation from the blisters on his belly. After the shower, he shaved the stubble off his face, working with care around a split in his lip and a bruise like a massive hickey on his throat.

Back in the forward cabin, he managed to round up clean underwear, jeans, and a T-shirt, but not without a hunt. He'd have to do laundry soon, an oddly comforting notion. No matter how tedious, it was something he knew how to do, something the outcome of which he could control. Hadn't been much of that recently.

Outside, the rising sun was melting through a layer of wispy marine cloud. Thick legions of Douglas fir towered through the mists. The air was still and quiet. There was an early morning chill. Davey zipped up his jacket and stood gazing across the bight, where a white swirl of gulls was making breakfast of a herring ball, the herring chased to the surface by feeding salmon or seals, possibly Gunner.

"Everything feeds," Davey muttered to himself. It's what his father had said of the cancer cells eating his brain: "It's nothing personal, just the natural course of events. Everything feeds."

Boomer's cabin smelled like coffee and sweet cinnamon. Linda was the only one up. She was in the kitchen. Coffee was burbling on the stove and cinnamon rolls baking in the oven. Linda the nurturer. It seemed almost criminal that she wasn't yet someone's mother.

"Good morning," she said, smiling. She had a delicate mouth and nose and big liquid blue eyes. She was like a joyful forest sprite in contrast to the lumbering grizzly bear of her lover.

Davey helped himself to coffee. "Thanks," he said.

They spoke in murmured voices. In the front room, Eddie slept on the couch and Kevin on a mattress on the floor. Boomer was, no doubt, still sleeping up in the loft.

"Sorry about last night," Davey said. "Don't blame Boomer. That was my show. I brought the guys here without asking him about it."

Linda gave him a hug. Davey had always felt awkward with hugs that weren't romantic embraces, but Linda did hugs as naturally as she drew breath.

"Don't make it a habit," she said. "There are a limited number of times I will tolerate coming home to a houseful of drunks."

She kissed him on the cheek and then went to the gas range, donned a pair of oven mitts shaped and printed like salmon, and pulled a tray of cinnamon rolls from the oven. The delicious smell was overwhelming. Linda set the tray on the counter under the window.

"You've been in a fight," she said. It was a statement, not a question.

Davey touched his face. "Yeah, I know."

"You must know how much Lawrence looks up to you."

Actually, Davey didn't know that. And he doubted its accuracy. Boomer was the stable one in their friendship, the anchor. Davey'd always seen himself as a bit of flotsam, tossed this way and that by wind and tide, tugged unresisting along the path of the prevailing current. But he didn't know how to say that.

"This thing you're involved in is dangerous," she said. She removed the oven mitts and absently wiped the countertop with them. "I know it's not your fault, but that doesn't make it less dangerous. I'd hate it if

Lawrence were to get dragged in over his head. I'd hate the person who dragged him in, whether or not it was his fault."

The notion of him dragging Boomer anywhere struck Davey as highly improbable, but he didn't suppose that was what Linda wanted to hear.

"What kind of eggs do you want?" she said, taking a cast iron skillet from an overhead rack.

"You don't have to do that," Davey said.

"Of course I don't have to. Do you only do things that you have to?" She smiled at him. "If I don't make eggs for you, you'll pig out on the sweet buns, won't you?"

"I'll do that anyway, eggs or not."

She turned the gas on under the frying pan and turned toward the counter. "You do know I work for a law firm, don't you?" she said, breaking eggs in a bowl.

"Of course. And I will take advantage of that as soon as I hear what the crown counselor has to say."

"Yes, Lawrence told me that your meeting with her got delayed."

Waylaid was more like it, but if Boomer said delayed, delayed it was. "I'll try again today," Davey said. He refilled his coffee and went to the kitchen table, a 1950s resurrection of speckled Formica on stainless steel legs. He moved a crossword puzzle book to make room for his coffee mug. "I have to get Eddie and Kevin back to Nanaimo anyway, so I'll give Counselor Dennison another call while I'm there."

Linda added milk and spices and whipped the eggs. She was at the cutting board slaughtering mushrooms and peppers and onions with a large knife when the outside door opened and Cassie stepped in. She wore the same summer dress from the night before and rubbed the goose bumps from her naked arms as she closed the door. She stole quietly past the two men sleeping and made her way to the kitchen.

"Smells good," she said and took a cinnamon roll and a mug of coffee to the table. Her voice, like her face, was still puffy with sleep. The way she'd look and sound, Davey thought, if she woke up warm and soft beside him.

"I'm sorry," she said to him. "I meant to talk to you about it last night, but you went to bed before I got a chance."

Up close, he realized that her eyes were puffy from crying, not from sleep, and her voice was muffled by a swollen mucus membrane. The truth of her appearance, that she'd been crying over her missing parents and burned home, was less sexy than Davey's fantasy, yet somehow more intimate.

He smiled at her softly and shook his head. "I don't have a clue what you're talking about."

"I've been sleeping in *Small Wonder*," she said. She tore a small piece off the roll and put it in her mouth. "Using Keith's bunk."

Davey felt himself blush and looked away. She'd been in the aft berth when he'd gone nude from his cabin to the shower and back. He tried to remember if the door to the aft cabin had been opened or closed. Cassie mistook his embarrassment for anger.

"I'm sorry," she said. "I knew I shouldn't have."

"No, no," said Davey. "It's okay. You're welcome to it. It's just, ah, now that I know, I'll make sure I'm clothed when I wander around."

It was Cassie's turn to drop her eyes and blush.

Linda slid the omelette onto a plate and set it in front of Davey. "Thanks," he said. "Nicely timed."

Linda smiled and patted his shoulder.

Cassie nibbled the cinnamon roll and sipped coffee. She cleared her throat and asked Davey how he'd ended up with Kevin.

Davey touched the bruise on his neck and his split lip. "Couple guys were doing this to me when he came along and convinced them to stop. He has a bit of a funding problem, and I thought his good deed was worth at least a ticket home."

"At least," said Cassie. She was dissecting her cinnamon roll and consuming it in tiny bites.

Davey polished off his omelette in half a dozen furious gulps, as if showing Cassie how it was done. He had no desire to hear what Cassie thought the handsome young Kiwi was worth.

"My goodness," said Linda. "Hungry boy. You want another, Davey?"

"Uh-uh. I want one of those cinnamon buns before Ms. Denton here tears through the whole batch."

Cassie looked as if she thought he might be serious. Maybe his puerile mood of jealousy had infected his voice. Time to change the subject.

"I understand you guys went up to your parents' place yesterday?" he asked.

"We tried," said Cassie. Her voice was flat, despondent. She had to be in agony over her missing parents. She had more worthy concerns than the state of Davey's ego.

Linda poured herself a coffee and brought it to the table. "The police still have it cordoned off," she said.

"Did you talk to them?" He sliced his roll in half with a knife and spread butter on each half.

"No. Cassie wants to find out about her mom and dad before she talks to the authorities."

Davey listened while Linda told him about her and Cassie driving around northern Vancouver Island, from Alert Bay to Zeballos, from

Port Hardy to Sayward, seeking out everyone Cassie could think of to whom Frank and Lorraine might turn for help. Everyone had heard about the explosion at the Denton's isolated fish farm, and they were all aware of the massive scale of the subsequent police investigation, but sorry, no word from or about Cassie's parents.

"Today, we're going to canvass their friends and relatives from Campbell River down to Victoria." She looked over Davey's shoulder and said, "Good morning."

"Morning," said Kevin. "Coffee smells great."

Cassie smiled. Davey turned. Kevin was in jeans, barefoot and shirtless, curly haired and dimple cheeked.

"Would you like eggs?" said Linda.

"In a bit, sure, soon as I wake up. But don't bother yourself, I can do my own." He helped himself to coffee and brought it to the table, where he put a hand on Cassie's shoulder and asked her how she was.

"I'll do, thanks," she said. "And thanks for listening last night. It helped. No offense, but I think it was easier talking to a stranger than it would've been to a friend."

"Glad I could be of some little help. Even if it took being a stranger."

Davey finished his cinnamon roll and dusted off his fingers.

"Now one of those," Kevin said, "I could manage before I wake up."

"Got to have eggs first," said Davey. He pushed away from the table and left.

Chapter 11

*I*t was about eleven thirty by the time they got to Nanaimo. Davey pulled Boomer's pickup to the curb in front of Boomer's Boatworks and parked behind Eddie's blue Toyota. Eddie stepped onto the sidewalk and stretched the kinks from his limbs. Being the little guy, he'd got stuck in the middle of the bench seat where his legs'd had to compete with the gear stick and the range selector.

"Long weekend's half over," he lamented. "They always go by so fast, don't you think?"

From the driver's seat, Davey gave him a rueful look. "Keep the doors locked till I get back. I don't want to find another 'we got the Indian' note."

"That what they said? 'We got the Indian'? Fucking racists."

Davey shook his head. "Just lock the door."

Kevin was standing beside the open door of the truck. He held out his hand. "Eddie Roe, it was a genuine pleasure making your acquaintance."

Eddie looked at the offered hand for a moment, then gave Kevin a friendly slap on the shoulder. "Nothing personal, Kiwi, but my people don't put a lot of stock in handshakes. Trusting handshakes over the years has cost us dearly."

Kevin dropped his hand. "Fair enough. I'll keep that in mind."

Eddie watched Boomer's truck till it disappeared up Stewart Avenue, then went to his Toyota pickup. He unlocked the passenger door and folded the back of the seat forward. From behind the seat, he took the soft leather case that held his Enfield .303 hunting rifle and a box of ammunition.

"Sons a bitches want another dance," he muttered as he carried the weapon into the boatworks and locked the door behind him. "Gonna be a service charge."

From the perch in the corner behind the reception desk, Captain Kidd greeted Eddie with a loud squawk.

Eddie glared at the bird. "Don't you talk to me," he said. "The way you let those goons walk in here like they own the place. Oughtta trade you for a can of dog food is what."

The parrot clucked softly and preened the underside of its wing.

"There you go," said Eddie. "Hide your chicken head."

He stepped through the connecting door into Boomer's office and uncased the rifle. He filled the clip with eight bullets, slid one into the chamber, set the safety, and leaned the rifle in the near corner, where he could reach it from the big leather chair behind the desk. He liberated the bottle of Glenfiddich from the bottom drawer, poured a healthy bit into a slightly stained coffee mug that said Boat builders raise stiffer masts, and sat back to think things through.

He liked Davey, he really did, and he respected that as long as this was Davey's show Davey had to handle it Davey's way even if that involved pussyfooting around with some crown counselor. But as of yesterday afternoon, when those goons had walked in like they owned the place, it was no longer Davey's exclusive show, was it?

It never occurred to Eddie to take the matter to the police. Aside from Keith's alleged dying request not to go to the cops, Eddie was perfectly aware that the police enforced a white man's law. He didn't see this as discriminatory or racist, simply a fact of life. The white man had, for centuries, seen himself as humanity's torch, bringing enlightenment to the barbarians. And no doubt, the road to enlightenment is paved with pain and humiliation. Burn a pagan and send a soul to God's heaven, praise the Lord.

Came a point, though, when a barbarian just had to do what a barbarian had to do. Eddie pulled the phone toward him and dialled a long-distance number that connected him to his homeland, the arrowhead-shaped archipelago that the white man called the Queen Charlotte Islands.

"Air Haida," said the phone, "Tom speaking."

"Hi, Tommy, it's your Uncle Eddie here, down in Nanaimo. How's life in the float plane business?"

"Same old, same old. Billy's still taking all the interesting flights, giving me the milk runs. George is still drinking most of the profits. Anything worthwhile happen to Nanaimo since I was last there? Sink in the ocean, nothing like that?"

Tommy didn't much like Nanaimo. He was one of the people Eddie had pulled from an alley after some good old white boys had had some fun with him. Praise the Lord.

Eddie chuckled. "Nah, city's still here, bright and shiny as ever. You know, Tommy, wasn't so long ago, in your great-granddaddy's day, if things got a bit slow up there in Haida Gwaii, they'd send a raiding party down here, eh, raise a few war clubs with the Kwakiutl."

"What are you saying?"

"Seems to be some foreign boys down here getting nasty with us locals. And for a change, they don't have the law on their side, at least not in any official way. Might be good to let them know we got some sting left in us. Good for them, good for us."

"Mom would kill me."

Tom was the only child of Eddie's sister, Nadine. Nadine was even smaller than Eddie. Tommy was about six foot four, with shoulders like the rear end of a tractor. But he was right; his mom would kill him.

"Yeah," said Eddie, "if she ever found out, she'd kill you. So when can you get here?"

"Have to talk to George and Billy. See if I can borrow a plane for a couple days."

"You do that," said Eddie. "And tell them the more the merrier, eh."

Chapter 12

"So what did you and Cassie talk about last night?" Davey asked.

Something in his voice warned Kevin that it wasn't just a conversational question. He looked over. Davey was watching the road, but Kevin didn't think the set of his jaw and the frown on his forehead had to do with the traffic.

"Nothing much," he said. "Talked about her folks, how she's trying to track them down. Essentially, she just wanted a shoulder to cry on."

They were south of the city, passing over the deeply gorged Nanaimo River. A billboard advertised the Bungee Zone, where you could get tied to an elastic band and jump off a bridge. Jump for free if you jumped nude and enjoy the bonus of having no underwear to clean afterward.

"Look, buds," said Kevin, "if I stepped on your territory, I'm sorry. You know, if you and Cassie are . . ." He waved his hand back and forth.

"No," said Davey. "No, no." Three times, like Peter denying Christ. "Nothing like that. I'm a decade older than her. I mean, I like her. She's a nice kid."

Kevin smiled. "Davey, don't tell me you're too old to notice that she's gorgeous."

Davey grinned. "Yeah, she is, isn't she?" Then he shrugged. "But you know, there's nothing between us. Fact, I don't even think she likes me very much. Even if she did, we're miles apart. Not just the age thing. She's got a master's degree in her near future. I barely made it out of high school."

Kevin turned his head to look out the side window. Davey was as deeply in love as he was in denial. He was probably right about it never working between them, but since when had that stopped people in love? As Davey turned left off the highway, Kevin wondered if he could use that bit of knowledge to his advantage or if it was simply an unwanted complication.

Nanaimo's municipal airport was just off the highway. Davey drove through a couple of acres of parking over which was scattered a handful of cars. In the field beyond, an eclectic array of planes sat on paved aprons—from frail little ultralights and squadrons of Cessnas to midsize jetliners and forestry service water bombers.

Davey parked beside the barracks-like terminal building. "They'll have shuttle service to Vancouver International," he said. "From Vancouver, there should be daily flights heading your way. You sure that's enough to see you home?" he asked, referring to the envelope plump with cash.

"I don't feel right about this, buds. Feel like I'm getting paid for a job not done."

"Twice you pulled my sorry ass out of the fire for me. I happen to think my sorry ass is worth at least that much." Davey grinned. Kevin tried to grin back, but it didn't work out.

"Don't worry," said Davey. "After what happened last night, I don't want any part of this. That was way too close. Soon as possible, it'll all be in the hands of a crown counselor. It'll be her problem, not mine, and most certainly not yours. Go home, Kevin. Drop me a card at Christmas."

It was clear that Davey was unwilling to further jeopardize a kid from New Zealand, and the truth burned in Kevin's mouth like a canker sore. He'd faced a similar dilemma a few years ago when he'd infiltrated a native land-claim protest and had been ordered to stir a little violence into a peaceful demonstration. His solution at that time had been to refuse the order, which had resulted in him being removed from the assignment. It hadn't helped his conscience when the shooting had started without him and two Mounties and five natives lay wounded on the ground, one of them fatally. And now, if he disobeyed orders and got removed from this assignment, how clear would his conscience be when Davey's body floated up in the harbor?

And it would. Davey's body, not Kevin's conscience. Without a watchdog, Davey wouldn't last a day against Lazuardi. Davey couldn't even imagine the depths of Lazuardi's resources or the lengths Lazuardi would stretch those resources to get what he wanted. Davey's naivety was demonstrated by his notion that Counselor Dennison could throw some sort of magic force field around him to keep him from harm.

Kevin kept his good-byes cheery while his mind raced. There was little chance that Cronk would give him the green light to tell Davey the truth. And he wasn't going to get himself canned again for a higher principle. He had to find another way. He lifted his backpack from the truck bed and stood watching Davey drive away. What would it take, he wondered, to get himself recruited by Lazuardi? Shaking his head as if to clear it of such nonsense, he went into the building and found a public phone.

It was a small building; fifty people would be a raucous crowd. But between flights, it was churchlike quiet. The phone was beside a small café where a handful of people held whispered conversation. Across the hallway, bored attendants at two airline booths spread gossip and giggled. Kevin faced the wall and spoke softly into the phone.

"Jones dropped me," he told Inspector Brian Cronk, then gave a swift report on his activities since his last call.

Cronk asked, "Is Lazuardi at this place on the Oyster River?"

"I believe not, sir. That bunch seems to be run by a man they call Sebastian. Five foot fuck-all, hundred twenty soaking wet, blond hair over blue eyes."

"Good. I'll put that on the wire. If he works for Lazuardi, he's got a record somewhere. Anyone else we should be interested in?"

"Couple of locals. One Cuchera, early twenties, five nine-ish, one sixty, dirty blond over brown. And one Rockwell, thirty-something, six three, six four, well built, shoulder-length dark brown hair. Also, a goon named Marco, Incredible Hulk look-alike."

Cronk grunted and said, "The two locals are Donny and Norm. They've been through our revolving door a time or two. Don Cuchera raced stock cars till he found out he could make more money supplying the other drivers with whatever they needed to take the edge off. Norm Rockwell, wannabe biker. Do anything to show the hell's angels how tough he is. The hell's Lazuardi doing with a couple losers like Rockwell and Cuchera?"

"Like you say, sir, they're losers. Lazuardi can use them and lose them, no skin off his nose."

"And what about this Sebastian? Any notions on how he fits in?"

"Maybe a subcontractor? Lazuardi knows we're sitting on him, so he wants to stay at arm's length from any rough stuff. Hires a bunch of local throwaways to hunt down Stoddard and get his stick back. But these guys, you got to add them all together to get half a clue, so he puts this Sebastian in the driver's seat."

"That plays," said Cronk. "If none of Sebastian's crowd has actually met Stoddard, that would explain the mistaken identity. He and Jones could certainly fit each other's physical descriptions. Speaking of Jones, did he ever explain why he hasn't gone to the police?"

"He doesn't know why. Keith Stoddard warned him away from the police, told him to talk to Counselor Dennison."

"Says Jones."

"Frankly, sir, I believe him. Was Counselor Dennison able to shed any light on it?"

"She has no light to shed. Jones demanded a private meeting, his time and place, and didn't do the courtesy of being there."

"That's because Chambers and Monkton altered his schedule. Sir, I believe that if we simply lay it out for him, he will return the favor."

"That's negative, Constable. That *is* negative. We've still got an officer somewhere out in the cold. Until we find her, I'm not going to bet her life on Jones's good character."

"And what about Davey, sir? In the last two days, Lazuardi has taken two swings at him. We just going to stand back now and let Lazuardi have at him?"

Cronk must've picked up a note of desperation in Kevin's voice. "Listen up," he said in his best inspector voice. "I forbid you to contact him again. Might as well take out a public ad explaining the entire operation. You understand *forbid*, Constable? Not too ambiguous for you?"

Ten minutes earlier, Kevin had wondered how he might get into Lazuardi's camp. He'd dismissed the idea as rhetorical nonsense. But down in the basement of his brain, a problem-solving mechanism had exercised itself by gathering scraps of information and stitching them together. The result was a gossamer plan, transparent and full of holes.

"In that case, sir," he blurted before the plan could disintegrate under its own weight, "I believe I can penetrate Lazuardi's crew."

"Bullshit," said Cronk. "It took three months for Operation Download to place an operative on Lazuardi's doorstep."

"Yes, sir, but three months ago, Lazuardi wasn't desperate to get his flash drive back. I've got a scenario based on information I got from Cassie Denton last night. If you could bear with me, sir, hear me out."

A few minutes later, Constable Purcell hung up the phone. He closed his eyes and drew a deep breath. Cold sweat broke across his shoulders. Okay, buds, he told himself, you called the tune, so you better get out there and dance.

Kevin used the phone to order a taxi and then went into a deserted men's room. He opened his backpack, took out his 9 mm service weapon and buried his badge in the pack—the weapon he'd need; the badge would only get him in trouble. Now he had to get rid of the backpack. There were no public lockers. He could abandon it in the washroom, but one of the bored attendants might just notice if he went out empty-handed. *Excuse me, sir, don't forget your luggage.*

He stuck the gun in the back of his pants and pulled his army surplus jacket on over it. He carried his backpack to the Air BC booth and booked onto the next flight to Victoria, boarding in two hours.

"If I leave my kit here," he asked, "could you see it gets on the plane, love?"

"I could probably manage that," she said, smiling as she tagged the backpack and took it into the booth.

Chapter 13

*D*avey almost nailed Eddie's Toyota. His mind was on the letter Boomer had given him rather than on his driving. He came in to the curb too fast and had to slam on the brakes. The Beretta automatic and the stubby revolver came sliding out from under the seat. Kevin must have put them there. Hiding them from Boomer. Grinning, Davey tucked them back under the seat.

He took the letter from his hip pocket and glanced through it again. As Boomer had observed, it read like a love letter. Two pages of Keith's bold block letter printing. Two pages of endearments spiced up with graphic anatomical suggestions.

Then there was the PS.

Ps baby. remember our talk about Erin? You can get her number off that colorful little guy they call Captain Kidd. She's all keyed up to meet you at Victoria Central. Love, K.

Erin was Keith's I'll-straighten-him-out ex-wife. Why would she be keyed up to meet his stripper girlfriend? And how was Lily supposed to get Erin's number from a parrot?

Davey got out of the truck and folded the letter back into his pocket. He stepped to the front of the building and rapped on one of the porthole windows until he got Eddie's attention. When Eddie let him in, he looked at the macaw. He pulled out the letter and directed Eddie's attention to the PS. The two men stepped up close to the bird's perch. Under the sudden scrutiny, Captain Kidd took a couple of side steps and squawked in discomfort.

"What're the bands on his leg?" Eddie asked.

"Registration number," said Davey.

"Both of them?"

Davey shrugged.

Two bracelets circled the bird's left leg. One was metallic silver in color and stood out. The other was the same grayish-brown color as the parrot's horny skin. With murmured endearments, Davey gently lifted the bird's leg and worked the bands off over its claws. The metallic band was embossed with a combination of numbers and letters. On the brown plastic one there were only numbers. Ten of them.

"Phone number," said Eddie.

Davey nodded. "'Get Erin's number off that colorful little guy they call Captain Kidd.'"

Erin lived in Toronto, area code 416. Davey found 416 on the band and wrote out the sequence from there. Then he stood staring at the phone on the reception desk.

Erin harbored an intense dislike for Davey, a dislike that was prone to spill over into hatred, convinced as she was that Davey had undermined her efforts to straighten out Keith. Davey pulled out his cigarettes and put one in his mouth.

"You better call from Boomer's office," Eddie cautioned, "if you plan on lighting that."

"Right. Sorry."

Boomer's receptionist, Catherine, was a nonsmoker, and Boomer enforced a rigid rule against smoking in her work area. Davey took the phone number and his filthy habit into Boomer's office.

"Hello?" Erin answered pleasantly, taking Davey off guard. He'd irrationally expected her to be annoyed from the start, as if she could psychically determine that the call was from him.

Davey had a sudden wrenching image of Keith's daughters, maybe sitting at the table having a snack, maybe wanting to speak to their daddy.

"Hello?" she repeated. "Who's there?"

"Hello. Sorry, it's long distance." A feeble excuse considering he could hear her as well as if she'd been there in person. "Is this Erin?"

"Yes, it is." Her voice was still pleasant, mildly curious, as if the caller might be a relative she couldn't quite place. Surprise!

"Hi, Erin. It's Davey here. Davey Jones."

She got rid of her pleasantness with a drawn sigh. "Jesus Christ," she said, perhaps pleading for divine intervention. "What are you two playing at this time?"

Not much. We just pissed off some people with armed helicopters who shot Keith's guts out, so I buried him off the back of our boat.

"I just called to ask if you've heard from Keith recently."

"Ah, poor Davey. Did he dump you? Run off with *Lily*, did he?"

Davey's grip tightened on the phone. He bit his tongue to hold back a retort. "You want me to beg, Erin? All right, I'm begging. This is serious. We're in some very serious trouble here."

"Well, congratulations! Isn't that what you've dedicated your lives to? The pursuit of trouble?"

Davey forced his grip on the phone to relax, forced his mouth to stay shut. He needed her cooperation. He couldn't afford to tell her what he thought of her life's dedication to dispensing misery in pursuit of control. He listened to her breathe as she calmed herself.

"Yes," she said. "He sent a letter with his last support payment. A letter and a key. In the letter, he wrote that if someone named Lily White, of all things, got in touch with me, would I please give her the key."

"A key for what?" Davey asked.

"He didn't say. It's a gold-colored key, similar to the one I use for my mailbox. Why can't you ask him?" she said, and a trickle of worry spilled from her voice. "God, did he get himself put in jail or something?"

Don't I wish?

"As I said, Erin, we're in serious trouble. And maybe we did get into it all on our own, but that's not a great comfort. That key he left could offer some comfort. Has Lily gotten in touch with you yet?"

Silence streamed down the phone line from Toronto. Davey crushed his cigarette to death in a big cut-glass ashtray and said, "What do you want, Erin? You want a signed confession that I sabotaged your marriage?"

"No, Davey, that doesn't require a confession. What I want is for Keith to be all right. Can you sign *that*?"

"Not without the key," Davey said softly.

"What does it open?" said Erin. "Or should I ask?"

"To be perfectly honest, I don't know."

Erin's silence begged for elaboration, but Davey was loath to spin the lie further and terrified of the truth, so he kept shut. Finally, Erin said, "Very well, then. I'll mail it this afternoon."

"I'd rather you didn't mail it, Erin. It could take a week to get here. I'd rather come and get it. I'll see if I can get a flight tomorrow and call you back."

From Toronto came another contemplative silence. It lasted long enough for Davey to wonder what he'd do if she hung up on him. She didn't, though. She said, "Don't take too long to call back. I've got an appointment this afternoon."

Davey's fingers trembled a bit as he hung up the phone. Eddie poured some whiskey into a coffee mug and handed it to him. Davey took the mug and stared into it.

"So did you?" asked Eddie as he poured a drink for himself.

"What?"

"Sabotage their marriage?"

"For Christsake, Eddie, what kind of question is that?"

"Good answer." Eddie chuckled. "She did steal your best pal, though, didn't she?"

"You know better than that, Eddie. Keith was a stealer, not a stealee. No one ever took any part of Keith that he didn't want them to take."

"Someone took his life," said Eddie.

"Well, yeah," said Davey. He lifted the mug and drank the whiskey. "Someone took his life."

Davey went back to Catherine's desk to use the phone book and used the reception phone to call Air Canada. They'd be happy to book him on a seat to Toronto in eighteen days. Or he could camp out at the airport and sacrifice small animals to the patron saint of standby seats.

"Try a travel agent," Eddie suggested. "That's what they get paid for."

The girl at the travel agency took it as a personal challenge to get Mr. Jones to Toronto and back all in the course of the following day. She came up with an itinerary that would keep him on his toes, changing planes in Edmonton, Regina, and Ottawa. Then she got lucky for his return flight. A cancelled rugby tour had opened up two dozen seats on a direct flight from Toronto to Victoria. Davey arranged to pick up the tickets at the airport in the morning.

To accommodate his tobacco addiction, he went back to Boomer's office to call Erin with the flight information. Erin offered to meet him at the airport so he wouldn't have to grope through the city looking for her. He was thanking her for her thoughtfulness when she hung up on him.

Chapter 14

*K*evin Purcell paid off the cab outside a corner store on Boundary Avenue, across from the Nanaimo Regional General Hospital. He went into the store and bought a newspaper and a large root beer slushee. Outside, he strolled down the sidewalk sipping the drink through a straw and glancing across the street.

The hospital and its grounds covered half a dozen city blocks in the middle of a residential zone. The main building towered like a castle; outbuildings crouched like serf hovels at its feet. The buildings were surrounded by parklike grounds and tree-shaded parking lots. Apartment blocks encroached on all sides like regiments laying siege. Kevin stopped at the end of the block. He drew a long noisy drink through the straw. On the opposite corner, a wooden signpost aimed arrows at the outpatient clinic, the rehab center, the emergency ward, and the main entrance. The main entrance seemed the best bet.

The landscaped grounds were well used by the cliff dwellers from the apartments. Scores of people strolled among the trees or lounged on the sun-soaked lawns, escaping their little caves, getting some green space around them. Kevin found the main entrance and selected a tree-shaded area about sixty meters from it. He sat on the lawn close to a rhododendron bush and began leafing through the newspaper while keeping the hospital entrance in his line of sight. If Inspector Cronk came through for him and if the hospital administration came through for Cronk, Collin Chambers and Jermaine Monkton would be discharged sometime that afternoon.

Chambers, no doubt, was eminently dispensable, one of Lazuardi's throwaways, to be used and discarded with nary a further thought. It was unlikely that Lazuardi would trouble himself to retrieve Chambers. Monkton, though, would have had access to the commodity of information. That alone would make him less disposable. By no means indispensable but, like toxic waste, to be disposed of in a prescribed manner after careful consideration, not simply abandoned on the street. Most likely, Lazuardi would send a car for them, but if they did get a cab, the cabbie was going to have one hell of a story for his grandkids.

An hour passed. Kevin flipped the paper back to page 1 and started through it again. Like petitioners to the castle keep, the population trickled in and out of the hospital: pregnant women, cradling their precious distensions; visitors of the stricken, wearing grief on their faces like old familiar wounds; discharged survivors on wheelchairs or crutches, grinning in bewildered relief; ambulances with busy lights, hurrying to the emergency entrance, dodging staff members who'd snuck out back for a quick smoke.

Kevin turned another page, deep into the want ads for a second time, and wondered if Cronk had changed his mind. Maybe the inspector, after talking to Kevin, had said, "To hell with him. Let him sit and watch the hospital all day. Make sure no one steals it."

His concentration waned, and he almost missed them. When he saw them, they were already seated on one of the benches that lined the walkway to the passenger pickup area. The Monk was lighting up a cigar. Chambers was touching the gauze pad on the side of his head as if searching for his ear.

Kevin stood up and tossed the paper and the empty cup into a trash can. He pulled his jacket on as he picked his way between trees toward the parking lot. From the jacket's right-hand cargo pocket, he took his pistol. He primed the chamber, engaged the safety, and returned the gun to his pocket. He kept to the shrubs at the edge of the parking lot, angling to get behind Monkton and Chambers.

A maroon-colored four-door Plymouth sedan rolled through the parking lot, passing not a dozen feet from him. He recognized the driver, Cuchera, the same kid who'd driven Sebastian the night before. He stepped away from the trees and followed in the car's wake.

The Plymouth stopped in the yellow-striped pickup zone. Monkton and Chambers stood and walked toward it. Kevin approached from the left rear, bent over as if with a stomach cramp. Chambers opened the right rear door for Monkton. The Monk's eyes slid over Kevin as if Kevin didn't exist. With his boss safely aboard, Chambers got in up front.

Kevin took two quick steps and grabbed the handle on the left rear door, thinking, *Don't be locked. Please, God, don't be locked.* It wasn't. His left hand opened the door, and his right hand drew the gun from his pocket. In a second, he was sitting in the backseat beside Monkton, his gun snugged up against the Monk's head.

He slammed the door and said, "Hi, buds, how's everyone this gorgeous sun-dappled day?"

Cuchera's head snapped around. "*You?*"

Kevin grinned at him. "Just smile at the nice people, buds, and drive off nice and easy. Me and your boss here, we got things to talk about."

Twenty-five minutes later, the Monk punched a number into a cell phone and put the phone to his ear. His eyes, dark and dull as coal dust, never left Kevin's. "It's Monkton," he said into the phone. "Get VL."

Despite the open windows, the air in the car was cloy with the hot humid scent from the three naked men. Kevin wondered how much longer he could keep smiling into those coal dust eyes. The inside of his mouth was dry as dust, and his stomach felt like a vat of acid. His heart galloped and sweat prickled his upper arms and his thighs. If he were any more scared, he'd throw up. But that was none of the Monk's business, so Kevin showed him nothing but the cocky grin plastered across his face and the bore of his gun.

"We got a problem," Monkton said into the phone. Kevin made a gimme motion with the pistol. Monkton told the phone, "It wants to talk to you."

Kevin took the phone in his left hand. "VL?" he said, forcing a chuckle through his grin. "Lucky for you that your last name doesn't start with a D."

"Who is this?"

Kevin's scalp tingled. There he was, Vincent Lazuardi, the Lizard, inside the little folding phone. He said, "The guy who took out Goofy here. Twice."

"You refer to Mr. Monkton?" said Lazuardi, an oriental lilt keeping his voice half an octave too high to be tough.

"Monkton, Monkey, Goofy, whatever. If he's the best you got, I'm better. That means whatever you're paying him, I'm worth more."

After a brief pause, Lazuardi said, "Whatever business you have with Mr. Monkton, I fail to see what it has to do with me."

Kevin didn't hesitate. He dared not. "In that case," he said, "good day, buds." He pressed the End button and tossed the phone on the seat.

Monkton's expression hadn't flickered since Kevin had jumped into the car and placed the gun to his head. Not while Cuchera had followed Kevin's directions to this deserted gravel pit in the hills behind Nanaimo. Not when Kevin had prodded the men from the car and made them strip and stand naked under the sun while he'd searched clothes and car. Not when he'd disarmed the three guns he'd found and heaved the weapons far into the mounds of gravel. Not when he'd pocketed the two large Cohiba cigars he'd found. Through all that, the Monk's expression could have been a photograph pasted to his face. A photograph of a predator watching prey.

Now it flickered. A slight knitting of the brow, a brief tightening around the lips. A flicker of concern that perhaps this suicidal maniac was not entirely bluffing.

"Tell you what," Kevin said, disgusted, "it is one *royal* fuck to make a living in this racket. Okay for you boys with your steady gig, but freelance, man, one fucking shit wipe after another. First it's Jonesy. Put you guys in the hospital for him, wreck your fucking car for him, turns out he's got no money. Believe that shit?"

Kevin gave his head a sorry little shake: *no* one believed *that* shit.

"Keith and Frankie got the money. 'Cept Keith's dead and you guys got Frankie on ice. Jonesy's got a fucking computer file. The fuck am I going to do with a computer file? This is a cash business, am I right?"

Kevin nodded. Fucking-*A* he was right.

"Now *your* boss ain't *in*terested. I mean, how the fuck could he *not* be interested? Puts me in a *fine* position, that does. I got all fucking outlay here and no fucking return. And now I got to do you guys or I'm a fucking laughingstock."

Fine beads of perspiration blossomed across Monkton's upper lip. *That's right,* Kevin thought. *Believe you're about to die, punk.*

He said, "Now I got to do this thing that I ain't getting paid for and I don't hate you guys or nothing so I got to carry the guilt of it for the rest of my life. Is that fair?" Kevin allowed a trickle of hysterical madness to destabilize his voice. It didn't take much acting. "You tell me," he almost squealed. "You tell me. Is that fair?"

Monkton's eyes went to the phone on the seat. *There you go,* Kevin thought. *Call your boss again, punk, and this time remember you're on my side.*

A sudden buzzing noise from the front seat surprised him. He couldn't quite stop the reflex to turn his head. He knew instantly that he'd made a mistake, but an instant was all it took. Monkton's hand slapped the pistol as Kevin squeezed the trigger. The gun fired into the roof of the car with a flat clap that boxed Kevin's ears. In a heartbeat, two hundred odd pounds of naked Monkton were on top of him, pressing him into the corner, restricting his fighting space. The two men up front joined the melee, Chambers pummelling his head, Cuchera clawing his face. There was a sharp pain in his right wrist and the gun was gone. Squirming, he got a leg free and started kicking. Then the gun was placed against his head.

Oh shit.

He stopped struggling. Cuchera continued to claw at his face, the kid releasing his fear with guttural little groans as he worked. Luckily, Cuchera was a fingernail-biter. Monkton, holding the gun in one hand, used the other to corral the kid's arms and push him away.

"Answer it," Monkton said.

Kevin's ears were ringing from the gunshot, dampening the buzzing tone that had initiated this mess. A car phone. Unbelievable.

"Answer it!" Monkton yelled, his breath a sour spray in Kevin's face.

The ring tone stopped. The voice of Collin Chambers said, "Yeah . . . Yes, sir."

There was the click of a switch being flipped, then Lazuardi's voice came through a speaker and filled the car. "Guy who took out Monkton, you still there?"

Kevin looked at the gun in his face, looked into Monkton's eyes and forced the grin back onto his lips. "For now," he said.

"So," said Lazuardi, "what is it you want?"

"Well, for starters, I want Monkton to get off me and give my gun back."

There was a protracted pause followed by a soft tittering chuckle. Even the Monk's stony features showed a ghost of a smile.

"Mr. Monkton," said Lazuardi, "am I to understand that there has been a reversal of fortune?"

"There's been a reversal of the gun barrel."

Another tittering chuckle. "Very well, then. I'll leave you two to sort out your differences."

"Stoddard's dead," Kevin blurted and then spoke rapidly into the ensuing silence. "Sebastian killed Stoddard, but his partner, Jones, has got the file, and Jones will dance with whoever has the girl and I can deliver the girl."

Chapter 15

Cassie stepped onto *Small Wonder*'s deck. It was nine o'clock. Sunset had bled into the forested hills to the west half an hour ago, leaving a purple sky pinholed with a handful of stars. Cassie stepped softly into the cockpit, trying not to rock the boat, careful to stay out of the cone of light shining up from the hatch. She listened to the sounds of his presence: the quiet rustle of paper, the light tinkle of ice cubes against glass, his gentle baritone as he mumbled something to himself. She smiled.

She frowned. He didn't know she was there; it wasn't too late to turn and leave as softly as she'd come.

"Don't be an idiot," she whispered. "You're just asking for a ride to Victoria."

But the quiver in her belly and the heat in her throat called her a liar. What if he guessed how she felt about him, and he said go away little girl, I'm busy?

"So what?" she whispered. "He's a drug runner. Who cares for his opinion?"

Another lie.

"Advance or retreat, little girl, but don't lurk in the shadows like a thief."

Before her mind was made up, her legs carried her to the companionway. She took four steps down and stopped. He was sitting at the salon table, bent over a chart, not yet aware of her presence. He wore faded jeans and a white T-shirt that clung to the girth of his chest, the round bulk of his shoulders and arms. His bare feet were crossed under the table. His hair, dark and damp from the shower, was in curly disarray. Most men she knew never missed a reflective opportunity to whip out a comb and preen themselves. She found the curly disarray sexy. It was the way he'd look in bed.

He rubbed his eyes and shook his head, a gesture of fatigue or frustration. Possibly both. "Lost fucking cause," he muttered.

Cassie realized that she was stealing a piece of his privacy. Like a thief. She knocked with her knuckles on the bulkhead. "Permission to come aboard?"

Davey looked up, surprised. His surprise gave way to a smile that dimpled his cheek and crinkled the corners of his eyes, a handsome smile that seemed to her awkward and forced. Maybe she'd made a mistake.

"Of course," he said. "By all means."

As she moved, she was aware of the light fabric of her dress clinging to her legs. She saw his eyes follow the lines of her legs and felt suddenly too warm. She dropped her eyes to the table and saw that it wasn't a chart he was studying, but a street map, a map of the city of Victoria. The map was pinned to the table by a whiskey bottle and a sweating glass, a smoking ashtray, and a gun.

"My goodness," she said, "don't we look Chandleresque."

Davey's eyes swept over the table. "You think? Without the misogyny, I hope."

"Oh? Was Raymond Chandler a misogynist?"

Davey shrugged. "His female characters all seem to be bimbos or bitches."

Cassie wondered what she'd stepped into. She certainly hadn't meant to open a literary critique. "Interesting observation," she said.

"And likely unjust. I've only read two of his stories."

"That's two more than I've read. I just said Chandleresque because it seemed a cool thing to say."

Davey laughed. "Had me going. You've no idea how intimidating a university education can be to we uneducated masses."

Davey's laugh seemed to be as forced as his smile. He was teasing her, and Cassie's blush began to burn with embarrassment. Maybe this was a bad idea. Maybe she should escape while she still had a pinch of self-esteem to spend on begging a ride from Linda.

"Sure I do," she said, a boxer wading in to take more punches. "That's exactly why I'm devoting so much work and money to it. How else is a girl like me going to be intimidating?"

Davey said, "You're kidding, right?"

Cassie was unsure of his meaning. Was he mocking her? "Anyway," she said, "uneducated people don't leave messages in Latin."

Davey cocked his head and frowned.

"*Illegitimus non carborundum?*" she said, reciting the words with which Keith had ended his message on Linda's answering machine.

Davey nodded and smiled. A small smile, without dimples or crinkles, but a real smile, kept honest with a touch of sadness.

"Means, 'Don't let the bastards grind you down,' according to Keith." Davey shrugged. "Nothing wrong with Keith's education. He had a degree in computer sciences. Still, he probably knew about as much Latin as Gunner does."

Cassie watched him covering the pain of his loss with a sad little smile. His sudden vulnerability took her off guard. She'd never thought of Davey as being vulnerable.

"I'm sorry," he said. "I'm a lousy host. Let me get you a drink." He started to rise, evidently forgetting about the overhead cupboard until his head cracked against it.

"Ouch," Cassie said, her brow furrowed in sympathy. "I didn't come out here to bother you."

"No bother." Rubbing the top of his head Davey went to the fridge and pulled out a bag of misshapen ice cubes. From a cupboard, he selected, inspected, and rejected three smudged glasses. A fourth he wiped out with a paper towel. He poured the drink and turned toward her.

They were standing close, almost touching, pushed together by the confines of the cabin. Or something. She studied his face, the split lip, the bruises, the dark stain on the white of his left eye. *I can make him better,* she thought.

His eyes were glistening, the pupils enlarged, like portals to a dream. The pulse in her throat grew heavy. Warmth tingled in her belly. *He can make me better,* she thought. *All he has to do is touch me and we'll both melt into a dream and be better.*

Davey turned away and set the drink on the table. He cleared his throat and said, "Boomer tells me you got some good news about your folks. It's about time we got some good news."

Cassie gave her head a little shake and took a deep breath. She picked up the glass and took a drink, then coughed and laughed. "At the risk of sounding like a bimbo, I need that watered down a bit."

"Oh, sorry. I didn't even . . . Ah, there should be some soda here somewhere."

"Water's fine. Really."

Davey took her glass to the tap, and Cassie took another deep breath. *This ain't a dream, little girl, where a kiss makes everything better.*

"I called some friends in Port Alberni," she said to his back, "who told me they got a call today from Aunt Toots."

"Aunt Toots?" Davey said as he returned the diluted scotch to her.

"Mom's sister. Her name's Florence. She plays trumpet in a jazz band. She got the name Toots in her high school band. Jazz players need nicknames. It's part of the guild covenant."

Cassie sipped the scotch. That was better. She gulped. Much better.

"Our friends in Port Alberni," she continued, "said Aunt Toots was asking about me. She told them Dad was trying to find me. So I've been trying to contact Auntie, but haven't got hold of her yet."

If she were half a step closer, her breasts would brush his arm. The whiskey swirled in her head, all mixed up with the scents of him.

"That's why I came out here," she said. There was an edge in her voice that she hadn't meant to put there. "Auntie lives in Victoria, and Boomer said you were going to the airport in the morning, and I hoped I could hitch a ride to Victoria, where it might be easier to track Auntie down. That's why."

"No problem," said Davey, smiling.

What was that about, the smile? Was it invitational? Or was he amused by her discomposure? Or was she being oversensitive and picking up signals that weren't there? Cassie gulped down her drink and made another.

Above the galley counter hung a framed pencil sketch of the *Alaska Prince,* one of four unsigned sketches hanging on the bulkheads. They were all of small coastal freighters plying the beautifully rugged BC coast. They were very well-done. You could almost hear the call of the swooping gulls, feel the mist on your face, smell the green of the forest at the water's edge and the briny scent of the sea. Cassie wondered who'd drawn them.

"How did it go in Nanaimo?" she asked.

"Well, let's see. Sent Kevin on his way home. I couldn't get hold of Dennison. Her office is closed, of course, but I'd hoped for an answering service that could reach her. No joy. I got Eddie to promise he'd stay with friends," Davey said and almost bit his tongue off. Neither Cassie nor Linda knew about Eddie's little adventure the previous evening, and Davey had promised Boomer it would stay that way. Fortunately, Cassie didn't ask why Eddie should stay with friends.

"And," he said, "I made arrangements to fly to Toronto."

"Boomer mentioned that. What's that all about?"

Davey told her about the key Keith had sent to his ex-wife and how Davey suspected that the key opened a locker at a bus depot or train station called Victoria Central. He gestured at the map spread across the table. "There doesn't seem to be any Victoria Central on this map. You live down there, don't you, during semesters? Ever hear of Victoria Central?"

"It's a post office."

"A what?"

"Post office. Like Postal Station A. Victoria's main post office is called Victoria Central." As she spoke, Cassie ran a finger over the map, tracking down the post office. She tapped a pink fingernail on it.

"That makes sense," Davey said. He could smell the shower on her, the soap and shampoo and the heat of her flesh. She brushed against him. Was she flirting with him, or was that nothing but a lecher's pathetic fantasy? He took a step away from her. "Keith's got mailboxes in towns all over the island," he said.

They made small talk through another scotch. Cassie admired the sketches, and Davey explained that Keith's ex-wife had drawn them years ago. The ships were freighters that their fathers, Keith's and Davey's and Boomer's, had crewed on together.

"She's talented," Cassie said.

"Oh yeah, Erin has many talents."

Cassie started to yawn and said she'd better turn in if she was going to be ready for the road at first light. Davey suggested that she sleep in the house tonight and not to worry as he wouldn't leave in the morning without her. He said he'd prefer if she didn't sleep in Keith's bunk. She blushed and gave him a funny look, a look that could've been either hurt or disdain. What was he supposed to say? That he didn't trust himself not to sneak into her bed in the middle of the night?

When she was gone, he had another scotch, but the whiskey tasted sour and flinty, as if he was comparing it to the warm stirring scent of Cassie. He paced the cabin, explaining to himself that Cassie was not for him. She was a bright young woman with a promising future. He was a salvage operator-cum-drug-runner who'd taken thirty-two years to accomplish not a damn thing.

The small cabin wasn't designed for pacing. Besides, the conversation stank. He returned to the scotch on the table. Any port in a storm. He drank and stared at the open map. He tapped his finger where Cassie had tapped hers. Victoria Central. A post office. A post office with thousands of boxes.

He got up and stepped toward the aft cabin, surprised that his legs took a minute to get the idea. He gave the whiskey bottle a suspicious look. In Keith's cabin, he started pulling drawers. There weren't many; it didn't take long to find the bundles of envelopes. Keith had been keeping his mail for years. Fodder for the book he was going to write someday. *Fuckin shot, man.* Book cancelled.

Davey took the bundles of mail into the salon and dumped them on the table, covering the map. Davey himself regularly got two pieces of mail a year—Christmas and birthday greetings from his mother. For the last few years, the cards had been identical: a basketful of puppies on the outside and bundles of joy on the inside. She must've bought them by the gross. He'd never bothered keeping them.

A lot of Keith's letters were from his daughters, addressed to a post office box in Nanaimo. As he set them aside, a crayon drawing slipped from one. He picked it up and looked at a child's depiction of a sailboat under a fat yellow sun, with a smiling stick daddy at the helm. He stared at it and thought, *Your daddy's dead.*

He stuffed the drawing back into the envelope. He poured another drink, and his hand shook so that the neck of the bottle rattled against the rim of the glass.

While drinking too fast, he waded through dozens of envelopes from Keith's friends and relatives, addressed to Keith at half a dozen different post offices scattered throughout Vancouver Island. His concentration started to blur. Too much scotch, among other things. Things like the way Cassie's dress clung to her legs and the way her hair lay in soft curls on her shoulders.

Things like, *Your daddy's dead.*

He almost missed the envelope, placing it in the discard pile before his brain registered the words Victoria Central. He snatched it back. Keith's name and the address were written in a soft looping hand that made the dots into little *o*'s. There was no return address. Davey ripped the flap off his cigarette package, wrote on it Keith's box number at Victoria Central, and stuffed the flap into his wallet. He stared at the envelope for a moment before picking it up and extracting the letter—a single page written in the same curvy feminine hand. It was undated.

Dearest Keith, it began. Davey's eyes slid to the bottom. *Love ya to pieces, Lil.*

As in Lily.

Davey read that she'd got a gig at JJ's, up in Campbell River, and that she hoped her *special K* could come spend some time with her because she positively *loved* being his *private dancer.* She was getting a new CD, the one B had mentioned, and it promised to be so *hot* that it would smoulder and burn, baby . . .

Who are you, Lily? Who the hell are you?

The letter swam out of focus. His head was suddenly too heavy. He folded his forearms on the table and laid down on them. The movement caused a wave of alcohol to roll across his head the way surf rolls across the beach. He thought he might vomit and didn't really care. He thought about Cassie and cared too much.

"Your daddy's dead," he muttered, and the alcohol surf curled and sucked him into its undertow.

Chapter 16

"All right, people," said Flammond from the front passenger seat, turning his crew cut head, looking toward the back, "listen up now."

There were very few things Norm Rockwell could do well at five thirty in the morning, and listening up sure as hell wasn't one of them. Norm was sitting on a bench seat in the back of the van. It was pitch-dark. The driving motion threatened to put him back to sleep, something pretty much guaranteed to piss Flammond right off. So he forced his eyes to stay open and tried to listen.

"We have a target and a location," Flammond said, "but no timetable. I want us set up on-site with zero pissing around. Better to hurry up and wait than piss around and be late."

Yeah, yeah, yeah. Norm pulled out his cigarettes. At least a guy could smoke in the van. He'd go bonkers if he had to do without all the way to Victoria. On the seat beside him, Twitch nudged him in the ribs. Norm lit a smoke for both of them. In the dim glow from the cigarettes, Norm looked at Twitch. At the frizzy dirty blond hair that Twitch tried to rubber band into a ponytail with ludicrous results, the too-bright eyes bulging from deep-set sockets, the sniffling nose and hollow stubbled cheeks, the sweaty sheen on his forehead.

"How you doing?" Norm whispered. "Hang on a few more hours? Soon as we hit the city, we'll get you fixed."

"I'm good, Norm. I'm on top of it." Twitch tried to whisper, but his voice jerked up and down with its own private brand of St. Vitas' dance. "I'm all fucking over it."

"Mr. Rockwell," barked Flammond, "are you having a problem taking me seriously?"

Nothing new under the sun. Flammond had barked at Norm before. Would've ended there except for Twitch.

"Seriously?" Twitch snickered. His exaggerated whisper sounded louder than a shout. "Guy out of a Sergeant fucking Rock comic book wants to be taken seriously?"

"Mr. Bartell," said Flammond, "stop the vehicle."

Oh shit, thought Norm. But inside he was chuckling. *Sergeant Rock* comic book. That wasn't bad. Fact, that was pretty fucking good. Sometimes, it almost seemed that Twitch still had it together.

The driver, Ricky Bartell, pulled the van to the side of the gravel road. Flammond opened his door and stepped out. He looked in at Norm.

"Mr. Rockwell, exit the vehicle."

There were guys at the lodge, if they had ordered him out onto a deserted gravel road in the wilderness, Norm would've feared being the main attraction at a roadside execution. But Flammond wasn't one of them. An ex-paratrooper, Flammond was one of those heavily muscled short guys, his T-shirts always stretched to the limit by his chest and arms. Rumor had it that he'd gotten drummed out of the paratroops for getting too gung ho on some jigaboos in some shithole called Somalia. Maybe it was from rumors like that or maybe from the fact that he'd been trained to step, combat-ready, from a moving aircraft out into the wind and the night, but Flammond didn't have to act tough; toughness came off him like a scent.

Flammond led Norm about thirty feet down the road, out of casual earshot of the van. "I was given three men to help me do this job," he said. "My pick. You were at the top of my list. Your junkie friend wasn't even in the top hundred."

Norm looked down at the cigarette in the cup of his hand. Of all the guys he'd met since being recruited by this mob—some he feared, some he despised, most he cared nothing about—Flammond was the only one he truly respected. Twitch's joke aside, Flammond's opinion mattered to him. But Norm had learned to resist feelings of respect. Having too much respect for someone could get a guy chewed up and spat out. Hell's angels had given him that if nothing else.

Flammond crouched down and scooped up a handful of gravel. He rolled the gravel between his hands while he spoke. "I admire loyalty, Mr. Rockwell, although I believe yours is misplaced. You're not stupid enough to be blindly loyal, so I assume that junkie did something to earn it. Okay, fine. Good for him, good for you."

Flammond had sieved the gravel down to half a dozen hazelnut-size stones. As he spoke, he pitched them one by one into the dark forest. They made chalky sounds as they slapped through unseen leaves.

"I allowed you to bring him for one reason: we're not going back to the lodge." *Pitch.* "Its location was compromised when the Indian escaped.

And after the last two days worth of fuckups, it's not a healthy place to be. Lazuardi has run out of patience with Sebastian. That's between you and me." *Pitch.* "Your loyalty to the junkie probably just saved his life, so now you're even." *Pitch.*

"Once we take the girl," he continued, "the only thing between us and twenty years in prison is a phone number. It's going to be dicey for a few hours." *Pitch.* "The junkie wants to have fun with me, fine. Only an idiot would take offense at what comes out of his mouth." *Pitch.* "But if I think for one second that his presence is compromising the job, I will terminate his employment. Permanently."

Norm followed Flammond back to the van and knew that Flammond could do it, could kill a guy dead quick as pitching a stone. Twitch would never even know.

Half an hour later, they were southbound on the highway. Dawn was shedding light on the eastern sky. Up ahead, the sign on a Mohawk gas station flickered to life, advertising a convenience store. The sign said Casper's, like the friendly fucking ghost.

Flammond got Bartell to pull into the gas station and handed him some money. "Four coffees," he said, "and some doughnuts for the blood sugar level."

Had Norm looked out the back window, he probably would have seen the dun-colored Chevy pickup that stopped at the stop sign on the connecting side road. In the dawn's early light, if his eyes hadn't locked onto the babe in the passenger's seat, he almost certainly would have recognized the guy behind the wheel, and there would have been no need for the drive to Victoria. But Norm was sitting forward with his elbows on his knees, blowing smoke at the floor, thinking that he was pretty cool for a guy about to add kidnapping to his rap sheet. By the time Bartell returned and everybody got their coffee fixed the way they liked it, the highway was empty, the dun-colored pickup a dozen kilometres ahead of them.

"Is it short for Cassandra?" Davey asked.

To the east, the sky was growing brighter by the minute. Beneath the truck, the blacktop hummed past at a hundred and twenty kilometers an hour. They were skirting Courtenay on the Inland Highway. A rock-and-roll oldies radio station from Seattle was fading in and out. "No," she said. "Cassiopeia."

"You're kidding."

"I happen to like it," she said, a touch defensively. "In fact, I prefer it to Cassie. I'm just not enough of a bitch to make everyone call me Cassiopeia."

"Don't get me wrong, I like it too. It's just unusual. Especially for someone who does a lot of boating. Wasn't Cassiopeia the one who pissed off Poseidon by claiming her daughter was more beautiful than the Nereids? Suppose Poseidon holds a grudge?"

"That was another Cassiopeia. I don't have a daughter."

It was a four-lane highway with a wide grassy median. The forest had been cleared back a couple of hundred meters on either side of the road, presumably as a landing strip for vehicles that launched themselves off the roadway at a hundred and twenty kilometers an hour. Slag heaps piled in the clearings looked like clusters of giant beaver lodges.

"What did you do," she asked, "before you worked for my dad?"

Davey chuckled. "Sorry to disillusion you, but the amount of pot Keith and I moved for your father does not a living make. We both have real jobs." The chuckle dried up inside him. *Had,* he reminded himself. *Had* real jobs.

Cassie reached across the seat and touched his arm. The gesture took him by surprise. He looked down at her hand and wondered what his expression must be to elicit such a response. He'd have to watch out for that—the way Keith's death snuck up ambushed him. He didn't like to be ambushed. When Cassie drew her hand back he missed its touch.

"Keith taught computer courses at North Island College," Davey said, with a note of pride in his voice, as if he'd had anything to do with it. "He was the one installed all the high-tech gizmos in *Small Wonder.* I don't understand most of it. Like some kind of parallel universe phenomena, the computer age seems to be slipstreaming around me on a wavelength I can't quite tune into. But Keith was a natural. He instructed in everything from entry level to advanced programming. Could've been a Silicon Valley millionaire. That's what his wife was counting on. She thought he was selfish when he opted for lifestyle over megabucks. I just thought he was crazy."

As they traveled south the pavement became more worn and the bordering clearings had turned into meadows. Chain-link wildlife barriers had been erected on either side of the highway. Cassie looked out the side window. Sometimes, in the early morning, you could see herds of mule deer or Roosevelt elk grazing in the meadows.

"What about you?" she asked after a while.

"Nothing so brilliant," he said. "I got a degree in nothing and became a beachcomber. Do some log salving, some underwater stuff, pick up the odd tow job."

"With *Small Wonder?*"

Davey laughed. "That would turn some heads, wouldn't it? No, I've got a small tugboat, *Precious Little*."

"*Precious Little?*" she said. Her lips pursed in a little smile. "*Small Wonder?* Is there a pattern here?"

"A tribute to dear old Mom, who believes it's small wonder nothing's become of my life since I show precious little in the way of ambition."

The sun climbed into the clear summer sky, dragging the temperature up with it. Just past Nanaimo, Davey pulled into a gas station to top off the tank and refill his coffee mug. Back in the truck, he removed his Windbreaker.

"Not even your mom and dad make a living off the pot, do they?" Davey pointed out. "They have the fish farm for an income. Whatever they make from the pot is fun money. Same with us. Allowed us to take the summers off. Financed a couple of weeks in the tropics in the middle of the winter."

South of Nanaimo the scenery changed. About 80 percent of Vancouver Island's one million people live in the 20 percent of its territory, between Nanaimo and Victoria. Between the two major cities, the highway runs a gauntlet of townships, one leading into the next. Forested slopes and river gorges give way to concrete malls and neon signs. Totem poles stand on street corners, brightly painted and varnished, as glitzy as the neon. These are tourist totems; they have little in common with the carved cedar logs of Eddie's ancestors that lay under the moss in cathedral groves of ancient rain forests.

"Whereabouts in the tropics?" Cassie asked.

"Different places—Rio, Belize, Tahiti. If you're wondering whether our current problem is related to something we did on some vacation, forget it. We've never had anything to do with anything but pot. And we've never had anything to do with pot if we didn't know where it came from."

The highway climbed the Malahat Summit, swooped down around Finlayson Arm, and branched to the east and the north. The east branch went to Victoria. Davey headed north up Saanich Peninsula. A short time later, he turned into the Victoria International Airport. The control tower rose above a flat-topped building, giving the place the aspect of an aircraft carrier, a notion reinforced by its location on the peninsula, nearly surrounded by the ocean.

"Maybe I should take your aunt's number," Davey said.

Cassie jotted it down on his cigarette box. "In case Auntie's not home," she said, "I booked a room at the Knightsbridge Inn. It's a little hotel downtown. What time do you expect to be back?"

"Nine-ish."

"Okay then. Well, good luck"

"Okay then." Davey opened the door and got out. Cassie slid behind the wheel. Davey imagined leaning in and brushing her lips with a kiss. For an instant, it seemed the natural thing to do. But the instant vanished. He stepped back and said, "Good luck to you too. See you tonight maybe."

"Good then. See you later."

Chapter 17

"Keep going," Flammond told Bartell. "Slow and easy. At the end of the street loop around and head back. Just a couple of peace-abiding JW's checking out the neighbourhood."

They were on a short dead-end side street on the Esquimalt side of the Gorge, a long narrow inlet that separates Victoria from Esquimalt. It was one of those holier-than-thou neighbourhoods, lousy with manicured little parks that weren't needed because the houses all sat on large wooded lots. As the van headed back up the street, Flammond turned his head to look down one of the driveways. Norm took a look. The house sat fifty meters off the street, barely visible between the trees. A small two-story house, white with blue trim, surrounded by a covered veranda. The kind of house a little girl could open up and put dolls in.

"Outstanding," murmured Flammond. "Let's look alive, people," he said. "Time to punch the clock and go to work."

Bartell stopped at the stop sign, made a left turn onto the connecting street, then another left into the parking lot of one of the trimmed and flowered little parks. The park was quiet, the herringbone parking lot empty. On Flammond's instructions, Bartell parked the van at the back of the lot, near the public washrooms, facing the street.

Flammond took a pair of walkie-talkies from the catch-all compartment between the front seats and handed one of them to Norm. They were cheap department store toys, good enough to serve the purpose at close range, easily disposable and virtually untraceable.

"Remember," said Flammond, "zero vocal response. We're not setting up a public broadcasting station. Do you remember the code?"

"I got it," said Norm.

"Good. Mr. Bartell, do you have the chloroform?"

"Got it." Ricky Bartell patted his jacket to make sure. He and Flammond had changed into conservative slacks and sport jackets over crisp white shirts. Bartell had a round cheeky face topped with thinning brown hair. Guy looked more like a cherub than a hitman. Hard to credit all the skeletons supposed to be in his closet. Until you looked into his flat brown eyes. If eyes were supposed to be windows, Bartell's looked out from a place that had been boarded up for sometime.

"Any questions, people, now is the time," said Flammond. His eyes briefly held Bartell's, Norm's, and Twitch's in turn. No one had questions. With his eyes locked on Twitch's, Flammond said, "You *will* stay straight, mister." His eyes still on Twitch's, he held his hand out to Norm.

Norm picked up a ream of *Awake!* pamphlets from the floor of the van and passed them forward. Flammond gave half of them to Bartell. "Mr. Bartell, shall we go spread the word of our Lord, Jesus Christ?"

With the Jehovah's Witness pamphlets prominently displayed, the ex-paratrooper and the contract killer strolled down the quiet tree-lined street, portraying the peaceful comportment of those who know that the good lord is smiling on them in all the glory of his morning sunshine.

"You *will* stay straight," Twitch mimicked. "*Mister.* Asshole doesn't even know my name."

"Let's keep it that way," said Norm. If Flammond knew who Twitch was, he'd use it against them, same as Lazuardi had, same as Sebastian had. "Flammond's sharp. Anyone can straighten out this mess, it's him. Play our cards right, we'll get out of it with him."

Twitch laughed. "Counting on a comic book soldier. How fucked is that, Norman?" He made a gimme gesture with his fingers.

Norm reached under his jacket. From an inside pocket, he drew a small glassine packet of white powder. Twitch tried to open it, but his fingers were shaking too violently.

"Careful. Let's not spill it all over the fucking van. Here, let me get that."

Norm got the packet open and held it up to Twitch's nose. When he was finished with the cocaine, Twitch sniffled and pinched his nose. "That ain't much," he said. "I could use, you know, just a bit more."

"No way," said Norm. He brushed a white smudge from Twitch's face. "Just enough to fly level, that was the deal. Flammond finds out, he'll leave what's left of us in an alley in a dumpster. We get paid for this job, you can spend the rest of your life with a needle in your arm, that's what you want."

Twitch turned the packet inside out and licked it with the unselfconscious demeanor of a dog licking crumbs off the floor. His fingers were steady now, his movements more relaxed. But there were only two packets left.

The plan for the Denton girl was to get to her through her aunt. Flammond and Bartell were going to get into the aunt's house, either when she opened the door to chase off a couple of Jehovah's Witnesses or, if she wasn't home, with a good old-fashioned break and enter. According to information that had surfaced last night, the Denton girl would show up at her aunt's place sooner or later. The part Norm wasn't thrilled about was the *later* part.

The walkie-talkie went *click*. Norm grabbed it and depressed the Send button, returning the click. It was answered by two clicks, a pause, and two more. They were in the house; the aunt wasn't home.

Twitch was rubbing the glassine packet between his thumb and forefinger. Norm took it from him, lit it with his lighter, and dropped it into the ashtray. He lit cigarettes for both of them and sat back to wait. His job now was to watch the street and click the Send button on the walkie-talkie if anything suspicious developed. They had food and drink in the van and a washroom right out the door. What they didn't have was enough cocaine to keep Twitch flying level for more than a day. But that never became an issue. Before they were finished their cigarettes, Flammond and Bartell appeared at the corner and strolled toward the van.

"A lucky break," Flammond said as Bartell started the engine. "Since the old girl wasn't home, we did her the service of checking her answering machine. Her niece was considerate enough to leave the name and room number of the hotel she's staying at."

Stepping from the shower, Cassy towel-dried her hair and wrapped the towel into a white turban around her head. She took a second towel from the rack and rubbed her body dry, then used a corner of the towel to wipe condensation from the mirror that covered the wall above the vanity counter. She looked at herself in the streaked glass.

"What say, girl? You up for another rejection?"

Her reflection frowned at her. "Why on earth do you care? We're talking about a beachcombing drug runner who's made an art form of underachieving and for whom lung cancer seems a satisfactory ambition. Not exactly everything you dreamed a man could be."

She shook her head. "So why can't I stop thinking about him?"

Her home had been attacked, for God's sake, by armed men in helicopters. She had no idea what had become of her parents. Keith's shredded body had emptied itself all over his sailboat. These things had really happened. Their ugly images were burned into her mind, igniting flares of anger and fear and worry. But where was the red curtain of horror and rage? Where was the inconsolable grief?

She'd been close to it that first night, when she'd help Davey bring *Small Wonder* down the inside passage. It was a night spent staring into some dark airless gulf of hysterical panic, held back only by her responsibility at the helm. And yes, by Davey's presence beside her. His presence hadn't made everything all right, hadn't erased the nightmare images, but it had loosened the grip of panic, like the closeness of a dive buddy's octopus when your air supply fails a hundred feet under the water.

"There you go," she told her reflection. "He rescued you, snatched you out of harm's way, delivered you from evil, all that good stuff, and now you've got some weird sort of knight-errant-damsel-in-distress syndrome."

Her reflection ran its eyes over her body, raising a warm pleasant tingle in her breasts, her belly, the insides of her thighs.

Who was she kidding? Davey had been igniting her jets for years. And not just on her solo flights. More than one sweaty college boy had grunted through his Trojan moment while she'd closed her eyes and thought of Davey.

Cassy realized her jets were heating up; she was pressing the towel against her ignition button.

"*Damn* him." She turned away from the mirror and tossed the towel over the rim off the tub. "I'm here to find Mom and Dad, not to play little girl dizzy with Davey bloody Jones."

Her tote bag, a doeskin affair with a big cannabis leaf embroidered on either side, was the only luggage she had, which restricted her travel wardrobe to a change of underwear. She put on bra and panties. She'd hand-washed the blue dress in the bathtub when she'd first arrived. As she took it down from where she'd hung it on a curtain rod above the radiator, she found that it'd dried to a wrinkled crispness. By drawing the fabric over the edge of the writing desk, she managed to press it into serviceable condition.

Obviously, she had to go shopping. She needed more clothes. Luggage would be a good idea as well. Anyway, if she didn't get out of the hotel room for a bit, she'd end up throwing things. She slipped the dress on, brushed her damp hair, and dabbed on a touch of makeup. She glanced at her watch. Nearly noon. Davey's wasn't even in Toronto yet. Be nine hours before he got back to Victoria, perchance to the Knightsbridge Inn.

"Perchance," she muttered as she laced her sandals on and shook her head at herself.

When she opened the door, she saw a big long-haired, rough-cut guy opening the door across the hallway. *Biker convention,* she thought. Her parents had a number of biker friends, so she knew their tough image was largely a marketing ploy. Despite their rowdy posturing, most of them were just regular guys. She made just enough eye contact to let him know she wasn't intimidated, then turned to close the door.

Her arms were grabbed, and a hand was clamped over her mouth. The prickly heat of adrenaline poured through her body. She was half-shoved, half-carried back into her room. She bit down on the hand, bit hard. There was a yelp and the hand was pulled away, leaving the taste of blood on her teeth.

That's when she should've screamed. She'd heard it a dozen times in women's workshops at university. If you're attacked, scream. Make as much noise as you possibly can. But Cassiopeia Denton wasn't a screamer. Screaming wasn't a natural reaction for her. She hadn't screamed when helicopters had dropped fire on her home or when Keith had hobbled down the trail with his insides leaking out. And she didn't scream when three men dragged her into her hotel room. She fought back.

She twisted against the restraining arms. She kicked at the legs around hers. Her left arm came free. She felt flesh against her palm and gouged with her nails. Someone grunted. A fist glanced off her cheek. She felt long coarse hair, clutched it and pulled. Someone cursed. Something covered her mouth again, and again she bit down on it. But this time, she didn't taste blood; she gagged on the cloying taste of chloroform.

Oh shit.

Her muscles went limp and her vision collapsed into the vanishing point.

I'm sorry, Davey, I should've screamed . . .

Chapter 18

*D*avey looked at his watch as the plane taxied toward the runway. It was nearly three. He hadn't bothered advancing his watch through the time zones; it was still set to Pacific Daylight Time. In Toronto, it was nearly six, but he would only be in Toronto for another minute or two. As if the pilot had the same thought, the jet sprinted down the runway and arrowed into the sky in a manner that left Davey's stomach alarmingly abaft.

"Don't fly much?" asked the man seated inboard from him, an overweight businessman in his late forties with short brown hair in mild disarray. He was looking at Davey's hands, which were clenching the armrests.

Davey ginned sheepishly. "Not much."

"Takes getting used to," the man assured him. "You can convince your brain that it's safe, but your body knows that being strapped into a steel tube five miles above hard ground or deep water sort of limits the old survival options." He chuckled to make a joke of it.

Davey smiled to be polite and asked the guy if he wrote ad copy for air travel. Then he looked out the window, examining the wing for signs of metal fatigue, until the flight attendant came around with the booze. Davey took a scotch. His seatmate, a big florid man in a light brown suit that he'd been wearing too long, took a Jack Daniel's.

"Wheaton Graines," he said, offering a plump pink hand. "I'm in cereal. Get it?" He chuckled as if he'd just gotten it himself. "Wheaton Graines? In cereal?"

It was the sort of line that should've been limp and frayed from overuse, yet the guy seemed genuinely amused. Davey found himself chuckling along. He decided that Wheaton was one of those luminous people, of the type who is unselfconsciously delighted to be a part of human diversity. Davey found the luminosity to be refreshing and somehow cleansing.

"Davey Jones," he said, shaking Wheaton's hand. "I'm in ocean salvage."

"No shit? Davey Jones? In ocean salvage?" Wheaton got another chuckle out of that.

While they made small talk, Davey's right hand stole into his jacket pocket and wrapped itself around the key. His fingers worried at it, pressing their flesh into its little teeth. Its acquisition had been easier than he'd imagined it would be. For much of his hopscotching trip to Toronto he'd agonized over the responsibility of telling Erin about Keith.

Keith's dead.

For hours, he'd practiced saying it and he never did learn how. Then, face-to-face, as it'd dawned on him that Erin wasn't even going to ask about Keith, he'd experienced a disorienting letdown, as if he'd struggled to the top of a ladder only to have it turn into a slide.

She'd been waiting for him at the arrivals gate, her soft green eyes ignoring the looks she drew from men and women alike, Erin being among those genetic lottery winners whose uncanny beauty drew looks of curiosity rather than admiration, as if such beauty were a defect of sorts. She was wearing a gray suit with pleated skirt over a cream-colored blouse. She had small pearls on her ears and around her neck and a slender gold watch on her wrist. Davey was stunned to see the wedding band still on her ring finger. He thought it must be a new man's, but no, it was clearly the same band Keith had had made for her. He wondered if she'd put it on for the benefit of this meeting. Rub it in his face a bit.

"Davey," she'd greeted him, putting an edge on the two syllables as if she'd clipped them with a sharp pair of scissors. Her eyes had danced over his face, taking in the split lip and fading bruises with neither curiosity nor concern. "I believe you're after this," she'd said. With a flip of hair the color of sunshine, she'd given him the key.

"Thank you, Erin, I, ah . . ." His face had got hot and his throat had filled with sand, certain that the questions were coming: How is Keith? What's he gotten up to now?

"Kindly tell him," she'd said, still clipping with those scissors, "that in the future, I would appreciate it if he kept his childish pranks to himself."

It was as if she didn't give a good goddamn. He'd wanted to scream at her. *You knew! You knew who he was when he gave you that ring! But you never fell in love with* him, *did you? No, you fell in love with the man you* wanted *him to be?*

But that had been nothing more than his emotions scrabbling at the ladder collapsing beneath them. Davey Jones didn't scream at people in crowded airports. He'd simply stood there and watched her march away.

"Roger, wilco, over and out," he'd muttered, as he'd tumbled down the emotional slide into a dark tarry pool of depression. The tar was a gooey concoction of emotions—dark slippery feelings that would neither hide nor show themselves, a viscous brew that would neither let him breathe nor drown him.

The mood had rendered tasteless his restaurant meal and tried its best to drag him into the airport bar. He'd managed to resist, knowing that if he started drinking, there was a good chance that he'd be sitting at the bar when his plane took off. The depression had tagged along with him into a coffee shop, where it had sat with slumped shoulders and downcast eyes and wondered how that worked. How could a person love another so intensely that it seemed an integral part of the glue holding the universe together and then, a few years later, not give a good goddamn? The depression had followed him onto the plane and kept him solemn company until Wheaton Graines in cereal had observed that he didn't fly much.

As talk of weather and salmon fishing exhausted itself, Wheaton unfolded a pair of glasses and prepared to immerse himself in a trade pamphlet with a stylized *K* in the corner. An unsolicited smile crept over Davey's face. Maybe it was the Wheaton Graines, he thought, not the Plasticine feelings with which people moulded love and hate and everything in between, but the Wheaton Graines and Kellogg's that kept the universe from splitting at the seams. After all, giving a damn seemed to flap around in the winds of change while corn flakes were clearly there for the long haul.

Davey Jones, philosopher at large, gazed down on the vast empty spread of prairies and longed to be with Cassie. The longing was a strange, alien feeling and he understood it not a bit. But it was real, a solid thing with dimension and mass, and it wasn't at all unpleasant.

By the time the plane touched down in Victoria, Davey had passed the responsibility of holding the universe together back to whatever manner of gods looked after that sort of thing. Davey had a few less godly things to take care of. As he strolled past the baggage carousel, he noticed Wheaton heading for the bar. The big guy was surprisingly steady on his feet considering the amount of JD he'd knocked back. Seemed Wheaton's luminosity burned on alcohol. Good for him.

Davey lit a cigarette and went to one of the cabs idling at the curb. A sign on the window told him it was a smoke-free vehicle. He looked at the tail pipe puffing out free smoke, shrugged, and dropped his cigarette.

By the time the taxi got him to Victoria Central post office, the streetlights were flickering on against a purpling sky. He trotted up broad concrete steps and pushed through glass doors into a large hall lined with hundreds of mailboxes. He quickly discerned the number sequence and hunted down the box Lily had sent her letter to. He experienced an elated sort of relief when the key actually worked.

The box was crammed full of advertising flyers and the little weekly newspapers they give away to boost circulation. Among the junk mail was a single envelope. It was addressed to Keith Stoddard, but Davey recognized the block letter printing; Keith had sent it to himself. The postmark bore Monday's date, the same day Keith had left the message on Linda's answering machine. He'd been busy last Monday, as if he'd suspected that his time on God's green earth was growing short. Davey tore open the envelope.

HI LILY. SORRY I HAD TO MAKE THIS SO HARD TO FIND BUT I HAD TO, AND I KNEW YOU'D FIND IT.

FIRST OFF, THE STICK WON'T COPY. THEY'VE PUT IN AN ERASE COMMAND. I TRY TO COPY, IT ALL GOES BYE-BYE. BUT THAT'S THE LEAST BAD PART. WE ARE ON THE STICK, LILY. THEY KNOW ABOUT US. THERE'S ONLY ONE WAY THEY GOT THAT INFORMATION AND I DON'T HAVE TO TELL YOU WHAT THAT IS. I'M KEEPING THE STICK. HOPE THAT'LL KEEP THEM FROM DOING ANYTHING TERMINAL. MEANWHILE, I'LL TRY TO CONTACT MARCIE. SHE'S THE ONLY ONE I TRUST RIGHT NOW.

IF YOU DON'T HEAR FROM ME BY THE TIME YOU FIND THIS GET IN TOUCH WITH DAVEY JONES. TELL HIM THE TRUTH. HE OFTEN MARCHES TO A DRUMBEAT ONLY HE CAN HEAR BUT HE'S A SOLID SORT AND I TRUST HIM TO THE ENDS OF THE EARTH. ONCE HE KNOWS WHAT'S GOING ON TELL HIM THE STICK IS IN MY SEA CHEST ON TREASURE ISLAND. IF THAT DRAWS A BLANK STARE TELL HIM HE HAS TO BACK UP SEVEN YEARS. TELL HIM THIS ONE TIME HE HAS TO GO BACK AND TAKE IT FROM THE BOTTOM. GOOD LUCK.

PS. ANY CHANCE, WHEN THIS IS OVER WITH, YOU AND I CAN GO OUT ON A REAL DATE?

Davey glanced around the hall, almost as if he hoped to find someone standing there who could explain things to him. The hall remained empty. His eyes dropped to the letter and read it through again.

What the hell did it mean? He'd spent the day flying back and forth across the country looking for answers, and all he'd gotten out of it were more riddles.

There were three people he knew of who might be able to decipher the riddles: Keith, who was in a position to tell only the fish at the bottom of Queen Charlotte Strait; there was Lily White, who'd left town with the police on her heels; and there was Crown Counselor Marcie Dennison, the only one Keith trusted.

And while he was trusting her, he died.

Davey folded the letter back into the envelope. He went to put it in his hip pocket but changed his mind. Instead, he locked it back in Keith's mailbox. Outside, he started walking. As he walked, he tumbled the letter through his mind.

Keith and Lily, with whom Keith apparently hadn't had a real date, had somehow gotten hold of a memory stick, a flash drive, whatever the hell they're called. Keith was going to make a copy. Copying the drive wasn't on, but in the course of his work, Keith discovered that they knew about us. Whatever it was they knew, Keith decided he'd be better off keeping the stick to stop them from "doing anything terminal." Got that one wrong too. Anyway, he put the stick in his sea chest—that big old footlocker for a memory tick?—and hid it in the Treasury on Granville Island—

Wait a minute, cried a voice in the back of his mind. *Wait just a minute.*

Shut up, Davey told the voice. *I'm thinking.*

Keith wasn't a fool. He must've realized that the treasury wouldn't be secure for an indefinite time period, so—

Wait a fucking minute! screamed the voice in his head. *"He has to back up seven years!" Seven years ago you didn't know the Treasury on Granville Island from Timbuktu.*

Shit.

Davey came to a stop in the middle of the sidewalk and stared at a crack in the concrete until he realized that people were giving him funny looks. As he got his legs moving again, he cast his mind back seven years. That was the summer Erin had left Keith in favor of a place where people grew up to become responsible adults. The summer Davey's father had left life in favor of a tumor that grew up to become a responsible cancer. It was a summer of prodigious consumption of alcohol and pot at Boomer's Bight, where Keith and Davey had leeched off Boomer's stability. God knew that neither Keith nor Davey had had any stability to call their own that year. Their social life had consisted of befriending Gunner, the seal who hung out on the drying reef in the middle of the bay, and getting philosophically stoned with Boomer. One relationship required them to supply the odd fish carcass; the other was their due through a lifetime friendship. Both were extremely low maintenance, the only kind either Keith or Davey had had the emotional energy for.

That was also the summer they'd bought *Small Wonder* and the summer Boomer had introduced them to Frank Denton just as Frank was looking for people to help get his August harvest to the marketplace. It was the summer Keith had pointed out that if they were going to take advantage of being born in an island paradise, they'd best get on with it because, unlike the stage, life didn't give you a chance to go back and take it from the top.

This one time he has to go back and take it from the bottom.

While his mind was lost in thought, Davey's legs, it seemed, knew exactly where to go. He approached the Knightsbridge Inn from the back side, cater-cornered. Across the alley behind the hotel was the parking lot. Boomer's pickup was easy to spot, an exceedingly sore thumb sticking out from amid the rows of shiny compacts and minivans. It was Boomer's truck, but it was driven by Cassie Denton, who had a room at the Knightsbridge Inn. As if he needed an excuse, Davey told himself that Frank Denton would be a fourth person who might be able to answer the riddles, and there was a good chance that Frank was already with his daughter, or at least that Cassie knew where he was.

Davey circled the block and found a late-night grocery where he bought a bunch of flowers. On his way back to the hotel, he realized that if Frank and Lorraine were there, he'd look like a fool. He dropped the flowers into a trash can.

"For Christsake, Jones," he said, "when did you start worrying about looking foolish?" He pulled the flowers from the trash, straightened them out, and brushed them off, ignoring the glances of passersby. "These are for Cassie, Cassiopeia, not her parents."

Conceived by an architect whose studies apparently included Ivanhoe, the Knightsbridge Inn was a smallish hotel with a capricious assortment of gables and dormers, merlons and embrasures. The exterior concrete was stamped in a design meant to resemble medieval masonry. The interior was equally Knightsbridge, its cozy lobby all dark leather and polished wood. Coats of arms hung on the walls and, yes, a suit of armor stood guard at a hearth. Davey felt disappointed that the concierge wore a quiet charcoal suit rather than a Beefeater's scarlet livery.

"Good evening, sir," the clerk greeted Davey in a soft British accent. "How may I be of assistance?"

"You have a guest by the name of Cassie, or Cassiopeia, Denton?"

"One moment, sir." The concierge consulted a very un-Knightsbridge computer screen. "Ms. Denton. Yes indeed. Shall I call her, sir?"

"Yes indeed. Tell her Davey's here."

"Davey. Very well, sir." He tapped three numbers into a phone and held the receiver to his ear for about ten seconds. "I'm sorry, sir, but Ms. Denton seems not to be in her suite at the moment. Shall I take a message for her?"

"She should be there," Davey blurted, a bit too loudly. "Maybe she's in the shower or something. Could you please keep trying?"

"That shan't be necessary, sir." The concierge gave Davey a commiserative smile. The sort of smile that knew perfectly well how infuriating the gentler sex could be when it made up its mind to be fashionably late. "A flashing light has been activated on her telephone to alert her to the fact that a message awaits her."

Davey left the Englishman to his clerking duties and strolled through the lobby. The hotel had no nightlife of its own, and those patrons who'd gone out on the town hadn't begun to trickle back yet, so it was just Davey, the concierge, and the suit of armor. Since the concierge seemed busy, Davey kept company with the suit of armor. Arrayed around it was a display of medieval weaponry, all of it blunt and heavy, clearly designed for the purpose of bashing crippling dents in suits of armor. Davey exhausted his curiosity over the chivalrous practice of dressing up in iron and getting bashed upon by blunt instruments, and Ms. Denton had apparently yet to be alerted by the flashing light on her telephone.

Maybe she hadn't noticed it, Davey thought. He was about to mention this to the concierge when another thought occurred to him. Despite her extended invitation, she'd come here to see her parents, not Davey Jones. If Frank and Lorraine were in hiding, they might be reluctant to stroll into a downtown hotel. More likely Cassie would go to them.

But the truck.

So what? Aunt Toots came and got her.

Would she have left a message for him, or had Davey Jones vanished from her mind like air from a popped balloon? Davey asked the concierge. The Englishman consulted a pigeonholed section of wall behind the desk. He zeroed in on pigeonhole 312 and pulled an envelope from it.

"Keith," he read, eyebrows arched, "Stoddard . . ."

Chapter 19

The concierge kept talking, but Davey stopped listening. It was as if he'd been stricken with a particularly virulent strain of flu. He leaned against the desk as his legs swayed beneath him.

"Nothing, I'm afraid, sir, for David," the Englishman concluded.

"It's Davey," he said, "not David." His mind had gone on standby. It was circling in some stratospheric holding pattern, leaving his tongue to deal with the crisis. Without a mind to worry it, his tongue lied freely. "Keith Davey Stoddard. She always calls me Davey. Keith is for when she's mad at me. Keith Stoddard she saves for furious."

"I say." The concierge looked embarrassed. He cleared his throat. "My sympathies, Mr. Stoddard, if I may. Clearly, the matter has caused you some considerable distress." He passed Davey the envelope. "I'm sure it's none of my affair, sir, but in my experience, these things have a way of sorting themselves . . ."

Davey left the Englishman to explain his experiences to the bouquet of flowers. He hurried out the door and gulped at the cool night air, forcing his mind down out of its holding pattern. His fingers trembled as he tore open the envelope.

We have the Denton girl, he read under the cold blue light of the street lamp. *If you want to see her again, go to the boat shop in Nanaimo. Stay by the phone.*

With the letter crumpled in his fist, Davey sprinted around the building, across the alley, and into the parking lot. It wasn't a long run, even for a smoker, but he was gasping for wind when he reached the truck. It wasn't exertion that winded him, it was fear. It was fear that broke a prickle of sweat across his shoulders, fear that weakened his arms and his thighs, fear that blocked his mind so that he pushed the button under the door handle three or four times before he realized that the damn thing was locked. He ran to the passenger door and found it locked as well.

Smash the window, he thought. He glanced around and saw no one. There was a bit of ruckus coming from down the alley, but it was just the sound of teens horseplaying the night away. Davey was looking for something to put through the window when it occurred to him that getting into the truck was only half the problem. He'd still be unable to start it.

He closed his eyes and forced himself to be still.

Think!

Okay. He needed the keys to the truck. Surely the people who took Cassie would realize that. If they wanted him in Nanaimo, they would have to give him access to the truck. He searched the nooks and crannies where people are prone to hide car keys—the tops of the tires and the space behind the bumpers. He even crawled under the truck and ran his hand along the differential housing and the axles. The search proved fruitless.

So maybe these guys didn't realize he needed the truck. Maybe they'd never even thought about it. Was that possible? Could they have made such a stupid mistake, leaving him stranded in Victoria?

Sure. It was one of those idiot things you do when you've lost your game plan and you start making things up as you go along. Davey knew what that was like. He had an intimate relationship with it. But so what? These guys were screwups. Hardly breaking news. What did it mean for Davey?

Meant he was stuck in Victoria while Cassie's well-being depended on him getting a hundred kilometers to the north. The instructions they'd left gave no time limit, but the very desperation of the act suggested urgency. He thought of Cassie in the company of men like the guy who'd prodded his belly with a burning cigar, and sweaty tentacles of fear snaked up his chest toward his throat. He fought it down. Cassie wouldn't benefit from his panic.

Think!

A locksmith? That would take time. And Davey might well have to prove it was *his* truck. What about renting? Would there be a car rental agency open at ten o'clock on a Monday night? The concierge would know. He started back toward the hotel. If all else failed, he'd hire a taxi. Cab fare to Nanaimo would be a lot more than the hundred and thirty bucks in his wallet, but to hell with that. His first worry was getting to Boomer's Boatworks; how he'd pay for it was a distant second.

He was at the edge of the parking lot, about to cross the alley, when someone called out, "Hey, pops!"

Four teens angled across the alley, blocking his exit from the lot. He shuffled to a stop.

"Hi, pops. Nice night for a walk."

The boy who did the talking was the oldest, maybe nineteen. His left arm was draped around a girl who didn't look more than fifteen. There were two boys in the sixteen to eighteen range. All four had their hair sheared to a fine stubble. They all wore baggy clothes, patched in a manner that suggested deliberation rather than deprivation. Hip clothes, his hair, hip-hip hooray. But of course it was neither their hair nor their clothes that pissed Davey off. It was the fact that they were going to mug him.

Their faces were pale under the mercury lighting, their lips bright purple. Davey thought it wouldn't have surprised him—horrified him, yes, but not surprised him—if they'd opened their mouths to reveal dripping vampire fangs. While the leader stood smirking with one lanky arm possessing his girl, the other two moved behind Davey. He heard them shuffle into position at his back. *Mutt and Jeff,* he thought.

"How's it hanging, pops?" With his free hand, the leader held a pack of cigarettes to his mouth, drew one out with his lips, and lit it with a flick of his lighter.

"Not so good," Davey said. "Been a real shitty day."

"Jeez, pops, sorry to hear that." The cigarette remained in the left corner of the kid's mouth. A thin curl of smoke kept his left eye closed. In a tanned leathery face, it might've looked tough. But the kid had smooth adolescent skin turned fish-belly blue by the street lamps, and it looked silly.

"Hate to be the one to tell you," he said, "but it just got shittier."

That searing wit elicited a stereo snicker from behind Davey. From close behind him. He looked at the girl who was smiling around a mouthful of gum. Her oval face and big doe eyes would've been pretty with a fraction of the makeup and a decent haircut. Davey wondered if she was already turning tricks for her boyfriend or if that was still in her future.

"Maybe not," Davey said, looking at the leader. "Maybe you're just the guy I'm looking for."

The boy's smile faded, replaced by a look of effort as he struggled to comprehend this sudden change in the script of a mugging.

"How'd you like to earn a hundred bucks?" Davey asked.

The cigarette slid across the boy's mouth and back again, displaying hours of dedicated practice. He finally removed the thing.

"You got a hundred bucks, pops, you outta just hand it over before you get hurt."

Davey shook his head. "Here's the deal. I won't hand it over. Day's been way too shitty for that. I'll fight back. You'll probably win, but I *will* do some damage. Break bones, bite figers, gouge eyes. Think about it, fellas. Think about a broken rib stabbing into your lungs or an eyeball hanging down your cheek. We can avoid all that and you still get the hundred bucks if you can open that truck and get it started." Davey pointed to show them which truck.

The boy flicked his cigarette down the alley. It hit the rough blacktop with a small explosion of sparks. "Why?" he asked.

That threw Davey a bit. He frowned. "Why? For a hundred bucks."

"Locksmith probably do it for half that."

"I'm in a hurry," said Davey.

The suspicion in the boy's voice and on his long narrow face momentarily struck Davey as absurd. Then he understood. There was only one reason this upstanding young man would consider Davey's request valid. He said, "It ain't my truck."

The boy grinned at him. Nodded. "Up front," he said.

Davey shook his head.

"How do I know you got a hundred?"

"How do I know you can do it?"

The boy lit another cigarette, two handed this time, his girl put aside for the time being. A change had come over him, a seriousness, akin to pride, that fit him awkwardly. "Oh, I can do it," he boasted. "Fuckin'-A I can do it. Gotta make sure I'm getting paid for it."

Davey pulled the two fifties from his wallet. He crumpled one into a ball and tossed it to the boy. The other, he returned to his wallet. He put the wallet in his pocket and patted it. "When the engine's running," he said.

The boy straightened out the fifty and examined it. He grinned and winked.

At the truck, the boy reached into a cargo pocket in his pants that swallowed half his arm. He pulled out a long white handle. With a whispery click, a foot of slender steel sprung from the handle. Davey realized the kid could've shown the knife a couple of minutes ago and annihilated Davey's threat of broken bones and hanging eyeballs.

The boy slipped his blade into the window slot on the driver's side door, wiggled it back and forth, opened the door, and said, "Love these old Chevies."

Inside the cab, he pulled the hood release, and the hood popped up an inch. He reached under the dashboard, tugged, and brought his hand out, holding a five-foot length of wire. "Hope you didn't want to listen to the radio, pops."

Mutt and Jeff got a big yuk out of that.

The youth stripped the ends of the wire and took it to the front of the truck, where he pushed the hood open. He fiddled under the hood for half a minute. Holding one end of the wire, the other presumably attached to something under the hood, the boy said, "Hop in, pops, and put her in neutral. Give her a little juice when she starts turning."

The boy touched the running end of the wire to the positive battery terminal, and the engine started turning. Davey gave it a hit of gas. It fired up and settled into a smooth idle. Davey was impressed. He also determined that if he ever owned a vehicle, he'd double up on the theft insurance. It was just too damn easy.

The boy slammed the hood closed, stepped around the open driver's door, and leaned against the inside of it. Davey said thanks and handed him the other fifty dollar bill. The boy took it and stuffed it in his pocket.

"'Gradulations, pops, just stole yourself a heavy Chevy."

Instead of stepping away, the boy drew closer, pressing in on Davey's space. The cab was infused with the odor of unwashed clothes. The boy began stropping his knife blade on Davey's thigh.

"You're right about it being a shitty day, pops. Price just went up. Inflation and all."

Behind him, Mutt and Jeff brayed.

"Supposing I take a look at that nice plump wallet, see what you can afford."

Angry blood rushed to Davey's temples and started pounding. "Let it go," he hissed through clenched teeth.

He wasn't angry about the money. Later, he'd need it to buy fuel, but at the time, he didn't even glance at the gauge. He didn't give a shit about the thirty lousy bucks in crumpled fives; it was about being pushed around. It was about being a tin duck in a shooting gallery. It was about being teased with a sense of grasping just a thread of control and then having it snatched away. It was about everyone, including Keith—hell, *starting* with Keith—who'd been jerking his strings for the last few days.

"Just let it go," he said.

The kid turned the knife blade so that the sharp part cut through the denim of Davey's jeans. It bit into his thigh, and his body jerked away. His wallet slipped from his fingers and fell to the floorboards.

"Don't be nervous, pops. It's just a scratch. You just reach on down and fetch that wallet. Then we'll have a little talk about eyeballs hanging down and such."

Neither, Davey realized, was it about the money for this young man. It was about control, albeit from the other side. He hadn't agreed to help

Davey because of Davey's threat. His knife could've dealt with the threat. No, he'd done it to put on a show for his little gang. Now he had to prove it. To his gang and to himself. If that involved punching his blade through someone's abdominal muscles and digging around in their soft guts, so much the better.

With the headache still pounding at his temples, Davey leaned forward to the right of the steering wheel. His hand ignored the wallet and reached under the seat, searching for the pistols that had been left there. He felt the stubby muzzle of the revolver and turned it till his fingers found the grip. As he sat up, he cocked the hammer. He placed the muzzle against the boy's forehead, right above the bridge of his nose.

There was a brief powerful urge to pull the trigger. His finger tried so hard that his hand cramped up, but his mind wouldn't let it happen. In a few seconds, the part of him that wanted to was subdued by the part of him that couldn't.

The boy stared cross-eyed at the gun. His mouth was open, drooling.

"Just let it go," Davey whispered.

The boy closed his eyes and took a deep breath, and then he spun and dashed off into the night, weaving between parked cars. His entourage scattered. Davey was alone, staring with some dreadful form of fascination at the gun at the end of his arm.

Chapter 20

"These guys at the lodge," said Eddie, "they ain't the brightest sparks in the fire."

Eddie Roe and his three companions were sitting around the big desk in Boomer's office. They were all dressed in similar fashion: various styles of denim jeans and jackets over various colored checkered shirts. Eddie wore his crinkled brown cowboy boots; the other three wore leather hiking boots. The air was full of tobacco smoke and coffee steam.

"That supposed to make them less dangerous?" asked Billy Tsimka. Billy's long hair was lightening toward gray, and his dark face was creased around the eyes. He'd touched his de Havilland Beaver floatplane down on Newcastle Channel at dusk, about three hours ago, bringing the entire staff of Air Haida down from the Queen Charlotte Islands. Eddie had met them at the float and helped carry their luggage up to the Boatworks. They'd decided it would be better to stay there rather than go to Eddie's place, where his middle class white neighbors might get nervous should they glimpse four Indians packing rifles in the night.

"Dangerous is flying with you, old man," said Tommy Clayton. He was the youngest of the Haida and, ten inches taller than his uncle Eddie, the largest. His big hands were wrapped around a .30-30 Winchester repeater. He worked the lever to open the breech and peered inside. "It's near midnight," he said, as if he kept a clock inside the rifle. "We going to hit the warpath or we going to sit here like old squaws chewing hide?"

"My sister's kid," Eddie said, laughing. "What about you, George, you got any thoughts on this?"

"Yeah," said George Winnitkish. About the same height as Eddie, George was growing portly with middle age. "First off, the young buck's too damn anxious to shoot at something. Second, Billy'd like it better if he could fly his Beaver up there and *crash* their damn lodge. Me, if I had a decent tooth left, I'd be happy to go home and chew a hide. But it's your grievance, Eddie, and you were always there for me." George grinned, showing off several blanks where teeth had come and gone. "Could be fun, being able to hit back for a change."

Eddie Roe could've told Davey a thing or two about having his strings jerked. Eddie belonged to a race of people who'd had their strings jerked not for a few days but for several generations. Again, though, Eddie didn't see this as a racial thing, at least not in any philosophical context. It was a tidal thing, part of the ebb and flow. For countless generations before the White Tide, the Haida had been the wealthiest, most prestigious nation on the continent. Perhaps someday, the Great Spirit would turn the tide back in the Haida's favor. But Eddie had about as much faith in the Great Spirit as most white folks had in their God. So he made what peace he could with the White Tide, and when he couldn't make peace, he made war, which, all too often, involved patching up friends and nephews after a gang of good old white boys had had some fun with them.

He could have told Davey all this, but he never would. It wasn't in Eddie's nature to talk about such things. Eddie's nature was more given to do whatever he could whenever the opportunity presented itself. And now, for a change, someone had jerked his strings without the sanction of parliamentary decree. For once, he could jerk back and, as George had pointed out, maybe have fun doing it.

He looked at his hulking nephew and his two old residential schoolmates. He felt a war cry build strength deep in his soul, way down where all the generations held council. It expanded through his lungs and gathered at the base of his throat. It was a glad thing, pulsing with its own life, like a child seeking birth. But before he could bear it forth, the sharp tinkle of breaking glass came from the back of the shop. Eddie's hand darted out to the light switch. The office went dark.

Davey made a mental note to add the cost of the broken window to his debt to Boomer. Not until he'd arrived at the Boatworks had he considered the problem of getting inside without Boomer's keys. In fact, since leaving Victoria, he'd considered nothing. The pathways of his mind were littered with trap doors that would open without warning and chute his thoughts into dark airless dungeons where Keith died over and over and Cassie screamed as burning cigars were pressed into her smooth flesh. So he'd stayed out of his mind and let his body do the driving on autopilot. At the Boatworks, his body had parked the truck and jiggled his mind awake and asked, *What now?* There'd been a moment of cold panic until he'd remembered the ground-level window in the storage room.

As he crunched over the broken glass, Davey hoped no burglar happened by in the night to take advantage of the ex-window. He shuffled through the dark shop, feeling his way by cautious instinct, until his left shin cracked against the bottom step. Cursing and rubbing his shin, he hobbled up the stairs. On the landing, still bent over rubbing his shin, he felt around for the doorknob, found it, and pushed the door open. That was when they took him.

Someone with the strength of a bear grabbed his jacket, pulled him into the office, and spun him face-first into the wall. A large hand in the center of his back pinned him there. The cold steel muzzle of a gun pressed against the hair behind his ear. Then the light came on.

"Davey?" said Eddie's voice. "I'll be damned. It's okay, Tom. This here's the Davey Jones I was telling you about."

The gun barrel dropped away from his head, and the hand from his back. Davey turned and met Tom, whose chest and shoulders blocked out most of the room. He carried a lever action rifle one-handed as though it were a large pistol. When Tom stepped aside, Davey saw Eddie and two other men, all of them holding hunting rifles.

"What's going on, Eddie?"

"Told you I'd stay with friends. So I got a couple of hunting buddies to come down from the Charlottes is all."

"Deer season doesn't open till September."

"Figured to get in some limited entry up Oyster River way."

"Do your friends know what they're up against?"

Eddie chuckled. "Been two hundred years since we last knew what we were up against."

He looked at Davey's leg and asked if Davey had cut himself breaking through the window. Davey gave a brief account of what had happened in Victoria, how he'd ended up with no keys, had hired a mugger to steal the truck for him and then had a wage dispute with the hired help.

"Goddamn unions, eh," said Eddie as he fetched a first aid kit from a drawer in the sideboard. "Better get some HP sauce on that cut."

"Some what?"

"$H2O2$. Hydrogen peroxide. It ain't likely that your mugger sterilizes his knife after every use."

Eddie dabbed hydrogen peroxide around the cut. Davey jerked as the antiseptic bit into his wound. "You want to come along with us?" Eddie asked. "See if Cassie's staying at their lodge?"

Davey frowned, troubled by the notion of Eddie's friends and their deer rifles against an army of goons with machine guns. "I thought you said you couldn't remember the exact location of that lodge?"

"Eh," Eddie grunted from the back of his throat. "Red man skookum tracker. Easy track down white eyes."

The other three Haidas cracked up laughing. Davey shook his head and reminded himself that these men had had their sense of humor forged on a different anvil than his; he'd never been ripped from his home and incarcerated in an institute with a written mandate to "remove the Indian from the child."

"We going to do this thing," asked Tom, demonstrating the cross-cultural nature of youthful impatience, "or we going to powwow all night?"

Davey looked at Eddie. "They said they'd contact me. Told me to stay by the phone."

Eddie nodded, looked at his nephew. "Patience, Tommy. Better learn about it. It's all we got left."

They waited. Davey drank coffee and smoked with them and listened to their plan. It all seemed surreal. He thought it was a good plan. He also thought it was a crazy plan. At one point, he found himself grinning like a fool because he thought he was a kid again playing cowboys and Indians due, he thought, to a combination of too little sleep and too much caffeine. Either that or he truly was crazy. They worked out a script for Sebastian's phone call that might buy them some time, tossing lines back and forth and laughing harder as each line became more ridiculous. At twelve thirty, the phone rang and took all the fun out of it.

It was the phone on Catherine's desk, out in the reception area. Eddie went out and answered it. He told the caller that no, Keith wasn't there, but Keith had called, eh, and sent Eddie over to cover for him and explain that he was stuck down in Victoria and someone had gone down to pick him up but it'd be awhile, eh.

Eddie listened for moment, then said, "Yeah, well, he said he got the truck there, you know, but he got no keys for it."

He listened for a moment and hung up. "We got three hours."

Eddie went back to Boomer's desk and opened a drawer. He pulled out a spare set of keys with the truck key among them. He tossed them to Davey. "We better go," he said. He was no longer smiling. "Before I chicken out."

Chapter 21

*M*arco shut off the vacuum cleaner. Its high-pitched whine was replaced by the rumble of the helicopter up in the clearing. It was two thirty in the morning. He'd pretty much finished the housekeeping, except for the mess out in the stable, which he couldn't get at until the disposal team showed up and took care of their business out there. He unplugged the vacuum cleaner and wrapped the cord. The task was made awkward by the soft cast on his broken right wrist.

Marco didn't much like housekeeping. Made him feel like a fucking maid. But Sebastian had told him to take care of it, and Marco would cut off his leg with a dull knife if Sebastian told him to. There was just himself, Sebastian, and the chopper pilot left at the lodge, no one he could bully into doing it for him. If the chopper pilot laughed at him for doing housework he'd saw through his fucking leg.

The housekeeping wasn't in consideration of the landlord; it was to minimize the amount of forensic evidence left behind. All that DNA crap, they could build a case on a piece of hair or a fingernail clipping. At least they said they could. Marco didn't know how much of that crap he believed, but he did know that in a court of law no one was likely to ask for his opinion.

"This affair," said Sebastian, "hasn't gone off exactly as we'd planned it, yet it appears it will come out nonetheless successful. Good fortune has no substitute."

Sebastian was sitting on a big couch upholstered in bold patterns of browns and reds. Earth tones, they called it. Matched the carpets, drapes, and other furniture. The couch was horseshoe shaped, but it had half a dozen segments, so you could do it any shape you wanted. It faced a big granite fireplace. There was a vast coffee table made from a single slab of varnished fir, complete with a heavy border of bark. Marco had recently polished it. On the edge of it was the communications device in the small briefcase that was never far from Sebastian's reach.

"The poor inspector," said Sebastian. "I put it in his lap for him and still he almost blew it. Although who would've thought Stoddard would stick his nose into that computer drive? Come to that, who'd have thought he'd turn out to be such a resourceful runner?"

Marco didn't know who would have thought that and, quite frankly, didn't give a shit. Marco had larger concerns. Sebastian had once put himself at considerable risk to extricate Marco from a nasty little situation in Kosovo, where they'd been employed in another sort of housekeeping—a brutal bit of business known as ethnic cleansing. In that situation, Marco had lost part of his tongue as well as the use of several facial muscles. Had Sebastian not intervened, Marco would have spent any number of long days dying piece by piece. He owed Sebastian more than merely his life. Now Sebastian was promising riches beyond his wildest dreams. Problem was, Marco's dreams had never been about riches, and he'd always considered drug pushers to be lower life forms, like Albanian Muslims. Marco's larger concern was that he felt honor bound to stand by Sebastian even though Sebastian was about to take over Lazuardi's drug empire. Marco was about to become a drug pusher, and he wasn't at all sure he could reconcile that.

From the direction of the clearing three hundred meters up the hill, the thrum of the helicopter wound down like a toy with a dead battery. Evidently, the pilot was satisfied that the aircraft was warmed up and ready to fly.

Sebastian laughed and clapped his hands. "This may very well come out even better than planned," he said. "While you and I are being escorted aboard the yacht to await Lazuardi's wrath, Lazuardi will be meeting with Stoddard and the inspector on the beach. No matter how that turns out, Lazuardi will be finished. His contacts will be desperate to deal. We can set our own conditions. And we will have a bought and paid for inspector in local drug enforcement. In fact, he may well emerge with a promotion. Well earned, wouldn't you say?"

Marco didn't care to say thank you. He cared that he'd never again see the forests of his native foothills. He cared that the only homecoming awaiting him would be a stone cell and a firing squad. But Sebastian wouldn't want to hear that. And Marco, lest we forget, owed Sebastian more than merely his life.

Marco pushed through the batwing doors into the kitchen. On a plate, he stacked layers of corn chips and sharp cheddar, sprinkled it with chopped olives and onions and green and red peppers. He heard the front door open and close. He heard the pilot tell Sebastian that the disposal team was here; he'd seen the headlights coming up the road. Marco put the plate in the microwave oven, set it for three minutes, and leaned back against the counter. Two and a half minutes later, he heard a knock on the door and the sound of voices, but the hum of the microwave covered whatever was being said. He was feeling indulgently sorry for himself when the microwave pinged.

When Davey had first heard the Haidas's plan, he'd liked its audacity, the simple brass balls of it. That had been a couple of hours ago, down in Nanaimo, in the familiar setting of Boomer's Boatworks. Now in the early-morning darkness, as he crouched beside the broad steps leading up to the front porch of the lodge, his mouth was dry and sour and the plan had already gone wrong.

The plan had assumed that Billy, driving Eddie's pickup, would be challenged at the entranceway. The plan had never dreamed that Billy would be allowed to drive right up to the front door. It was possible, Davey thought, that Eddie wasn't a skookum tracker after all and had led them to the wrong place. But it was just as possible that these people had planted a listening device in Boomer's office and that they knew every brass ball of the plan and that Davey and the four Haidas had just stepped into a trap.

Davey was clutching Billy's big bolt-action .30-06. Eddie and his .303 were on the other side of the steps. It was too quiet. No guards. Not even a vehicle in sight. The doubt in Davey's head became more insistent. A bug in Boomer's office. That would explain how they'd learned about Davey going to Toronto via Victoria. They'd staked out the airport, seen Cassie drop him off, followed Cassie to the Knightsbridge Inn. And now they'd laid a trap for five fools playing cowboys and Indians. Davey imagined an army of goons moving through the dark forest, surrounding them with machine guns and assault rifles.

Shut up, he told himself. *Just shut up! It's too late for that shit!*

Too late because Tom and George, rifles in hand, had already split up and sprinted around each side of the house. Too late because Billy, with the pistol tucked under a blanket robe, was already crossing the porch, knocking on the door.

The door opened slightly, spilling a narrow band of light across the porch and down the steps. Someone said, "It's about fucking time you guys—" The voice stopped as if it had stubbed its toe. "Who the hell are you?" it asked.

"Billy Tsimka of the Kwakiutl Nation." Billy's voice was a slow, deep eddy of respect and long-suffering sorrow. "I'm sorry to bother you at this time of night, but I noticed your lights on, eh, and I want to make sure you are aware of my people's land claims in this area . . ."

It was understood that these people would not be sympathetic toward native land claims, but it was hoped that they would know enough about the situation to realize that a native blockade would quickly attract the attention of both the media and the Mounties. It was a believable intangible, something it was unlikely they'd have contingencies for. Hopefully, it would throw them off stride, cause them to hesitate.

When Billy got to the part about the roadblock, the guy at the door exclaimed, "Ah, shit."

From deeper in the house, another voice asked what the problem was. Davey recognized it as the voice of the man they called Sebastian. How many more were in there? Davey peeked over the deck of the porch.

The young man at the door turned away to answer Sebastian. Billy drew the pistol from beneath his robe, pushed the door open wide, and stepped across the threshold.

Eddie and Davey sprinted up the steps, through the open door, prepared to cover a dozen men, rifles pointing at empty space, disoriented on finding only two. There was Sebastian, dapper in a gray suit and open-necked cream shirt, seeming to be in control even with his hands on his head, and the young man who'd answered the door, aviator glasses clipped to the neck of a white T-shirt, short black hair slick with Brylcream.

Davey recognized the open layout from Eddie's sketch. They were in a large open games room. To the left, upholstered furniture gathered around a fireplace and a large-screen TV. On the other side, a bar overlooked a billiard table, shuffleboard, and casino-style card table. Farther back, batwing doors led to the kitchen. There was a large dining area over which a broad staircase led topside to the guest rooms. Eddie pointed up the stairs.

To Billy, Davey said, "If they move, kill them."

He'd started toward the staircase to follow Eddie when he heard a ping from the kitchen. He changed direction and crashed through the batwing doors. A muscular man in blue slacks and a shirt with the sleeves rolled up was bent over pulling something from a microwave oven. The man looked over his shoulder and Davey recognized Marco from the Oyster Bay rest stop incident. He lifted the butt of the rifle.

The .30-06 was a heavy gun. He thought he'd swung it gently, as if delivering a bunt down the third base line, but fear had put something extra into it. The hollow *whack* sounded more like a heavy hitter catching all of a hanging curveball. The big guy crumpled to the floor, pulling nachos and melted cheese down on top of himself.

Back in the front room, Sebastian and Ah Shit were facedown on the floor, hands clasped behind their heads, Billy Tsimka and the Beretta automatic watching placidly over them.

"There's one in there," Davey said, pointing to the kitchen. "I think he's out of it, but stay alert."

He sprinted up the stairs, prepared to cover Eddie's back. But Eddie's back didn't need covering. The upstairs was empty. The six small suites were neat and tidy, as if no one had ever stayed there.

By the time they got back downstairs, George was inside. He was helping Billy wrap duct tape around the ankles and wrists of Sebastian and Ah Shit. George looked at Eddie. "You better go out back," he said. "Found three people in a barn. They're hurt pretty bad."

Davey looked at him.

"There's a young woman," George said, "and an older couple."

The Dentons, Davey thought, *all three of them.* Cassie and her parents. Hurt pretty bad. Davey felt hollow, numb, as he followed Eddie out the back door.

The stable was beyond a couple of riding paddocks, about thirty meters from the house, up against the forest. It was a lean-to style building, with the higher wall facing the house. It was lit from within, a rectangle of light showing where the sliding door stood open. At the door, Davey's nostrils cringed at the goatish stench of human waste. In a stall off to the left, Tom was kneeling in a bed of straw beside three people chained to the wall.

Clothed in filthy rags, Frank appeared to be dead except for the saliva that bubbled slowly at the corners of his mouth. Lorraine was curled up beside him, her puffed up eyes staring at nothing, her fingers picking at Frank's hair.

The young woman wasn't Cassie. She had black hair crusted with filth, falling around a face that would've been beautiful if it weren't covered with swollen welts. The only thing she wore was a tattered denim shirt, streaked with blood and filth. She was sitting with her back to the wall. With both hands, she held the shirttail between her legs. Beneath her glazed eyes was a layer of terror that had learned the futility of this token resistance to impending rape. Eddie was kneeling beside Frank, taking the pulse at the base of his throat, lifting his eyelids to peer beneath.

"Lorraine?" Davey said. "Lorraine, it's me, Davey. Do you know what they did with Cassie?"

Lorraine picked at Frank's hair.

"Lost in space," said Eddie.

Davey turned to the black-haired woman. "Lily? Is that your name? Lily? Do you understand me?"

"They're all lost in space," said Eddie. "Drugged to the moon and back. Frank's the worst. He needs a hospital. Soon."

Davey wondered if they were too late for Cassie. Maybe they'd drugged her to the moon and she hadn't come back. He took the thought and crumpled it into a ball. He found a black hole in the bottom of his brainpan and tossed it in there.

"I saw a phone in the house. I'll call for an ambulance."

"And get the keys to these fucking shackles." Eddie continued to examine Frank as he spoke. "Go with him, Tommy. There are bedrooms upstairs. Bring some blankets."

Back in the lodge, Davey found Sebastian and Ah Shit on the couch, sitting awkwardly with their hands bound behind them. The big man from the kitchen was still in never-never land. Billy and George had gotten him situated in a large armchair. There was a cast on his right forearm and the front of his shirt was decorated with nacho chips and stringy globs of melted cheese. Under the light, Davey noticed the scar tissue around his mouth. Sebastian had mentioned something about an incident in Kosovo. There was a trickled of blood dribbling from his left ear and damned if Davey didn't feel a pinprick of guilt. He suppressed it with the image of Frank and Lorraine and Lily.

"Where's George?" he asked Billy.

"Went out to watch the road, eh. These guys were expecting company."

Davey nodded. He turned to Sebastian. "These people you're expecting, do they have Cassie?"

The diminutive blond man wore a smile, but it was an odd smile, as if he was watching a comedy that he didn't quite get. "I take it," he said, "that you didn't get the message."

"What message?"

"I quite honestly don't know the content of it. I seem to have fallen out of favor with the powers that be. But I'm sure you were supposed to receive instructions pertaining to the welfare of the young lady they took in Victoria."

Jesus Christ, what had he done? He'd bet everything that she would be here and that he would bust in and rescue her at gunpoint and be her hero. But she wasn't here. His last link to her was through the phone at Boomer's Boatworks, and that link was the price of his bet. A band of numbness tightened around his head.

"Hey, Davey?" said Tom from the bottom of the stairs. His arms were loaded with blankets. "You find the key?"

Davey closed his eyes and rubbed his forehead to ease the numbness. There were three people who needed help here and now. He looked at Sebastian. "Key for the shackles?"

Sebastian's smile deepened. "So you *are* Davey, not Keith Stoddard." He chuckled softly, apparently starting to get it.

"The *key*, asshole."

Sebastian inclined his head to the right. "In my pocket."

Davey dug a key ring from the pocket of Sebastian's suit jacket and tossed it to Tom. Then he looked at the phone in the briefcase on the coffee table. The handset and touch-tone faceplate appeared normal. But there was a dial with nine settings and a row of switches. Davey lifted the handset and held it to his ear. Dead air. He pushed a few of the buttons at random. Nothing but dead air.

"How do you work this thing?" he asked.

"It's not the sort of phone on which 911 will alert the emergency service of your choice."

Davey recalled the number they'd left when they'd taken Eddie. The number that rang through the first time and then, thirty seconds later, was not in service.

"Activate the third switch," said Sebastian, "and dial 895-4."

"What will that do?"

"I'm not entirely sure. But it should be enlightening. And there's a chance, an awfully good chance, that you will learn something about the girl from Victoria."

That was enough for Davey. He followed the dialing instructions. There was a ring tone, just one, before it was answered.

"For God's sake, Sebastian, what is it now?" said a voice with a slight Oriental lilt.

Davey said, "Sebastian can't come to the phone right now."

"Who . . . ? No, let me guess. You must be the one they call Stoddard. Since you have access to this phone, I conclude that you are, for the moment, in control of our little retreat on the Oyster River. Well done, sir."

"Where's Cassie?"

"Cassie? Ah yes. Cassiopeia Denton. Such a charming name. As a matter of fact, she is sitting at this moment not twenty feet away from me. If it gives you any comfort, she is among friends. Beside her sits an imposingly large man, appropriately known as Boomer. On the other side of him is a pretty little lady with the most gorgeous silky blonde hair, whose name I understand to be Linda."

Davey's hand tightened around the receiver. He tried to moisten his lips, but his tongue was dry and sticky. "You're at Boomer's Bight?"

"Boomer's Bight? Is that what you call it? How enchantingly coastal. I understand that to drive from where you are to where we are takes about half an hour. In the interests of fair play, I will grant you a full forty minutes. Don't be late now. And I needn't mention, need I, that you have to come alone?"

"I'll come," said Davey, "and I'll come alone. But I want you to know something."

Davey took the phone away from his face and placed it against Sebastian's. "Tell him," Davey said. "Tell him who's with me."

Sebastian frowned at him.

"Tell him!" Davey placed the muzzle of the rifle to Sebastian's temple.

Sebastian shrugged. "With him," he said into the phone, "are the Indian named Eddie and three others."

Davey pulled the phone away from Sebastian. From the earpiece, he could hear the squawk of the voice at Boomer's cabin, but he was no longer interested in what it had to say. He hung up.

"I have to go," he told Billy. He gave Billy his rifle back. Billy offered the pistol. Davey shook his head. "Tell Eddie there won't be an ambulance. He'll have to get them to the hospital in his truck."

He hurried out the door, sprinted past a startled George, and ran down the road to where he'd left Boomer's truck.

Chapter 22

$\mathcal{E}$ddie's Toyota pickup was crowded. George was behind the wheel. The dark-haired girl was on the seat beside him. She seemed to be the least injured. Although unresponsive, she seemed to understand what was happening. Frank and Lorraine lay wrapped in blankets in the back of the truck. Eddie was with them, prepared to provide cardiopulmonary assistance should one of them arrest. Also in the truck bed was the big man with the cast on his arm and the cheese on his shirt—Eddie's old handcuff buddy, Marco. After seeing the blood trickling from his ear and the rodent-red color of his eyes, Eddie decided Marco needed a hospital as well.

Tom shut the tailgate and stood back. "That's a load," he said. "I'll hang around here, keep an eye on Blackie and Blondie until you can send the Mounties up."

Eddie wasn't crazy about Tom staying behind. "They were expecting someone else, Tommy. Be best if you weren't around when they showed up."

"The boy's right," said Billy Tsimka, stepping away from the truck. "Can't just leave them tied up in there. If there's a fire or something, they're toast. So to speak." He chuckled. "Don't worry about the young buck," he said. "I'll keep him out of trouble."

When the truck's taillights disappeared down the roar, Tom and Billy went into the lodge and regarded their prisoners. The blond guy seemed calm enough, as if he'd either accepted his fate or was confident of imminent rescue. The black-haired fellow, though, wasn't calm at all. His face was pale and shiny with sweat; his breath was short and shallow.

"Take it easy, boy," Billy said to him. "Don't go cardiac on us. Eddie's the only paramedic. Soon as they hit Campbell River, they'll send up the Mounties. You'll be eating breakfast in a nice comfy jail cell."

Davey's foot eased off the gas pedal. For fifteen minutes, he'd been driving with reckless urgency, fishtailing across the loose gravel on every curve. It wasn't the immovable size of the trees on either side of the road that slowed him down or the irrecoverable depth of the ditches. It was doubt.

He couldn't remember fifteen minutes worth of gravel road on the way in, and he began to wonder if he'd taken a wrong turn somewhere. There were no landmarks, just pitch-black forest on either side of the headlamp beams. A wrong turn, he knew, could lead him up into the Strathcona Mountains where he might spend days circling through mazes of unmarked logging roads. Doubt was turning into an agony of indecision when the surface beneath the tires changed to pavement.

He put on speed and shortly came to the community of Oyster River, an incongruous cluster of urban homes on small city lots misplaced in the wilderness as if by some absent-minded realtor. When he came to the stop sign at the highway, he almost rolled through, confident that there would be no traffic. He was surprised by headlights approaching from the left and put his weight on the brake pedal, jerking the truck to a stop. But the approaching vehicle turned off the highway into the community. It passed under the wash of the overhead lights, and Davey saw that it was a big humpback garbage truck.

As Davey proceeded down the highway, he found himself thinking about the people who got up in the wee hours of the morning to go around picking up the world's garbage. People who earned regular paychecks and had lists of regular things on which to spend them. It was a lifestyle he'd always viewed with a certain degree of disdain. Now he couldn't for the life of him remember why.

Crabbe-Levy Road came up on his left. Casper's Mohawk station slept in the dark on the corner. Davey made the left turn, but he didn't proceed down Crabbe-Levy. He guided the truck into Casper's parking lot and came to a stop. Boomer's was only a few minutes away, and he still had fifteen minutes left in his deadline.

Deadline. *Good word,* he thought as he killed the lights and drew the stick into neutral. He rolled down the window and lit a smoke.

"God, I'm tired," he said. "Too tired. Is that what it comes down to, Dad, in the end? You just get too tired?"

The last time he'd seen him, his father had asked him to smuggle a beer and a cigarette into the hospital for him. Davey had promised to do it, but he'd died before Davey had gotten back to him.

How good would that be, to sit quietly on the shore in the sun and have a beer and a smoke with the old man? Mom always fretted about their lack of communication, but she never understood. It was she, with her constant chatter, who never communicated. Anyway, that was his story, and he was sticking to it.

A sudden gaping ache opened up in the middle of him. He clutched his forehead to hold back the tears of it.

"No regrets," he said through gritted teeth. That had been his father's deathbed pronouncement, no regrets. It had taken Davey seven years to realize it was complete and utter bullshit; there were regrets all over the fucking place. And then he realized that someone was standing beside the truck, pointing a gun at his head.

Tom and Billy exchanged puzzled looks when they heard the growl of the big diesel engine. Billy went to the broad front window and looked out just as headlights turned into the driveway and splashed across the front of the lodge.

"What is it?" asked Tom.

From his awkward seat on the couch, the blond man grinned at him. "If you really want to know, stick around," he said. "I'll introduce you."

Tom looked at his elder for guidance. Billy shook his head. "I believe it's time to slip out the back, Jack."

Billy closed the phone into its briefcase and took it with him out the back door. They crossed the yard to the verge of the forest, where huge veiny boles of Douglas fir and Sitka spruce rose from a thick understory of bracken and salal. Billy tossed the briefcase with the phone in it as far as he could into the underbrush. Keeping to the edge of the forest, they hurried around the lodge, heading for the road. When they reached the front, they found their route cut off by a big garbage truck filling the driveway.

The truck's air brakes chuffed and the engine settled into a deep-throated idle. The cab doors swung open, and Billy touched his young companion's arm and motioned for him to hunker down among the bracken.

Two men stepped down from the cab and strolled into the light from the headlamps. The driver was a heavily built black man; the passenger a young white man, about Tom's age, with a lanky frame and a spray of acne scars on his face. Both of them wore loose-fitting blue coveralls.

"That's the beauty of it, kid," the black man said as they strode toward the lodge. "Big as it is, no one notices a garbage truck, especially when it's driven by a nigger. White folk see a nigger driving a garbage truck, they figure God is in his heaven and all is right with the world."

The white man stayed on the front porch while the black man opened the door and stepped into the lodge. Billy and Tom could see through the window into the front room. They saw the blond man talking to the black garbage collector. The black man raised his hands and shook his head. Apparently, all was not right with the world.

The black man stepped out onto the porch and drew his partner away from the door. They walked to the end of the porch, bringing them within thirty feet of the two Haidas. The black man said, "Dude claims they got set upon by wild injuns, shit you not. Says a couple of them are running loose in the dark here as we speak."

The white man made a grunting sound that could've been the retarded cousin of a laugh. "What you wanna do?"

"Hell, we contracted to take out four packages, not to chase wild injuns through the night. Things get this fucked up, you generally want to take a walk, except we'd have to return the down payment, which ain't exactly possible at this particular point in time. So here's what we got. We got the blond dude, Joshua, who's one of the packages anyway, so that's okay. The other guy, he ain't in the contract, but we can't just leave him sitting there."

The man took a deep breath, as if adjusting on his shoulders the weight of such executive decisions. He stared into the night, and Billy was certain that he stared straight at him. A frigid chill pierced Billy's soul. His grip tightened around the stock of his rifle.

"Way I figure it," the guy continued, "if the man wants to bitch, we can give him a bit of a discount, but this here ain't our fault. Wild injuns took the others, don't you know. Long as we leave the place clean, the man can't bitch too hard."

Both men went into the lodge. Words were spoken, and the two on the couch leaned forward, perhaps expecting to get the tape cut from their wrists. The sanitation engineers stepped behind the couch and reached into their coveralls. But they didn't pull out knives to cut the tape; they pulled out pistols with long slender barrels that ended in bulbous silencers. The pistols pointed and jerked. From the back of each head came a little puff, as if they'd been hit with dust balls. With their hands still taped behind them, the blond man and the black haired man tumbled forward off the couch.

"Oh shit," said Tom. He started to rise. "Did you see that?"

Billy patted his arm. "Easy, lad. They got no night vision. They won't see us if we stay still."

The sanitation crew brought out the body of the blond man first, hauling it by the arms and legs while they passed the time with shoptalk.

"Low velocity hollow-point .22 at the base of the skull, kid, that's your ticket. The big cannons? Macho bullshit. Blood and bone and brains all over the Jesus place."

"Ready? One, two, three, hup!"

The blond-haired body arched up and tumbled into the scoop at the back of the truck.

"Your .22, see, is less likely to break out of the skull. She just bounces around up there, keeps all the mess on the inside."

The two men went back to the mess inside, evidently content to be gainfully employed.

Billy shook Tom's arm. "You still with me?"

Tom opened his mouth, closed it, and nodded.

"Twenty feet to your right, there's a break in the underbrush. It's away from the light from the window. We can hunker in there until this psycho show hits the road."

But the break in the underbrush turned out to be a trail. Crouching under the cover of the dark forest, Billy Tsimka and Tommy Clayton, from boringly peaceful Haida Gwaii, hurried up the trail. It didn't matter where the trail led, only that it led away from the garbage collectors. They had no idea that a young helicopter pilot, after warming the engine and completing a preflight check, had left his helicopter in the clearing and taken the same trail down to the lodge and his ill-timed meeting with the disposal team.

Chapter 23

"Don't move!" said the man with the gun. "Don't fucking move!"

Davey looked past the big chrome revolver and focused on the man holding it. He'd been in the car at the Oyster Bay rest stop, the big guy whose hair hung from his head like shanks of oily hemp.

"I got him covered, Twitch," the guy said. "Go in and check him out. Make sure he's got no surprises."

The passenger-side door opened and a tall gaunt man with frizzy hair yelled at him not to fucking move, just in case he hadn't heard the first guy. As the man named Twitch got into the truck, he brought with him an odor that suggested decay, similar to the odor that had hovered around the deathbed of Davey's father.

Under the dome light, Davey got a good look at Twitch. At sunken eyes bright with some inner fever. At hollow cheeks and thin lips and jagged rot-pocked teeth. At spastic muscles twitching under crepe paper flesh. He realized that Twitch, like his father, did indeed have a cancer of sorts—a cancer with which he was injecting himself. Davey realized that he was sitting beside a junkie with a large automatic pistol in his jittery hands. Happy days.

Skeletal, palsied fingers roamed over Davey's body, after which Twitch declared, "He's clean, Norm," as if Twitch knew the meaning of the word.

Norm was holding his pistol through the open window, inches from Davey's face. "All right, you prick, you've caused enough grief. Slide over. I'm driving the rest of the way."

Through the shadow cast by his lank hair, Davey found the gleam of Norm's eyes. "I'm going to finish my smoke, Norm, then I'm going to drive down the road a ways and visit some friends. That's the way it is, Norm old pal."

"Fuck *you*, Stoddard!"

"That's not an option, Norm. You familiar with the word *option*?"

"*Fuck* you. Any more shit and I'll blow your fucking knee off." Norm moved the barrel of his gun to show Davey where his fucking knee was.

"Get that from the movies, did you, Norm?" Davey took another drag from his cigarette. Maybe he was baiting Norm. Maybe he *wanted* his knee blown off. Get himself taken out of the game.

No. No injured reserve list in this game.

He said, "Your boss and I have an understanding, Norm. If you so much as give me a haircut without his say so, you'll end up feeding the fish. You know that, don't you?"

"Fuck you," Norm said. Vocabularily challenged, no doubt. But his *fuck you* had lost much of its conviction. Poor Norm probably didn't know whether he'd be fish food or not and didn't feel adventurous enough to find out.

Davey's cigarette was almost down to the filter, but he took a few more puffs just to make a point and then flicked it into the night. He ground the transmission into first and started rolling.

Norm jumped into the back of the truck and ordered Twitch to bring the fucking car, man. Twitch trotted away, and Davey gunned the truck up behind him. With a startled look, Twitch leaped out of the path.

When Davey turned into Boomer's driveway, the headlights swept across Linda's white Prelude and a sleek dark-colored motor home. The second he stopped, the truck the door was pulled open and the snout of an assault rifle sniffed his face.

Assault Rifle was a short compactly muscled man with a facial expression as stoic as his bristly haircut. On his instructions, Davey reached out and grabbed the top of the door with both hands, then slowly pulled himself out. Assault Rifle patted Davey down while Norm muttered that he'd already done that. Assault Rifle asked for Davey's hands one at a time, took them behind Davey's back, and clipped them into a metal bracelet. Only then did he turn his attention to Norm and Twitch.

"You two are supposed to be watching the road," he said, conveying heavy censure with little change in vocal inflection.

Norm dropped his eyes. "Just making sure Stoddard behaved himself."

"We have three of his friends against the wall. He'll behave. You came looking for a pat on the head and a scratch on the ear. Dogs are rewarded for doing their duty, not for leaping about pissing on the floor. Don't let me see you again before you are summoned."

Norm turned and walked to the car. He opened the driver's door and yelled at Twitch to move over. The car sprayed gravel as it backed out of the driveway and headed up Crabbe-Levy. The man called Twitch sang out the window: "Just a-working for a living."

"Strange man, your Twitch," Davey said.

"None of your concern," Assault Rifle assured him.

"Working for a living," Twitch sang, rocking back and forth on the seat, jittering to a beat only he could hear. "Working for a living."

"Fuck's sake," Norm yelled, "get a fucking grip!"

Twitch sat sniffling, wiping his nose with the length of his forearm. "I'm sorry, Norm," he whined. "I need a little something. Know what I'm saying? Starting to hurt, man. Know what I'm saying?"

"Too fucking bad. Get used to it. You got one left, then it gets cold, turkey."

Twitch gave a stuttering laugh. "Ha-ha. Good one, Norm." He wiped his nose again. "You can get some more, right?"

"Don't count on it. This Lazuardi ain't Sebastian. Ain't keen on his employees using the product. Until this Stoddard business is done, we won't see any pot, never mind coke."

"*Fuck* coke!" Twitched wailed. "I don't *want* coke. Coke ain't *doing* it no more. I need the good stuff. I really need it. Really, really need it."

Norm made a fist and lobbed it across the seat. Twitch ducked with the lazy reflex of someone who, over the years, had gotten used to ducking. Norm's fist glanced off his cheek.

"Shut up!" Norm yelled in the wake of his fist. "Okay? Just shut the fuck up!"

He fucking hated it when the junkie's mewling got under his skin and made him blow a gasket. Liked to think he was always in control, Twitch's rock of fucking Gibraltar. Truth was, he was still smarting from Flammond's reprimand. Even more than he hated losing his temper, he hated that he cared what a little fuck like Flammond thought of him. He hated the way Flammond made him feel toward Twitch—that their relationship was a sticky, stifling goo that wouldn't scrape off. Disgusted with both Twitch and himself, Norm took it out on the car. Gravel rattled off the fenders as he fishtailed through the parking lot of the closed gas station. He sped into the dark shadows behind the building and skidded to a stop, took the final glassine packet from his pocket, and tossed it into Twitch's face.

The car doors flew open. Faster than the speed of thought, Norm was hauled from the seat and thrown to the ground. His face was pressed into the gravel. Powerful hands groped over his body, found the .357, and took it away. His heart was thumping like a frightened rabbit. He heard Twitch crying on the other side of the car.

Assault Rifle guided Davey onto the veranda and around to the front of the cabin. In the starlight, the wharf was a blotch on the water. Out at the T, men stood in a group, cigarette tips glowing among milling shapes. The dark bulge of a boat lay fast against the dock.

A couple of steps into the cabin, Assault Rifle grabbed the handcuffs on Davey's wrists and brought him to a halt. The cabin was gloomy. There was only one light burning, off by the kitchen entrance. Linda, Boomer, and Cassie were sitting together on the couch. Davey counted four men standing in the shadowy parts of the room, all of them clearly armed.

"Well, well," said a voice from off to Davey's right. It was the voice he'd spoken to on the phone forty minutes ago. "We meet at last."

Davey looked to his right, but the owner of the voice was ensconced in a deep armchair in the darkest corner of the room, a shadow within a shadow.

"Before we carry these proceedings further," said the Oriental lilt, "there is something you should know, something about which you are apparently misinformed." The voice produced a high-pitched giggle. "I'm afraid that your name is not Keith Stoddard but rather Davey Jones. Keith Stoddard, you see, has been dead for some several days now."

Oh shit, thought Davey. He said, "Don't tell Norm. It'll ruin his day."

Assault Rifle chuckled softly, but the voice in the shadow said, "What on earth are you talking about?"

"Nothing."

"Hmm," the voice mused, considering nothing. "Tell me, Mr. Jones, why the charade?"

"Your Sebastian insisted on it."

"Did he? And you had no opportunity to enlighten him?"

"I've been busy."

"Hmm. Busy, I understand, looking for the property that Mr. Stoddard stole from me. Pity you didn't appeal to us with your dilemma. We might have worked together on your search, with far less unpleasant consequences."

Davey saw no point in voicing his doubts about that. He'd had a plan once, but that seemed long ago in a universe far away. What was it boxers said? Everyone's got a plan until they get hit? That was a two-way aphorism, wasn't it? Sure, all he had to do was land a punch. Throw this bunch into total disarray. Arms raised in victory. Conquering hero. Crowd goes wild.

"Unfortunately," the shadow in the armchair was saying, "I now face a dilemma of my own. Do I continue to deal with the man who played Sebastian for a fool or do I liquidate my assets and accept my losses?"

The implication of assets being liquidated acted on Davey's mind like a pinprick, waking it from its lethargy. "Your Sebastian made a fool of himself," he said. "And now you're playing me for a fool. You've gone to a lot of trouble and expense to get that flash drive back. I don't believe you'd walk away from it when you're so close."

"Hmm. A hollow hypothesis since I have no idea whether I'm close or not."

"You know the police don't have it. You know that I went to Toronto yesterday, and you probably know that a key was given to me. You don't need Sherlock Holmes to figure it out from there."

"Yet clearly you do not have the stick with you."

"Clearly. If I had it with me, my friends and I would be dead by now."

"Hmm. You are suggesting that you will tell me where it is if I let you all walk away?"

"Is that your offer?"

"No."

"I didn't think so. You know there were four men with me tonight. Sebastian confirmed that. Two of those men took Frank and Lorraine Denton and Lily White to the hospital in Campbell River. The other two men boarded a boat. They have the stick with them. Right now they're heading around Quadra Island on their way to a group of small islands called the Octopus Islands. They'll leave the stick on one of those islands. I take it that's your boat tied to the dock. I'll go in that with your people. My friends will follow in the sailboat."

Boomer was frowning at him. Davey gave his head a slight shake, hoping to convey to Boomer that it was all bullshit.

"When we reach the island," Davey said, while his eyes tried to tell Boomer different, "the sailboat turns away. She has a top speed of about eight knots, so if I don't produce as promised, you'll have time to chase her down."

"Hmm. How flattering that you consider me so honorable that I shan't go after them in any event."

"At the speed of the sailboat, we won't get there till midday. It's never crowded up there, but there will be boats on the water. Once you have what you want, it won't be worth your while to draw that sort of attention."

After what seemed a long moment of silence, the shadow voice said, "Hmm. What say you, Mr. Monkton? Is Mr. Jones finally telling the truth, or is he leading us another merry dance?"

A figure by the staircase pulled something from his jacket pocket. A match flared and touched the tip of a cigar. The cigar was sipped into a bright red glow.

"Shall I ask him?" said the cigar smoker.

Davey recognized the voice. The burns on his stomach began to sting with a high-pitched sympathetic resonance. This was the guy who'd made those burns.

"I'm afraid, Mr. Jones," said the man in the armchair, "that you have not enamored yourself of our Monk."

"Be still my aching heart."

The armchair guy laughed. "I like you, Mr. Jones. You are breathing fresh air. As Mr. Stoddard before you. I liked him too." The laughter ended with a sigh. "Alas, deceit, betrayal, treachery. A poor recipe for lasting friendship. Do you, Mr. Jones, offer the same recipe?"

"I'm too tired to dance anymore," said Davey, which wasn't a lie. His eyes were dry and gritty, and his body was soggy with exhaustion.

After a moment of silence, the voice in the armchair said, "Mr. Flammond?" There was no more casual amusement in the inflection. A decision had been made. "Mr Flammond, are you familiar with these Octopus Islands?"

"I know where they are," said Davey's short muscular escort.

"You will accompany Mr. Jenkins and the ladies aboard the sailboat. Take two men with you. Make sure that one of them is the new man. Let's see if his heart is really in this trade."

"No." Davey shook his head. "My friends go by themselves." But no one was listening. Everyone but Davey seemed to know what to do. Even Boomer and Linda and Cassie took directions from the muzzles of the guns as if they'd had rehearsals. The cabin emptied outside, everyone moving across the veranda toward the wharf.

"The junkie's singing," said Corporal Archambault, leader of the Emergency Response Team. "Says someone named Stoddard went in there about fifteen minutes ago. I thought Stoddard was dead."

"You believe everything a junkie tells you?" said Chief Inspector Brian Cronk. The corporal looked more like a combat troop than a cop—camouflage uniform, flack vest, coal-scuttle helmet over face paint. Acted like one too, submachine gun lying cocky on his hip. Somewhere along the line, drug interdiction had become the War on Drugs, said so in the movies, and wars needed soldiers, not cops. Cronk rarely carried his service pistol.

"It'll be a guy named Jones," Cronk said. He was sitting in his car, talking out the open window. "Everyone thinks he's Stoddard."

Archambault was standing beside the car, shifting his weight like a racehorse at the starting gate. Cronk wondered if Archambault's warriors were any better for society than the pathetic junkie named Twitch or Rockwell the wannabe biker. God help the society that ran out battles for the soldiers because they'd find their own, bet your life they would. And if they couldn't find them, they'd make them.

Twitch and Rockwell were being questioned, each in one of the two big panel vans that had brought the ERT and their equipment. The vans were pulled into the deep shadows behind the service station. They'd only just arrived when they'd been surprised by the car careening into the parking lot. But the takedown had been quick and efficient. They were, after all, an emergency response team.

"Unfortunately," said the corporal, "the junkie knows squat about the setup down there, and the biker's telling the world all about his rights."

"Straightening him out on that are you, Corporal?"

Archambault frowned, as if he didn't know whether or not Cronk was kidding him, not sure if Cronk was advising or discouraging the use of rubber hose and electrodes. He moved some gravel with his foot. "We could be all over them," he said, "before they realize their sentries are taken."

"That what those two are? Sentries?"

Cronk's cell phone rang. It was Detective Steinhauser, who'd taken an ERT up to the lodge on the Oyster River. Steinhauser reported that the place was deserted—hastily it seemed. In a shed out back, there was grim evidence that hostages had been held. Cronk was telling him to stay and secure the place in case someone returned, when Steinhauser started shouting. There was more shouting and, in the background, the sound of an aircraft.

"Call you back, Brian," said Steinhauser. "We just had a fucking helicopter take off from the woods out back, you believe that shit?"

Cronk told Archambault about the helicopter. "Not likely coming our way, not if it's got the Dentons, or what's left of them. Still, keep your head up."

"It's a go, then, sir?"

Cronk nodded. "Remember, there're four hostages now, not three. And don't forget we've got a man in there."

"Right. Purcell, Kevin. Hope he's smart enough to lay his gun down when the shooting starts."

"Corporal? Be careful. They're not all as useless as the junkie and the biker here. One of them is a veteran paratrooper. At least three have mercenary training. They'll be armed for Armageddon."

For an awkward second, Cronk was afraid Archambault was going to salute. Thankfully, the corporal simply grinned. "Then, sir, that's what we'll give them," he said and trotted off to gather his team.

Chapter 24

$\mathcal{D}$awn was prying the sky off the mountain peaks forty kilometers to the east across Georgia Strait. Watery light was spilling through the crack, bluing the sky, chasing off the stars. Davey could make out the shapes of objects that had been merely shadows twenty minutes ago. Out on the cross pier, opposite *Small Wonder*, was tied a rigid-hull inflatable about twenty-five feet in length, with two big outboards strapped to her bum. Sitting on the beach, about thirty meters from the cabin, was a black helicopter of the type useful for dropping gasoline bombs on pot plantations.

Good shit.

There were five armed men posted on the wharf. Along with the entourage from the cabin, it made for quite a congregation when they all gathered at the T-junction. The inflatable boat was a Zodiac in gunmetal gray, powered by a pair of 225s, capable of maybe fifty, sixty knots.

While the gunmen milled about getting organized, Davey contrived to shuffle up close to Boomer. "That was all bullshit," he whispered. "I'll do what I can to give you some distance, but try to do something before you hit open water. Put her aground on the point if you can."

Boomer was scowling in the direction of *Small Wonder*, where Cassie and Linda were being goaded aboard. The man doing the goading looked up. Davey's mouth dropped open.

"Ah no," he said.

Kevin, the kid from New Zealand, turned quickly away.

"Fuck sold us out," Boomer growled.

"Pisser, ain't it," said the man named Flammond. "Come on, big guy, time to go."

Small Wonder's lines were slipped. Her diesel gurgled as Boomer eased her away from the wharf and turned her seaward. Cassie and Linda were sitting together on the starboard bench. Opposite them, the Kiwi traitor and a man named Bartell displayed pistols. Flammond carried his assault rifle out to the forepeak.

A large hand closed on Davey's shoulder. He turned and looked up into the dark craggy face of Dominic Slavos. The last time he'd seen Slavos, in the truck bay on the crowded ferry, seemed like an ancient memory, something that had happened years ago or maybe something he'd only dreamed about.

"Another boat ride together," Slavos said, his face slashed with a smile. "No trucks this time for hiding, yes?" With a short-barrelled submachine gun, Slavos motioned for Davey to precede him.

The Zodiac's twin outboards came to life with a predatory growl. Up in the bow, the man they called the Monk was fiddling with some sort of tubelike device. Standing at the center helm console was Chambers, a white patch where his right ear had been. Quite the reunion.

Davey stopped near the tie rail at the edge of the wharf. Slavos's hand went to his shoulder and pushed. Davey resisted. The push became stiffer, more aggressive. Davey relaxed and let Slavos push him off the wharf.

The frigid water parted with a splash and closed around him with the muffled effervescence of air bubbles rushing to the surface. With his hands shackled abaft, he sank like a sackful of unwanted kittens. He let himself sink about eight feet before stabilizing his descent by kicking his legs. He wasn't willing to bet his life that any of these thugs would go deeper than that to get him.

Two splashes broke the surface above him. He felt, rather than saw, the two men swimming down to him. Davey let them grope around in the dark water, waiting until his lungs began to hurt before letting them find him. They dragged him up beside the Zodiac. Slavos reached down and grabbed the handcuffs, dragging Davey over the inflated pontoons in a manner that threatened to pull his arms from their sockets. Gasping for air, he lay in a cold wet heap on the aluminum sole. The engines roared, and the Zodiac darted away from the wharf.

Cedric Flammond took position in the bow of the sailboat and saw that it was good. No one could get close to him without coming into the fire zone of his C-7 assault rifle.

Dishonorable discharge notwithstanding, Flammond still thought of himself as an airborne sergeant. Like all worthy combat sergeants, he was able to make quick accurate assessments on the capabilities of individuals, and he knew that his three hostages were not the curl-up-in-a-corner type.

There was the smallish blonde with the frightened doe eyes, who moved not at all like someone frozen with fright. The Denton girl was a wildcat with a length of steel cable in her. What Bartell had done to her might have bent that cable but, clearly, hadn't broken it. And the big guy with the red beard, the one they called Boomer, was nothing if not capable. They'd taken the man's home without a fight only because of the gun at the Denton girl's head. When confronted, Red Beard had assessed, decided, and reacted with an agility rare in soldiers, let alone civilians. It made him a dangerous enemy.

How these people had become the enemy was an abstraction of null consequence. They were the enemy, and Flammond's task was to maintain control of them with a minimum of bloodshed. Only alive could they be used to make Jones perform. And only if Jones performed would the operation be successful. And Flammond harbored a deeply personal reason for wanting this operation to succeed.

His years of dedication to the airborne had in the end been worth nothing but a discharge, a *dishonorable* discharge, for doing what he'd been trained to do—intimidating the enemy. Judged by politicians from the comfort of their parliament buildings. Judged by the very people who'd sent him to that sweltering fly-infested asshole of a country to stand between two armed camps of crazed rebels and take sniper fire from both sides as often as not with Canadian ammunition because he wasn't allowed to defend his ordnance with deadly force. Judged by politicians and abandoned by a corps of officers whose "orders" had been so obfuscated with ass-covering political correctness as to be indecipherable by the time they reached the front line. The whole debacle had made of Flammond what they call a highly motivated individual.

From the moment he'd left the court martial, stripped of everything that defined him, Cedric Flammond had begun looking for someone like Lazuardi. Someone with the resources and the agenda to give Flammond an opportunity to show the people who'd stripped him that they'd made an error.

It was true that Lazuardi's troops were fuckups rather than soldiers, but that in itself gave Flammond a degree of satisfaction. He was, far and away, the best player on this team. Success depended on him maintaining a level of performance high above that of the incompetents around him. Word would get out; his future would be secure. The world was full of Lazuardi's willing to pay for the types of services Flammond could offer.

From his station on the bow, Flammond kept glancing at the receding wharf. The Zodiac hadn't left yet. Flammond wondered if there was a mechanical problem. He was about to tell Boomer to stop the sailboat when he saw a wake of white foam, indicating the departure of the powerboat. The sailboat had a head start of over half a kilometer but that clearly wouldn't be a problem. The foaming wake of the Zodiac zipped across the bay. The powerboat would fetch them up quickly.

Flammond's attention was wrenched away from the progress of the Zodiac. The Denton girl started crying hysterically, tripping Flammond's mental fire alarm; the Denton girl was not a caldron of hysterical tears. Before anyone could stop her, she darted down into the cabin.

What was she up to? Sabotaging the engine? Even holing the hull, he thought, wasn't beyond her. He couldn't allow her to be down there by herself. "Mr. Bartell, go see what she's about."

Ricky Bartell grinned and nodded. Flammond wasn't a proponent of rape; he understood the moral repugnance of it. But the soldier in him recognized its intrinsic intimidatory value. If anyone could cow the young woman, it would be her rapist.

A moment later, Flammond was given reason to rue his decision by the muffled *pop* that could only be a pistol shot. The new man, the Kiwi, was raising his pistol when Boomer moved. A fist like an anvil hammered into the Kiwi's head and felled him. Boomer picked up the Kiwi's gun.

Flammond almost squeezed the trigger, but he too could think on his feet. A split second before killing the man, he realized that Boomer couldn't get a clean shot at him around the mast. He moved his C-7 a few inches until it pointed at the blonde. He shook his head. Boomer scowled at him, but he lowered the gun.

Okay. They'd had their little rebellion, their little uprising. They'd gotten it out of their system, and Flammond was still in command. Whatever had happened below could be dealt with when he got backup from the men in the Zodiac. He glanced out and saw that the Zodiac was coming fast. It would be alongside within thirty seconds. He'd be content to simply keep a lid on things till then.

Davey braced his shoulder against the helm console and levered himself to his feet. He saw *Small Wonder* heading out along the north arm of the bay, ploughing along joyfully at about ten knots. The Zodiac was planning at about forty. He had to think of a way to slow the powerboat down, give Boomer more time.

But he was having trouble thinking. The forty-knot wind cut through his sodden clothes like a volley of icicles. His body was shivering to the point of convulsion. Without the protection of a dive suit the North Pacific was nothing but cold—deep, debilitating cold.

As he tried to channel his thoughts away from being cold, Davey glanced around at his shipmates. Slavos, sitting in the stern sheets, gave him a smile and a wave with the snout of his submachine gun. Chambers, with a death grip on the helm, was squinting into the headwind. The one they called the Monk was crouched in the bow, admiring the piece of equipment he'd assembled. It was Davey's first look at a real one, but he'd seen pictures of them. He understood the acronym was LAW. Stood for light antisailboat weapon. Your basic disposable fucking bazooka. Things just got better and better.

Something off the port bow caught his attention. A small phosphorescent ripple about two hundred meters ahead. *Small Wonder*'s wake, he realized, just kissing the top of Gunner's Rock.

In his haste to catch the sailboat, Chambers was cutting across the center of the bay rather than following the deep channel along the north arm. In fact, it was unlikely that Chambers knew anything about the deep channel or of Gunner's Rock. If he knew about it, he'd have to slow the boat and steer a wide loop to port, which might give Boomer time to run aground on the headland. Davey opened his mouth to inform Chambers of his navigational error.

He didn't though. Another ripple ran over the crown of the rock, showing it to be only inches under water. Steering the Zodiac around the rock *might* give Boomer enough time to make a move. On the other hand, steering the Zodiac into the rock at full speed would give Boomer all the time in the world.

He saw that the Zodiac was angling slightly away from the ripple, away from the peak of the rock. The reef sprawled all over the center of the bay, but on this tide, most of it would be deeper than the Zodiac's one or two feet of draught. Davey realized he might have to give Chambers a little guidance. He stood close to Chambers and stared at the spot where he'd seen the ripples. The boat closed quickly. Fifty meters. Forty. Twenty.

"Thanks for the lift," Davey said, and he leaned on Chambers's shoulder.

The wheel didn't turn much, but at forty knots, it was enough to lay the boat on her thwarts. His arms unavailable for balance, Davey stumbled across the canted sole. He saw that Slavos had let go of his submachine gun to reach for the grab lines. Up in the bow, the Monk was fumbling with the LAW of objects in motion. The pontoon caught Davey at the knees and tripped him into the achingly cold water.

Chambers corrected the helm. The correcting maneuver brought the boat over top of Davey. Turbulence from the propellers sucked him upward. One of the props plucked at his jacket, then hit his left leg. The leg was kicked to the side and went instantly numb, as if it was no longer there.

The turbulence sucked him up into the wake trough. His face broke the surface, and he saw the Zodiac turning steeply at full speed, no doubt coming around to fetch him. He captured a lungful of air and was starting to slide back under when the boat hit Gunner's Rock and leaped off the water. The Monk's rocket gun fired. Unfortunately for the Monk, it fired into the Zodiac. As the sea closed over Davey's head, it was lit by a dazzling flash. A deep muffled *whumph* boxed his ears. The shock wave put a gentle hand on his chest and pushed him backward.

In stunned disbelief, Flammond saw the Zodiac swerve erratically, leap off the water, and then explode. It was totally unbelievable, like something out of a stupid cartoon. Cedric Flammond, for the first time since boot camp, forgot about the weapon in his hand. By the time he recovered, the blonde with the frightened doe eyes was hauling on a rope. The foresail came unfurled and flapped at his head.

The boat veered left. The sail billowed with the wind of the boat's momentum. The force with which the sail shoved him took Flammond by surprise. Before he could grab the lifeline, the sail stiffened and pitched him overboard.

He refused to acknowledge the frigid shock. He kicked away from the hull, away from the churning propeller, and oriented himself to the shoreline about twenty meters away. There was no point in trying to reboard the sailboat; if Jones was anywhere near that explosion this gig was over. He let go of his rifle and began swimming toward the shore.

Davey's vision was streaked from the white flash of the explosion. His ears were deaf from the clap of it. He folded his legs against his chest and strained to pass the shackles under his feet, all the while sinking, the sea pressing at his mouth, his nose, determined to invade him and rid him of the air he carried. By the time he got his hands in front of him, panic was pressing at his mind, determined to invade him and rid him of thought. He'd sunk too deep; the surface was impossibly far above, a distant planet rumored to be full of air.

But panic did its job, covering the crippling pain in his leg, the numb fatigue in his muscles. He kicked with his legs, pulled with his hands, disoriented and blind, up and down and sideways all the same in the weightless fluid, panic insisting that the struggle was important, not the direction. His hands broke through into the air, where they encountered an object like a nightmare that kept his head inches under the water. His lungs felt like they were ripping open. He flailed with the strength of panic, but the object wouldn't move, or rather, it moved with him, staying over his head. Then his flailing arms slipped around it. Using its floatation, he pulled himself up. His face broke the surface. His lungs erupted, spewing out stale air, gulping furiously at the fresh cool morning.

Davey clung to the seal, its fur sleek as satin and warm to the touch. It smelled musky and wild. It was on its side. He thought it was dead, but its body convulsed, and it raised its head from the water and its nostril flaps chuffed at the air. It took two breaths, and then its head fell back into the water. Davey did what he could to keep its nostrils out of the water, but it took no more breaths.

It floated though, and its buoyancy kept Davey above the greedy depths. And it stayed warm to Davey's touch, shielding him from debilitating hypothermia. Davey kicked shoreward or, rather, waved one exhausted leg. His left leg, the one hit by the propeller, had gone useless on him. But the tide was flooding, the current moving him shoreward faster than he could have swam anyway.

As his ears cleared, Davey became aware of a ruckus. He heard the growl of a helicopter engine and the sharp staccato popping sound of light arms fire, and he had a chilling vision of Eddie and his Haida warriors pitting their deer rifles against the automatic weapons. He thought he should hurry ashore and help them, but the thought was vague and indistinct, like the stuff that makes up time.

Saltwater burned his lungs, waking him. His face jerked up. Choking, he coughed the water out of his throat, his nose. His feet were dragging on solid ground. He pushed with his good leg until he was mostly out of the water. He slipped his arms from around Gunner's neck, rolled onto his side, and vomited. He puked until his stomach cramped and his throat burned raw. He rinsed his mouth in the ocean and rolled onto his back. Gunner lay at his feet, a mottled brown bulk rolling back and forth in the lapping waves.

Sporadic bursts of gunfire came from the direction of the cabin. The helicopter idled on the beach. None of it seemed very important. Things had begun to drift away from him, as if he'd spent the night smoking Frank's homegrown sun-ripened ganja. He was near the wharf, and he wiggled around until he got his back braced against a piling and enjoyed the sensation of leaving his frigid body and gathering in a warm fluffy cloud under the roof of his skull.

Half a dozen men spilled from the cabin, firing as they backed toward the helicopter. Davey watched blandly until he was distracted by another helicopter flying in across the bay. It was low to the water, bouncing around as if the pilot were drunk. Then he realized that *Small Wonder* was motoring back into the bay. He didn't really want to see that, so he turned back to the gun battle.

Two of the retreating men dropped. One became a deathly still pile of loose clothing. The other lay on his back clutching his belly and screaming at the sky while his heals crabbed the sand. Looked painful, whatever he had.

Davey watched it all as if he was wrapped in a quilt on the couch forcing himself to stay awake for the end of the movie. Way down inside, a part of him realized that this was not a good thing. He should've been crazy with pain, shivering from the cold and the fear and the stress. But that part of him was deeply buried in the comforting folds of the quilt.

The second helicopter came in swinging like a punch-drunk boxer. It eventually managed a shaky hover directly over the chopper on the beach. One of Lazuardi's soldiers looked up at it and pointed toward the cabin and then dove for cover as the helicopter dropped straight down. There was a god-awful clatter when its landing skids touched the cycling rotor of the helicopter beneath it. One quick touch, then it jumped up a couple of meters before coming down like a drop hammer. Amid a deafening cascade of sparks and screaming metal, the stacked-up helicopters yawed slowly, irrecoverably to port. The spinning rotors bit into the ground, and the air was filled with sand and rocks and bits of broken steel.

The metallic screams of the crash ended abruptly. There was a long eerie silence. Even the gut-shot man had shut up.

A loudspeaker broke the silence. It came from the cabin, and it told everyone to stand up slowly with their hands on their heads. Since Davey could neither stand nor raise his hands, he didn't bother. The men on the beach who could did.

Armed men came running from the cabin. They wore army helmets and dark camouflage and flack vests with the word police stenciled in day-glow yellow on the back. They swarmed around the men on the beach, pushing them to the ground and cuffing their hands. One of them noticed Davey and pointed a machine pistol at him.

"I killed him," Davey tried to say, but his throat was raw. His eyes were blurred with tears.

The police looked Davey over and muttered, "Sweet Jesus. Stay put. I'll get a medic."

So Davey stayed put.

A pounding noise came from the helicopter that had dropped out of the sky. It was lying on its side, and the door on the upper side jumped a few centimeters with each blow. This quickly drew the attention of the police, several of whom aimed weapons at it. The door groaned for a moment, then popped open. The police were shouting at the two men who crawled out of the wreck, but Tommy Clayton and Billy Tsimka paid them no heed as they stood on the side of the helicopter and whooped at the sky.

One of the police pointed seaward and yelled above the chaos, "Get that boat out of here!"

Davey watched *Small Wonder* slide up to the wharf. Linda leaped to the dock and secured the breast line. Davey saw Kevin tied to the mast. He saw Boomer help Cassie disembark. Her face was buried in his massive chest.

Two police were trotting out toward them. "You can't stay here," one of them said. "This is a restricted area."

Boomer told him to pound his meat. "This is my dock. That's my house you just shot the shit out of. So take your restricted area and go pound your meat with it."

The two police shuffled to a halt halfway along the float. They seemed unsure as to what came next.

Linda's eyes found Davey. She stared at him for a few seconds, then turned and spoke to Cassie. Cassie pulled away from Boomer and looked in the direction of Linda's pointing arm.

Cassie broke into a sprint. The two police were blocking her way, telling her she couldn't go there, it was a restricted area. Without breaking stride, she dove into the water. A dozen quick darting strokes and she was on her feet, plowing up through the shallows, running to Davey.

"I killed him," he tried to tell her, but she was too far away, receding, unable to run fast enough to catch him as he plunged with dizzying speed down a warm tunnel of darkness. "I killed Ben Gunn."

Chapter 25

$\mathcal{D}$avey's mind rose slowly through layers of sleep, reluctantly folding each layer and placing it aside before moving on to the next, pausing between the layers to linger over cottony memories, which could have been lint left by dreams. There was a dazzling image of Keith, whole and laughing. An image of Davey's mother dressed in her garden dungarees, complete with floppy hat and soiled pink gloves, shaking her head and clucking her tongue. There was the impenetrable security of his father's lap, the textured wool sweater fragranced with pipe tobacco and salt air. And a shimmering image of Cassie's face suspended in a soft cone of light . . .

His mind set aside the last bit of sleep, and his eyes blinked open. He saw a hospital room, the color of daylight diffused through white curtains. His body stretched to flush the atrophy from its muscles. He felt an overall leaden sort of ache, but no particular pain. He found himself attached by a tube to a drip bag, no doubt doping him with painkillers.

"Hey hey," said Boomer's voice.

He looked over and saw his substantial friend sitting beside a shaded lamp in the corner, a crossword puzzle book on his lap and a cockeyed grin on his face.

Davey's mouth was coated with a sticky residue of antiseptic flavor. He cleared a buildup of mucus from his throat and croaked, "Where's the water closet?"

"Just a minute." Boomer set his puzzle book aside and stood up. "I'll get a nurse."

"Minute'll be too late." Davey swung his legs off the bed and sat still for a second as a little whirlpool went spinning off the top of his head. He saw the bathroom door off to his right. Using the drip bag stand as a crutch, he stood up and gingerly tested his left leg. There was a curiously painless ripping sensation beneath the pressure of the bandage. Boomer came up beside him and took his elbow. Just as they reached the john, the ward door opened and a uniformed Mountie poked his head in. He gave them a curt nod and disappeared.

Boomer made a disparaging face. "Here comes the force," he muttered.

In the bathroom, Davey was mortified to find his loins wrapped in a diaperlike garment. Thank Christ it was clean. He ripped it off and tossed it in the trash. After a lengthy, gratifying piss, he went to the sink and washed his face and swished out his mouth before limping from the washroom to meet the force.

A tall, well-built man in his fifties. Neatly trimmed ginger-brown hair. Gray slacks to match his eyes, short leather jacket over light brown shirt, open at the collar. One of those good-looking people the Mounties seemed stocked with, as if they recruited through model agencies.

"Mr. Jones?" asked the force. His voice was as clear as his pale eyes.

"Yeah, it is." Davey got back into bed, arranging the pillows so that he could sit.

"I'm Inspector Brian Cronk, RCMP drug interdiction unit."

Davey was pleasantly light-headed from whatever drug dripped into his arm, and it made him cocky. He figured the cop was there to list the crimes he was going to be charged with and maybe even to claim *Small Wonder* as spoils of war. Davey had no intention of making it easy. "Can you prove it?" he asked.

Boomer grunted. Cronk's eyes called Davey a punk, but he pulled a wallet from an inner pocket and offered his ID.

Davey studied the ID and returned the wallet. "What can I do for you, Brian?"

"My friends call me Brian. You can call me sir or officer or inspector."

"Ouch," grunted Boomer.

"Right," said Davey. "Officer in the war on drugs. How is that working out for you, guys? Caught one of your shows this morning. Nice touch, the helicopter crash."

"That wasn't this morning," Cronk said. "That was two days ago."

Davey blushed. The cockiness went out of him. He looked at Boomer. Boomer nodded. So that was why he was in the hospital—he'd just had two days surgically removed.

"So what do you want with me?" he asked.

"To finish what Mr. Stoddard and Mr. Denton started."

That threw Davey off the scent. He looked to Boomer for edification.

"Keith and Frank were working with the cops," Boomer said. "Least that's what they say." He nodded toward the cop and left it up for grabs as to how much weight to put on what they say.

Cronk's eyes were fixed on Davey's face. It wasn't really a stare, more as if the cop's eyes were a pair of hawks that found Davey's face a convenient place to roost. "Your freinds," Cronk said, "were contacted by a major player in the drug trade, an individual of Hong Kong origin seeking to open a base of operation here on our lovely coast."

"On Vancouver Island?"

"Sure. Lax immigration policies, thousands of kilometers of remote coastline, ineffectively patrolled, easy access to Vancouver's international trade routes, five thousand kilometers of open border to the American Dream. Make no mistake, Mr. Jones, this is a prime location for these people."

Cronk was making points on his fingers. Davey got the feeling he was getting the drug interdiction recruitment speech.

"Also," Cronk continued, "the area has little organized competition. The local drug trade has remained largely in the hands of small-time independents like yourselves. So along they come with their carrot and stick, thinking easy pickings. Carrot's a bagful of money. Stick shoots bullets. Going to organize your slack asses.

"But they don't know you guys, do they? Can't understand that you guys don't want to be organized. Organization takes too much effort. You're West Coasters, and West Coasters are lethargic sons of bitches. Can't organize a softball game, never mind a drug deal. Money doesn't work because, like farmers and fishermen, you're not in it for the money. It's a lifestyle, not a living. And threats, by nature, provide only short-term management."

Davey wondered if he was supposed to feel better now that it was all explained to him. But the cop wasn't finished yet.

"Your pals, Stoddard and Denton, contacted us through the office of the crown counselor. Claimed they'd been contacted by one Vincent Lazuardi, our player from Hong Kong. Offered to help us get up close and personal with Lazuardi."

Davey shook his head. "Keith and I were like brothers. He never said a word. Not a hint."

"We insisted," said Cronk. "In this sort of thing, obviously, the fewer people who know about it, the safer for all concerned."

"Must've missed that part," Davey said, the words bitter in his mouth. "The part where it turned out safer for all concerned."

Cronk's eyes roosted on him for a few seconds and then said, "They helped us insert an undercover officer into Lazuardi's organization. The officer got into a position to access a computer flash drive, which is said to contain files pertaining to Lazuardi's networks. Last we heard, the officer was going to copy the drive and return it unmissed. We lost contact for two days. Then the Denton's place went kaboom. They tell me you were there at the time, so I won't bore you with details. After that, the screwups came hard on the heels of each other."

No details needed for that either; Davey had been *there* at the time as well.

"Now," he said, "you want me to finish what Keith and Frank started? I take it then that the battle of Boomer's Bight did not net this Lazuardi-san?"

"Oh, we got Lazuardi, bet your life we did. But Lazuardi wasn't our main target. His memory stick was. The stick remains at large, and Stoddard left a message telling you where it is."

Davey looked at Boomer. Boomer shrugged and said, "They listened to the tape on Linda's machine."

Davey nodded. Looked at Cronk. "I hope you're not counting on that stick for a conviction. There's a spot on Granville Island where Keith and I stashed pot when we had business in Vancouver. We called it the treasury. It's the only place I can think of that he would refer to as Treasure Island. I checked it out when I first got the message. It was empty. Some wino could've found it, taken it for his collection of memory sticks. Who knows? I tried to arrange a meeting with a Counselor Dennison to tell her about it, but the meeting never happened."

Cronk's raptorial eyes roosted on Davey's face, calling him a liar. Davey wasn't sure if Cronk knew he was lying or simply assumed everyone lied to him. But he was sure that he wanted to open Keith's sea chest before the police did.

The ward door opened, and a starch-white nurse bustled in. The scene obviously caught her off guard. Her expression of surprise quickly turned to one of disapproval.

"This is a hospital, Inspector, not a police station. You were to inform us the moment Mr. Jones woke up."

She drew the privacy curtain around the bed, all five-foot nothing of her, throwing the two big men into hasty retreat. She recorded Davey's vital signs and changed the dressings on his wounded leg and his burned abdomen. When she was done, she opened the privacy curtain, went to the window, and drew the blinds open. The window faced east, down a suburban hillside, down to the sun-dappled waters of Discovery Passage. It was the hospital in Campbell River.

The nurse stood holding the door open, her eyes locked on Cronk's. "His doctor will be here shortly," she said. "The doctor will determine whether or not he is well enough to be interviewed."

Cronk opened his mouth, shut it, and walked out. The nurse glanced at Boomer but evidently decided that he didn't pose a threat to her patient. Off she bustled.

"How are Frank and Lorraine?" Davey asked.

"Not good. They look like zombies. They're down in Victoria, neurosciences ward at the Royal Jubilee. Cassie's down there with them."

Davey stared out the window, across the passage to the islands of Quadra and Cortes and the myriad of smaller islands that clustered at the feet of the snowcapped Coastal Range. One of the geographically youngest places on the planet. According to Keith, the gods had used the rest of the world for practice and then done coastal British Columbia when they'd got everything right.

"I've made a fucking mess of it," Davey lamented.

"Don't take credit that ain't due," said Boomer. "Keith and Frank got this ball rolling."

"Did they really?" Davey wondered out loud. He glanced at the closed door, remembering that there was a Mountie listening just outside.

"Pull a chair up," he said. "Let's have a quiet bedside talk."

When Boomer was seated close to the bed, Davey lowered his voice and asked him if he'd talked to Cronk.

"Yeah. Him and the prosecutor, Dennison. We all did."

"How did he come across? He on the level? The Hong Kong thing, all that?"

Boomer shrugged. "Got no reason not to believe him. Pushy asshole, but I guess cops are supposed to be."

"How about Dennison?"

"She's okay. Reefed Cronk's sails a few times when he got too pushy."

"Good cop, bad cop?"

"I don't think so. She wants to get this Lazuardi creature behind bars. Likely make her career. She don't want Cronk pissing off the witnesses or taking short cuts that might get Lazuardi off on a technicality."

Davey scratched his cheek. When had he shaved last? The morning he'd taken Cassie to Victoria. Three, four days ago?

"What's with Kevin?" he asked. "What's his story? He a cop?"

"Uh-huh." Boomer leaned forward on his knees and frowned at his hands, as if they'd done something to disappoint him. "He was tailing you. They claim they didn't know which side you were on, so they sicked him on you to keep tabs. He followed you onto the ferry, over to Granville Island, back to the ferry. Saw you talking to a person of suspicious demeanour—his words, not mine—then lost you."

"And found me in the head, too late to help me with Dominic."

"Who?"

Davey shook his head. "Just this guy. So how'd Kevin end up on Lazuardi's team?"

Boomer's right hand curled into a large fist. "I plan to ask him about that one of these days."

"Did he help you out on the boat? I seem to recall him being tied to the mast."

"Didn't get much of a chance to do one thing or another," Boomer said. He brushed at his fist with the fingers of his left hand, as if removing bits of debris. "Was Cassie who saved our asses. She went crying below. One of the goons went down to see what she was up to. She was up to getting her hands on that old Llama of yours. When we heard the gunshot, we didn't know who'd shot who. The Kiwi looked at the goon out on the bow, and that's when I gave him a little pop in the head."

Boomer groomed his fist, a fist too massive to ever manage anything remotely like a little pop.

"The guy on the bow," Boomer continued, "still had his rifle on us, but then the Zodiac blew up and distracted him. Linda let go the jib in his face. He went overboard. I took the Kiwi's gun and went below. What a mess. Guy lying there in a puddle of blood. I thought she'd killed him, but he was just passed out from the pain. She shot him in the crotch. Messed up his parts something awful. Mean to say, his genes ain't ever getting in the pool."

Boomer chuckled. Davey shivered.

"Then," Boomer said, "Cassie found out the Zodiac had blown up. She went a little crazy. Wanted to shoot everything in sight. I had to wrestle the gun away from her. She was plenty happy when she saw you on the beach."

Boomer dropped his head and studied his fist again. "Gunner got killed, Davey. Washed up on the beach beside you. He must've been on the rock when that boat blew up."

Davey nodded quietly for a moment. "He kept me afloat, his body did. Saved my life. If Ben Gunn doesn't die, I drown."

"Yeah," said Boomer, "Ben's life for yours." He made it sound like a poor trade. Then he repeated the name. "Ben Gunn." His eyes narrowed as he made the same association Davey had made. He whistled softly and whispered, "I'll be damned."

"Exactly," said Davey.

"Jesus, Davey, it's a reef, a big old piece of waterlogged granite. Spends eight hours a day completely submerged."

"So he must have waterproofed the chest somehow. It's there, Boomer. It has to be."

"So why not tell the cops, let them look for it?"

"For the time being, I'd like to keep this between you and me."

Boomer glanced toward the door. "You think something's not what it's supposed to be?"

"I don't know. Maybe I'm just paranoid. But if Cronk's story is straight, why didn't Keith just send me to the cops? Why all the Treasure Island shit? The trip to Toronto—damn! What happened to the clothes I was wearing?"

"They were bloody rags, Davey. I trashed them. Brought you some clean stuff from *Small Wonder*."

"Before you trashed my clothes, did you go through the pockets?"

"Course I did. Stuff from your wallet is spread all over my table drying out."

"There was a key."

"Yeah. Along with a handful of change. You want I should bring it to you?"

Davey shook his head. "The key opens a mailbox in Victoria. There's a letter in the box. I need you to get that letter and give it to Counselor Dennison."

That afternoon, Davey finally met the elusive Counselor Marcie Dennison. Chief Inspector Cronk ushered her into the room, a dark-haired woman of indeterminate age. One of those women who, somewhere around thirty-five, put the aging process on hold for a couple of decades. She carried a brown leather satchel the size of a small suitcase. It was bruised and scarred, and the flap on the top of it hung with a limp sort of uselessness. It thumped to the floor beside the bed, and Dennison extended her hand.

"I'm Marcie," she said. Her hand was cool and smooth, her grip firm.

The lawyer pulled a chair up beside the bed and sat. She leaned forward to rummage through her briefcase, and the neckline of her salmon-colored silk blouse opened a peak. She came up with a pad of yellow paper filled with notes, a well-chewed pen, and a small tape recorder, which she placed on the bedside table and activated. There was a whisper of nylon as she crossed her knees to make a lap for her notepad. Her skirt was pleated plaid, and her feet were shod in pink sneakers.

She spoke to the recorder, telling it the time, date, location, and subject. Cronk remained a hovering background presence while Marcie led Davey through a reconstruction of the attack on the Denton place, the escape on the boat, and Keith's death and burial. "Which means," she said, "that we have no body, and so no postmortem and so no official cause of death."

"Cause of *death*?" Davey said. "Two bullets through him back to front. Exit wounds here and here, big enough to put your fist in. Shredded lungs leaking from this one, shredded intestines from this one. If I had to take a wild guess, I'd say that could be the cause of death. What do you think, Counselor? Go out on a limb with that?"

The lawyer nodded, but it was a gesture of mollification rather than agreement. "Unfortunately, unless by some miracle we recover the body, all we have is your word."

That'd be the word of a known drug dealer.

"Cassie saw him," Davey said, and even to him it sounded peevish.

Dennison shook her head. "Ms. Denton was in a state of shock. She remembers both you and Keith covered with blood. Beyond that, her recollection is based on what you told her."

"I didn't kill Keith."

"No one's suggesting you did. Not yet. When you're on the stand, the defense will suggest exactly that, if they're any good. You have to be absolutely positive about how he died."

"I didn't kill him," Davey repeated. But suppose he had? Suppose that, despite the grievous wounds, Keith had still been alive when Davey had wrapped him up and sent him to the deep?

No. No way. The still lungs, the still heart, the glassy eyes. He was dead. Shot to death because . . . *they know about us, Lily. There's only one way they got that information.*

"Are you okay, Davey?" the lawyer asked. "You look a little pale. We can take a break if you need to."

Davey shook his head. "I'm fine."

What he needed was a chance to talk to Dennison alone, without Cronk's presence and without Cronk's knowledge. Because the only one Keith had trusted was Marcie, not Inspector Cronk. Because they knew about Keith and Lily, and there's only one way they got that information. Hopefully, Cronk would, sooner or later, have to go take a leak or something.

Davey answered questions. Dennison jotted notes. Cronk roosted with his eyes, letting Davey know Cronk thought he was full of shit, even when Davey was telling the truth. *That's okay,* Davey thought, *because you're not telling the whole truth and nothing but the truth yourself, are you, Inspector Drug Inter-fucking-diction?*

The interview consumed most of the afternoon. Davey never got an opportunity to talk to the counselor alone. He had to interrupt the interview twice to use the washroom, but the inspector's bladder was evidently made of sterner stuff.

As the day wore on, Davey got to explore new exotic levels of exhaustion, which, along with nicotine withdrawal, produced an ugly trollish headache. Although it was within his mandate to terminate the interview, he avoided exercising that prerogative, hoping for a moment, a few seconds, to talk to Dennison alone.

The moment never came. Cronk stayed to the end and beyond. Dennison packed up her battle-scarred briefcase and left, wishing Davey well and promising to be in touch again, and still Cronk stood there, his gray eyes roosting. Davey couldn't take it. He used the remote control to lower the bed. His eyes closed, and he drifted into a weightless void. He never did hear Cronk leave.

"He knows where it is, Kevin, bet your life he does. But why the hell is he lying about it?"

Constable Kevin Purcell shifted in his chair, squinting under the glare of fluorescent lamps. Cronk's office had windows on every wall. Three sides looked out over the open squad room. The two guys on the night watch had picked the farthest desk on which to play cards. The fourth wall looked three stories down to the inner harbor. Across the way, the Provincial Parliament buildings were lit up for the night, as if boasting of the province's hydroelectric surplus.

Kevin stared at the light show and said, "He's not working for Lazuardi. That's something I *would* bet my life on."

Cronk nodded. "I agree. So let's find out what he's up to, shall we? He's getting discharged tomorrow afternoon. From the time he leaves the hospital you're going to baby sit him."

Kevin touched the left side of his jaw. It was still tender from its meeting with Boomer's fist. "I don't think he likes me very much."

"He doesn't have to like you. You're not soliciting his vote. It's enough that you know each other. A bit of tension between you might even prove useful."

Kevin shook his head and stared out the window, not trusting himself to look at his boss. His taste for undercover work had taken on a bitter tinge. He'd never forget the look on Davey's face when Davey saw he'd been betrayed. It hadn't been a look of anger or disgust; it had been one of pity, as if Kevin had become some sort of lower life form.

"We'll call it witness protection," Cronk was saying. "We didn't round up all of Lazuardi's people. Flammond never showed up, and there could well be others. To make sure, we've arranged bail for some of the lowlifes. Considering what he's been through, Jones might be glad for your company when he learns that some of Lazuardi's soldiers are still on the loose."

Already arranged. A done deal. Kevin wasn't there to discuss the matter; he was there to receive orders. Short of resignation, Constable Purcell would do what he was bloody told.

"Since you've taken the trouble to create an actual threat," he said, "can I count on backup?"

"We can't afford to have a team sit on their hands up there for God knows how long. And without Lazuardi's leadership, the threat will be largely imaginary. But I'll work out something with the Campbell River detachment if it makes you feel better."

Purcell wondered about the definition of *largely imaginary* but thought better than to ask.

"Your contact," Cronk said, "will be our liaison officer, Staff Sergeant Lohman. You know Tim Lohman?"

Oh yeah. Everyone knew Tim Lohman. The fat fool who thought sober was an alternative lifestyle. Just the guy to back him up for a largely imaginary threat—a largely imaginary cop.

Purcell simply nodded.

Chapter 26

The marine cloud refused to burn off. By two in the afternoon, it hung above the hills like a gray flannel sheet. Tiny spits of rain dotted the windshield as Boomer slowed the truck and turned off the highway onto Crabbe-Levy Road.

"What did Dennison say," Davey asked, "about the letter?"

Boomer grunted. "Said thanks."

"That's it?"

"What's she supposed to say? I give her evidence that one of her cops is in bed with the bad guys, she's supposed to discuss it with good old Boomer? Maybe ask my advice?"

"Did you warn her to keep Cronk out of it?"

"Yeah right. Then she told me about deblistering fiberglass and vinylester skinning."

Davey shrugged off the sarcasm and tapped the tip of his cane against the truck's floorboards. The cane was a gift from Boomer, a handsome branch of twisted hazel wood with a brass handle done in the likeness of a seal. Touched as he was by the gesture, he couldn't find a niche in his self-image for hobbling about on a cane.

Boomer said, "Forget about it. It's in Dennison's hands now. It's her job. She's got ways and means. Let her deal with it."

"Cronk gives me the creeps."

"Here's a flash for you: cops are supposed to give drug runners the creeps."

"Ha-ha."

"Anyway, you got your own brand of problems."

"What's that supposed to mean?"

Boomer guided the truck into his driveway and came to a stop behind Cassie's white Suzuki Samurai. Davey's insides tightened up as if torqued with a wrench.

"I thought you took her up to her folks' place?" he said.

"I did." Boomer shrugged. "Said she wanted to clean the place up. And spend some time alone to get her head around what happened."

Davey stared at the little jeep, alarmed by unfamiliar feelings the way a wild thing is alarmed by strange scents. His alarm fluttered toward panic when Boomer shifted into reverse instead of turning off the engine.

"You're not leaving right away?" Davey said.

"Time to get back to work. Eddie's been pulling the load by himself for long enough."

"At least come say hi to her."

Boomer grinned. "Like I said, you got your own brand of problems. Go deal with them."

"You bastard, you set me up."

Boomer shook his head. "Swear to God, I didn't know she was here. Course, I ain't real surprised."

Davey looked up as Constable Kevin Purcell's gray Caprice rolled into the driveway. He looked back into the truck. "You'll be here Sunday?"

"I'll be here," Boomer said. "And you wait for me. Don't be going down there by yourself."

Davey hobbled up onto the veranda and limped around the house, coming to a halt as he stepped onto the seaward side. Cassie was sitting in one of the wicker chairs. She looked at him for an awkward second and then turned and gazed out at the bay. Davey started toward her.

"I wanted to stay away from you," she said, and Davey stopped. "When I thought you'd been killed . . . I went putrid inside. Everything in the center of me decayed into a pulpy rot. I never want to feel like that again."

Davey had no idea what to say. His mind, the part that formed thoughts and words, was a feverish blank. He stood looking at her, astonished by the physical impact generated by her presence. This was all new territory for him, an uncharted landscape of alien feelings, feelings with which he had no idea what to do.

"God damn you!" she hissed. Then she stood and rushed to him, folded herself around him.

He breathed in the scent of her hair and her warm flesh. She was the symptom and the cure, and he held her like his life depended on it. Pressure built behind his eyes.

He'd been a child crying over something childish when his father had told him that tears were precious, and the only shame was in handing them out too easy, like penny candy from a rich kid trying to buy a personality. So Davey struggled against the tears, but it was no contest. Even as they slipped from his eyes, though, their source remained a mystery to him. And he suspected that the mystery was part of the deal, that the territory was uncharted because it was unchartable. A dark exotic territory that everyone entered as if they were the first and blundered through in a constant state of being, more or less, lost. Cassie's head tilted back and their lips came together, and Davey thought that being lost was not a heavy price to pay.

An hour later, Davey was lying on the berth in *Small Wonder*'s aft cabin, gazing at the low ceiling. The length of Cassie was warm and smooth against his left side. Although the water was still, he could sense the boat's flotation. It was a sensation that nicely complemented the soft weightless afterglow of lovemaking. Yet his mind tumbled and churned, unable to shut itself off and enjoy the moment. It kept probing into the future. The near future when he would dive Gunner's Rock. Could Keith's sea chest possibly be there, or was he jamming together pieces that weren't meant to fit? And the further future when he might have to reexamine what the hell this Davey Jones guy was all about. He'd worked hard to develop the underachiever's contentment with being just this guy, but how long would a young woman on her way to a master's degree be happy with just this guy?

Come to that, why did he care? He'd never cared before. It'd never occurred to him to care what anyone thought of his education or his occupation. Was that part of being in love? He had nothing with which to compare it. No chart to follow.

He thought of Keith and Erin and he wondered if what he felt for Cassie would pass, like a virus. He was appalled that it might.

"Doesn't matter," she murmured.

Her head was cradled on his left shoulder. He peeked down. Her eyes were closed. Her cheeks moved as she smiled.

"You're fretting about something," she murmured. "I can feel it. Whatever it is, it doesn't matter. Not right now. Right now, all that matters is the way our bodies feel against each other."

Finding no compelling argument, Davey's mind shut up.

Afterward, they crowded together into the cramped shower stall. By the time they finished playing with the soap, the hot water had run out and they had to rinse under cold. They warmed each other with vigorous towelling, and then Davey laid face down on the berth while Cassie applied a fresh dressing to the sutured gash on his leg.

As she worked, she quietly admitted feeling guilty about leaving her parents. "I just couldn't stay. It was too depressing. They didn't even know who I was."

Davey couldn't rid his mind of the image of the breathing dead people chained to the wall of the shed in a pile of filthy hay. "What are the doctors saying?"

"You know doctors. Anything's possible, nothing's certain."

"If it's any consolation, I'm selfishly delighted you decided to come here."

Cassie slapped his butt. "It wasn't my first choice, wise guy. I got Boomer to drive me home. Up to the farm? Thought it would do me good to spend some time alone, lose myself in cleaning up the mess. When Boomer drove away? I realized it was a mistake. It wasn't home anymore. It was a nightmare place, all burned and broken."

She snugged the bandage. "Too tight?"

"Not for me."

"I started looking for Lord Greystoke. Like everything would be okay if I could just find my cat. Then I was crying, standing in the ruins crying like a lost little girl. I cried until I thought of you. No specific thoughts, just you. I got in my car and started driving. All the way here part of me insisted that it was a bad idea."

"Was it?" Davey's voice was muted by a tightness in his throat. "A bad idea?"

She gave him another slap. "All fixed better. We should get supper going."

Despite the clouds and the odd spit of rain, it was warm enough for them to dress in shorts and light T-shirts as they rowed the dinghy out to the mouth of the bay and fished the bottom for sole. An hour later, the galley was aromatic with fillet of sole poached in a lemon herb sauce and dressed with black beans and rice. There was a garden salad from Casper's produce section and a bottle of Chardonnay from his agency liquor store.

"This is good," Davey said. "This is really good."

"You've been saying that a lot." Cassie's head was bent slightly over her plate. A comb of abalone shell held her auburn hair off her face and guided it down over her right shoulder. Her liquid hazel eyes glinted at him. God, but she was lovely.

"Been a good day," he said.

With the tip of her tongue, she licked a drip of sauce off her fork. "And it's not even over yet."

"Be gentle, girl. I'm thirty-three, not twenty-three."

"But I'm twenty-three. Still seven years away from my sexual peak."

"Oh boy."

"Is that oh boy as in good, or oh boy as in oh no?"

"Maybe it's oh boy as in seven years is a long time."

Cassie bit her bottom lip and concentrated on corralling a forkful of rice. "Getting a wee bit ahead of myself, am I? Sorry," she said, clearly and deeply embarrassed.

"Look," Davey said, feeling dumb as a man, "I didn't mean that the way it sounded." But of course, he did. How else could he mean it? Seven years *was* a long time, long enough to be a commitment. Way too long for something as ephemeral as love to last.

"No, you're right," Cassie said. "They say that, except for brain cells, every cell in our body is renewed every seven years."

"Is that what they say?" Davey uttered.

"In a way, that makes seven years a lifetime," she said, dissecting the flaky white meat of the sole, chattering to hide her discomfort, Davey so much in love with her it could blow him to pieces. "Seven years ago," she said, "I was sixteen. Talk about a different lifetime. Adolescence is pretty compelling evidence in support of the theory that we, at some point, interbred with aliens."

Davey laughed. The sound of her voice was part of it, part of this thing that threatened to burst him at the seams, blow him to pieces without doing him the mercy of killing him. Part of it was the slender geometry of her fingers on the knife and fork, and the shy, almost furtive, way her mouth took the food and chewed, being dainty for his benefit. Part of it was the way her eyes skidded aside when she realized he was watching her and then returned to his, smiling, swallowing, covering her lips, clearing her throat, cocking her head, murmuring, "What?"

You could blow me to pieces, he thought, *and leave me scattered like dust in the cosmos.* He said, "If you don't care for avocado, I'll disemburden you."

"Back off," she said, threatening with her fork. "I'm saving it for last."

"Suppose we were suddenly drowned by a tsunami from an earthquake. The image of that uneaten avocado would haunt your ghost through eternity."

"No way. The paradise I'm going to has groves of avocado trees."

"Of course. Silly me."

"And my friends can come and pick from my groves anytime," she said to show him she harbored no hard feelings.

"Your turn," she said. "Where were you seven years ago?"

Davey scooped the last bits of pulp from his half of the avocado shell.

"Seven years ago, I was way past sixteen," he said. "Miles past sixteen. Sixteen was something I vaguely remembered hearing rumors about."

"You're belaboring," she said. "I'm neither that young nor you that old."

Davey licked the green fruit off his spoon. "Some people find it bland."

"I find it soothing," Cassie said, frowning at him. "A massage for the taste buds. What happened seven years ago that you don't want to talk about?"

"A massage for the taste buds. I like that." He emptied his wine glass and switched to scotch. "Massage for the brain," he said and drank up, avoiding her eyes the way she'd avoided his a minute ago.

"Davey—"

"Seven years ago," he blurted, the words like burrs in his throat, "my father died."

Cassie touched his arm. "I'm sorry."

"Got cancer and died. The son of a bitch."

"The son of a bitch? Sounds like maybe you two had histories left unresolved?"

Davey felt a little smile touch his lips. Cassie had a major in ECE, early childhood education, kiddie psych, where every child, no doubt, had a "history" with his parents.

"He was my hero. That simple and that corny. My hero. I wasn't prepared for the event of his mortality, the fact that he was a mere mortal."

"Well, there you go." She put a light touch in her voice but maintained contact with his arm. "It's a lapse in your classical education. Heroes always die. They die covered in glory, but they die. It's in their job description. Only the gods are immortal, and no one ever confused them with heroes."

Davey rounded up rice with his fork.

"Like Gunner," Cassie said. "Boomer told me that he saved your life. It doesn't get any more hero than that."

"Gunner died from being too close to an exploding boat," Davey said, spreading the rice into a sunburst shape on his plate. He'd lost his appetite. "He died because Keith and I gave him a fatal dose of trust in mankind. A wild seal wouldn't have let that boat get anywhere near him."

"Does it make you feel better blaming yourself?" Cassie didn't clarify whether she was talking about Gunner's death or the death of Davey's father.

"I don't think my feelings matter one way or the other. He's still dead."

"They matter to me. Your feelings. They matter a lot to me."

Davey looked at her. She was still touching his arm. He realized something, and it took him by surprise. Crept up and snuck a little smile onto his lips. "I'm glad," he said. "About the feelings. I'm glad they matter to you."

"You look surprised."

"Every minute with you is a surprise," he said and loved her for blushing.

He told her about that summer seven years ago. Told her that he'd been rocked by the death of his hero within days of Keith being blindsided by the death of his marriage. Told her how the two of them had drifted, flotsamlike, into Boomer's Bight. "Ever since high school, Boomer was the rock among us. Keith and I were always getting caught up in one current or another, but not Boomer. Currents break around Boomer."

Cassie listened with a gentle, quiet attention while Davey spoke of prodigious consumption of alcohol and pot, he and Keith lying busted as shipwrecks on Boomer's sturdy shore. It was early September before they'd sobered up long enough to found Gunner's Rock Maritime Salvage Society, D. Jones & K. Stoddard, Esqs., just days before Keith had had to return to his teaching position at the college. Without Keith's paycheck from the school district and, later, the cash infusion from transporting Frank's produce, the salvage business would have foundered before getting very far off the ways. But before that, there was Gunner's Rock itself and, before that, Gunner.

Evening cast its gloaming blanket over the water and tucked it in among the shoreline trees. *Small Wonder*'s cabin grew dim, but Davey was loath to burn a light. The deepening shadows were part of the mood, like the wine shimmering in Cassie's glass, the movement of ice as it melted in Davey's scotch, a comforting mood he didn't want to tamper with at the risk of damaging it. Being comfortable in conversation was a rarity for Davey, and he wanted it to last. With his fork, he absently toyed with his leftover black beans and rice, unconsciously separating Christians from Moors as if drawing up battle lines.

He told her how they used to swim out to the reef, he and Keith, almost daily. By noon, the reef was usually high and dry. Davey and Keith would climb onto the rock, strip off their wet suits, and lie there in the sun drinking beer they'd drag with them in a mesh bag.

What he didn't tell her was the way he and Keith could talk out there about stuff that guys can't always talk about. Stuff you're afraid of. Not stuff you pretend to fear, like heights and darkness and spiders, but the stuff you really fear. The stuff you solder closed in the morning and carry like a weight in the back of your head all day and hope to hell it doesn't open like a can of mealy worms when you close your eyes at night, but you know that sometimes it will, which only exacerbates the fear. The name of the fear is insecurity, and it has grave doubts that, at end of the day, you'll have been strong enough or brave enough or wise enough to do what had to be done.

Davey didn't tell Cassie any of that. It was stuff he and Keith could talk about on the rock because the rock, like a slate, got washed clean every day by the tide. It wasn't stuff you wanted hanging out there waiting to come back at you.

He told her about the seal that visited the rock, oddly unperturbed by the presence of humans. "Every time we swam out there, he'd come around to see what we were up to."

"You're sure it was always the same one, are you?" she asked.

"Had a scar on his left flank." Davey drew with his finger a large crescent on his left flank. "Looked like a close encounter with a killer whale. Bite-shaped pink pucker carved through his fur. We started taking food out for him—herring, cod, the odd salmon. Within a couple weeks, he was climbing up on the rock with us. By summer's end, he was pretty friendly. He'd play water tag with us, laughing at our clumsy swimming abilities."

"Laughing?" Cassie said.

Davey shrugged, smiling. "He'd bark at us while swimming circles around us. Wasn't hard to imagine he was laughing." It was a good memory, maybe a great memory. Didn't translate worth shit; memories never do. The essence of them is a private thing that lives inside the memory itself and dies a little bit if you take it out. Like the old adage says, you had to be there. But Cassie smiled anyway for him, if not with him.

"Did you name the seal after the rock," she asked, "or the rock after the seal?"

"Gunner the seal before Gunner the rock."

"Why Gunner?"

"Funny you should ask," Davey said. The scotch and the wine were getting along wonderfully, having a fine old time swimming through his head. "That's just what I was leading up to, in my shy quiet way."

She laughed. "I always imagined you were. Shy and quiet."

"I am. Don't expect this sort of sparkling conversation every evening."

"I won't," she said, her eyes a-twinkle. "In fact, I can think of all sorts of uses for evenings aside from conversation."

"Oh boy," Davey said and took a drink. He gently removed her hand from his thigh. "Pay attention. I'm going to tell you why we're going to dive Gunner's Rock on Sunday."

"We are?"

"Yes, we are. Boomer and I are. Of course, you're welcome to join us."

Now she was frowning. "What about your leg? I mean, what's the hurry? Shouldn't you let your leg heal before doing any diving?"

"Leg's fine. And the hurry is that Gunner's Rock is what Keith called Treasure Island. That's where the sea chest is, where the memory stick is, where, I believe, all manner of things are, things that answer all manner of questions, questions that our Royal Mounties might rather remain unanswered."

Cassie's frown was getting serious. Davey ploughed ahead before she could pepper him with objections.

"The day we named the seal, we got pretty drunk, Keith and Boomer and I. I mean, we tied one on, then tied another on top. Before that night was over, we'd shortened his name, *shortened* it to Gunner. We've called him Gunner ever since. I'd forgotten that we'd originally called him Ben Gunn."

Davey watched Cassie's face for a reaction. Nothing.

"Have you never read the book *Treasure Island?*"

She shook her head.

"And you consider yourself educated?" Davey rolled his eyes at the sad state of modern education. "In the story, Ben Gunn is the old marooned pirate who's been watching over the treasure."

"Thus, Keith put his chest out on that little drying reef and called it Treasure Island? You don't think that's a bit of reach, darling?"

Davey shook his head. "He tried to tell me. Keith did. On the boat. I thought he was babbling about getting shot in the chest with a gun. But I wasn't listening. I was too scared to listen. He was telling me that his sea chest was with Gunner."

Cassie's frown remained sceptical. "Let's be careful we're not projecting something we want over top of what really was."

"There's more," Davey said. "Keith liked to tell anyone who would listen that Shakespeare had gotten it wrong when he called the world a stage. On a stage, he said—Keith, not Shakespeare—he said if you blow it, you can go back and do it again, take it from the top. In the real world, if you blow it, it stays blown.

"That key," he said, "the key Keith sent to his ex-wife, opened a mailbox where Keith had left a message for Lily White. The message was for her to tell me that this one time I had to go back and take it from the bottom."

"The bottom?" she said.

"Have you ever been to the bottom of Gunner's Rock?"

Comprehension dawned in her eyes. "My god. The wolf eel that lives down there. Boomer calls it Willie. William Shakespeare. Keith put the chest in Willie's cave."

"How did you get so wise so young?" Davey said.

"I think I was Merlin in a past life," she said.

"How come no one was ever a peasant in a past life?" he asked.

"Really dahling," she said, "reincarnation for the masses? What an appalling notion."

"Silly me," he said, drawing her close till their lips nearly touch.

"Of course you are," she said into his mouth. "But lucky you, you now have the wisdom of Merlin at your beck and call."

"Lucky me," he breathed. He kissed her cheek, her ear, her neck.

"Oh boy," she murmured.

Chapter 27

*T*wo hundred kilometers to the northwest, the cloud cover was thicker. It hung close to the surface, socking in the logging town of Port McNeill. From the shore flats, grounded herons squawked about the weather. Foghorns moaned through the harbor like lamenting ghosts. A stone breakwater curved like a protective arm around the harbor. Scattered along its length, a handful of men in rain gear were casting through the drizzle with that single-minded determination common only in fishing and gambling addicts.

Cedric Flammond studied the scene from the window of his ground floor hotel room. The small hotel was perched on the hillside two blocks up from the waterfront. His window afforded a view of the approaches along Broughton Boulevard and Beach Drive. Brightly clothed tourists mingled with forestry workers in red suspenders and checkered shirts as they drifted among the shops and restaurants. Mallicheck's dark pinstripe suit stood out as sharply as his silver Mercedes, parked at the mall on the corner among pickup trucks and campers. Flammond watched the lawyer stride up the sidewalk toward the hotel. He shook his head and dropped the stained orange curtains across the window.

Mallicheck stepped gingerly into the dim room. Looked around with obvious distaste as he took in the frayed carpet, worn bedspread, and lumpy upholstery.

"Budget restraints?" he said, ostentatiously careful to allow nothing but the soles of his shoes to come in contact with the room.

"They take cash," Flammond said. "They don't require a guest card filled out or a credit card number left. They don't expect their guests to sign out. Did you bring what I asked for?"

Mallicheck reached under his coat.

Flammond said, "This is a logging town. Your suit stands out like a neon sign. People are going to remember you, wonder what the hell a guy in that outfit is doing at the local piss-tank hotel. Maybe you're not worried about being the center of attention, but my smiling face is likely on the bulletin board of every cop shop in the county."

"Don't flatter yourself," Mallicheck said, pulling a thick envelope from the folds of his overcoat. "Your freedom has less to do with your prowess than with their lack of interest. My apologies to your ego."

Flammond opened the envelope and riffled the wad of cash in it. From his shirt pocket, he took a folded piece of paper. "A shopping list," he said, handing it to the lawyer. "Have it together by tomorrow night."

Mallicheck unfolded the page and glanced at the list. "Can I buy these items without a scuba certificate?"

"Don't try to buy it all in one place. There must be dozens of dive shops on Vancouver Island. Pick up a little here, a little there. If anyone asks, you're buying gifts for your scuba-diving brother. You won't be able to get the tanks filled, but I'll deal with that when the time comes."

"You want it delivered to the Denton farm?"

"Tentatively, yes. But first you need to apply the screws to your source. I want information, not fairy tales."

"The source was not the problem," Mallicheck said testily. "The information was good. The problem was Sebastian, known to the police as source Joshua. That problem has been rectified."

"History doesn't interest me, lawyer. I'm talking about the security of the Denton farm. You need to find out why a vehicle that was there yesterday is gone today. That's right, lawyer. Someone was there and removed a vehicle. A white Suzuki Samurai. That's the license number on the bottom of the paper. Find out who it belongs to and what they were doing there. Is the crew assembled?" he asked.

Mallicheck nodded.

"Send the answer with Rockwell tonight. If I'm not happy with what I hear, I'll move shop."

"How will I know what makes you happy?"

"You'll know if I'm not. Unless you hear otherwise by this time tomorrow, send the rest of the people and the equipment. Are we clear on everything?"

Mallicheck nodded.

"I have an appointment," Flammond said. As he pulled on his jacket and picked up his packsack, he became aware that Mallicheck was watching him with his head canted and his eyebrow cocked. Flammond glared at him. "Something else?"

The lawyer said, "You really believe you can pull this off, don't you?"

"What I believe is none of your concern. I'm paid for results, not beliefs. And you can tell Lazuardi that my price increases with every pointless question his lawyer pesters me with."

On northern Vancouver Island, the forested slopes rise steeply from the ocean so that the towns have limited useful waterfront. The log-sort took up most of the useful waterfront in Port McNeill. A small marina was crammed into a corner beside the government ferry dock. Flammond went to the marina and boarded a thirty-foot Bayliner cabin cruiser. He'd acquired the Bayliner the previous night, quietly removing it from a boathouse near Willow Point after ascertaining that the owners were on vacation in Europe. While the engine warmed up, Flammond stowed his gear and spread a chart on the table. On the chart, he located the small cove on Malcolm Island where the Logger had assure him they could conduct their transaction in privacy.

Flammond had spent the best part of two days finding the Logger. Such people exist virtually everywhere, plying a brisk trade in various commodities, including firearms, without troubling the bureaucracy with a lot of paperwork. Finding them was a matter of asking appropriate questions of certain persons in venues designated by reputation. Flammond's inquiries had started with an overweight bleached-blonde prostitute and ended two days later with the man they called the Logger, an ex-forestry worker who'd been forced into a career change by the plight of the island marmot.

Flammond's request had been an easy one to fill even on short notice. Small arms, nothing exotic. Along with the spear guns he'd found at the Denton place that's all he'd need. He was in command now, and under his command, there'd be no rocket launchers, no random hailstorms of automatic weapons' fire. That happy horseshit had no use outside of the movies. Anyone who couldn't do the job without spraying ordnance all over hell's half acre had no business with a weapon in his hand.

"And that, lawyer, is what I believe," he muttered as he steered the boat through the mist.

Chapter 28

*I*nspector Brian Cronk stared out his office window. During the night, a stiff wind had risen from the northwest and swept the sky clear. Saturday had dawned bright and breezy over the city of Victoria. Whitecaps chased one another across the mouth of the harbor and flags and pennants snapped smartly against the blue sky. Cronk stared without seeing while he chewed his fingernail to the quick.

A stab of pain brought his mind back into the office. He frowned at his fingertip. A drop of blood oozed out between the nail and the flesh. He licked it.

He looked out at the squad room. The war room, they called it, here at drug interdiction, and yes, Mr. Jones, it *was* a war, bet your life it was. It had its own rules of engagement. Anyone who had a problem with that was welcome to stay with the traffic bureau.

Desks were starting to fill as the troops filtered in; warfare doesn't take Saturdays off. Of course, the likes of Jones wouldn't know about that. To Jones's sort, every day was a day off.

As he watched, Marcie Dennison walked through the far door. She was dressed down for the weekend, in jeans and an old beige blouse with fray at the collar. She carried it nicely. As she maneuverd between the desks, the detectives stopped what they were doing to watch her go by. But they couldn't see the scowl on her face. Cronk's eyes went from her face to the large brown envelope in her hand, and he muttered, "Shit."

When she entered his office, Cronk forced a smile. "To what do I owe—"

"Don't," said Dennison, cutting him off. She opened her mouth, closed it, and shook her head. She dropped the envelope on the desk, a manila envelope with a tie-down flap, and went to a table in the back corner upon which sat a coffee maker and half a dozen mugs.

"Lawrence Jenkins gave me that," she said. "You better read it."

She picked up a mug that said *Cops have bigger nightsticks* and peered suspiciously into it. She wiped the mug with a paper towel and poured coffee from the pot. The coffee smelled stale.

Cronk untied the flap and pulled from the envelope a clear plastic evidence bag. Inside the bag was a sheet of paper filled with block letter printing. Cronk lowered himself into his chair and read through the clear plastic.

Bad news, Lily girl . . . did a little digging . . . they know about us . . . only one way they got that information . . .

Cronk skimmed through the letter, but saw little of it after that line. His face grew hot. Unable to trust his voice, he said nothing. His mind had locked up, like so many crooks before him, unable to decide between fight or flight, between deny or deal.

"I'm sorry," said Dennison. She sipped coffee and made a face. "I know you personally handpicked the guys on your team. But it looks like Lazuardi handpicked one of them as well. I've got to file this. I thought you should hear it from me first rather than from the internal affairs commission."

Cronk's mind broke the lock of panic and resumed thinking. Stoddard must have found evidence on the computer disk to indicate that Lazuardi knew about the undercover operation. Stoddard had concluded that a cop had gone bad. He'd probably warned Jones about it. Now Dennison was making the same conclusion. Cronk could see no way to tell her otherwise without revealing the truth. If that's what it came down to, he'd do it, but he wanted time first. Time to evaluate the extent of his compromise and to examine his options.

He set the letter on his desk and steepled his fingers over it, as if placing it behind bars. "Can you leave this with me, Marcie, until I make some inquiries?"

"Come on, Brian. You know what you're asking?"

"I'm not asking for it to disappear. You know I wouldn't do that. Just give me a chance to work it out. Once the commission gets this, they'll gut my team like a slaughtered cow. I got a staff sergeant who drinks on the job. I got a detective who likes dirty movies. I got a constable who grows a pot plant in his kitchen window." Not to mention an inspector who accepts cash payments from a disguised voice that calls itself Joshua, let's not forget that. But let's not mention it, either, not just yet.

"A pot plant," she said, "in his kitchen window?" She looked around the office. "Sorry, I must have the wrong place. I was looking for drug interdiction."

"Come on, Marcie. One pot plant isn't even illegal these days. And he's a good cop. They're all good cops. But they're human beings, not robots. A distinction the commission hates to admit."

Dennison pointed to the letter. "One of them sold out, Brian. They're not all good cops." She loaded sugar into her coffee, stirred, took another sip, made a face, emptied the mug into a potted philodendron.

"Okay," she said. "My clerk's off for the weekend. Be a pain in the ass to file it. So I'll leave it here for safekeeping until Monday morning."

"Thanks, Marcie. I owe you."

"Big time," she said. "And I'll need a written receipt for it."

After she left, Cronk read through the letter again. Must've been quite the trick, Stoddard getting into Lazuardi's flash drive. The thing would be littered with roadblocks. Stoddard must have gone in the night to the computer lab at the North Island College; being an instructor, he'd have easy enough access. He'd have thought himself quite clever when he'd broken the code, or codes, as the case may be. Bet your life he would. Proud as the ocean is deep. How long did that last? Cronk wondered. How far had he gotten, how much had he read, before he realized that Lazuardi knew as much about the undercover operation as he did?

We are on the stick, Lily. They know about us.

Had he broken a cold sweat? Had his mouth turned to sand? Had he dribbled in his pants?

Had he warned Officer White, or had he merely sent secret letters and cryptic recordings from a hidey-hole where he'd cowered with his tail between his legs?

There's only one way they got that information.

From a cop on Lazuardi's payroll? You sure that's where they got it, Stoddard? Know that for a fact, do you? Got a name to back it up? Inspector Brian Cronk, drug interdiction, that the name you got? Got any evidence at all? Or are we just jerking off on the wall here?

Get in touch with Davey Jones.

Trust Jones to the ends of the earth do you, Stoddard? Got your honor among thieves going on there, do you? How nice for you. How nice for Jones should he choose to start a little side action. How much of the operation did you tell Jones about while you were trusting him to the ends of the earth? Tell him that your girlfriend was an undercover cop, did you? Tell him that you and she were a couple super spies, did you, putting big bad Lazuardi in the bag?

Cronk crumpled the letter, plastic bag and all, and dropped it in the trash can beside his desk. He got up and went to the window, gazed out through the mouth of the harbor, out to the whitecaps galloping across the open ocean, from right to left at the moment, but the wind could change as quickly as a politician's mind.

He retrieved the letter from the trash can, laid it on his desk, and pressed it with his hands. The plastic bag had kept it from getting too wrinkled, but when Dennison saw it on Monday, she'd know he'd crumpled it up. Course, by then she'd know a hell of a lot more than that unless Cronk could come up with some hocus-pocus.

Davey Jones was not the leak no matter how badly Cronk wanted him to be, which was quite a bit. It got under his skin like a rash that a punk like Jones was going to walk away from this scot-free, but that seemed to be the current direction of the prevailing political wind. Cronk couldn't remember the last time anyone had done time for pot. Fine by him. Legalize the crap if that's the way you want it. Just don't let the punks thumb their noses at the law as they walk on by.

Cronk waved as if chasing an annoying insect. Forget Jones. He had bigger worries than Jones. Not many, but enough. For instance, Joshua.

It was unlikely that Joshua had put Brian Cronk's name on the memory stick. If Stoddard had found a name he would have shouted it from the rooftops. No, a name would have been too blatant, too crude, too much like a setup. Instead, he would have scattered around a few hints, something about the payments, just enough to get internal affairs commission interested, get their scent up, then let the nature of the beast take its course.

If that was the case, Cronk had some wiggle room. Joshua was counting on there being a trail for the commission to follow. There'd be no trail; Cronk hadn't spent a dollar of the money. In the neighborhood of three hundred and fifty thousand, he guessed, although he'd never counted it. He'd had no clear idea what he'd do with it in the end. An anonymous donation to drug rehab maybe. He'd kept it unreported for one reason only—the certainty that if he ever reported it, the phone calls would stop. The phone calls from the disguised voice that called itself Joshua. *"Like the trumpet dude who brought down the walls of Jericho. Ha ha ha."*

Certainly, Joshua was one of Lazuardi's people. Judging by the information he supplied, he was among Lazuardi's inner circle. Selling his boss down the river in the spirit of free enterprise. And while he's at it, why not get a choke chain on the head of drug interdiction. A choke chain forged link by link with packets of money. Joshua making sure he'd have a well-heeled inspector when he took over his boss's business, thinking himself clever. Cronk thinking himself more clever, cocky about being able to beat Joshua at his own game. Confident that when the time came, he could shake off the choke chain and turn on its maker.

"Wasn't even playing the same bloody game," Cronk muttered and threw the letter aside in disgust. "Son of a bitch *never* planned to control me. Planned to *bury* me. We'll see about that."

As long as Cronk's name wasn't on the memory stick, the only evidence was the money itself. Paper money. Smoke and ashes.

Against the unlikely event that his name *was* on the memory stick, he'd do every considerable thing in his power to ensure that he read it before anyone else did. Especially Jones.

Chapter 29

$\mathcal{B}$oomer's Bight faced east so the stiff westerly breeze didn't get into it. Out in the strait whitecaps leaped at each other and smashed themselves to bits on the headland, but the water in the bay was flat except where roving zephyrs made ripples that sparkled here and there like scattered handfuls of gems. The air was still and bright and almost too hot.

Davey was lying on a blanket on one of the pockets of sand that nestled between outcrops of rock on the shore. He was on his back, propped on his elbows. He wore sunglasses, comfortably tattered khaki shorts, and the bandage on his leg. His right hand held a tin of beer in an insulated sleeve. His left hand was close enough to feel the heat from Cassie's body.

She was lying on her stomach, head cradled on her arms, breathing the soft peaceful breath of sleep. Her tanned flesh glistened with sunblock between the bikini bits. The bits were yellow with green vines growing around them and pink flowers blossoming at interesting locations. Beside her on the blanket was a book—a dark green hardcover, ragged on the edges, spotted and warped with age. She'd borrowed it from Boomer's library. It was Robert Louis Stevenson's *Treasure Island*.

"God, it's hot," said Kevin Purcell. He opened the icebox a few feet to Davey's right, took out a bottle of water, and drank deeply.

"Muggy," said Davey. "Need a rainstorm to clear the air."

Purcell was wearing white sneakers under blue jeans under a white T-shirt all sweaty around the shoulder harness that held his 9 mm service automatic. Davey didn't invite the constable to relax his dress code; Purcell was old enough to dress himself. He wanted to wear a parka and mukluks, go for it. Besides, the cop's comfort was not on Davey's list of concerns.

"Long as there's no lightning," said Kevin. "Be wildfires from here to the Rockies."

"In the grand scheme of things, they say, wildfires do more good than harm."

"Oh yeah? Who says that?"

"You changing the subject?"

"What subject? Thought we were talking about the weather."

Davey gave him a look, wasted behind the sunglasses. "You were talking about the weather. I was wondering how you guys knew about Lazuardi's computer stick in the first place."

Purcell lit a cigarette, and Davey's napping addiction woke up and took a good sniff of tobacco smoke. His last cigarette had been when he was taunting Norm and Twitch, four or five days ago, but he wasn't fooling himself that he'd quit. Davey's father had gone smokeless for nearly ten years, but on his deathbed, the last thing he'd asked for was a cigarette.

"We're detectives," said Purcell. "We detect." He swallowed more water, capped the bottle, and dropped it back in the icebox. "Detection," he said, "is defined as the cultivation of snitches. They grow well in the dark. Call them informants, toss them the odd twenty so they can pretend it's their job."

"That how you found out about the computer stick? Someone close enough to this Lazuardi guy to know about his stick, you met him in a dark alley and gave him twenty bucks?"

"The 'odd twenty' was a manner of speaking. Twenty bucks, twenty thousand, twenty years. Everyone's got their price."

"I bet they do," Davey said. Right about then, his price was a cigarette or even a drag off a cigarette. In smokeless distress, he almost asked what the going rate for an inspector was. Instead, he said, "So Keith and his girlfriend, Lily, get invited aboard Lazuardi's yacht and manage to snatch this fabled memory stick. Keith takes it to the computer lab at the college to make a copy and instead finds something that scares him to death. Why did you ask him to copy it? Why couldn't he just hand the fucking thing over?"

"Had to make sure we had the goods," Purcell said. "Would've looked pretty foolish if we'd grabbed a file full of legitimate stock options or something. From Lazuardi's reaction, it seems we got the right one. But according to your statement, we may never know for sure."

Davey sat up, leaned forward to draw circles with his finger in the sand off the edge of the blanket. His first impression of Kevin Purcell had been the kid he'd met on the ferry, the young backpacker from New Zealand, slightly lost and completely busted. Even if that man was as phony as a Hollywood cowboy, Davey still thought of him as the real Kevin. The phony guy seemed to be this cop sitting next to him, cigarette smoke in his face, draped in a holstered gun despite the heat, glaring back at the glare, too tough to wear sunglasses, working on his leathery squint. Even with the squint, Purcell's eyes lacked the predacious intensity of Cronk's. Somehow, Davey found this more unsettling rather than less. He got defensive.

"After it all went wrong, your operation lay in smoking ruins, never occurred to you guys to talk to me? No one ever said, let's tell Jones what's going on? More fun to sneak around behind me, peek in my windows?"

"C'mon, Davey, naive doesn't fit you, worth shit. You must know what it looked like to us. Operation blown to hell, Frank's place burning, *Small Wonder* sails into the sunset without a scratch. You don't think you guys looked good for a double-cross?"

"Without a scratch?" Davey said, anger hot in his head, Keith dying again in his arms, blowing bloody bubbles in a doomed effort to draw air into the shredded remains of his lungs. "Without a scratch? You want to run that by Keith? He'll be glad to know we sailed off without a scratch."

Purcell shrugged. "We didn't know about Keith. Not till you contacted Counselor Dennison. And you told her no cops. Seemed to us, if you were little Mr. Innocent caught in the middle, you'd have wanted the cops, you'd have begged for the cops."

Unless, Davey thought, Keith opened that flash drive and found a rotten cop, a whole fucking barrel of rotten cops. After all, everyone has their price, don't they? Aloud, he said, "You continued to think I worked for Lazuardi after you found me strapped to a chair getting holes poked in me with a cigar by a nightmare named the Monk?"

Purcell made a snorting noise that was supposed to be a laugh. "Lazuardi didn't sick the Monk just on good guys. He'd do that if you'd got greedy and tried to hold out on him." His excuse was no more convincing than his snorted laugh. He crushed his cigarette into the sand, maybe trying to crush the image of the glowing tip of the Monk's cigar. "Didn't help," he continued, "when you went tearing off to Toronto. When this comes to trial, you know, they'll ask you about that on the witness stand, under oath, how come you went tearing off to Toronto. You stick to 'unrelated personal matter,' the jury's liable to put you in Lazuardi's boat before they sink it."

Davey looked at Purcell, glad that the dark glasses hid his eyes. Apparently, the cop who'd followed him had missed the quick exchange between himself and Erin. But sooner or later, the police would talk to Erin to inform her of Keith's death if nothing else. When they did, they'd learn about the key, the letter, the works. But until they learned it from her, they wouldn't get it from him. He needed time, time to find

Keith's sea chest. Because something in that chest had passed a death sentence on Keith.

"What about the report," Davey said, "from the cop who followed me?"

"No joy there, Buds. We had a tap on the phone in Boomer's Boatworks. We knew you'd booked not only to Toronto but back again, so you weren't running."

Davey blushed, glad for his dark tan, and looked away. They'd had the phone tapped. They knew about Erin and the mailbox key all along. Why had they let him lie about it?

"We faxed your picture to Toronto Metro," Purcell was saying, "and asked them to keep an eye on you. By the time they got a man with your picture to the airport, you were sitting in a coffee shop eating blueberry pie."

Two phone lines. He'd used the phone on the reception desk to book the flights. That phone had connections to the shop, the dock, and Boomer's office. But in Boomer's office, there was also a private line. He'd talked to Erin on Boomer's private line, which had apparently escaped the wiretap.

"There was no need to follow you," Purcell said. "Besides, we had our plate full right here."

Fifty meters down the beach, the unsightly sculpture of the broken helicopters lay with jagged bones sticking out at awkward angles, like a spoiled kid's abandoned toys. A fluorescent orange oil-containment boom had been strung around it to contain the pollutants while the government debated who should clean it up. The government would debate for three months before Boomer called a scrap dealer who brought in a crane barge and cleaned up the mess in three hours. But that Saturday in August, it was still offending the air with its punky odor of spilled lubricants and sheared metal. Seagulls flitted around it, squawking as if disgruntled that nothing had died for them to eat.

"Amazing they didn't all get killed," said Purcell, as if sympathizing with the seagulls.

And it was amazing. Even Lazuardi's pilot, down in the bottom of it, had sustained only a concussion and a sprained wrist.

"Bill Tsimka is licensed for fixed-wing only," Purcell continued. "Friend of his got a little two-seater chopper he's gone up and played with a few times. That's the extent of his training."

"Going to charge him?" Davey said. "Reckless endangerment?"

"No need to get pissy. Just making conversation."

Davey recalled the staggering flight path of the helicopter and imagined Billy wrestling with the unfamiliar controls. He recalled the two helicopters coming together, the sight of it as loud as the noise, the two machines stacked for a moment like breeding insects, and then slowly toppling, as ineluctably as a felled tree. Trained by the movies, he'd expected the crash to end in a spectacular explosion, but of course, outside Hollywood, most vehicles are specifically designed not to explode on impact. Did Billy know that? Had he counted on that and purposely crashed the helicopters, or had he simply lost control? Only Billy knew for sure, and it was his story to tell any way he wanted.

But that morning had been full of surprises for Davey. Not the least of which had been seeing Kevin, who Davey had still thought was a Kiwi kid on a poor man's vacation, a kid he'd grown fond of, consorting with Lazuardi's soldiers.

"How did you do it?" he asked.

Purcell didn't answer. Davey looked at him. The cop was staring vacantly out at the water.

"Your boss," Davey said, "the good inspector, told me it was virtually impossible to penetrate Lazuardi's organization. That without Keith and Frank to open the back door, you'd never have gotten in. Yet there you were."

"That's what our plate was full of the day you went to Toronto," Purcell said, apparently speaking to the ocean at large.

"So it took you one whole day to do the virtually impossible. Is that a Mountie thing or what? How does that work?"

Purcell squinted. "It was a wee bit hairy." No, Davey realized, it wasn't a squint; it was a grin, as if being a wee bit hairy was just fine with Constable Kevin Purcell. "A matter of crashing through the front door, then talking real fast to convince Lazuardi that I was too valuable to kill."

Davey cleared his throat, but when he spoke, the blockage still seemed to be there. "So you told him that Keith Stoddard was dead, that his goons were chasing Davey Jones, a sad sack who didn't know which end was up?"

Purcell didn't answer. Didn't have to. Davey knew that wasn't all of it. A little ball of ice formed in the pit of his stomach.

"And you gave them Boomer's place? Brought them here? Gave them Boomer and Linda?"

Again, no answer. But it wasn't finished yet. The ball of ice expanded through Davey's guts. Despite the hot sun, a chill prickled his shoulders.

"Not Cassie," he whispered.

Purcell glanced down at her. She appeared to be sleeping. To his credit, Purcell looked and sounded ashamed of himself. "We planted some information," he said softly, "with an aunt of hers. Information regarding her parents. We figured that would draw her."

"Then you told Lazuardi where he could find her? You asshole. You total asshole."

"You son of a bitch!" Cassie hissed. She exploded up off the blanket. "You fucking son of a bitch!"

Purcell turned away. When he looked back, he was blushing furiously, but he held his head up and spoke to her eyes. "I'm sorry we put you through that, but it was the only way. If I hadn't penetrated Lazuardi's crew, you two, along with Boomer and Linda, would have been on your own that morning with Lazuardi and his little army, and believe me, you would not have lived. And don't forget, those people went after you because of your father's occupation and your boyfriend's, not because of mine."

Cassie's breath was rapid and shallow, her body so tight it trembled. Davey stood up. He was alarmed by the force of her rage and uncomfortably aware that Purcell had hit close to the mark, that maybe Cassie was directing her anger at the wrong man.

Her eyes were pools of tears, her face contorted with the effort to hold them back. He held his arms out, stepped toward her. As soon as he touched her, her head collapsed against his chest.

"They raped me," she gasped. "Oh god, I'm sorry," she sobbed. "I couldn't . . . They . . . they raped . . ."

A cold fist squeezed around Davey's heart, making him numb and dizzy. He felt inept, unworthy. Powerless to reverse it, to make it not have happened, he felt he'd failed her, and he almost turned away in shame. But part of him understood that if he turned away, Cassie would think he was ashamed of her. So he stood trembling in his impotence and held her as she cried on his chest.

Chapter 30

Inspector Cronk left Victoria and drove north up the Saanich Peninsula. Just past the airport, he turned off the highway and entered Sidney, heading east toward the waterfront. Sidney was known for its high-end yacht basin, where the idle rich played boats, yet the town itself, with a perverse sort of snobbery, seemed to sit back from all the floating wealth and vacillate between quaintness and grubbiness. Along with cobbled lanes and wrought-iron lampposts were shops that looked like they'd been designed by the guy who did concrete bunkers, complete with battle dust, and display windows that seemed a bit too dark, like if you didn't know what was on display, then maybe it was none of your damn business. Cronk realized that his perception of Sidney was colored by the fact that it was home to Sonya, his ex-wife, but that still didn't excuse the place.

He turned his forest-green Buick down a quiet side street lined either side with cookie-cutter bungalows on postage-stamp lots. The houses were built in the 1950s, when they used stucco with bits of colored glass in it. The street dead-ended at a small park carpeted with patchy brown grass and littered with a few malnourished oak and spruce trees. The park was on a bluff looking out over Haro Strait. Cronk had spent more than a few nights in that park, watching to see with whom Sonya came home. But that was years ago, back when he'd still cared. He pulled into her driveway, the last one on the right, and turned off the engine.

He wasn't worried about the neighbors; they knew he used her garage for storage space and were used to him dropping in now and again. Nor was he worried about Sonja showing up; she made it a point to let him know when she was off on one of her "jaunts." London, he thought it was, this time. He went to the side door of the garage, sorting out the right key on his ring. His cell phone buzzed.

"Cronk here," he said to the phone as he opened the garage door.

"It's Staff Sergeant Lohman," said the phone.

The garage was dim. The windows were unwashed and largely blocked by stacked boxes. The air was cool, chilling the sweat on Cronk's shirt. He hit the light switch, and four naked bulbs sprang to life.

"What's up, Tim?" Cronk asked as he pulled a stepladder out of the corner and opened it beneath a steamer trunk perched in the rafters. "We get a green light from Kevin?"

The trunk was full of crap going all the way back to his school years. All kinds of crap Sonya hadn't let him throw out, insisting that he'd regret it. When he'd argued that he had no room for it in his bachelor suite she'd taken it on, adding his possible regret to the collection of other people's burdens she displayed on shelves in her mind in a room, Cronk was sure, kept bright and airy, unlike the dingy garage, where the trunk had lurked for years in the rafters as if waiting for Joshua's money.

"There's a message from him," Lohman was saying. "But I don't think it's the one you want. He requested that he be relieved from his assignment. Said a personal situation had developed that might interfere with the pursuit of his duty."

As Cronk listened to Lohman, he climbed the ladder, pulled the trunk between two rafters, and eased it down onto the top of the ladder. He was sliding it down the slope of the ladder when the phone slipped from his shoulder and clattered to the floor.

"Brian?" Lohman said to the floor. "How do you want to handle this?"

Cronk picked up the phone and stood over the trunk, frowning. *Personal situation?* What the hell, was he banging the Denton girl or something? God *damn* it.

"Look, Tim, I got a shitload of loose ends to tie together here in Victoria. I can't be running all over the island solving members' personal problems. Hop over there, will you, and hold his hand for him. Find out what his beef is. If it's legitimate, I'll arrange for relief. But I don't want our back turned on Jones, not for five minutes. You might remind Constable Purcell that he's a cop, not a social worker, and that Jones is a drug dealer."

Cronk pocketed the phone and opened the trunk, releasing the musty smell of old things. He started pulling out crap: school annuals, shoe boxes full of photos of strangers he'd once known, newspaper clippings of things accomplished by the stranger he'd once been, trophies of forgotten achievements. There was a University of Manitoba Bisons jacket worn by some kid named Brian. A Brandon Wheat Kings hockey puck that had scored a winning goal in some ancient, pointless contest. Crap. The only thing in the trunk that mattered was the money nestled under the false bottom, the evidence that would put him away, end his career in disgrace. Money to burn, and it was time to start the fire, burn the shit before it burned him.

He lifted the false bottom from the trunk and stood staring, unable to breathe. The space was empty; the money was gone. One lonely envelope looked up at him from the floor of the trunk.

He closed his eyes and forced air through his nose until the panic constricted into a pulsing heat in his temples. Could his ex have had at it? Sonya had had no curious interest in the trunk. To her, the trunk had merely been something of Cronk's over which she could feel a sense of control. Something for which someday Cronk would have to thank her. *So glad you kept all this* crap, *Sonya. To think, I was gonna shit-can the lot of it.*

But maybe he'd underestimated her. Who else would have access to the trunk?

Panic gave way to perplexity. If Sonja had taken the money, what the hell had she done with it? She was self-centered and overbearing, but she wasn't stupid. She wouldn't have stuffed it into a suitcase and put it on the plane to London. If she'd even gone to London. If she'd even kept the money. Her greed for sympathy was at least as strong as her material greed. She would find it very tempting to turn the money in and report him. *I knew the poor man was troubled of course, but I never* dreamed *he'd do anything like this.*

He bent to repack the trunk. He took out the empty envelope. As he crumpled it into a ball, he realized it wasn't empty. He opened it, pulled out a folded sheet of paper and a fifty-dollar bill. There was writing on the the bill. Printing actually. Block letter printing. HI BRIAN, it said, IF YOUR LITTLE GAME GETS ME KILLED I'LL SEE YOU IN HELL YOU BASTARD. KS.

Keith Stoddard. The bloody hell did you get onto this? Even if the money was mentioned on the memory stick, how did you know about the trunk in the rafters in the ex-wife's garage? Think yourself Sam bloody Spade, detective at large? You don't know shit, Stoddard. Never did, never will. All you had to do was make a copy of a fucking flash drive and hand it over. That's it. If you'd done that, everyone's at home right now having tea and crumpets. But oh no, not Keith Sam Spade Stoddard. Got to dig up a bit of shit here, a bit there, jump to conclusions like a cricket in a grass fire . . .

Cronk unfolded the sheet of paper. It was a computer printout. The sheet was divided into six sections, six photographs. Each one featured a naked Staff Sergeant Tim Lohman. Way more of Tim Lohman than anyone should ever have to see. But Timmy wasn't alone, was he? Oh no. Timmy had a couple of playmates. They also were naked. Looked to be about twelve years old.

In a small office in a back corner of the Campbell River RCMP station, Staff Sergeant Lohman hung up the phone. He stared out the window at the scenic view of the impound yard, where scarred, dusty, sun-baked vehicles, impounded for one reason or another, were lined up against a chipped, aging brick fence, like a used-car lot in some Hebron back alley.

"What do you think, Jackie?" he asked his friend, the only friend he could count on in recent months. His friend was sitting on the desk. The desk was small, metal, the brownish-gray color of all government furniture, as if they used the leftover paint from the naval yards. There was a matching file cabinet in the corner. The walls were slightly darker, a shade, Lohman suspected, designed specifically to camouflage dirt. As a liaison officer for drug interdiction, Lohman had been in Mountie stations across the country, but always in an office just like this, buried in the bowels of the station, near the rectum. Maybe there was just the one office and they moved it from station to station.

"What do you think?" he said. "Our inspector wants us to hop over there and hold our young constable's hand."

He gazed at the bottle of whiskey he was talking to, his friend from Tennessee, the good old boy, Jack Daniels. "But that won't do, will it, Jackie? No, I'm afraid that just won't do."

Lohman was a large man of the type engaged in a lifelong battle against overweight, a battle he'd recently lost interest in. He was among that jolly breed of fat men, pure sunny-side up. Ask anyone. Except his ex-wife. And maybe two or three others who'd gotten close enough to see behind the florid, cherubic mask that made him a shoo-in for Santa at the Christmas parties.

Aside from making him perfect for Santa, his weight and his ruddy face also marked him as a candidate for an early heart attack, something he was, no doubt, asking his friend, Jack Daniels, to help him along with. Had he been of a different disposition, he might have simply used his service pistol. But Lohman could no more blow his brains out than could Santa Claus.

He poured an inch of whiskey into a well-used glass and tossed it down his throat. Comfortably numb. That was the ticket. Let Jackie Daniels keep him in a state of numb comfort until his heart muscle blew itself to pieces. Then Lazuardi could take his filthy pictures and shove them up his filthy asshole.

If only it was *just* the pictures. Lord knew, the pictures were bad enough: Pornographic mementos of a night in paradise, cavorting with two—count 'em, two—juvenile prostitutes. It would've meant a disgraceful end to his career, but he could have lived with that. At least, in hindsight and with a little help from Jack Daniels, he *told* himself he could have lived with it. Except, it wasn't just the pictures.

By the time that bastard, Lazuardi, had shown him the pictures, the girls' brutally beaten bodies had been found. It mattered little that Lohman hadn't physically harmed the girls—at least, through a drink-blurred memory he didn't think he had. Forensics had come up with a clear DNA print from seminal fluid taken from the bodies, and Tim Lohman had no doubt whatsoever that the donor of that seminal fluid was Tim Lohman.

Lohman picked up the phone and dialled Purcell's cellular number. He explained to the constable that the inspector had more pressing concerns than the constable's personal problems and that the constable was a professional police officer and the inspector expected him to conduct himself as such, including putting aside his personal problems and concentrating on the job at hand. "Sorry, Kevin," he said.

"Yeah well, I don't guess I was expecting anything different. Thanks for trying, Tim."

Lohman hung up and poured another drink. "Believe it or not," he told the bottle, "I was like that once. A young cop full of piss and vinegar, champing at the bit to tear a strip off the bad guys and make the world a better place." The bottle didn't doubt him.

He dumped the bourbon down his throat and explained to the empty glass how it got confusing. "You see it all the time—the bad guys got you by the balls because you have to play by the rules and they don't. You try to level out the playing field. Bend a rule here, tweak one there. You don't see it coming, you just wake up one day and it's all fucked up."

Lohman didn't see any relationship between that and using the uniform as a bartering tool. At least, he didn't want to see it. Free meals, the odd bottle, young hookers—all these things were your due, all owed to you because you were out there, part of the thin blue line between civilization and savagery. That's the way he told himself he saw it, and he'd never found it difficult to lie, even to himself, and Jack Daniels didn't raise a lot of bothersome questions.

He would play it out to the end, pretending that he could save himself—pretend that it could work out if he got his hands on that memory stick before Purcell gave it to Cronk. Another lie, maybe, but it was far too late to do anything else.

"I just hope I don't have to kill him," he said, which at least was not a lie.

Chapter 31

*L*ohman staggered into Cronk's office, huffing and puffing, dishevelled and reeking of whiskey. He held a large brown envelope clutched to his chest two-handed, like a life preserver. Cronk had found the two girls, Lohman's photo partners, among the unsolved murder files. More pictures: the butchered young bodies in a dumpster in a Nanaimo alley. He was sure Lohman had nothing to do with the killings, but the fat fool had waddled happily into Lazuardi's trap, delivered by a dick he likely couldn't see over the rim of his gut. Cronk should have been disgusted, repulsed, revolted. Instead, he was afraid. It was the hollow fear of a driver on the highway who touches the brake and turns the wheel and finds that neither one of them work.

Cronk heard himself droning on about how he'd let it go this time, but woe betide Lohman if anything like this ever happened again. Lohman untied the flap on the envelope and upended it. An avalanche of fifty-dollar bills cascaded over the desk. Each bill was covered in block letter printing in blood red: hi Brian if your little game gets me killed i'll bring down the walls of Jericho to see you in hell.

"Hello? Excuse me? Inspector?"

The dream of Staff Sergeant Lohman and his fifty-dollar bills ran like weak paint off the walls of Cronk's mind. He blinked his eyes open into the hospital waiting room, plastic bright. His neck was cricked painfully to starboard and his right shoe was full of pins and needles.

"Inspector? Uh, Dr. Hastings left word that you wanted to interview Ms. White? She's coherent now, but we may have to sedate her again. If you want to talk to her, now's the time."

Cronk's eyes were puffy, gritty with kernels of sleep. He saw a white lab coat topped by a ridiculously young face. He looked at the name tag.

"That's *Officer* White to you, Dr. Simpson," he said, forcing the sibilants through the sleep sludge that coated his mouth.

"Right. Officer White. Anyway . . ." Simpson shrugged, raised a clipboard. *I've got things to do, pops.*

Plucking sleep from his eyes, Cronk watched the doctor walk away. If Simpson had been through med school, he must have started when he was twelve. Arrogant pup. Hadn't earned his degree in humility yet. Needed a few people to die on his shift.

"And a very good morning to you too," he muttered to himself, wiggling his right foot in an effort to relieve the paresthesia.

He peeked at his watch. It was nearly eight, Sunday morning. Thirty years ago, he'd be getting ready for church, looking forward to the routine, if not the sermon: He and his brother, with that pubescent determination to turn everything into a game, arguing over the proper way to knot a neck tie; Mom agonizing over her array of hats; Dad sequestered behind the Sunday paper with his own conditional brand of agnosticism . . .

The bloody hell had that come from, the memory so vivid it carried through the decades the smell of polished oak pews and the feel of sunlight taunting him though tall painted windows while the sermon flowed around him dull as porridge?

The answer lurked close by but Cronk ignored it. The answer was pointless or, worse, encumbering. The sort of answer that would zip around in his mind like a computer virus, opening circuitry that needed to stay closed—the insidious circuitry of remorse. He couldn't afford remorse just now. He'd forsaken its currency when he'd accepted the first envelope of Joshua's cash.

He pushed himself off the blood-colored vinyl chair. In his jacket pocket, his hand made a fist around the fifty-dollar bill and the page of dirty pictures.

From his ex-wife's garage, he'd gone back to Victoria, to his office. He'd needed to know how badly Lohman had been compromised, how badly and for how long. On the scanner, he'd cropped the photos to get facial shots of the two girls, then he'd contacted vice. Vice had come up empty; the girls were either new in town or new in the business. Brought in and taken out, Cronk suspected, for one job only. Then another thought had occurred to him, a grim thought. Its very grimness made it real, gave it substance. The photographs of Lohman and the girls were bad, but not that bad. If Lazuardi really wanted Lohman by the balls, he'd want something more damaging than pictures of Lohman prancing with a couple of hookers.

It'd been nearly midnight by then, and Cronk had needed to do some noisy rattling of chains. Fortunately, in the RCMP hierarchy, drug interdiction was currently considered sexy enough to have clout. By 0100 hours, he had a pissed-off but obedient detective at major crimes to help him access unsolved murder files. By 0140, they'd found the girls, both named Jane Doe. Eight weeks earlier, they'd turned up in a Nanaimo dumpster. The detective thought it odd that although they'd been beaten to death, their faces were virtually untouched. Cronk didn't think it odd at all. Lazuardi would've wanted them to be readily recognized.

So Lohman had been Lazuardi's man for two months, essentially the entire life of Operation Download. Lohman had known every detail of the operation; so too had Lazuardi. At least, every detail that drug interdiction had known. No one had known that Stoddard would go rogue, get Jones wound up, get himself killed, and leave Jones to clatter around in circles, knocking things over.

And where was Joshua while all this was happening? What had happened to Cronk's golden source? Had he got scared and gone to ground? Or had he got caught and gone into the sea? And how much of the whole sordid mess was on that computer file? Enough to lead Keith Stoddard to the money in Sonja's garage. Enough to make cellmates of Tim Lohman and Brian Cronk.

He'd come straight to the hospital from major crimes. If anyone, aside from Jones, knew where the memory stick was hidden, it would be Constable Laura White, a.k.a. Lily White, exotic dancer.

When he entered her ward, her bruised face managed half a smile. "Hi, boss," she mumbled through the right side of her jaw. Her hair was jet-black, shoulder length. A nurse or someone had brushed it down to her left, arranged it to hide most of the nastiness on the left side of her face.

"Good morning." Cronk tried a smile of his own, but it felt brittle. "They looking after you?"

"Yeah. You know."

Her bed was flanked by flower arrangements. There were cards from family, friends, the force. A small bouquet, he saw, with a thank-you card from Cassie Denton. He should've brought something. Hadn't even thought of it.

"Sorry, Laura, I've got to ask some questions."

"I know. Doubt I can help much. He gave me a drink. Mickey Finned. Dropped me like a hammer." Her right cheek twitched. Her left didn't move, just hid behind her hair, yellow and purple and puffy. "Can't believe I took that drink. Stupid."

"Don't blame yourself. You were set up. Lazuardi had one of us in his pocket. Sorry but true. You were sold out. We all were. Keith evidently accessed the file and found out. We know he tried to contact you, to warn you, but we don't know if he succeeded."

Laura shook her head once. A tear leaked from the swelling around her left eye. "Is Keith . . . ?" Her voice caught. She cleared her throat.

"Missing," said Cronk.

"Dead?"

"We don't . . ." Cronk's eyes drifted to the flowers. "Probably."

Another tear tumbled down her cheek. She didn't seem to notice.

"You didn't see him or talk to him," Cronk asked, "after he got the stick, the night on Lazuardi's yacht?"

"In my mind," she said, "I never got off Lazuardi's yacht." Her good eye glazed over as some nightmare memory rose to the surface. "I woke up in a barn chained to the wall."

"I'm sorry." He looked at the flowers again. They were common flowers, but he didn't know the names of any of them. He thought that maybe he should ask her. She would know. It would be a nice gentle conversation. Give her a chance to compose herself. He said, "Just one more thing, Laura. The stick. Keith hid it somewhere. Had you two made arrangements for a drop, a safe place where you could leave confidential messages?"

"No. Our cover, you know, we were lovers. There was no need to meet secretly." She wiped the tears from her right eye. Her left ran freely.

"That was our cover," she repeated softly, "so we could meet anywhere, anytime. We were lovers."

Chapter 32

*B*oomer steered *One Across* into the bay and tied up beside *Small Wonder* about eleven o'clock Sunday morning. *One Across* was a 1930s vintage motor launch, forty-three feet overall, originally commissioned by Canada Post to move the mail between isolated coastal communities. Boomer had acquired through barter the broken, scavenged hulk of her and had spent three years restoring her, refitting, as much as possible, with gear authentic to her pedigree. Her large wheelhouse peered over a high chesty prow. There was an outside helm station abaft her cabin. Her afterdeck was low and beamy, designed to facilitate cargo transfers at isolated camps where docking facilities often consisted of nothing but transient log booms. It made an ideal diving platform.

The sky was smudged with horsetail wisps of cirrus cloud. The clouds were coming from the northwest but feathering back on themselves, forecasting a change to south-easterly, the winds of rain. But at noon, when they boarded *One Across* and left the dock, the weather was still fine. The sea was calm and running with coho; the waters out in the strait were speckled with sportfishing boats. Boomer ordered the anchor dropped about twenty meters off Gunner's Rock, then he, Davey, and Cassie went into the cabin to help one another into their dry suits, leaving Purcell alone on deck.

When they'd told Purcell that they'd be diving, the cop had been displeased, but his protest had been silenced by Cassie's withering stare. It'd been a protest without much authority in it to start with. Since learning how Cassie had suffered the consequences of his actions, the cocky young Kiwi was gone, imprisoned behind a quiet, fierce intensity. As if to guard against his own escape, he'd added a short blunt shotgun to his arsenal. Boomer had noticed the change in him and had asked Davey what the problem was. Davey had told Boomer the truth—he couldn't talk about it.

Out on deck, Kevin Purcell ostentatiously ignored the three divers by studying their surroundings through a pair of binoculars. The three returned the favor, ignoring the cop as they donned weight and tanks, masks, gloves, and fins. Just as they were ready to get wet, Purcell stepped up beside Davey.

"When you're through with your fun and games here," the cop said, "you and I have to talk."

Davey stared at him until he heard the splashes of Boomer and Cassie stepping overboard. "Count on it," he said.

He inflated for buoyancy, adjusted his mask, bit into his mouthpiece, and stepped off the deck.

Forty-five feet beneath the keel of *One Across*, the three divers gathered on the silty seabed. Visibility was about fifty feet, not bad for that time of year when the summer sun tends to precipitate blinding plankton blooms. They kicked off and glided out over an alien landscape inhabited by fantastical cucumbers and spiky urchins, by feathery sea pens and phallic geoducks and angelically glowing nudibranchs. They approached the wall of Gunner's Rock beneath a swaying morass of purple kelp leaves the size of elephant ears. The jagged rock wall was softened with startling mosaics of starfish and anemone. Multicolored rockfish patrolled up and down, treating the vertical rock as their horizon, unperturbed by the three bubble-making creatures that had no business being there.

Two monolithic rocks rose up from the seabed, forming a gateway to the wolf eel's lair. As they passed through this natural portal, Cassie plucked a couple of unlucky urchins from the rocks.

The mouth of Willie's cave formed a horizontal oval, roughly two meters wide by one meter high. The wolf eel was at the mouth of the cave, watching them with his endearingly ugly face, looking like a grumpy, dentureless grandpa.

Davey took an end of the rope Boomer was carrying and secured it around his waist while Cassie used her knife to open one of the urchins. Scarlet globs of urchin innards drifted through the water at the mouth of the cave. Willie plucked leisurely at the floating bits of roe. Cassie backed up, carefully offering the morsels of urchin. Wolf eels are diver friendly, but their jaws are designed for crushing shellfish, so a prudent diver uses extreme caution when hand-feeding the creatures. When she'd drawn the whole six and a half feet of iridescent grayish-pink wolf eel out of the cave, Davey eased in behind it.

He activated his light and cast it around. The cave sloped upward at about forty degrees. It seemed to be no more than about fifteen feet deep. Davey determined that there was plenty of room for him and his equipment, then he began rising while Boomer played out the rope, and Cassie kept the wolf eel's mind off the invasion of its home.

The walls of the cave were featureless rock. There was no sea chest and no place for a sea chest to hide. Davey began to have serious doubts. He hadn't known what to expect, but he'd talked himself into expecting something amazing. He neared the end of the cave. It was as empty as the Treasury on Granville Island. But this time, Davey's disappointment wasn't watered down with relief; it was straight up and bitter. Then he saw that the cave didn't end, but rather doglegged into a vertical shaft.

He examined the dogleg to make sure he wouldn't become jammed in it and then let himself drift upward. His right hand purged air from his suit to keep his upward drift under control. His left hand held the lamp above him so that it would meet the roof of the cave before his head did. Instead, he rose into air. He'd come up into a natural diving bell—an air pocket trapped inside the crown of Gunner's Rock.

He returned air to his suit to make buoyancy and then shone the light around. He was in a small cavern lined with black glistening rock, too dark to make out the dimensions. Along one side of it was a rocky shelf about fifteen inches above the waterline. On the shelf was something amazing.

He stared at the sea chest for a long moment. There was giddiness in his skull, a tightness threatening to become a headache. His excitement turned into something akin to dread. Bathed in lamplight, the old locker seemed to radiate an implicit menace, as if opening it might resurrect something better left dead.

Don't be an idiot, Jones. It's an oak chest, that's all. Probably ruined now by the water it's soaked up. Just open the fucking thing.

He unhooked his weight belt and heaved it up onto the ledge, then wrestled himself up beside the chest. He removed his mouthpiece, but only for a second. He choked on the viscous, damply sulphuric stench of the ancient atmosphere, put the regulator back into his mouth, and took a deep steadying breath.

You're wasting air, Jones. Just do it.

He peeled off his gloves, lifted the curved lid, and shone his light into a nest of heavy-gauge black plastic. He dug through four layers of the plastic before he found the computer memory stick. It was wrapped in its own sheath of clear plastic. It was nestled amid a trunkful of brown padded envelopes.

He ran his hand through the envelopes. Most of them were sealed. He picked up one of the open ones and peeked inside it. A bundle, a brick, of hundred-dollar bills. He was holding in his hand several thousand dollars. He opened another, found another bundle of cash. Assuming all the envelopes contained the same thing, he was looking at hundreds of thousands of dollars. He caught himself wasting air again.

He made sure the computer disk was well sealed inside its plastic bag, then tucked it in through the convenience zipper at the crotch of his dry suit. He snugged the layers of plastic back over the plump brown envelopes and closed the lid on the sea chest.

Fifteen men and a dead man's chest, his mind sang as he fastened his weight, pulled on his gloves and lowered himself into the water. *Drink to the devil and done for the rest.*

The old pirate ditty was still reeling through his brain when he encountered Willie in the cave just below the dogleg. The creature didn't look pleased, but then wolf eels never do. Cassie and Boomer had either run out of urchins or the eel had lost its appetite. Davey eased by, looking at Willie's wrinkled face with what he hoped was an eelish expression of apology.

Outside the cave, he swam into water clouded with silt. Visibility was down to five or six feet. He followed the safety line through the murk and found it hitched to an outcrop of rock. No Boomer, no Cassie. Of course, they could be ten feet away, and he wouldn't know it. He unsheathed his knife and tapped the handle against his air tank. A loud clanking sound carried through the water. As he listened for a reply, he fumbled the bowline off his waist. No reply came. He tapped again. Perplexity began to trickle into the frantic feeling that is the forerunner of panic.

Think, don't imagine.

They'd had an equipment problem. Free-flowing regulator, something like that. Had to buddy back to *One Across.* Sure. Nothing to worry about. Situation copasetic. He abandoned the rope and started to rise.

When he got above the silt, he saw the boat's hull profiled against the sky, and he stopped swimming. Just abaft the boat was the profile of a person floating spread-eagled. The water surrounding the floater was opaque, inky. As Davey drifted closer, it became apparent that the inky stain was blood. The person was bleeding because his chest had been ripped to pieces. Bits of his insides hung down in the water like jellyfish tentacles. The floater wasn't large enough to be Boomer and wasn't wearing Cassie's bright yellow fins, but Davey found little comfort in that. Copaseticness was slipping away.

He heard a splash from the direction of the boat, looked over, and saw Purcell dive under. Davey thought Purcell was moronically taking his shotgun with him, then saw that it was a spear gun. And just where the hell had the cop gotten a spear gun?

Davey approached the boat cautiously. Without a mask, Purcell wouldn't see him until he was right there. It seemed a good idea not to startle someone armed and clearly nervous. He made the boarding ladder, tossed weight belt, fins, and mask up onto the deck, and scrambled up after them. He kept his tank on in case he had to get back in the water quickly.

Purcell surfaced twenty feet away. For a heart-stopping moment, he pointed the spear gun at Davey. He lowered it instantly and swam to the ladder.

"Where're the others?" he shouted as he climbed aboard, shivering, seawater sluicing from his clothes.

"I don't know. I thought they'd come up."

"What the hell happened down there?" Purcell was obviously frightened.

"I don't know." Davey hadn't arrived at fright yet. He was still stuck in bewilderment. "I went into a cave. When I came out, they were gone."

"You don't know a hell of a lot, do you?"

"I know there's a guy in the water with a big hole in his chest."

Purcell looked out at the guy with the hole in his chest. "One of Lazuardi's. He came up over the side and pointed this thing at me." He waved the spear gun. "I pointed the shotgun. I pulled the trigger first."

"Jesus. How do you know he's Lazuardi's?" Davey's mind wasn't getting the picture. All this Lazuardi shit was supposed to be over with. "Maybe he's just some guy out hunting cod or something. Ran low on air, couldn't get back to his own boat." Davey waved his arm at the sport boats out in the strait. There was one a few hundred meters away, bobbing around out at the headland.

"I recognized him," Purcell said. "He was in custody a few days ago."

A short barking laugh broke away from Davey, a bit of leakage through the barrier between logic and lunacy. "Wasn't much of a custody, was it?"

Purcell glanced at the floating body. "It is now."

"I don't fucking *believe* this."

"Shouldn't we be doing something? Looking for them?"

"Look where?" Davey swept his arm to indicate the sheer scope of futility.

"*I* don't know. *You're* the diver. What're they *supposed* to do?"

Davey gaped at the cop. "You think they write this up in the *manual?*"

"Don't be an asshole. What do you *think* they'd do?"

Davey was trying to think, but there was too much interference crackling through his brain, battering at the lunacy barrier. "Did you see any bubbles? Notice which direction they were heading?"

"Lots of bubbles. All over the fucking place. Then your cod hunter popped up and took my attention. After I dealt with him, I dove in and got his spear gun. I looked around but couldn't see much."

"Should've taken his mask. Can't see without a mask."

"Great! Thanks! I'll file that for future consideration!"

Something caught Davey's eye. Someone was coming out of the water, climbing up onto Gunner's Rock. He recognized the blue suit, the red beard. "Boomer!"

But Boomer was preoccupied. He was hauling another diver from the water. The diver wore a black suit, no yellow trim. Not Cassie. A man. He was gasping and choking. His mask was gone, his air hose severed.

"Pull the anchor," Davey ordered.

Purcell sprinted forward to the anchor winch. Davey went to the helm station and fired the engine. He had way on her before the anchor was hove. He was unaccustomed to her mannerisms and found her to have a ponderous helm and a tight-lipped throttle. But the water was calm and he knew the rock well, so he managed to nose her in between the kelp beds and hold her to the rock without smashing her to bits. Boomer threw his prisoner onto the deck and leaped aboard. Purcell took charge of the black-suited diver while Boomer shed his equipment and took over the helm.

"They got her," he said, answering the question that lay petrified beneath Davey's confusion. "Four of them. Came up behind us. This fuck tried to spear me. Doesn't know shit about shooting underwater. Let fly from thirty feet. Spear didn't even break my suit. Then he pulled a knife. Time I showed him the error of his ways the others were gone. Cassie with them. I'm sorry, man."

That was Davey's cue to speak up and remove his friend's guilt, to tell Boomer it wasn't his fault, it was Davey's idea to play hide-and-seek with the computer stick. But he couldn't speak. His head was full of the anguish in Cassie's voice. *They raped me, Davey. Oh god, I'm sorry . . .*

The boat at the mouth of the bay was easing closer. They were inside two hundred meters. Maybe they'd seen something. Davey picked up a set of binoculars and brought the boat in close. It was a white Bayliner cabin cruiser, about thirty feet long. There was a guy at the helm on the raised bridge, a big guy with long, ropy hair. Good old Norm.

"That's them." Davey shouted, pointing. "That's their boat." Even as he spoke he saw four divers bob to the surface beside the Bayliner.

Boomer poured the diesel to *One Across*. She growled and lumbered forth, her displacement hull shouldering aside the ocean, atremble with her effort to hold twelve knots. The motion rendered the binoculars useless, but even without them Davey could see the divers board the Bayliner. Cassie's yellow fins flashed as she was dragged up over the side. *One Across* was still over a hundred meters away when the Bayliner dug her hind end into the water to gain purchase, then leapt forward and planed off to the north at twenty-five knots.

Boomer brought *One Across* up. She was clearly outmatched in a footrace. He activated the VHF. "Time to call in the guard."

From the afterdeck, Purcell said, "I've got it."

Davey looked back. The diver lay on his side, coughing briny phlegm from his lungs. Too weak from his near drowning to expectorate it, it hung in a gelatinous streamer from the corner of his mouth. Purcell stood over him, one foot on the diver's side, like a conquering gladiator. Purcell's right hand pointed the spear gun at the diver's head. With his left hand, he picked up his jacket from the deck and pulled out a cell phone.

"What are you doing?" Davey asked.

"Calling my contact in Campbell River. I already called for help, so it's on the way. I'll give them an update. Describe the boat and its heading. They can sick the *Nadon* on it."

The *Nadon* was the high-speed police catamaran stationed in Campbell River. No question she could run down the Bayliner. But the men on the Bayliner had Cassie. Davey stepped over to Purcell, snatched the phone from his hand, and tossed it over the side.

"Christsake, Davey," said Boomer. "We need help. If there's a dirty cop, this won't be a secret to him. They can't all be dirty."

Purcell was glaring, his face flushed with anger as he stared at Davey. "What does he mean? What dirty cop?"

"Keith found out that Lazuardi had one of you people in his pocket."

"Who?" said Purcell.

"If he had a name, they killed him before he got a chance to tell me."

Purcell closed his eyes, rubbed his forehead, took a breath and held it, blew it out, and shook his head. It seemed more a gesture of sadness than anger. He looked down at his prisoner. "This shit knows where they're taking her."

Purcell moved his foot to the diver's chest and pushed him over until the air tank clunked against the decking. The diver's face rolled into view, and Davey recognized the young man who'd driven the car they'd had Eddie in, the kid who fancied himself a ladies' man. Purcell pointed the spear gun at his chest and asked the kid where his pals were headed.

The young man tried to grin, but in his state, it came out more of a grimace. "You're a cop," he croaked. "You can't shoot me. All you can do is read me my rights. So fuck you."

The diver's left arm was lying across the deck. Purcell pinned it with his foot. "Sorry, buds," he said. "That's old news. I just resigned my commission."

The spear gun was pointed at the diver's hand. The hand was encased in a neoprene glove. When Purcell fired the gun, the razor-sharp head of the bolt went through the neoprene as if it were tissue paper. It went through the hand, through flesh and tendon and bone, with equal ease. It went through the other side of the glove and with a muffled *thunk* buried itself in the deck planking.

The kid jerked as if he'd taken an electric shock. His left arm went into a palsied tremble. His eyes and mouth were opened wide. He gaped at the eighteen-inch shaft protruding from the palm of his hand. A sheen of blood was welling up around it. He tried to reach across to it with his right hand. Purcell stopped him.

"Jesus Christ," said Boomer, more in astonishment than disapproval.

"Good idea," said Purcell. "One in each hand and one for the feet. Just like Jesus Christ."

Singing "Nearer My Lord to Thee," Purcell forced the kid's right hand against the deck. The diver's shoulders were arched awkwardly over his air tank. Purcell fiddled with the spear gun. "How do you load this stupid thing, Davey?"

"Nooo . . ." the diver groaned. "The plantation." He dry-swallowed, panted a few rapid shallow breaths. "Where you grew the pot. The place we burned."

Purcell looked at Davey. Davey nodded. "Frank's place. They're taking her home."

Chapter 33

*D*onny "Wheels" Cuchera couldn't fucking *believe* they'd left him pinned to the deck of the stinking boat. Despite the blanket they'd placed over him, chills raced through his body like aftershocks. And although they'd removed his diving hood, his brain felt like it was being deep-fried. They'd promised him that help would arrive shortly, but their idea of shortly differed greatly from Donny's, fuck you very much.

He glanced at the shaft in his hand, looked quickly away. The sight of it turned his stomach, and he couldn't handle vomiting right now, if you don't mind. His throat was still raw from choking on saltwater. His hand felt like it was cartoonishly bloated, puffy and numb. Except right in the middle. The middle wasn't numb. The middle was the target of a hive of mad bees. Thousands of them. Each one probing with the poison heat of its stinger.

He heard himself sobbing and bit his lip. No way was Donny "Wheels" Cuchera going to start balling. He was tougher than that. He rolled onto his left shoulder, reached with his right hand, and gingerly took hold of the metal shaft. One swift pull and it's out. Just like that time he got a nail in his foot . . .

Standing screaming with a broken plank nailed to the bottom of his six-year-old foot while his dad yelled don't be such a baby and gave one quick yank and the nail was out and his dad tossed aside the plank with the bloody nail in it and went back to mending his gill nets, but it still hurt like a bitch, which is what his mom was when she'd run off with that truck driver who his dad was going to shoot down like a dog he ever saw him again . . .

Pull.

It wasn't at all like the nail coming out of his foot. The shaft didn't budge, but jagged pain ripped through Donny Cuchera like broken glass. He forgot about being too tough to ball; he would've wailed like a baby if he'd had the breath for it. Instead, he passed out.

For a long while, his body lay still, his mind mercifully blank. Then he began to twitch and moan softly as his fevered brain took him back into the water . . .

Over the side of the Bayliner twelve hours ahead of schedule—early afternoon instead of early morning; broad daylight instead of the narrow darkness they'd planned on, Flammond assuring them with talk of contingencies. The five of them making neutral buoyancy at twenty feet: Flammond leading the way, fluorescent tape up his spine and along the backs of his arms making him easy to follow; couple of Flammond's buddies from the army, Beale and Tallen, who kept to themselves and did nothing to make Cuchera feel like a turd, but succeeded anyway; and a guy named Mackie who was supposed to be Lazuardi's personal gofer. In the twenty-four hours Cuchera had known Mackie, he'd come to the conclusion that Mackie was a clinical fucking psychopath.

Cuchera and Mackie carried the spear guns, a pair of them, like *his* and *hers*, that they'd found at the plantation. Cuchera lagged behind. He was glad for the bulky neoprene suit and the mask covering his face. He felt safe inside the gear—anonymous—protected from his own insecurity as well as from the frigid tons of saltwater. The spear gun felt weird to him, but it felt right to the suit. It fit. It made him this other guy, this tough son of a bitch stone-cold killer, inside whom Donny was just a passenger. It was exciting. Donny didn't actually want to kill anyone, but he wanted desperately to have been a killer. He wanted the prestige of it, the respect of it. Now he had this alter ego or whatever they called it, this terror in the dive suit with the spear gun that really felt like it wanted to kill someone. He'd have respect by the fucking boxcar load. No more shit from assholes like Rockwell.

Flammond stopped near a rock face, pointed up to the right. The shadow of the wooden boat loomed against the sky. Flammond pointed to Mackie. Mackie left the group, kicked off toward the boat. His job had to do with the cop.

Flammond led off around the rock. Beale and Tallen followed his moves as if they were all hooked together, the three army buddies in their weird shimmering suits that virtually disappeared in the water. Cuchera lagged behind, following their bubbles and the tape on Flammond's back. He'd been told to stay out of the way, like he was a kid along for the ride.

There they were, on the bottom, twenty feet below. The girl in her yellow fins, feeding a wolf eel. One of the men a dozen feet to her left, holding a rope. Where was the other guy?

The three ex-soldiers drifted over top of the girl, invisible as ghosts, formed a circle, and descended around her. The wolf eel darted away. The girl struggled, silt rose clouding the water. The guy with the rope turned toward her. Cuchera saw the red beard around his mouthpiece. *If you have to shoot one of them,* they'd told him, *make sure it's the guy with the beard.* Cuchera burrowed deeper into his mind, giving himself to the killer in the dive suit.

Red Beard wrapped the rope around a rock and tied it off. He reached for the knife strapped to his leg. Me thinks not, sayeth the killer in the dive suit. He centered the spear gun on Red Beard's chest, squeezed the trigger.

The bolt shot through the water, cavitated a thin stream of pearly bubbles, slowed too quickly. The killer forgot that underwater a spear gun is an arm's length weapon. The killer slunk away, leaving Donny Cuchera to watch in dreamy horror as the bolt bounced uselessly off Red Beard.

Silt rose around him like thick brown fog. He reached for his knife, fumbling with the sheath, shaking weak with terror. Felt movement behind him. Tried to turn. His mask was gone, ripped from his face. He flailed blindly. Bubbles exploded from his air hose. His next breath was full of cold salty water. It pressed against his face, pushed itself down his throat. He came thrashing awake.

Awake. But the saltwater was still there, in his eyes and his mouth. He coughed, rubbed his eyes with his free hand, gradually became aware that someone was standing over him. About fucking time. He blinked and squinted, saw a big round man holding a bucket. Fuck threw a bucket of water on him.

"What happened here?" the guy asked. His face seemed to be a mile and a half in the air.

Donny thought, *You just threw a fucking bucket of water on me is what happened, you fuck.* But that's not what he said. He said, "I need help." His voice was a groan. "You got to help me. They left me here like this."

"Where did they go?" the man asked. "Tell me where they went, then I'll help you."

"They left me like this," Donny muttered. He rolled his head to the side and looked at his pinned hand. "I got a spear in my hand, you know?"

The pain had eased to a dull throbbing. He could look at the wound without getting sick to his stomach. He was feeling a little high, as if he'd just tooted some prime reefer.

"It's not fair," he droned. "I told them, you know. I told them they were taking the girl to the plantation." The injustice of it made him cry. "I told them," he whimpered. "I told them, and they still left me here."

The man stood looking around for a minute, no doubt sharing Donny's sense of injustice. Then he crouched down over Donny. "Do you know who I am?"

Donny squinted. The guy's face swam into focus. A round jowly face that sort of glowed, as if permanently sunburned. And Donny *did* recognize it. Three, four times he'd driven Lazuardi's people to meetings in the middle of nowhere. Meetings with *this* man. The guy was from *Lazuardi.* Thank the Lord fucking Jesus. Lazuardi wanted his ace wheelman back.

"Yeah," he said, hope giving him new energy. "Yeah, you're Mr. Lazuardi's friend."

"Shit," the guy muttered and stood up. He stood there on the deck of the boat looking around. Donny wanted to tell him that they could still do Lazuardi proud. They still stood a good chance of bringing these pricks down. Provided, that is, someone *get this fucking spear out of his hand!*

Then he saw that the man wasn't holding a bucket anymore. Instead, he was holding a stubby little pistol with a very large hole in the end of it. For a brief instant, understanding began to glimmer through the dense thickets of his mind. *Means to kill me,* he thought, and for the first time in a long while, Donny "Wheels" Cuchera was right; he died before the flat echo of Lohman's gunshot did.

Chapter 34

$\mathcal{T}$witch squeezed the trigger. Again and again and again. Ten times in rapid succession. Each time he squeezed, the automatic pistol nuzzled into his hand like the snout of an affectionate dog, and the flat clap of the shot seemed to come from some happy place inside him. Twenty paces away the twelve-inch target was shredded. It was the second full clip, the twentieth bullet that he'd put into the target. For the first time within his limited memory, Twitch experienced a swell of pride.

Twitch the Shootist. Right on.

He reached into his pocket for more bullets to reload the clip. The heroin racing through his nervous system made the bullets feel fat and unwieldy. They slipped through his fingers, dropped into the underbrush. He squatted, searching the ground.

Awhile later, he found one of the bullets, which was cool, since he'd convinced himself that he'd only dropped one to start with. He slid the magazine from the handle of the pistol and pressed the single bullet into the clip. He checked his pockets, wondering why he only had one. He was sure that Flammond had left him with a box of thirty. He'd come out just now to shoot a little target and only brought one bullet with him. What a fool! He laughed at himself. The good Lady H, man, she fuck with your head you're not careful.

He started back toward the house, strolling across the charred acreage that, two weeks earlier, had been verdant with west coast scrub and Frank Denton's natural-grown, sun-ripened ganja. Had Twitch been inclined to think about it at all, he would have accepted the sooty odor of burned vegetation and gasoline as part and parcel of the whole outdoorsy thing, man.

Frank Denton's house was slightly askew, as might be expected of a house built by a noncarpenter with home-milled lumber. It was neither square nor plumb nor evenly pitched. Most people who looked at it got a sensation of being slightly off balance. But not Twitch. In his years on the street Twitch had played house in a diversity of structures, from empty shells of condemned buildings to packing crates and park benches. It bothered him not at all that the kicked-in door hung broken on a single hinge or that glass from the windows crunched under his boots as he walked across the kitchen floor. Like most things in Twitch's world, the house existed for no particular reason, which left it free to be whatever it was. Twitch enjoyed that profound thought for a second or two until it popped and left his mind in the middle of a dark and empty space. This was a state to which Twitch had grown accustomed over the years; it had long ago ceased to trouble him.

His eyes fell on the limp condom lying in the center of the kitchen table. He picked up the condom and bounced it in his hand, gauging the contents. The pistol lay forgotten on the table; this version of Twitch the Shootist didn't shoot with a firearm.

Before Lazuardi's lawyer had bailed him out, Twitch had spent four days in the Nanaimo lockup. For Twitch, this was in the nature of a class reunion. He'd hooked up with Sailor, an emaciated street junkie with a 160 IQ, a PhD in physics, and HIV positive blood. Sailor was a regular visitor to the lockup. He'd been in the prison system for more years than it had taken him to achieve his degree. The system was built, managed, and operated by civil servants. Sailor's genius, doped up as it was, found the system embarrassingly simple to manipulate. Prison, by nature, was a conference of drug dealers, a wholesale supermarket for addicts who could make the right connections. Over the years Sailor had cultivated more connections that the phone company. He'd been impressed to learn that Twitch was working for the legendary Vincent Lazuardi and instantly saw the advantage in cultivating a personal connection into Lazuardi's pipeline. Sailor arranged for Twitch to get a private cot, special food, his own shitter and shower. And a couple of ounces of Lady H, packaged in a condom lubricated for your enhanced pleasure.

For nearly two days, Twitch had lived with that condom plugging his lower colon. A masterful act of self-control; Houdini had nothing on Twitch. Then early that morning, Flammond and the rest of them had gone off to do their commando shit, leaving Twitch to . . .

To keep an eye on the plantation and warn the boat if there was unwanted company . . .

To go into the forest and squat against a tree and grunt with near-rupturous effort until, ah, the orgasmic-like evacuation, and there she is, the sweet Lady H, in need of a bit of rinsing, but what the hell, all God's children gotta work for a living.

Twitch used a butter knife to squeeze a pinch of heroin from the condom. He carefully cut it with a bit of baking soda, just enough to make it smoke. He tamped the mixture into a pipe he'd fashioned from a gutted pen and a bit of tinfoil. He struck a kitchen match and held the flame under the foil bowl of the pipe. A tendril of pure white smoke rose from the powder. As he drew the smoke into his lungs, Twitch envisioned tiny crystals of heroin hitting his brain like fireworks on a dark night. Would be better with a spike, but sometimes, as little brother, Norm was wont to say, sometimes a guy just had to make do with what a guy had.

Twitch was pulling in another lungful of smoke when he heard the cat meow. It stood in the doorway, a huge gray thing swishing its tail and glaring with yellow eyes. Never in his life had Twitch experienced such a vivid hallucination. Was fucking scary was what.

He stared at the cat and scratched the scruffy stubble on his cheek while his heart raced with the heroin and the outrageous notion that such a realistic hallucination was pretty fucking close to being the real thing. Like maybe there was some line that kept hallucinations on one side and reality on the other, and maybe some, you know, cosmic event could blur that line so things could cross back and forth. And if that wasn't the be-fucking-all to end-fucking-all, Twitch didn't know what was.

Chapter 35

"Not much of a career move now, was it?" Brian Cronk said to the thing pinned to the deck of the boat.

He stepped gingerly around the gooey red-and-gray splatter in which lay Donny Cuchera's head. Tugging up the knees of his trousers, he squatted. Despite the spilled gray matter, he went through the motions, making it official, pressing two fingers against the side of the corpse's neck.

The carotid artery, of course, was still, but the flesh was warm and pliant. The blood around the head glistened wetly while that around the speared hand was crusting. Cuchera must have lain there for sometime with the spear in his hand. Man, that had to hurt.

From the regulator on Cuchera's air tank hung six inches of air hose. Cronk examined the end of it. Sliced clean with a sharp instrument. Hell of a way to end a dive.

"You, Donny, have had what they call a bad day. Don't suppose you care to tell me about it?"

The boat had a broad gunwale topped with a dark-grained plank worn smooth as marble. Cronk inspected it for grime and then sat on it. He rolled up his shirt sleeves. The clouds stealing down from the north hadn't lowered the temperature, merely raised the humidity. From his hip pocket, he pulled a folded sheet of paper and opened it out. It was the printout of Lohman's photo op with the two teenage girls. He waved it fanlike under his chin.

"Lohman have anything to do with this?" he wondered out loud. Maybe if he'd phoned and had Lohman picked up, Donny would still be drawing breath. Maybe. But that was an *if*, and at the end of the day *if* didn't mean a bloody thing.

Anyway, in Lohman's case, Cronk wanted to do the picking up in person. He had a question or two for Lohman. A question or two he wanted to ask before Lohman got into an interview room with an audience and a movie camera. A question or two about a voice on the phone known as Joshua. But at the Campbell River detachment, they'd told him that Lohman had left the office, destination unknown. Cronk had decided to hop down to Boomer's Bight, have a chat with Purcell re Lohman, find out about this developing personal situation, whatever. Maybe give Jones a shake, see what fell out. He'd found the Jenkins place deserted, Jenkins's pickup and Denton's Samurai in the driveway but no sign of Purcell's car. Jones's sailboat and Jenkins's tug were tied to the dock. Cronk had called out. No answer. He'd strolled out along the wharf to the boats. Found Donny Cuchera—failed race driver, failed car thief, short-lived gangster—drying in the sun.

"How about Purcell?" Cronk asked. "He have anything to do with this? Doesn't seem his style, does it? Still, where's his car? He drive off in it? Off playing Lone Ranger again? Or dead in the bay? What about Jones? Jenkins? Cassie Denton? What are they up to, Donny, while you're getting speared to the deck and shot in the head?"

A spear gun, presumably the one that had speared Donny to the deck, was lying on a coil of pale green rope toward the stern of the boat. Cronk stood up, pocketed Lohman's pictures, and picked up the spear gun. When the time came to spill his guts, evidence of tampering would be the least of it.

"He got the stick, didn't he? Jones? Bet your life he did. And your bunch took another crack at it, right?" He nodded.

"Flammond surface? Put you up to this? Make it sound like a big adventure?" Cronk waved the weapon. "Amphibious assault with spear guns? Everyone's James fucking Bond? That how it went, Donny, until it went wrong?"

As he spoke, he examined the spear gun. It was basically a rifle stock, made of weighted plastic with a grainy surface to make it less slippery when wet, black with bright yellow rings around it so that you could find it if the grainy surface didn't work and you dropped it in the muck at the bottom of the sea. There was a channel for a spear, no doubt much like the one in Donny's hand, and a cavity in the handle, currently occupied, for a compressed-air cartridge.

"Nothing personal, Donny. These things always go wrong. But Flammond had a contingency plan, didn't he? Bet your life he did. His sort always does. Know what that means, Donny? Contingency plan? Means you take a big fuckup and slice it up and dole it out until you've got a whole bunch of little fuckups running around tripping over one another."

Cronk's fingers encountered a smooth surface embedded in the grainy plastic on the bottom side of the stock. He glanced down. Saw a small brass plaque, fancy scroll writing inscribed on the brass. He ran his thumb over the embossed inscription. *Happy Father's Day*, it said. *Love you lots, Cassie.*

"What every daddy wants for Father's Day, I'll tell you that," he muttered.

He looked at the corpse. "She have this with her, Donny? Take Daddy's gift out hunting bad guys, did she? I don't think so."

He looked at Donny's body while his mind's eye followed Donny through his last few hours, playing it over and over until it ran smooth. When a reconstruction ran smooth it was usually close. You never got it perfect; there'd always be details you'd never know. But you could get it close. Close enough for government work, and fuck the jury.

"I think you had it to start with, Donny. Take it from the Denton's place, did you, on the way to work this morning? Lunch bag, coffee thermos, spear gun, hi-ho hi-ho. You, Flammond, what? Three, four others? Spear guns at high noon. All fun and games until someone's in the water with you cutting your air hose, shooting you with your spear gun, generally making you wish you'd stayed home and ordered pizza. That how it was, Donny?"

Jones gets the memory stick from wherever it's hidden. Flammond's bunch swoops in to grab it. Donny here runs into resistance. Or gets pushed into it by Flammond. Flammond takes the stick and runs, Purcell *et al.* hot on his tail. Or Purcell *et al.* floating out to sea while Flammond drives away in Purcell's car after making sure that Donny keeps it all a secret. Either way, Cronk suspected that everyone who could was heading for the Denton's place.

"Any idea what I'll find, Donny, if I go up there and take a look around?"

Donny "Wheels" Cuchera didn't answer. Cronk dropped the spear gun back onto the coil of rope, stepped over the gunwale onto the dock.

"Been good, Donny. Do it again sometime."

As he drove out Crabbe-Levy Road, Cronk pulled out his cell phone and punched in the number for Purcell's car phone. Gave up after a dozen rings. Started dialing the number for the Campbell River detachment. Hit End and tossed the phone on the seat.

"Bloody hell's the use?" he muttered to himself. "Donny's going nowhere, and you got things to do if you're not too late before you go all confessional on us."

Chapter 36

"That'll be Inspector Cronk," said Purcell, when the car phone started chirping. He was at the wheel of his Caprice, speeding northwestward on the highway alongside the Nimpkish River. "Or Staff Sergeant Lohman. They'll wonder why I'm not answering."

"I understand you resigned from the force," Davey said. He was sitting with his bandaged left leg stretched out across the backseat. His 9 mm Llama lay beside it. He'd fetched the pistol from *Small Wonder* when he'd changed out of his dry suit. His finger's rested lightly on the gun's oily black steel. "I also understand that Inspector Cronk moonlights for Lazuardi."

"That's bullshit. Brian wouldn't piss on Lazuardi if he was dying of thirst. Your bad cop is not Brian."

"He's not my bad cop."

"He's not anyone's bad cop! You got that all wrong."

"We'll see. But not until Cassie's safe. I'm not betting her life on the untouchable Brian Inspector Cronk."

"Funny," Purcell said into the mirror, "he wouldn't bet Constable White's life on Davey drug-running Jones."

"Funny," Davey said.

Boomer was following the exchange from the front passenger seat. He reached forward and shut off the car phone. "The cellular customer you are calling," he muttered, "is unavailable at this time."

"This is nuts." Purcell shook his head. "I can't believe I'm doing this." He took a deep breath and pushed it out. "No worries about resigning. Right about now, my badge is worth its weight in scrap tin."

"Their loss," muttered Boomer. Like a mediator calming a nasty contract negotiation, he produced a pack of Player's and offered them around.

Without thinking, Davey took one and lit it. It was his first smoke in days. It tasted vile. The first few drags left him dizzy and nauseous. He smoked the thing down to the filter.

Vancouver Island houses about a million people in twelve and a half thousand square miles. Roughly half of its land mass lies northwest of Campbell River, but only 2 percent of the population live there. The highway is a lonely stretch of blacktop winding and twisting through the inland mountains, literally a logging main that had been widened and paved, crowded by green walls of hemlock and spruce and Douglas fir. Posted here and there are roadside monuments the forest industry has erected to itself in the form of billboards proclaiming the conscientious dedication of its silviculture practices. And the cultured forest is there for all to see. Huge tracts of trees grow neat and orderly. Truly a fine forest. Much nicer than the tangled, jumbled wilderness nature makes of a forest when she's left to do it on her own.

As the highway drew them northwestward, the cloud cover thickened. It dropped over the tops of the mountains and pressed down on the towering conifer forests. Further up the island, the flat underbelly of cloud was charcoal black and stretched from east to west, forecasting not a summer squall but rather the omnipotent deluge that gives the rainforest its name.

The highway ducked under a railway trestle and climbed out of the Nimpkish Valley onto a high ridge, near the underbelly of the clouds. On the roadside, outcrops of purple rock shouldered their way up through the undergrowth. Five hundred feet below, the long water of Nimpkish Lake sped by on their left. The rain started up. Just a fine spray at first, misting the windshield as if they'd driven close by a waterfall. Purcell activated the wipers on a slow delay setting.

Boomer passed out another round of cigarettes and asked why the hell Lazuardi was doing this. "With or without his computer file, he's cooked anyway, right?"

Purcell explained that Lazuardi was singed a bit, but hardly cooked, facing weapons charges, reckless endangerment, an easy year or two and then deportation. Davey barely heard him. Davey didn't care *why*. Why had nothing to do with anything. It had no basis in reality.

"According to our source," Purcell was saying, "that memory stick contains information not only about his organization but also other organizations he's dealt with. If we can tap that information, Lazuardi will be on the bad side of some very nasty people who tend not to forgive and forget. Solitary confinement may be the only place he can stay alive. Oh yeah, he wants that stick."

There you go: Lazuardi wanted the memory stick; Davey wanted Cassie. You could ask why *ad infinitum*. But that was a child's game. Reality was much simpler. At the end of the day, you did what you had to do to get where you had to go or you didn't. Everything else was white noise. Static. Interference.

The car chattered over the decking of the Nimpkish River Bridge. The rainfall had increased to a steady drizzle, finding its pace like a runner at the beginning of a marathon. Purcell adjusted the speed of the wipers. Davey stared out the window. He watched the Port McNeill turn off speed past. He gazed at the rain-shrouded forest as the highway climbed and bent inland again. The forest between the highway and the ocean hadn't been logged for decades, but the highway itself had once been a logging road, and several old access roads still adjoined it.

About ten minutes past Port McNeill, Boomer pointed ahead. "It's the next road on your right," he said.

"I know," snapped Purcell.

He slowed the car and eased it off the highway, nosing it onto a gravel logging road about a lane and a half wide. Two cars passing would leave paint on each other and on the young conifers encroaching on either side. Due to infrequent use, the gravel surface wasn't pitted or rippled in the manner usually associated with logging roads. A patina of moss had created a thin patchy carpet over the gravel.

About fifty meters off the highway, Purcell stopped the car and drew the shifter into park. Large drops of water falling from the trees pelted the car. Purcell turned his head and started to speak, telling the two civilians how it was going to be. While the cop talked, Boomer pulled on a lightweight summer parka. He zipped it up and drew the hood over his head. Purcell was still talking when Boomer said, "I'll go on ahead. You wait for my signal."

"What?" Purcell snapped. "You been listening?"

"Not to you. According to buddy," Boomer said, unaware that buddy's brains were currently drying on the deck of his boat, "they left an armed guard here. But maybe you missed that part."

"At the *house*, Jenkins. They left a guard at the *house*. That's three kilometers down the road. We wait for you to walk all the way, we'll be late for the party." Purcell turned his bitter look on Davey and then back at Boomer. "We do this my way, or we don't do it."

Boomer's Remington 12 gauge lay on the front seat, pointing at the floor. Boomer picked it up and pumped a load into the chamber. It made a smooth sliding sound and a solid reassuring click. The sound of oiled steel moving to a purpose. Boomer carefully set the safety.

"Your way," he said, "has gotten people killed and tortured and raped. Time for a change."

He opened the door, admitting a waft of the peculiar odor of warm gravel suddenly wet and stepped out. He looked to his right, then his left, as if searching for something he'd forgotten, and then ducked down and spoke into the car.

"Look," he said, "unless that Bayliner can sprout wings and fly, the party won't start for at least another hour. And we don't want to be surprised by a guard hiding somewhere along the road here."

He closed the door, turned into the rain, and vanished between the boughs of the young evergreens.

The back of Purcell's neck was red; his ears were purple. Anger came off him in waves until the air in the car seemed to crackle with the static of his rage. Davey wondered if the cop was more pissed off at taking orders from a civilian or having Cassie's rape tossed once again into his lap. Maybe a little of both. When Boomer appeared on the road two hundred meters ahead and waved them forward, Purcell accelerated with a spray of gravel. Boomer held his ground, forcing Purcell to slam on the brakes and skid to a stop. Purcell opened his door and stepped out, but Boomer turned and disappeared again into the forest.

"Asshole," muttered Purcell as he got back in and slammed the door.

It was fifteen, twenty minutes before Purcell cooled off enough to try and draw Davey into a debate about a phone call that would bring down a troop of Mounties. It was a debate Davey didn't allow himself to be drawn into. No doubt Constable Purcell had the logical side of that debate. Davey just shook his head and let the drumbeat of the rain on the roof drown out logic.

He thought of Keith. *Fuckin' shot man.* The fear like cold wax on Keith's face as he died in Davey's arms. He thought of Frank and Lorraine and the young female cop chained to the stable wall, drugged to the moon, lost in space, maybe for the rest of their lives. He thought of Cassie. *They raped me. Oh god, I'm sorry.*

There was no logic to his thoughts, only feelings—a tangled, jumbled wilderness of emotions. The emotions seemed dim-witted and shabby next to Purcell's cultured logic, so Davey kept them to himself. He gazed at the snakes of water writhing down the windows and let his mind clench up tight, like a sphincter closing off the fluid evacuation of scared shit until Boomer materialized beside the car and pulled the door open.

"House is just around the bend," Boomer said, bringing into the car the smell of wet hair and clothes. "If there is a guard, he must be in the house. We can walk from here. Cut through the forest. Take us right up to the back of the house."

"Then what?" Purcell asked. "Gunfight at the O-fucking-K corral?" He turned toward the backseat. "We don't have to do it this way, Davey. It's still not too late."

Davey stared at him. Maybe it was the way his mind was clenched up, but he felt slightly stoned. A tight, rolling sensation gripped the top of his brain. He stared at Constable Purcell, and he saw Kevin, the kid on the ferry, the backpacker from New Zealand. For a brief moment, the dark tangle of his emotions opened up, like sudden sunlight in a clearing, and the feeling of being lost subsided. But in the time it took him to open his mouth, the light faded and overgrowth choked the clearing.

"Too late for *what?*" he said, lost again but bound to forge on. "At least Lazuardi knows what he wants. With you, guys, it's like you're all after something different. You all got your own agenda. And if some poor schmuck gets greased in the crosswalk because your agenda includes a hundred-mile-an-hour car chase to catch a fucking *shop*lifter, well that just too bad, isn't it?"

"Lazuardi," said Purcell, "is not a shoplifter. Keith Stoddard was not a poor schmuck in the crosswalk."

Davey shrugged, disappointed that what he wanted to say had come out so poorly, frustrated that such strong feelings were so hard to clearly pick out of the jungle. Made it tough to trust the damn things.

"I've got the stick in my pocket," he said. "If I have to give it up to get Cassie back I won't even hesitate. That's real. Everything else is bullshit."

Purcell frowned, gave his head a disappointed little shake, glanced at the car phone.

"If you guys are about done your discussion," Boomer said, leaning forward and reaching in behind the car phone, "maybe we can get some work done." He yanked and came up with a fistful of wires.

"Oh great!" said Purcell. "Real fucking swift. Just what the fuck . . ."

But Boomer and Davey were walking away, leaving the cop to tell himself how fucking swift that was. As he muttered, Purcell grabbed the riot gun from its mount under the dashboard and hurried after the two civilians.

Five minutes later, the three of them were soaking wet. They were knee-deep in wet salal, crouched behind the boles of fir trees that splattered them with water dropped from boughs forty feet above. They were about twenty meters behind the house, on a rise that allowed them to see over the roof.

From the house came a shouted curse, the crash of something thrown or knocked over. Lord Greystoke went streaking out the front door. A man followed, alternately cursing and imploring the cat to come back. He was waving his hands over his head. In his right hand was an automatic pistol. Davey recognized the man. Tall and skinny, frizzy hair of a dirty blond color. The junkie who'd been with the guy named Norm. Norm had called him Twitch or something equally stupid.

Chapter 37

"*W*as my kid brother started calling me Twitch," he told the cat, "when we was just boys."

Twitch was sitting at the kitchen table. He brought the pen casing to his lips and sipped wistfully on the opening. All he got was a bitter aftertaste. The smoke was gone. The foil bowl at the other end of the pen casing was cold; the last of the heroin was a stain of powdery soot. Well, not quite. Actually, the last of the heroin was inside the sardine that the big gray cat was scarfing down.

The propane fridge had run out of fuel who knows when, and opening the fridge door had released a stench that Twitch didn't even want to think about. But off the kitchen, he'd found a pantry stocked with canned and dried food. Aside from the open tin of sardines under the cat's fangs, the tabletop was littered with open cans of beans, chicken, ham, olives, pineapple, water chestnuts, peanut butter, plum jam, a handheld VHF radio, and a Glock 29 automatic pistol with a single 10 mm bullet lodged in the chamber.

"We spent lots a time together, me an' Norm. Mom was always chasin' us out when the uncles came callin', like we never knew they was johns. And a course the other kids never much played with us, account of Mom's johns. But never mind, she done okay by us, done the best she could."

As he talked, small frowns and small smiles flitted across Twitches face like intermittent clouds scudding across a summer sky.

"Was okay. We built a little fort in the pasture out back of the tenement. Yeah, a real pasture with cows and all. Lived in Surrey in the Fraser Valley. Surrey went from country to city like a bushfire, so fast that farmland got left behind, like unburned pockets, surrounded by apartments and strip malls and minimarts. Anyway, the farmer never minded us playin' there."

Twitch fell quiet and pensively plucked at his lip for a moment. Something stirred deep inside him, a tender ache that would be very fine if he could ever feel it. But it was quickly gone, borne off in a rush of heroin. Twitch shrugged, smiled.

"Mom used to throw him a freebie every now and again. Thing of it was, instead a barbed wire, that pasture had one of them electric fences. We was always joshin', me an' Norm, about if you peed on the wire you'd fry your little wienie. Well, one day I done it, just to see what would happen. Got a little jolt, a little tingle, no big deal, but I figured to throw a scare into my kid brother, the way brothers will, you know. So I dropped to the ground and started spassin' and twitchin' and droolin'."

Twitch laughed softly. "Poor little Normy, he went apeshit. Thought I'd taken the big lightenin' bolt to the sky. Went streakin' home, hollerin' his head off, busted in on Mom and a john. Tell you, I got walloped some for that one. Was after that Normy started callin' me the Twitch Man."

The cat looked at him, licked sardine oil from its whiskers, blinked a couple of times. The grateful look in the cat's eyes made Twitch feel important and appreciated. Twitch wasn't sure whether or not the cat was a hallucination and didn't really care. It was enough that the cat was his friend. Twitch had a very high regard for the value of friendship, it being such a rare coin and so quickly spent. The cat purred as if to thank him and dropped its fangs back into the sardines.

The empty condom lay in the center of the table. In a few hours, Twitch might regret having fed the last of its contents to the cat, but presently, it didn't mean much one way or another. While the perceptual part of his mind had been boosted onto a hyperplane, a lofty mesa where each of his senses had virtual texture, the planning part of his mind, the part that recalled instructions and arranged those instructions into activities, that part of his mind was filmed over with a stagnant sludge. When the VHF handset let out a loud protracted squawk, it meant no more to Twitch than it did to the cat.

The cat screeched and leaped straight up. It shot off the table, claws tearing at the floorboards as it sprinted to the door and out into the rainy afternoon.

"Fuck!" Twitch screamed.

He jumped up, sending the chair toppling behind him, and glared at the offending item, the thing that had scared his friend away. His mind was producing no real thought pattern, just a lot of blotchy red anger. When he picked up the handset to throw it against the wall, he had no idea his thumb was depressing the Send button, transmitting a single long carrier wave, which told Flammond, on the boat, that everything was under control.

As he headed out after his feline friend, who might have been nothing but a hallucination and so lost to him forever, Twitch the Shootist snatched the pistol off the table.

From their blind on the hill, Davey, Boomer, and Constable Purcell watched the tall, skinny guy with the frizzy hair pursue Lord Greystoke through the rain across the burned-out clearing and into the forest. Purcell waited a few minutes, then started down the slope to check the house for other occupants. "If that guy comes back," he said, "or anyone else shows up, toss a pebble at me."

The house was a simple rectangle, the back wall about sixty feet long. The corners were softened by plantings of pieris and fatsia shrubs. Between the planters, the ground was moss-covered bedrock. There were four windows evenly spaced along the wall. Outside each window a flowerpot depended from the eaves. The pots were made of moss, the flowers in them thriving on retained water.

Purcell went east to west, staying low, peering through the lower corners of each window. He'd got to the shrubs on the west side of the house when Boomer tapped Davey on the shoulder.

Boomer pointed to the east, toward the trail that led through the forest down to the wharf, the trail along which Davey had dragged Keith. Less than two weeks ago. Seemed like two years. Keith stumbling along, leaving bits of himself on the trail like a nightmare version of Hansel and Gretel. *Fuckin' shot, man.*

Davey shook his head to get rid of the static. He saw movement between the trees. Several people were coming up the trail. He picked up a small rock and tossed it, aiming for the ground at Purcell's feet, hitting him in the back. Davey waved at him. Purcell hurried back up into the trees.

"Any ideas?" asked Boomer.

"Yeah," said Purcell. "We stay hidden until they get into the clearing between the forest and the house, then Davey, you let them know you got the stick. Jenkins and I'll let them know you're not alone, that a gun fight would be in no one's best interest."

Davey gave the cop a suspicious look. Would Purcell so easily give up the memory stick?

Purcell read his look. "You were right," he said. "Cassie has to be safe before anything else matters."

"Thought the water drowned that fucker," muttered Boomer. He was looking at the trailhead where the short muscular man called Flammond had crouched beside a tree.

Flammond stared at the house for a long minute, then he summoned the others with flicks of his wrist. Cassie came into view, dressed in her black-and-yellow dry suit, her hands fastened at her back. Two men flanked her. A fourth man, the one Davey knew as Norm, brought up the rear.

"Shit," said Purcell. "They're suspicious. Frizzy was probably supposed to be meeting them instead of chasing cats through the fucking bush."

Norm and Cassie's two keepers drew pistols and faded off to the sides of the trail. Flammond advanced low and fast across the thirty meters of open ground between the forest and the house. He disappeared around the front of the house.

Davey stood up. Purcell grabbed the hem of his jacket. "The hell do you think you're going?"

"To get Cassie," Davey said. He yanked his jacket a couple of times, but the cop wouldn't let go.

"They'll kill her," Davey said, his voice shaking, his head full of images of the bullets going through Keith. "God damn you, they'll kill her."

He twisted his arms out of the sleeves and left Purcell holding the empty jacket. His wounded leg, stiff from the long car ride and squatting in the wet, started to cramp up. He hobbled off, keeping to the edge of the forest, his eyes on the trailhead. He heard Purcell tell Boomer to follow that idiot and try to keep him alive while Purcell kept Flammond in the house.

"Hey, Normy!"

The voice came from the bush near the trailhead. Davey stepped behind a Douglas fir tree. He peered around the trunk, his cheek pressed against the gnarly bark, his nostrils full of the bulky, musty smell of green. A few seconds later, the guy called Twitch followed his voice out of the bush.

"Look what I got, Norm," he said, his voice high-pitched, almost giggling. A highly agitated Lord Greystoke struggled in Twitch's scratched bloody arms. "I found this neat cat."

Purcell couldn't keep Flammond occupied in the house because Flammond never went into the house. Flammond bypassed the house and slipped through the cover of the trees. He got thirty meters up the road before he glimpsed the gray Chevy Caprice parked amid the trees. He turned and sprinted back toward the trailhead.

"We're blown!" Flammond shouted.

Davey heard him, looked to his left, saw the ex-paratrooper sprinting toward the trail.

"Get her back to the boat!" Flammond yelled.

Davey froze. Fear went through him like a voltage. When he started running, his muscles were stiff, his left leg was still cramping. He took half a dozen steps before his feet got tangled and took him down. He slid and rolled down the slope, a dozen meters before his feet got back under him. The whole time, his eyes were locked on the group at the trailhead.

He saw Flammond rip Lord Greystoke from Twitch's arms. As the cat ran, Flammond snapped three quick shots at it. The third shot seemed to knock the legs out from under it. Twitch screamed, pulled a pistol from his jeans, put it to Flammond's head, and fired. A misty spray erupted from Flammond's crew cut. Flammond crumpled to the ground.

One of the men with Cassie let her go, raised a pistol, and shot Twitch twice. Twitch spun away into the base of a tree. Norm screamed "Nooo . . ." He raised a gun and shot point-blank into Twitch's killer's face.

The fourth man let go of Cassie, crouched, and spun as if to make a run for it, wherever *it* might be. He found himself looking into the barrel of Purcell's riot gun.

Purcell was ten meters away, running with the gun at his shoulder, yelling, "Police! Police!"

The man dropped his gun, went to his knees, bowed his head, and held his hands out to the side.

The guy shot in the face was still standing when Davey went by him. Davey shoved him aside. He crumpled to the ground. Davey grabbed Cassie around the waist, tackled her to the side of the trail, and rolled with her into the ferns. She struggled away from him, got to her feet, and delivered a solid kick to the side of his head.

"Davey!" she cried. She dropped to her knees beside him. "Oh Jesus, I'm sorry!" She took him into her arms, pressed his face against wet neoprene. "I'm sorry, baby. I thought you were—"

He shut her up by crushing his mouth to hers.

Chapter 38

*B*oomer loaded the woodstove with paper and kindling and tossed in a match. The stove belched out a puff of white smoke, then drew it back in. Kindling crackled. Boomer checked to make sure the draught was open, then closed and sealed the glass door. He stood over the stove rubbing his hands. Davey, shivering, joined him. The shivering, he suspected, was a reaction to shock rather than cold, but either way, the fire was comforting.

The stove squatted on a brick pad on the floor between the living room and the kitchen. The two rooms were open to each other and shared four windows. Three of the windows were broken. A wind had risen, and gusts were tossing handfuls of rain through the broken panes. Leaf-patterned drapes fluttered as if dodging the rain.

Cassie brought a wicker basket from the table and set it down beside the stove. She stood and put her arm around Davey's waist.

"You guys are soaked," she said from the dry comfort of her dive suit. She spoke softly, as if there was someone nearby who might be disturbed. "I'll get you some dry clothes," she said and walked off through the kitchen, down the hallway toward the bedrooms.

Davey looked down into the basket. He watched the rise and fall of Lord Greystoke's chest, the only sign that the cat was alive. There didn't seem to be much blood. Some seepage in the bandages wrapped around the two-inch stump that had been Greystoke's right foreleg and a spatter of blood on the towel on the table where they'd patched him up. But then, how much blood could a twelve-pound cat have in him?

The antiseptic smell of the bandages blended with the damp mousy smell of the disused house and the conglomerate odors from the tins on the table left from Twitch's last meal. The combination of odors seemed to press with unpleasant pressure against Davey's solar plexus, the sort of pressure you could only get rid of by vomiting. Or maybe the nausea, like the shivering, was a reaction to shock. A bit of mental indigestion. Acid reflux from the image of the three bodies lying in the rain under the trees by the trail. Upon ascertaining that the shot men were indeed dead, Purcell had insisted that they remain where they'd fallen until an investigative unit arrived, which would have been on its way, he'd said, had either his tax-funded car phone or his personal-expense cell phone been operational.

Norm and the other man were sitting on the floor, back-to-back, near the wall farthest from the broken windows. Their hands were cuffed behind them, each to the other. Purcell had had one set of cuffs on him; the other set he'd brought in when he'd moved his car down from the road. Norm had his head down, crying softly on his knees. He was moaning something to God: appeal, lament, or accusation—maybe a bit of each. Davey picked up enough to understand that Twitch had been Norm's brother.

Norm's partner had a stunned expression on his face, as if he'd woken up and found himself on Mars. Purcell was trying to get him to acknowledge that he understood his constitutional rights as Purcell had explained them. The guy just sat there shaking his head. Purcell demonstrated how to nod instead of shake. "Do this," he said, nodding. "Not this," he said, shaking. It appeared hopeless.

"Someone's here." Cassie's voice came from a back room. It hurried down the hallway, muffled by the walls. Cassie followed close on its tail.

"Someone's here," she repeated, stepping into the front room. Her arms were full of folded towels and clothes. She looked for a place to set the burden down. Her expression was desperate, as if this was a daunting decision. Finally, she dumped the bundle on the kitchen countertop and said, "Someone's here."

Davey and Boomer rubbed their hands over the stove and looked at Purcell. *You're a cop,* Davey thought. *You can stop this, right? That's your job, isn't it?*

Purcell asked his prisoners if they were expecting anyone. Norm moaned to God into his knees; the other guy stared like a blind man and shook his head. Purcell told them to stay put, then picked up his riot gun and went to a window.

Davey shook his head. Boomer shrugged, went to the table, picked up his Remington shotgun, and joined Purcell by the window. Davey bit his lip so he wouldn't whimper. He got his pistol off the table. He was shivering again. It was the cold; two steps away from the stove, it was freezing cold. Even the pistol was wet and cold. He glanced at the bundle of towels and dry clothes.

A green sedan drifted into the parking area in front of the house. Despite the gloom of the day, it showed no lights. It looked ghostly through the vicious downpour. It stopped about twenty feet short of Purcell's car and sat there swiping water off its windshield. The driver turned his head to study the house. His features were unclear through the gloom and the water cascading down the windows. As gloomy as it was outside, it was much darker in the house. The guy in the car would see nothing but dark empty windows. He watched them for a full minute before he opened the car door.

As soon as the car's dome light came on, Purcell let out an audible sigh of relief. "He's a cop," he said. "Kid on the boat must've told them where to find us."

He tossed his gun onto the table and stepped out the door. "Staff Sergeant Lohman," he called out. "It's me, Constable Purcell."

Staff Sergeant Lohman pulled his bulk from the car but didn't step away from it. Davey shivered and swallowed bile. He hissed at Purcell to come back, but Purcell had already stepped off the porch into the rain. Purcell was explaining the situation to Staff Sergeant Lohman, as if Purcell knew what the situation was.

"Davey?" said Boomer. "What's the matter, Davey?"

"It's him." Davey was backing away from the window. "He's the bad cop."

"Ah shit," said Boomer.

Cassie picked up Purcell's riot gun and disengaged the safety.

Lohman hadn't moved from the crook of the open car door. The car was shielding him from the house. His right hand was on the roof of the car. There was a revolver in it, pointed roughly in Purcell's direction.

Davey told Boomer to watch him. He wasn't thinking; his mind was numb, as if from the cold. He said he'd get behind him, but the words seemed nonsensical, as if he were speaking some strange, exotic language. He moved through the hallway, into a bedroom, drifting, like in a dream. Had to be a dream: It was a little girl's bedroom. Dolls and stuffed toys on the dresser and huddled in corners as if sharing secrets. Four-poster bed covered with a bedspread full of hobbits, round and jolly with long-stem pipes and hairy toes, meandering among thick green tree trunks and whimsical toadstools. Peaceful hobbits, minding their own business, before Baggins got them messed up in that whole ring thing.

He could easily be asleep in that bed. He and the hobbits, minding their own business. The bed would smell like Cassie. Not just her perfume and shampoo and the heat of her flesh. It was the bed in which she'd grown up; it would smell like the beginning of her. It would smell like her laughter and her tears as she discovered the world into which she'd been born. It would smell like her first joy and her first pleasure and her first pain and her first fear. It would smell like the wonder that moulded the woman from the girl.

In his dream, the room flashed by and smelled of nothing. He pushed open the window and kicked out the screen. He crawled gun-first out into the rain and fell onto moss-covered rock, wet and slimy. He headed around the west end of the house, stumbling through planters whose soil had turned into muck. He peeked around the corner, saw Lohman's back, a target too big to miss. Purcell was standing near the front of Lohman's car. Lohman was telling Purcell that the constable was hereby to consider himself on probation and needed to surrender his weapons.

Davey stepped away from the house. The rain hit him like a fury. He raised his gun. "Not so fast, Wheaton," he said.

Lohman turned his head. His right hand started sliding the gun across the roof of his car. Stopped when he saw Davey's gun.

"Davey?" said Purcell. "Easy, Davey. This is Staff Sergeant Lohman. He's our liaison officer. What he said is true. I broke some rules. I got some explaining to do. Meanwhile, I'm on probation. That's how it works."

"Uh-uh," Davey said, shouting because he was out of breath and because the rain was too loud and because if he were dreaming no one would hear him. "No, he's Wheaton Grains, in cereal."

"What the *hell* are you talking about?" Purcell shook his head. "Put the *gun* down, Davey."

Davey's legs had kept walking, the way they do in a dream. He was nearly to the back of Lohman's car when he stopped, about fifteen feet from the target too big to miss.

"Davey," Purcell said, "put the fucking gun *down!*"

"He followed me to Toronto. You said no one followed me. Well, Staff Sergeant Wheaton Grains Lohman here, he followed me."

Lohman turned his head back toward Purcell. Purcell was frowning at him. Purcell didn't tell Davey to put the gun *down.*

"Think about it, Constable," said Lohman. "You're already up to your neck in shit. He's a drug dealer. He's holding a gun on an RCMP member. You are a constable of the RCMP. Your duty is clear."

Purcell continued to frown. "That true, Sergeant? You follow Davey to Toronto?"

"Of course. We weren't about to let him run across the country without an escort."

"We who, Staff Sergeant? We, drug interdiction? Or we, Vincent Lazuardi Enterprises?"

Maybe Lohman saw that Purcell was unarmed. Or maybe he hoped that Purcell was armed. Maybe he hoped Purcell would shoot him in the back and have done with it. He said, "Fuck it," and turned the gun deliberately, almost slowly, toward Davey.

Or maybe it just seemed slow because it was happening in a dream. How else could he shoot a cop unless it was only in a dream? He kept the pistol centered on Lohman, a target too big to miss, and squeezed the trigger. The dud made a sound like a wet fart.

Whether dream or reality, Davey lived the next second of his life up on that hyperplane of which Twitch had been so fond, where sensory input was magnified to a granular clarity and time seemed to thicken, densify, as if it were some vast woven fabric being sucked into the black hole of Lohman's gun.

The moment was shattered by a scream. The scream was swallowed by two explosions. Sparks and glass sprayed from Lohman's car. Lohman's gun fired wildly as he ducked and covered from the shotgun blasts. Purcell sprinted forward and slammed the car door into Lohman. The car rocked under another tandem blast from the shotguns. Lohman pushed back against the door. Purcell bounced off. Lohman lay prone on the ground, raising the gun two-handed. Davey lunged, arms outstretched. His hands touched the hot steel of Lohman's gun. He felt the cylinder turn, watched it turn, saw the dull gleam from the cute little nubs of brass-coated lead burrowed in their holes in the cylinder snug as eggs in a nest. He tried to twist the gun, but his hands felt too weak, as if he'd left them back in the dream.

There was a blinding flash, a deafening roar, the acrid smell of burnt gunpowder, a whiff of burning flesh. Hot powder on his right cheek felt like fire sizzling in the rain. Shocked stupid, he watched the hammer lift, the cylinder come around again.

But the next shots didn't come from Lohman's gun; they came from above and behind Davey. Two shots, nearly simultaneous. Two holes appeared magically in Lohman's forehead. He grunted, his breath hot and smelling like stale whiskey. His eyes opened wide as if seeing something amazing and then glazed over.

Davey rolled onto his back. Brian Cronk was leaning against the fender of Lohman's car. A gun slipped from Cronk's hand and thudded to the ground. Cronk crossed his hands over his stomach and slid down until he was sitting in the muddy gravel.

Purcell squatted beside him, pulled Cronk's jacket open. He hissed, "Jesus," and closed the jacket back over the dark stain spreading across

Cronk's belly. Boomer hurried over and joined Purcell, trying to staunch the flow of Cronk's blood. Or maybe just hide it.

Cassie was leaning over Davey, fussing with the powder burn on his cheek. Just a powder burn, not a bullet hole. Because Lohman hadn't fired at Davey, Lohman had fired at Brian Cronk. Cronk had gotten the bullet hole. He was sitting against the car, leaking out of the bullet hole, staring at Davey.

Davey reached into the pocket of his jacket, into a pocketful of cold grainy mud. He pulled out the memory stick. The cap had come off, the USB port was plugged with mud, it was bent nearly in half. Cronk shook his head. Davey thought maybe he was laughing. It was hard to tell, the way the rain poured down.

Chapter 39

*D*avey stood over the stove again, shivering. He thought he might never again in his life feel warm. Cassie brought ointment from the first aid kit on the table where she'd operated on Greystoke and applied it to Davey's cheek. Norm and his companion, shackled back-to-back, struggled against each other to get a view of Boomer and Kevin Purcell carrying Cronk down the hallway to the bedrooms. Boomer came out, grabbed the first aid kit, and hurried back to the bedroom. Outside in the rain, Lohman waited with the other bodies for the crime scene investigators.

Cassie helped strip Davey to his underwear, cursing softly when she saw blood seeping through the bandage on his left leg. "You've gone and broken it open," she said in the same voice she'd some day use to scold their children. Lucky kids. She towelled him dry and helped him into track pants and a sweatshirt of her father's.

Boomer lumbered into the room. He picked up a towel from the stack Cassie had left on the counter and wiped his face and hair. From a broom closet, he got a large flashlight and tested its beam against the wall.

"How is Cronk?" Davey asked.

Boomer shook his head. "Medevac chopper's on its way. I'm going out to make sure it's got a landing pad. But I'll be surprised if he's here to see it."

Kevin Purcell had come out of the bedroom in time to hear Boomer's pronouncement. He glared at Boomer for a moment, then turned to Davey and said, "He wants to see you."

Davey didn't particularly want to see him. Davey could easily go through the rest of his life seeing no one else dying. But the dead would have their last requests, wouldn't they? Davey stepped toward the bedroom. Cassie took his hand and came with him.

Purcell held out a hand. "He said just Davey."

Davey looked at Cassie, nodded, squeezed her hand, and let go. As he stepped by Purcell, the cop held out a sheet of paper.

"Brian had this in his pocket."

It was the sheet with the pictures of Lohman and the child prostitutes. Davey looked away, disgusted.

"Lohman was your bad cop," said Purcell, "not Brian."

Purcell watched Davey as if he was expecting something, something like an apology. Davey said, "He wasn't *my* bad cop."

They'd put Cronk in Cassie's bedroom. Davey stood in the doorframe, where you're supposed to stand during earthquakes, and looked at him. He was lying on Cassie's bed with his eyes closed, his hair plastered to his head in a ginger-brown helmet. Lying on the bed where Cassie's girlhood secrets hid among the hobbits on the bedspread. The hobbits were pulled up to Cronk's chin, hiding the leakage from his belly, and Davey had a thoroughly selfish regret: he'd never be able to share that bed with Cassie without seeing Cronk die in it.

Cronk opened his eyes and smiled. "Sorry," he said, as if he'd read Davey's thoughts. He spoke through gritted teeth, same way Keith had spoken when he'd got shot in the guts. Davey stepped into the room.

"You got the stick?" Cronk asked.

Davey nodded. "It's broken."

Cronk shrugged. "Things break. It happens. Some can be fixed," he said and looked down at his belly. "Some can't."

"Should I write that down?"

"Always the punk, Jones, aren't you?"

Cronk's skin was pale and waxy. There were beads of sweat on his face, as if the wax were melting. Or maybe it was rainwater rather than sweat; he looked cold. Keith had been cold.

"You asked for me," Davey reminded him.

"Did you find the money?" Cronk asked.

Davey felt his face grow hot.

"Ah ha," said Cronk. "Your cool's slipping there a bit, Jones. You might want to get a handle on that."

Davey wanted to hate him. Whether he was the bad cop or not, it was his operation. His hands were soaked in the blood of it. Davey stared at him, waiting for the hate to kick in. But it didn't. Cronk was no longer a hovering presence. His eyes had lost their hawklike intensity. Now they seemed the shade of gray that was simply without color.

"Quite the little digger, your Keith." Cronk looked as though he was enjoying himself despite the teeth-gritting pain. "Bet your life he was. Dug up all kinds of things, not the least of which was three and a half hundred thousand dollars. Give or take. Dug that out of my trunk. Ah, now you're listening."

Cronk tried to wet his lips, but his tongue was coated with a sticky white film. Davey offered to get him some water. He shook his head. "Tummy's got a hole in it. Won't hold water no more. Like Keith's theories. Quite the digger, your Keith, but he hadn't a clue what he'd dug up, had he? Not really."

Cronk coughed a horrible raspy cough. The white film was stringy between his lips. Davey stepped out and went to the bathroom across the hallway. He soaked a facecloth in cold water and then wrung it out till it was just damp. Back in the bedroom, he wiped Cronk's lips. Cronk bit the cool damp facecloth and sucked softly.

"Thanks," he said, smiling. "I needed that."

"You need rest," Davey said. He was desperate to hear what Cronk was going to tell him and equally desperate to be struck deaf.

"Few more minutes," Cronk said, "I'll get all the rest in the world." He suckled more moisture from the facecloth and continued.

"Dug a hole into Lazuardi's computer drive, your Keith. Dug down into the nasty bits. Found pictures of Staff Sergeant Tim Lohman, liaison officer, drug interdiction, letting Mr. Happy out to play with little girls. Keith realized that whatever Lohman knew, Lazuardi knew, and Lohman knew everything. Keith hard-copied the dirty pictures, but where could he take them? If Lohman was compromised, who else was? Best take them to the top, right? To the inspector in charge, fellow name of Brian Cronk."

Cronk paused to moisten his lips and catch his breath. Davey found himself holding his.

"It's Sunday night," Cronk said, "week before the August holiday. He's scared, your Keith, carrying his own death warrant. Hanging back, staying to the shadows, watching everything, seeing the chief inspector receive an envelope of cash. That was the last payment. Stoddard and White had the stick. The operation should've been over. He must have seen me, followed me, that's the only way it plays. I was getting careless. The money never meant anything to me anyway. It was just a way to stay in touch with Joshua. Joshua was my source, my tour guide to Lazuardi's empire. Voice on the phone was Joshua, but he held my hand, led me through the magic kingdom. Price of admission was that I compromise myself so that when he takes over his boss's business, he's got a friend in high places."

Cronk took another break. His breathing had become more laboured. Words were slurring off his tongue. Davey took the facecloth and gently wiped the sweat from Cronk's forehead.

"Why are you telling me this?" he asked.

"Got to close the case," Cronk said. He coughed. "Someone should know."

"Why not Purcell?"

Cronk closed his eyes. His face contorted in pain. "Didn't get Purcell's friend killed, did I? Got your friend killed. Keith Stoddard, good little digger. He'd have been fine had he come to me. But how could he know? Saw me take a bribe, followed me to Sidney, watched me stash the money. Must have thought he was alone in the wide world. Now he's waiting for me in hell."

"No one's going to hell," Davey said. He took Cronk's hand. "Medevac chopper's on the way. You'll be in the hospital before you know it."

Cronk's eyes stayed closed, as if he lacked the energy to lift his eyelids. Each breath was a contest.

"Joshua too," Cronk hissed. Davey thought he'd tried to laugh. "Your native friends, they heard a hit man refer to Sebastian as Joshua just before he killed him. Remember Sebastian? He must've been my Joshua. It all goes round and round. Bet your life it does," he murmured, and then he stopped breathing.

"Boomer!" Davey yelled.

But Boomer was busy outside. Davey could hear the helicopter chopping through the rain. He ripped the quilt off Cronk and lowered him to the floor, kneeled beside him and started performing chest compressions.

"Purcell!" he yelled just as Purcell rushed into the room.

Purcell kneeled by Cronk's head and started breathing into his mouth. Cronk's eyes opened halfway and saw nothing.

Chapter 40

*L*ord Greystoke sat on the steps of the porch in a patch of warm September sunshine, grooming the stump of his right foreleg. Davey leaned forward and gave him a scratch on the head.

"Looking awfully goddamn smug for a gimp," Frank said to the cat. Frank was sitting in a wicker chair, tapping the tips of his canes on the deck of the porch. Frank's hands had an uncontrollable tremor, and his skin had a yellowish hue. He'd lost weight and he'd never carried extra; his white shirt looked like it was on a wire hanger.

He said, "Ain't that right, Tripod? You and me, the brothers gimp."

Cassie slapped her dad on the shoulder. "Don't call him Tripod. You'll hurt his feelings."

"It's a cat, daughter of mine. Cats don't have feelings. Cats torment things and then kill them." He waved a cane in the direction of the door. "Never mind correcting your betters, go get changed. Traipsing around in your goddamn underwear when your mom's about to put supper on the table."

Cassie laughed and ruffled her father's hair before heading in to the house. Her underwear was the thermal johns she wore under her drysuit. She and Davey had been doing three dives a day for the past week, cleaning and inspecting the net pens, preparing to bring the fish farm back on line again. Davey had stopped at *Small Wonder*, down on the dock, where he'd showered and changed into jeans and a T-shirt.

Frank levered himself with his canes out of the chair. Davey made a move to help, but Frank's expression said, "Don't even think about it."

"C'mon," he said. "Let's walk." As he hobbled across the yard, Davey fell in step with him.

"That cop was here today," Frank said. "Purcell."

Davey wondered if Frank knew that Purcell's game had gotten Cassie raped. No, if Frank had known that, he'd have met Purcell with his shotgun.

"He came to let us know that Lazuardi fled."

Davey stopped, put a hand on Frank's shoulder to stop him. "What?"

Frank looked at him and nodded. "He made bail and bailed. Too bad about the computer file. Might've kept him locked up. With him on the loose, it all seems kind of pointless."

The accusation was not very subtle. Davey had destroyed the memory stick and so had rendered useless the sacrifices made by others. Not Davey's fault, but still, it's what you get when a second-stringer tries to do the job. To make amends, he's helping the Dentons fix their house and put their fish farm back in order, but let's not forget that he's banging their daughter in the bargain.

"Asked him about that reward," Frank said as he resumed his hobbling walk. "Didn't know shit about any reward."

"He's a constable," Davey said. "A constable under review for conduct unbecoming. I'm sure there's a lot he doesn't know shit about."

"In *cash*? Hundred eighty thousand in *cash*? You sure that money ain't gonna come back and bite my ass?"

"That's why they call it a cash reward," Davey said. "Don't worry, Frank, it's good money. Inspector Cronk told me about it."

Frank hobbled a few more steps, then stopped and stared out at his charred acreage. "Cronk was a good cop. Won't hear me say that a lot. Hell of a cop, Cronk."

Another not-so-veiled accusation, Davey thought. The good cop Cronk having given his life to save the second-stringer Jones from his own fatal mistake. Maybe he should remind Frank that Cronk was the author of the whole operation. Maybe tell him about Cronk's true involvement with the money, not to mention the violation of Frank's daughter. Maybe he should, but he wouldn't. Didn't seem any point in it. Cronk had paid the ultimate price, and Frank was certainly entitled to blame someone for his ruined health. Davey happened to be there. He also happened to be sleeping with Frank's daughter.

"It was three hundred and sixty thousand bucks," Davey said. "The reward."

Frank raised his eyebrows. "Guess you figure you earned Keith's share, do you?"

"Actually, I told Erin about it. Linda hooked us up with an estate lawyer and we put it in a trust fund for Keith and Erin's daughters."

"So that's what she meant," Frank said. "Well, aren't you *just* the little philanthropist?" he said, but it didn't feel like a compliment.

He took a joint from his shirt pocket and lit it. "I can smoke this shit legally now," he said. "Got a medical exemption."

He offered the joint to Davey. Davey shook his head and said, "I don't."

"Helps my nerves and my appetite," Frank said. "Doctors figure it does the job better than any prescription drugs they could give me." He took another hit and said, "Still illegal to buy it, though, so I got to grow my own. Ain't that a hoot?"

"A hoot," Davey agreed.

"He brought a message from her. The cop, Purcell, he brought a message from Erin. She headed back east this morning. Said to tell you thanks. Said she wants to keep in touch. For the daughters, you know. Said she hoped you could help her daughters understand that part of their father that she never could. Understand." Frank shook his head, as if he didn't. After a moment, he said, "That Erin, huh? Some kinda pretty, that one."

"So are ice sculptures," said Davey.

"That right? Hottie with a cold heart? Ain't that the way of it? That why Keith left her?"

"She left Keith," Davey corrected. But he said it with little conviction. Since Erin's visit, the subject of Keith's ex-marriage had become yet another thing for Davey to be unsure of. It'd been easy when he'd thought of Erin as nothing but a siren bitch who'd seduced Keith and left him broken on the rocks. But he'd just spent a few days with her. He'd shared with her a mutual grief over Keith's death. He'd come to see that she did give a damn, that in fact she'd felt about Keith the same way Davey felt about Cassie. It disturbed him deeply, the evidence that that feeling, love, if that was the name of it, might not be enough.

"Odd," said Frank, giving voice to Davey's thoughts. "Seemed to me that she was still in love with him." He puffed on his joint and said, "But then, love can be a whore."

"Nicely put," said Davey, but his sarcasm never made it through the smoke crowning Frank's head.

Frank frowned at the joint in his hand and said, "You and Cassiopeia, that ain't serious, right?"

A hot flush burned through Davey's body. Not trusting himself to speak, he bit his lip.

"I mean," Frank continued as he licked his thumb and forefinger and crushed out the joint, "I know you two got this thing going. You saved our asses. Conquering hero, all that good shit. So have some fun. Long as you're taking precautions, no harm, no foul. But next week, she goes back to university. She'll be surrounded by guys with futures, you know what I mean? You're a nice guy, Davey, but let's face it. You're a salvor with a rusty tug who lives on a sailboat. Cassiopeia's summa cum lauding her way to a master's degree, maybe a doctorate someday. Be a real hero and don't mess that up for her."

That night, Davey lay awake in the bunk in the after cabin, debating in his head whether or not to tell Cassie. Obviously, she would find it disturbing, but if she didn't know about it, it could be downright dangerous for her.

He snugged his arm around her shoulders, kissed her forehead, and said, "Lazuardi jumped bail."

Her body stiffened against his. "Should we be worried?"

"They say he's a businessman and that revenge is bad business. But they've been wrong before. So I think I'm going to worry whether I should or not."

She pressed herself tighter against him. He could tell by her breathing and the sudden tension in her body that she was wide-awake. Maybe he should have saved it until the morning. She ran her fingers through the hair on his chest and pressed against him.

"I'm not," she said after a while and sounded like she meant it. "We gave him a licking. We beat him up good. He won't be back for more."

"'Beat him up good'? You learn that in university?"

"No," she said. She kissed his ear, and her hand moved down his belly. "There's lots of things I didn't learn in university."

For the next half hour, Cassie showed Davey some of the things she didn't learn in university. Afterward, they were lying quietly cuddled together when Cassie asked Davey why his father was his hero. The question seemed to come out of the blue, and it took Davey by surprise. It was a question he'd never been asked before, not even by himself, and the answer momentarily eluded him.

The answer, when it came to him, was as surprising as the question. "Because he was out there, flailing away to cut a path through the goblins for me, without knowing where I was or where I wanted to go or even what my goblins looked like."

Cassie laughed. "You just posted a perfect job description for a father." Then she whispered, "Think it's a job you'll ever apply for?"

Davey blushed, glad for the darkness. "The mother would have to summa cum laude a PhD," he said. "No kid of mine's going to be stuck with my brain."